Praise for Corin

'A heart-rending story of courage
endures even when all hope has
I thoroughly enjoyed it!'
Anita Frank

'This novel has everything – a tragic love story, thrilling
wartime adventures, a very brave heroine, icy-cold danger,
a beautiful setting and a dashing love interest'
Kerry Barrett

'What a wonderful book . . .
I can't wait to see what Corin writes next!'
Kathleen McGurl

'An unforgettable and epic story of love, bravery
and hope in the most challenging of circumstances'
Kate Galley

'A wonderfully evocative story'
Suzanne Ewart

'A captivating novel about love and sacrifice that
manages to be both thrilling and moving'
Neema Shah

CORIN BURNSIDE grew up in a house full of books and has been scribbling stories for as long as she can remember. A passion for history, travel and the natural environment colours her writing and provides inspiration for her story-telling.

She has recently returned to the UK to live in the beautiful Eden Valley, after spending ten years in the heart of the French Pyrenees with her husband and The Princess, a demanding Hungarian Vizsla who helps with plot holes in exchange for cheese.

Also by Corin Burnside

Her Forgotten Promise

The Memory Keeper

CORIN BURNSIDE

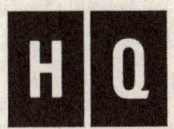

ONE PLACE. MANY STORIES

HQ
An imprint of HarperCollins*Publishers* Ltd
1 London Bridge Street
London SE1 9GF

www.harpercollins.co.uk

HarperCollins*Publishers*
Macken House, 39/40 Mayor Street Upper,
Dublin 1 D01 C9W8

This paperback edition 2024

1
First published in Great Britain by
HQ, an imprint of HarperCollins*Publishers* Ltd 2024

ISBN: 9780008603403

This book contains FSC™ certified paper and other controlled
sources to ensure responsible forest management.

For more information visit: www.harpercollins.co.uk/green

Printed and bound in the UK using
100% Renewable Electricity by CPI Group (UK) Ltd, Croydon, CR0 4YY

For my mother, Ann Aldridge, with love.

Prologue

1941

The Merlin engine coughed and stuttered, the propellor slowing for a moment before picking up its revs again. It was enough to make the Spitfire drop even lower, and fresh beads of perspiration popped onto the pilot's face, running down into a green silk scarf turned black with sweat.

'Come on, you can do it, not much further and we'll be home free,' the pilot muttered, alternately cursing the machine and crooning to it, as if it were a living, breathing beast. Glancing down through the thickening cloud, the choppy, grey water of the English Channel seemed close enough to touch. With a feather-light movement on the stick the nose of the plane lifted slightly. 'That's my girl. We don't want to get wet feet, do we?'

Pain and exhaustion made it almost impossible not to surrender to oblivion. To close heavy eyelids and allow sleep to win. But that way led to disaster, and the pilot thumped a hand on a thigh, biting back a cry, fighting off the swoon of agony.

Trying the radio for the umpteenth time brought the same crackling hiss; the hail of fire from the Messerschmitt must have knocked it out, along with damaging the rudder and what felt like most of the undercarriage. Still, the pilot had seen planes with worse damage make it back and land safely.

A dark smudge gradually grew clearer, swathed in a bank of cloud, lit by the hazy sun reflecting off the Perspex of the cockpit. Relief brought a blur, making the pilot blink hard and sit a little straighter, grunting at the movement.

'We're going to make it.' Yelling now, willing the Spitfire on as if it were a horse at the end of a hard race, keeping the adrenaline going. 'Come on, one more push and we'll be home safe.'

A low-lying area of coastline appeared through the fog for a moment, with a meandering river snaking its way to the sea. A couple of small houses and a farm seemed to grow out of the ground as the land came closer, revealing a marshy area of bog and canal-like waterways. Stands of stunted trees, bent from years of being battered by the wind and storms, resembled groups of old men crowding together gossiping. Then as quickly as it appeared the whole area was swallowed up as the fog swirled in from the sea.

It was enough to raise the pilot's spirits and determination, though. The momentary sight of a pair of coastal gunnery defences squatting on either side of the estuary, guns pointing out to sea, evoked a sob of relief. Fear subsided, replaced by an exhausted euphoria, leaving limbs trembling and a desire to laugh out loud. They would be celebrating another successful mission in the mess tonight.

It was all worth it; the fear, the danger, the exhaustion, even the pain.

This. This was what made it worthwhile.

Chapter 1

'It were a Spitfire, I know it,' Terry Bristow said emphatically, throwing up distorted, swollen hands to emphasise his point. 'Can't mistake the sound of the Merlin engine, see. That's what made me look up.' He squinted into the distance, as if still searching for something. 'But it were in trouble, even I could tell. Too low, and stuttering like it were runnin' out of fuel or some such.'

He coughed and hawked a large wad of phlegm onto the gravel in front of him. I took an involuntary half-step backwards before stopping myself.

'And you saw the plane crash, Mr Bristow?' The old man nodded. 'Was anyone else there who saw it too?'

'No, just me. Da was doing the milkin', and Ma was makin' breakfast, I reckon, cos that's what they allus did then.' He inspected the gob of spittle between his boots and rubbed it into the ground with his toe. 'They ne'er believed me, you know. Ma and Da. I got a belting every time I tried to tell 'em. Got told to stop makin' up stories.' Now his faded blue eyes searched my face. 'But you believe me, don't you, Dr Dawson?'

'I want to believe you, Mr Bristow,' I said. 'It's just that we need a bit more corroborating evidence of a crash site before we can get authority to start digging.' I put a hand up to quell his protestations. 'But if as you say, you saw the plane come down in 1941 and sink into the marsh then I'm happy to do some investigation work first and see if there was ever a recorded crash near here.'

He nodded. 'I do say. It were me tenth birthday, see. Not likely to forget that, am I?'

My pulse jumped. 'Well, that makes it a day to remember,' I said. 'What date is your birthday?'

'Seventeenth February.'

'That's a huge help, Mr Bristow. Hopefully, we can find out where the plane came from and who the pilot was.' I gazed out across the flat Kent marshes, shading my eyes from the sun's reflection on the river. The fresh breeze made each wavelet glitter, and my eyes water. I hugged my jacket closer, tucking hands into the deep side pockets, wondering vaguely if the wind ever dropped. This was a sparse and lonely place, and it seemed a crying shame that a new road might carve it up, if the planners had their way. I turned back to Mr Bristow. 'I believe there was a gun battery near here, during the war?'

He pointed at a squat, square block of concrete on the edge of the marsh, which appeared to be slowly sinking into the mud. He seemed immune to the cold, a flannel shirt with sleeves rolled up to his elbows and an old waistcoat all that protected him from the elements.

'Aye, there were two of 'em back then. One on each side of the river mouth.' He turned back and looked at me. 'They was firin' at it, at the Spitfire. That's why it crashed.'

My attention sharpened.

'Mr Bristow, that's an extraordinary accusation to make after all this time. You were ten, you said? How could you possibly know what they were firing at? It's surely more likely they were firing at an enemy plane chasing your phantom Spitfire. Don't you think?'

He shrugged and a mulish expression crossed his face.

'I know what I saw,' he repeated. 'There were only one plane and it were shot down by our own side. You'll see, if you ever make the effort to look for it.'

He spat again, tipped his flat cap and stomped away, leaving me staring out at the place where the river joined the sea, my mind a hive of possibilities and questions.

Was the Spitfire running from a German – a lone wolf on the hunt for a plane limping home from a mission, perhaps? And if so, what happened to the enemy plane? Did it get shot down by the coastal gunners?

And the Spitfire pilot. Had he got out over the water, before the plane crashed? If so, did he survive? Was he able to get ashore unaided, or did a local fishing boat come to his rescue?

Before meeting with Terry Bristow, I had taken a cursory look at crash site records, in my role as an archaeologist. They had yielded numerous reports of planes coming down in the area and just off the coast. Unsurprising, considering Romney Marsh was under one of the direct flight paths to airfields in the south of England. There was still a huge amount of work to be done to discover where all those planes were, and to record the remains of aircrew that had gone down with them.

I turned and followed Mr Bristow back along the track to the road, wanting to believe his story. His youthfulness at the time didn't put me off, I could imagine how much of a thrill it was for a small boy to see the iconic Spitfire overhead. It was something nobody would be likely to forget. But the plane being a victim of friendly fire I hoped would be proved wrong – *if* we got the go-ahead to start a dig, and *if* we could find the crash site.

So many hoops to jump through before we get to that point.

I stepped up the pace, a kernel of excitement bringing a shiver along my hairline. The black cloud enveloping me lifted an inch or two for a moment.

Chapter 2

New South Wales, Australia – 1938
Bella

Bella Gardner swore under her breath, swung her weight as far to the left as she could and prayed Mini would respond. The horse changed legs without checking, veering onto the line of the ball at a gallop, ears flat to her head, nose outstretched, muscles straining to follow her rider's instruction. Bella flung her arm out and swung the polo stick under Mini's neck, where it clipped the ball, changing its trajectory so it flew wide, missing the goal by inches.

She raised her stick in the air in a victory salute, standing in the stirrups and allowing Mini to gallop on around the ground. The scoreboard remained at 7–6 and the bell rang for the end of the match. The home crowd surrounding the polo field cheered and clapped as she passed them and she couldn't keep the grin off her face.

What a match and what a result. Bindalong retaining the Mackenzie Cup for another year meant everything.

Mini dropped to a walk, sides heaving, neck lathered in sweat. The horse knew her work was done, and Bella marvelled at the intelligence of her favourite polo pony. She jumped off, loosened

6

the girth and nose-band, and walked back to the pony lines, Mini following. Her teammates, Jim, wearing the number 2 shirt, and Grant, number 3, equally sweat-drenched and excited, came over and congratulated her.

A lad with the number 1 on his back ran to meet her, a wide smile splitting his freckled face. His horse, a stocky roan with a thin tail, stood forgotten, blowing hard. He threw an arm around her.

'Bella, that was bloody brilliant – what a save!'

'Well, someone had to do it, after you let Jack ride you off the ball like that,' Bella said, pulling off her helmet and shaking out her red hair. Her shirt, with a large 4 on the back, stuck to her skinny frame and she pulled it away, trying to cool down a little. 'You made it far too easy for him, Aiden, and if I hadn't been on Mini, I would never have got to it in time and he would have scored. I sure as hell didn't want the final to end in a shoot-out, did you?' Aiden's grin disappeared and a worm of shame nipped her stomach at her mean words. Why couldn't she let go of her brother's lack of competitive spirit? Still, he had almost cost them the final and retaining the trophy. She pushed his arm off her shoulder. 'And for Christ's sake, see to your horse, you've not even undone the girth. You're a disgrace.'

She stalked away, irritation prickling under her skin. The brief high of saving the goal dissipated as if it hadn't happened. She tied Mini up to the rails in the shade of a stand of white gums, took the heavy stock saddle off her back, and unwrapped the bandages that protected her pony's legs during a match. Mini's dark bay coat was streaked black with sweat and Bella set to with a bucket of water and sponge, checking her over for injuries and soreness at the same time. Her spirits rose again as she worked, the routine act reviving her. As the name suggested, Mini was the smallest of her team of four polo ponies, but by far the best. Fast, nippy and as brave as her rider, she understood the game as well as Bella did.

'Here, let me finish that for you.'

Bella looked up as Greg Boyd, her father's horse trainer, approached and took the sponge from her. The rest of the ponies were cool and comfortable, thanks to his ministrations, and she smiled her thanks, stretching her tired back while watching him work.

'Can you keep an eye on her off-hind, for me? That galah, Clark, clipped her with his stick when I rode him off,' she said. 'It might need a cold hose and some liniment tonight. I'll come and check her later.'

'Will do,' he said, pushing his hat to the back of his bald head. 'Go and get yoursel' a drink. You deserve it after that save.'

'Wasn't Mini marvellous? I swear that pony would do it on her own, if she was allowed. She's so bloody quick.'

Greg grinned.

'Well, her rider ain't no slug either. The pair of you make a cracker of a team.' His grin faded and he nodded towards Aiden's team of ponies, tied next to Bella's. 'Don't be too hard on the lad. Jack has years more experience, and knows every trick in the book. And Aiden hasn't had the chance to practise like you have.'

'I know, I know,' Bella said, swiping at a patch of Paterson's curse with her whip, decapitating it of its purple heads. 'He's so infuriating, though. It's like he doesn't care if we win or not.'

Greg laughed, then shut his mouth at her look. He bent to the task of washing off Mini's legs and belly, dodging her kicks as the mare objected to the water. 'Stand still, will you,' he muttered. 'I don't need two bitches giving me a hard time.'

Bella turned away, smiling in spite of herself, knowing she was meant to hear the words. Dear Greg. She wouldn't stand for it from anyone else, and he knew it.

Walking up the shallow steps into the old wool shed that was used as a bar on match days, she was greeted by her father. John Gardner no longer played sport, arthritis in his knees making even walking difficult. These days, he leant on a stick, but still came to watch his children play polo at the club his own father had set up forty years earlier.

8

'Well done, Bella. That last play was a beaut,' John said, as they sat with a cold drink at one of the long trestle tables. 'You read the game well today, and we'd have struggled in a shoot-out for sure if you hadn't seen where the ball was headed at the end and prevented the draw.'

Bella flushed with pleasure at his praise. It felt hard won, as if she had to try twice as hard as Aiden; her father reluctant to acknowledge her skills. He had played 4 and been one of the best players in NSW in his day, so she took his words and kept them warm, wishing her mother had been there to see her play. Her biggest cheerleader who gave her the self-belief that she could do anything she put her mind to.

'I like that feeling of being last man, guarding goal,' she said, eager to discuss the match further. 'I figure I was too hard on Aiden at the end, though; I couldn't have bested Jack either, his horses are so much bigger and stronger than mine.' She dropped her head, thinking back to the last play of the final, then looked up at her father. 'He hasn't had the practice time I have, being away at school until this year.'

John Gardner shook his head.

'Aiden hasn't got such a good game brain as you, yet, but that'll come with experience. He'll learn there's more than brawn needed in polo. And once he's finished school next year and back here full time, taking over Bindalong, he'll soon get it. I have high hopes for him – Bindalong team will make its mark with him as captain, you'll see.'

Why did he have to do that? It always came back to her brother; as if her life and dreams didn't matter. Bella swallowed the bitterness in her throat and kept her thoughts about Aiden's future to herself, making a space on the bench for Grant and Jim as they approached, carrying glasses of beer.

Her brother wandered into the shed, his mop of red hair lit from behind by the lowering sun, identical in colour to Bella's, and a legacy of their mother's Scottish forbears. She hated that people often mistook them for twins. Aiden collected a glass of lemonade as he passed the bar, and came over to sit with them. The chat was all about the day and who did what, who scored the best goal and who would win the rosette for best pony.

They were soon joined by the rest of the teams, and rivalries were left at the door. Cold beers were passed around and friendly discussions became raucous, the language growing coarser as the beers went down. It was stifling, the tin roof sucking up the sun's rays and roasting everyone inside, until they spilled out onto the shaded verandah where the air at least had a hint of movement.

A reminder that summer was around the corner and this was the final game of the season.

'What'll I do now, Dad?' Bella said, as they sat on the steps outside the shed. 'Life's going to be so boring once the horses are turned away for the summer.'

'What's happened to the plan of going overseas and studying in Edinburgh? You promised your grandmother. Her letters are full of all the places she wants to show you.'

Bella dug her heel into the dust, dragging a trench in front of her. Part of her couldn't wait to get away, but days like this reminded her how much she would miss life here – where the Gardner name opened doors. Her mother had persuaded Dad to allow her to travel to Scotland to see Granny Mack, her maternal grandmother. He thought it was completely unnecessary, but had agreed in the end. Since Mum's death, Bella was surprised he hadn't changed his mind and demanded she remain at home, and a tiny part of her acknowledged she was terrified to leave and explore the unknown. But it was her mother's dearest wish that her children have the chance to discover their roots and she couldn't let her down.

'I've missed the boat this year. The soonest I can start university in Scotland is next September. Granny Mack will have to wait.' She gazed ahead at the small hills in the distance, the russet and grey slopes dotted with gum trees and bush scrub. The lowering sun caught in reflection on the surface of the dam that fed water to the station, the mirror-flat water turning rose-pink until the red orb slipped behind the hills. 'Maybe I should stay and help here? There are all the youngstock to break – I could do that, with Greg?'

It was a forlorn hope, she knew, but worth another go.

'I'm not letting you anywhere near those animals until they're broke and safe.' He scowled and grunted as he tried to rise. 'Come on, help your old man up. It's time for the presentation.'

That evening, the family had dinner with Greg and the rest of the station hands. It was a tradition to celebrate the end of the polo season and the beginning of the summer. A long table had been set up on the covered verandah, and sixteen sat down to a meal of home-bred mutton, and potatoes roasted alongside the meat. The Mackenzie Cup had pride of place on a side table, along with the rosette Bella had won for Mini being judged Best Pony.

'Seeing as no bugger wants to buy our meat, we may as well enjoy it ourselves,' John said, as he carved thick slices onto platters.

Susan Gardner, Aiden and Bella's stepmother, stood behind him, looking as out of place and fearful as a cat at a dogfight. At a curt nod from her husband she placed the loaded plates onto the table and asked everyone to come and eat. Conversation became desultory until they had finished eating and alcohol began to loosen tongues. The talk was all about the looming drought and the recession.

'Gonna have to pray we get some rain, otherwise we'll be shooting the buggers if we can't sell 'em,' Liam Connaughy, Bindalong's foreman, said, his voice, as ever, sounding as if he'd been gargling with gravel.

'Enough shop talk, Liam. Tonight, we're celebrating the end of the season, and the Bindalong team winning the trophy again. Aiden and Bella have done a bloody top job in their first season.'

John struggled to his feet, shaking off Susan's guiding hand and raising a beer in a toast to his children. The assembled group raised their beer bottles and cheered and clapped. Aiden flushed under his freckles, looking, for once, pleased to be the centre of attention.

Bella accepted her father's words with a nod, hiding the fury in her gut. She hated the way her stepmother tried to turn him into an invalid. Always hovering, always suggesting he was doing too much and should rest. Thank God Dad didn't have any truck with it. Susan would more than likely be happy to see him in the ground, and then she could run off back to Sydney and spend his money.

'*Over my dead body.*'

She smiled benignly and jumped as someone whispered in her ear.

'What're you hatching now?'

Greg slid onto the bench beside her, an eyebrow raised and a grin pulling at the corners of his mouth.

'I've no idea what you mean,' she said.

'Bella Gardner, I've known you since you were ten, and that innocent expression has only ever meant one thing – mischief.'

'You're imagining things. I was just enjoying seeing Dad and Susan entertaining everyone.' She gave him her brightest smile. 'This is always the best night of the year – the end of winter, the beginning of the summer season. How could I not love it?'

'Hah! For one thing, it's the end of polo for six months, and for another, you hate Susan, so don't try and sell me your bullshit.'

Greg nudged her with an elbow, trying to get a rise from her, she knew. Determined not to take the bait, she turned the tables.

'You might have known me for the past eight years, but I've known you the same amount of time. You hate it as much as I do. You're not interested in the other livestock or planting grain, and the only horse-work you'll be doing is trying not to get dumped on your arse by one of the colts you've got to break. Am I right?'

She laughed at his expression. This year's crop of three-year-olds had a couple of mean colts that were already proving a handful.

Greg shrugged and dropped his head.

'Yeah, it's gonna be hard, and I'm not getting any younger. Maybe I'll let one of the others start them, while I work that filly of Trilby's. She's a good sort and has a great temperament.'

Bella patted his knee.

'You do that. You need to look after yourself, old man,' she said, and jinked away from the hand that tried to slap her leg, laughing.

Greg laughed with her and rose.

'Once I've got her going sweet, I'll let you get on her – who knows, maybe she'll be another Mini – she's got the same bloodlines.'

'You're too kind, sir. I just wish Dad would let me have a go with the youngsters, he's so unreasonable about the subject.' She frowned, knowing well the reason. 'I'm not Mum.' She drew a breath, then dragged a smile onto her face and raised her glass. 'Anyway, here's hoping for another Mini – imagine a whole string of them? I'd be untouchable.'

Greg squeezed her shoulder in sympathy and raised his own bottle of beer.

'I'll drink to that,' he said. 'Which reminds me – I need another beer. G'night, Bella, I'll see you in the mornin'.'

He hobbled away, his shorter leg giving him an uneven gait. Aiden wandered over and nodded at Greg as he passed him. He sat down in the vacated place, jamming Bella against the wall. She watched Greg go, wanting him to stay and make her laugh. Her brother burped loudly and leant against her.

'Shit, have you been drinking?' Bella shoved him off her. 'Dad'll skin you alive if he realises you've been on the grog.'

Aiden put a finger against the side of his nose and gave an exaggerated wink.

'I won't tell him if you won't,' he slurred. 'An' why shouldn't I have a beer to celebrate our win today? Every other bugger is, and I'm nearly seventeen, almost an adult.'

'Really? Well, why don't you act like it, then? All that money getting you a fine Pommy education, and you still act like you're twelve.' Taking the almost empty bottle off him, she slid it along the table out of his reach. She put her hand under his chin and forced him to look at her. 'Things are bad enough around here, without you setting Dad off on one.' She dropped her hand. 'Bloody Susan doesn't help – I can't stand her. I should have applied for university sooner, then I would be on my way to Scotland in a few weeks instead of kicking my heels around here for another year. God knows how I'm going to bear it without going crazy.'

'Well that's your own fault. Don't go blaming Susan, she's done nothing wrong. I dunno why you don't like her,' Aiden said, his eyelids drooping as he evaded her gaze. 'She's kind, and if you made the effort, I reckon you two could get along.'

Bella held her temper in check – just.

'There is nothing about that woman that I like or want to like,' she said, her tone cold. 'How can you think she could ever replace Mum? I don't understand you – it's like you've forgotten she existed.'

Aiden sat up.

'You know that's not true,' he protested. 'Mum was the best, and I miss her every day, but that doesn't make Susan a bad person. It's you that treads all over Mum's memory, going all out to try and kill yourself in any way you can.'

Bella's temper finally got the better of her. She put her face right up to his, smelling the beer on his breath.

'Don't you dare say such a thing. You're about as much use as a wet weekend, and Mum would want me to carry on doing the things she loved.' She pushed him away from her, again, almost knocking him off the bench. 'Now get the hell out of my way.'

14

Chapter 3

Jennifer

'Jennifer.'

I stopped and waited, took a calming breath and dragged a smile onto my face. Dominic Smith-Hayes, the head of our archaeology team and my boss, sauntered up to me.

'Good morning, Dominic.'

Civility at all times, Jennifer. Even though the sight of him put my teeth on edge.

He halted in front of me, just a fraction too close. I took a step back. He didn't seem to notice.

'Morning. God this is a cold hole, isn't it?'

He was tucked up in a sheepskin car coat under a spotless hi-vis vest with a shiny hard hat on his carefully gelled hair, looking out of place among the rest of us, who were ready to get our hands dirty and had dressed accordingly. Behind him, keeping a distance from the two of us, was a group of strangers, who also stuck out like sore thumbs. These were the new volunteers then. My fingers itched. All I wanted to do was get started on the dig but it seemed I was to be nurse-maid to the newbies.

He flicked a glance their way and I gave them a small nod. One or two nodded back. A girl put a hand up in a half-hearted way.

'This is Dr Dawson, who'll show you the ropes. She's in charge here, so if you've got any questions, she's your man.'

'Please, call me Jennifer,' I said, mentally cringing. 'Right, come with me and we'll check you're all kitted out with everything you need.'

The arrangements for them to volunteer had all been in place before I knew about it. Our usual crop of students being in the middle of exams and dissertations, Dominic took on this group after being contacted by a charity working with members of the armed forces who had suffered trauma in battle.

While I applauded the commitment and support offered by the charity, I knew I was not the best person for the job. Too focused on my work, too impatient – and that's on a good day. There had not been any of those in the past few months. My amiable and easy-going assistant, Alan Bowes, high-tailing off to France on a twelve-month sabbatical to work on another project hadn't helped.

Under normal circumstances I would be in my element – the start of a new project was always exciting and I loved the feeling of uncovering something which had been buried for decades.

Not this time.

How could I lead this dig when all I wanted to do was shut myself away and wallow in grief?

I dreaded the next few weeks.

I took a breath and kept my gaze on Dominic.

'Keep me posted if anything exciting happens,' he said. 'I've got a meeting and might not make it back today.'

Yeah, because you'd rather schmooze and beg for funding than get your hands dirty doing real archaeology.

I said nothing.

Dominic threw a parody of a salute and walked away.

Why did he always do things like that? Try as I might not to get riled up, he rubbed me up the wrong way every time he opened his mouth and out came another glib comment that he thought was clever or funny. Or the way he could belittle others without seeming aware of doing so, as in this instance. I felt like slapping him but made do with shaking my head and apologising to the group. They looked at each other and shrugged; water off a duck's back.

'He's a bit of an arse-hole, isn't he?'

The speaker was one of the men. Solid, twentysomething, I guessed. He looked as if he took his fitness seriously judging by the shape of him, though he leant on a stick. He frowned at the sheepskin clad back of Dominic retreating to his BMW. Could the man be any more of a cliché?

'I'm sorry,' I said again.

I led the group to one of the Portakabins set up at the edge of the dig site, handed out buckets, trowels, brushes and gloves, and gave each member a sticky label.

'Please write your name on these and wear them for the first few days. I'm terrible at remembering names, so don't be insulted if I get yours wrong, it's nothing personal.' I looked around the group. 'If anyone has difficulty with kneeling, digging, or anything else physical, now's the time to tell me. There are any number of jobs we can give you to do. Finds washing, logging finds, bagging up are all time consuming and need close attention to keep our records straight.'

A couple of men and one of the two women raised their hands. One of the men sat in a high-spec wheelchair and the other two had visible physical difficulties. The woman wore heavy make-up and dark glasses which failed to hide the network of scars across her face. I wondered fleetingly what the rest of her body was like.

'Right, stay here and I'll get someone to take you over to the finds hut and show you what to do. The rest, come with me. At this early stage of the excavation, we're still machining at the moment so you'll mainly be watching and waiting. But it'll give you time to get the feel of this place and see what goes on – if you're interested.'

There was a general murmur from the group. One or two of the men hung back and a short, wiry, red-haired lad, who might still be in his teens, lit up a cigarette.

'There's no smoking allowed anywhere on-site,' I said, quickly. 'If you want a fag, go outside the gate – and pick up your dog-ends, you're on someone's private land and will treat it with the same respect as you would want your own home treated.'

'Fag-ends are the least of what's in Ginge's gaff,' one wag piped up.

'Fuck off,' came the reply, but 'Ginge' nipped out the cigarette and replaced it carefully in its pack.

God, I must sound like a harridan.

I felt old enough to be the mother of most of them. Alan would have made a joke and got them all onside by now. I sent a quick text to Yvonne Miller, my assistant, to say she had three extra pairs of hands for the finds hut waiting in the main Portakabin, and she replied with a smiley face.

We walked on towards the site of the main dig where the digger driver and a couple of my colleagues stood, talking. The giant yellow machine looked out of place, but in such a watery, flat environment it was a necessity to get deep enough to find the Spitfire – if it was even there. The geophysical survey of the site revealed a series of shadows at one side of the field, very close to the banks of the waterway that ran down to the main river. It might be the plane, or it might be old farm equipment that got bogged and had been abandoned to sink into the marsh.

So far, the exploratory holes had yielded nothing and quickly filled with water. The team had already made a start on the visual scanning and metal detecting, going by the fresh heaps of wet soil piled up in what looked like random parts of the field. As we approached, the driver climbed back into his machine, started the engine and manoeuvred it into position for another attempt.

'Wait here, please.' I halted the group and walked over to speak to George Faulks, our geophys expert.

He put his thumb up as the driver dropped the bucket and lifted the first sod, then turned away and approached me.

'Anything promising this morning?'

He shook his head.

'Not even a rivet, so far. Though we know it'll probably be at least twenty feet down so geophys won't be much use. Still, I hope we'll find some evidence closer to the surface.' He grinned at my expression. 'Don't look so glum, it's early days, and we might not be looking in the right place. The geophys findings showed a wide area where we might potentially find something.'

'Yeah, I know. But patience is not a virtue of mine.'

He laughed and agreed it was frustrating.

'Who're the gang?' he said, nodding towards the group, who looked bored and cold. 'They're not like your usual students.'

'They've been sent by a charity that works with ex-military personnel.' I lowered my voice. 'I always assumed soldiers were the same size and shape – you know, Arnie Schwarzenegger types. Most of this lot don't look like they would know one end of a rifle from the other.'

George laughed again.

'Bit judgmental there, Jen, don't you think?' he said. 'I assume they've undergone some kind of trauma and this is meant to help in their recovery?'

I nodded, hoping he didn't notice the flush I could feel running up my neck. He was right – I was being judgmental. What did I know about these people and what they had gone through in their careers?

I wondered what it must be like to be related to someone who served in the armed forces. If Ben or Rosie had decided it was a career they wanted to pursue, I would have done my best to dissuade them. One or two of this group didn't look any older than Ben, yet must have seen and done things I couldn't begin to imagine.

. . . and yet, they were alive and getting on with their lives . . .

That night, as he had every night for the past six months, Ben came to me. This time he was very small and crept into my bed and snuggled up next to me, on the other side to Peter, his tiny feet cold against my thigh.

'I had a bad dream, Mummy.' Even as a little boy, he knew to whisper so as not to waken his dad. 'I was shut in a box and you couldn't find me. It was scary. Why couldn't you find me, Mummy? Why did the man put me in a box?'

It was a recurring fear of his as a child which shattered my already fractured heart. I brushed away his tears and hugged him, burying my face into his sweaty neck and inhaling the little boy smell of him. He fell asleep in the crook of my arm, and I lay, not moving in case it disturbed him.

My boy, my firstborn.

I woke with tears on my face and a Ben-shaped hole ripping me apart.

How is it possible that I'll never see you again, never hug you again, never laugh at your atrocious jokes, or have my mood lifted when you smile. You were my world for twenty-one years; how can I carry on without you?

Chapter 4

Bella

'I'm heading down to Sydney tomorrow for a couple of days. Do you want to come with me?'

Bella's head shot up from the book she was reading in the shade of the porch, and she grinned at her father.

'Oh, yes please, that'll be fun. Are we staying with Uncle Gavin? I haven't seen him and Aunt Pegs since . . .' She faltered, cringing inwardly and cursing herself, unable to look her father in the eye, wary of his reaction. She changed tack. 'Please let me be pilot, I haven't flown for ages.' Hoping it wasn't a fruitless question; it seemed as if he wanted to keep her wrapped in cotton-wool these days.

His face took on the closed, pinched expression she had come to recognise, and Bella rose, her head hanging.

'Sorry, Dad.'

He scowled and turned away, clearing his throat.

'Yes, you can fly. Why do you think I asked you along?' he growled, ignoring her apology. 'These knees can't cope with piloting anymore, and everyone else is busy.'

His smile looked more like a grimace to Bella, and she

managed a small grin back, but she could have kicked herself for speaking without thinking first. Still. Even if it was true that he only asked her so he didn't have to fly himself, it was an exciting prospect. Getting off the station for a few days, and having the chance to pilot the Curtiss Robin for the entire flight to Sydney lifted her out of the foul mood she had been in since the ponies had been turned away two weeks ago. Her mind flitted back to flying lessons with Mum, practising take-offs and landings over and over again at the bumpy airstrip until she could do both with her eyes closed.

She kissed his cheek briefly, then picked up the book and ran into the house, stopping in the doorway for a moment.

'I must pack, and we'll need a hamper,' she called. 'Then I'll go and check the plane.'

'Woah, there's no rush. We don't have to leave until tomorrow after breakfast.'

'Still. It's best to be ready to go by tonight. The Robin's not been out for weeks, the brakes are bound to be locked on, and I'll fill it with fuel and water.'

And she fled, excitement bubbling in her veins.

They set out the following morning, the sun low in the sky, but already with the promise of heat in the day to come. Bella sang as she pulled the throttle back, and the small plane lifted off the rough airstrip cut into one of the paddocks on the edge of the main homestead. She loved the feeling of her stomach being left behind as they climbed steeply, and considered whether she felt more at home flying or galloping flat strap down a polo field on Mini. Both made her feel whole, as if this was what she had been put on earth for.

As the sun climbed, the small cockpit grew hotter, and Bella opened the side windows as far as they would go, to catch some cool air. She couldn't remember the last time she felt this happy and decided flying was even better than the thrill she got from polo. The plane felt like an extension of her own body, something she controlled without even thinking about it.

As they flew over the Razorback, a line of small hills about an hour out of Sydney, Bella noticed a bank of black clouds building in front of them. She raised her hand to get her father's attention and pointed ahead.

'Looks like a bit of weather up ahead,' she mouthed, turning in her seat.

Her father pointed at the ground.

'Let's land until it passes,' he yelled.

Bella frowned, frustration rising. They were close to Camden, where there was a small airfield, but who knew how long they would be stuck there if the storm hit.

When had her father become so cautious? She knew the answer, of course. Well, she was the pilot, it was her call, and she knew she could easily outrun whatever the weather wanted to throw at them.

They had crested the line of hills and Bella made her mind up. Pushing the throttle as far as she could, she nudged the stick to put the small plane into a shallow dive. It shot forward, skimming the hills as its speed increased.

Her father's slap on her shoulder came as a shock, but she kept her attention on flying the plane.

'I can get us to Sydney before this storm hits,' she said to herself, gritting her teeth and concentrating on levelling out without losing too much speed.

She could almost feel the fury building behind her, and Bella flicked a glance over her shoulder. Her dad's face was bright red, his eyes fixed on her, a furious scowl etching deep trenches in his forehead. He hunched lower in his seat, his arms gripped around his body. There was nothing he could do to stop her and she knew he knew it.

She looked away again, and sat a bit straighter. When would he start to respect her and stop treating her like a child? She could get them to Sydney, safely. All he had to do was believe in her.

'This is the last time you ever fly this plane,' he yelled, loud enough for her to hear his words.

A lead weight landed in Bella's gut. Her only hope of changing his mind was to prove herself. She concentrated on flying fast and straight for Sydney Airport.

An hour later, after an increasingly bumpy ride with the small aircraft being buffeted like an empty bag in a wind, they landed at their destination, just as a huge hailstorm hit the coast, battering everything in its path.

Bella taxied off the gravel runway and stopped outside the main building. She switched off the engine and listened to it tick as it cooled, her ears ringing, while her heart hammered. She wanted to punch the air, yell, dance a jig; anything to release the tension in her body.

John Gardner climbed slowly out of the plane without saying anything, shook off Bella's helping hand, and hobbled away.

She watched him go, still fizzing with adrenaline but aware that he might not speak to her for the rest of their trip.

Sod him. I knew I could do it and I did. I don't care if he's mad at me, I would do the same thing again tomorrow.

Following in her father's wake, she skipped a few yards and then broke into a quick run towards the building, hailstones stinging her face as the storm finally got into its stride.

Her father barely spoke to her while they were in Sydney, staying with his sister Pegs and her husband, Gavin. His mood hung like a black cloud over everyone.

'What's up with your dad?' Aunt Pegs asked Bella on their final morning, as they prepared breakfast.

Bella shrugged. A worm of shame and embarrassment wriggled in her stomach for a moment. This visit had been long anticipated by her aunt and uncle, and she had managed to scupper the family reunion.

'He's furious with me,' she said.

Pegs raised an eyebrow and fixed her with a questioning glare.

'You don't say? What did you do to make him so mad at you this time?'

'We had a disagreement about where I should land the plane.' She felt the need to explain, to get Aunt Pegs onside. 'Since Mum . . .' She swallowed, still unable to emit the words. Tried again. 'The storm made Dad panic. He wanted us to land at Camden and wait until it passed.' She shrugged again. 'I *knew* we could reach Sydney before the weather hit us. Who knew how long we'd have been grounded at Camden. He's changed, Aunt Pegs. It's suffocating.' She looked her aunt squarely in the eye. 'Bloody Susan doesn't help. She treats him like an invalid . . . as if he's an old man who can't look after himself. I can't bear being around her, and don't understand why he married her so soon after losing Mum.' Turning away to hide the angry tears threatening to fall, she picked up a pile of crockery and began to set the table, setting her teeth at the memory of the words her father had flung at her in the plane. 'The person he wants me to be is not who I am. I *need* to fly, need to challenge myself.' She slammed plates down on the polished oak dining table. 'I've got to prove I can do all the things Mum did.' With the last plate set, she placed her hands flat on the table and dropped her head. 'And that I'm better than Aiden.'

The last came out as a whisper, without conscious thought.

She realised, for the first time, that she had spoken a truth she had never allowed herself to acknowledge. To admit how constrained and chained by her gender she felt, and how much she resented her brother. She railed against the fact that, even though he was younger than her, and had neither the same sharp mind nor her competitive spirit, Aiden was the golden child. *He* would inherit Bindalong. *He* would be invited to play on regional polo teams while she had to watch from the sidelines. *He* would be allowed to apply for his full pilot's licence. *He* would have all the advantages while she was expected to marry, have a brood of children and play the good wife.

She suspected her mother had felt the same way.

'I'm sorry my row with Dad has spoilt our visit,' she said. 'I just wish he would have more confidence in me.'

'Dear girl, don't you see he's terrified? After what happened to your mum – dying the way she did – he can't help it, and you surely can't blame him?'

Bella had been there when the young horse her mother was riding for the first time took fright at a snake, reared up and came over backwards. She would never forget the sound of the horse crashing to the rock-hard ground. The thump and grunt as its breath left it and it struggled to get up, followed by a smack as a foot caught her mum on the side of her head. She closed her eyes for a moment, trying and failing to dispel the memories.

Her mother's broken body.

Blood soaking into the dust.

Her father going out to the paddock afterwards, grabbing the horse and whipping it until it was covered in bloody welts, its shrieks of agony reverberating through her head long after he took a shotgun and killed it.

Afterwards his roaring at the men not to touch it.

The carcass lying in the paddock until the crows and dingoes picked the bones clean.

She had never told Aiden what he did; hated him for his cruelty.

Aunt Pegs drew her over to where a pair of chairs were placed under a window. She pushed her gently into one, and then sat in the other.

'Your mother was an extraordinary woman. She could do anything she put her mind to, and was the perfect match for your dad – she stood up to him, encouraged him – *loved* him.' Aunt Pegs's eyes filled, but she brushed away the tears. 'And he loved her right back; far more than I think even he realised, until she was gone. I've never seen John so broken as he was at her funeral.' She paused, as if remembering the day, just over a year ago, when her sister-in-law had been laid to rest. Raising her gaze to meet Bella's, she continued. 'But he's a man who needs a woman around him, and Susan came along at the right time.' She put a hand up to quell Bella's remonstration. 'I know she will never replace your mum – and neither should she. But if she can make your dad happy again, then perhaps you should cut her some slack.' She took Bella's hands in her own, her pale, manicured nails and ring-covered fingers so different from Bella's brown, work-roughened ones, the nails bitten almost to the quick. 'As to wanting to prove yourself; I think everyone who knows or meets you recognises what a strong-minded, independent young woman you are. You have nothing to prove – to your father or to anyone else, for that matter.' Aunt Pegs sighed. 'But for better or worse, you are part of a family that counts tradition as one of the most important things that keeps it together. You know your dad will never let you take precedence over Aiden, no matter how much you want to. It's just not the way things go – you do see that, don't you?'

'But that doesn't make it right, Aunt Pegs,' Bella said, her voice rising in frustration. She pulled her hands away. 'Why should it be the case, that just because I'm a girl I can't do all the things Aiden will be able to do, the moment he's eighteen? It's not fair.'

She heard the pettishness in her tone, aware she sounded like a spoilt child, but couldn't help herself.

Aunt Pegs fixed her with her familiar sharp gaze – head on one side, one eyebrow raised.

'Bella, I know what it's like to be the sister. Of course, I do. Many years ago, I was in the same position as you are now. Girls had even less independence, back then. Finish school, find a good match, get married. Be a wife and mother.' Her expression took on a distant sadness. 'Uncle Gavin and I would have loved to have our own children, but it wasn't to be. You and Aiden have been the family we never had, and I love you both as if you were my own.' She patted Bella's cheek, her eyes full of grief for a moment. Then she seemed to shake herself out of it and rose from the chair. 'Look, how about this for an idea. Why don't you stay with us for a while longer; get out from under your dad's feet and let the dust settle between you?'

Bella looked at her old, scuffed boots, thinking how out of place they were next to her aunt's smart town shoes. What could she possibly find to do in Sydney? It was a foreign land, where everyone had somewhere to go except her. Her aunt lifted her chin and winked.

'I thought you might like a visit to the racetrack at Penrith with your uncle? He's got a new car – if you speak nicely to him, he might let you take the wheel and do a circuit or two. I'll talk to your father, persuade him to get on a train for the journey home.'

Bella felt a grin pulling at her mouth and a giggle forced its way up her throat before she could stop it.

'Really? That would be beaut, Aunt Pegs, thank you.'

She hugged her aunt, her spirits rising a little. Things didn't seem quite so impossible, after all. And, perhaps, by the time she returned, her father would have forgiven her.

Chapter 5

Jennifer

Driving home, having checked everyone had left the site and it was secure, I couldn't prevent a sense of disappointment from washing over me. Test holes had been dug in all but two of the potential areas of interest in the field and nothing had turned up except a couple of rusty bits of metal, one of which had a Massey Ferguson badge on it. Some ancient farm machinery that had been left to rot into the ground, no doubt.

The volunteers looked bored stiff by the time they had been collected by someone from the charity in a minibus, and I wondered if we would see any of them again. One or two appeared interested in what we were doing but I couldn't blame them for not wanting to stand around getting cold for another day. Scott Hudson, the ex-Royal Marine with a pronounced limp, who had made me smile when he called Dominic an arse-hole, seemed keen, and asked some sensible questions about what we were doing. His enthusiasm might not survive for long, though, if we didn't find something soon.

It was getting towards dusk when I arrived home. The evenings were lengthening but with a commute of over an hour, there

29

wasn't much of the day left by the time I parked my estate car alongside Peter's ancient Land Rover in the drive. I sat for a while, not able to make the effort to go inside to the desert that passed for home nowadays.

At least getting back late meant we didn't have to spend many hours together, silence reverberating on silence. As this thought skipped through my brain, I swallowed the guilt sitting like a lead weight in my throat. These days during the long hours of darkness our bodies carefully stayed as far away from each other as possible while still sharing a bed. Wasn't grief meant to draw a couple together? Make them forget their differences and lean on each other through the most devastating time of their lives?

The study door was closed, which indicated Peter was in there, doing whatever it was that he did with his time. His current research was something to do with an obscure medieval monk who might have been the first person to discover penicillin, centuries before Alexander Fleming did. Peter was convinced of his theory, although proving it seemed impossible to me. My husband was nothing if not tenacious though, and would keep going to the bitter end.

I put my hand up to the doorknob and hesitated a moment too long before turning it. Walking on down the hallway to the kitchen, I felt defeated in knowing how to get past this wall which had grown between us.

The kitchen was warm, the range a natural draw for everyone who entered this, the heart of our home. At present, two dogs and a cat were curled up in a jumbled heap in front of it. Sally, the Jack Russell terrier, lifted her head and disentangled herself from her bed-mates, coming over to me with a shake and a wave of her feathery tail.

'Hello, you,' I said, scratching her behind her ear. 'At least you're pleased to see me.' She rolled over, exposing her pink belly, and rubbed herself along the rough hessian of the kitchen mat.

Ginger, the huge tom-cat, eyed me with hate and yawned widely, showing all his teeth. He was Ben's cat, and ignored everyone else, spending his time either on Ben's bed or fighting for space in the dogs' basket. His ears flattened and he hissed as his tail was stood on by the oldest of the three, Deefa, climbing stiffly out of the bed.

'I bet no one has fed you, have they?'

Spying the empty bowls still on the draining board in the utility room, I scooped cupfuls of dog food into them and put them in opposite corners of the room, knowing Deefa would relinquish his supper if Sally decided she preferred his to her own. Ginger jumped up onto the worktop and I shooed him off, then put his outside the backdoor and turfed him out after it.

Animals done, I tried to think what to make for supper. If only we could live off dried kibble, it would make life so much easier. Hunting in the fridge and freezer for something quick, all I could find was a pack of bacon and some mushrooms which had seen better days.

Carbonara it is then.

A door slamming upstairs told me Rosie was home. Quick feet pattered down the wooden stairs. My daughter sloped into the kitchen, pulling on an old denim jacket as she entered. She had become a pale version of the lively teenager of a few months ago. One of Ben's old scarves was wrapped around her neck and mouth, making her eyes seem even larger than usual. Dark rings beneath them accentuated her pale skin.

I wanted to hug her but knew it was off limits. Looking at her caused a physical pain; she was so like her brother. I turned away and opened the fridge door again for something to do – anything to make things seem normal.

'Mum?'

I pulled my head out and closed the door, trying for a bright smile.

'Hello. How's your day been?'

She shrugged, heaved a sigh, said nothing. We avoided eye contact, and she flopped down on the old sofa. Sally immediately jumped onto her knee and Rosie hugged her, burying her face into her wiry coat. Tears sat like tiny raindrops on her closed lashes.

Wait. Don't pull her into your arms and cradle her as you did when she was tiny, making everything better.

There is nothing I can do to make it better. Turn away again; breathe . . .

'I've decided not to go back to uni.'

A whisper. Emphatic.

Pause.

Don't jump in. Let her talk if she wants to.

I went and sat beside her, stroking Sally's head, receiving a lick as a reward. Tried to think how to react.

'Why?'

As if I didn't know.

She lowered her head, her hair hanging forward so I couldn't see her face; a tear dropped onto my hand. I pushed a stray lock behind her ear and tilted her chin so she had to look at me. Even then, she could barely hold my gaze, her eyes flooded with tears.

I pulled her in to me and let her cry, tears and snot mingling into my jumper. The dog whined and licked us both. Rosie gulped and sniffed.

'Poor Sal, she can't get used to such a load of sad sacks in this house, can she?'

I smiled.

'Do you want to talk? About uni?'

She pulled a tissue out of her sleeve and tried to fix her face, mascara drawing inky trails down her cheeks. I took it from her and wiped them away as best I could. It was the first time in as long as I could remember that she had let me help her. Always her own person, so independent, so strong-willed, so determined.

So lost – like the rest of us.

She let out a long sigh.

32

'It doesn't seem to matter anymore.' Picked at a hangnail, making it bleed. Sucked the red drop. 'Why am I bothered about a history degree? What use is it? It won't bring Ben back.' Bitterness lent steel to her words. She looked me in the eye. 'Sometimes I get so angry at him. How could he do something so risky? So reckless?'

I sighed. 'The grief counsellor has talked to us about this, hasn't she?' Rosie glared at me. 'It's a natural part of grieving.' How to help her, when I couldn't even help myself, was beyond me. 'The uni has said you can take as much time as you need. Perhaps tell them you want to put your course on hold for now.'

'They want to know if I'm going back for the start of summer term. I can't even think of it. Why can't they bloody well leave me alone?'

Anger at the thoughtlessness of some faceless administrator rose in my throat. I pulled her in to me again, gently rubbing her back.

'I'll help you write a reply, explaining why you're not coming back yet, if you want?' I breathed in the scent of shampoo. 'I honestly think you shouldn't burn all your bridges though. Give yourself some more time. Why not leave it until the end of the year and then see how you feel? If it still doesn't seem the right thing to do, then that's okay.'

She nodded against my shoulder, and I dropped a kiss on top of her head.

How could we continue navigating home life with three broken-hearted people in the house? It felt as if we had all built a barrier around ourselves, behind which we were untouchable. I had no idea how to break down the one I had built for myself, never mind Rosie's or Peter's. Our family was broken, and the one person who could fix it was gone forever.

Chapter 6

Bella

A week later, Bella returned home to Bindalong. The day at the speedway circuit had been the highlight, seeing so many airplanes together alongside the racing cars. It had reminded her of a day when her mother had taken her and Aiden to Sydney to see Amy Johnson land in Australia.

'Can you imagine how Amy Johnson must have felt when she arrived after flying all the way across the world?' Bella said to her uncle after she had landed the Curtiss Robin at the racetrack, her heart still hammering from landing in front of the other pilots who had already arrived and stood watching her. 'I remember Mum bringing Aiden and me to Sydney to watch her. I got her autograph, did you know?'

Uncle Gavin had laughed. 'I never saw you so excited, when you came to our house afterwards. You've forgotten that's where you all stayed, haven't you?'

'Did we? I can't remember anything else about that visit. Only Miss Johnson. She was so kind to me. When I said I wanted to fly airplanes like she did, she told me to follow my dream and not to listen to anyone telling me I couldn't do something because

I was a girl.' The memory burnt as brightly as the day it had happened when she was ten years old. 'And now I'm doing just that. I should write and thank her for her advice.'

The rest of the visit had been far less exciting. She had endured two shopping trips and an appointment at a hair salon with Aunt Pegs to have her hair cut, set and curled. Her aunt seemed to have taken it upon herself to turn her reluctant niece into a young lady fit to be seen in Sydney society.

It was arranged that Uncle Gavin would sit behind her in the Curtiss Robin, inducing a stomach-churning frustration in Bella, who saw his presence as nothing other than baby-sitting. But her father had been adamant; she could only fly home if she was accompanied, otherwise she must get the train and the airplane would stay in Sydney until the next time someone needed to go to the city.

'He's won, again,' she muttered, throwing clothes into the small valise she had brought with her from home.

'Darling, careful with that frock – it is silk, you know. You don't want your new wardrobe to look like dishrags before you even have a chance to wear any of it, do you?'

Aunt Pegs took the offending garment and smoothed it out on the bed, carefully folding the sky-blue silk tea-dress and placing it in the case.

'Aunt Pegs, where the hell am I going to wear something like that?' Bella asked. 'There's not much cause for tea dances round home. You know that as well as I do.'

'You're planning to go to university, next year, aren't you? Strange as it may seem, most of the world's women don't spend their lives in moleskin britches, boots and a check shirt,' said Aunt Pegs, lifting her gaze and smiling at Bella. 'One day, you will thank me for choosing this dress for you.'

'Hmm, you think so?'

Bella grinned and her aunt laughed.

'Well, as long as you don't wear it to muck out the horse pens,

I don't care when you wear it,' she said. 'Just promise me you'll try to enjoy the feeling of being feminine, once in a while.' Aunt Pegs patted her cheek. 'You never know – you might even get to like it. You're a beautiful young woman, Bella, and so like your mum. Don't hide in the shadows.'

Heat prickled along her hairline and Bella dropped her head. Being compared to her mother was impossible. Catriona Gardner was just Mum to her and Aiden, but to everyone else she had been a shining light in the community. How did Aunt Pegs ever imagine she could fill the same shoes?

Chapter 7

Jennifer

After two days of digging, we still hadn't found anything significant. The volunteers had dwindled to eight, which didn't surprise me – who wants to stand around in a wet, windy field all day with nothing to do?

Scott Hudson continued to show enthusiasm, offering to help with mundane jobs and asking questions about the process and what we expected to find. Surprisingly, the young redhead, Ginge, also turned up each day, methodically digging through the layers without complaint. I attempted to keep them busy, getting them to sift through the spoil for any aircraft debris or other finds.

On the morning of the third day, in the far corner of the field, closest to the river, the digger driver struggled to keep his machine stable. The ground there was almost a quicksand, the hole he was digging filling with water as soon as he scooped out each bucketful of sandy soil. The edges of the widening hole were fragile and fell in constantly, making the driver's job even more difficult.

'We can't go any further with this machine,' George said, as we watched the huge bucket dip into the watery sludge for the umpteenth time. 'The driver's getting very twitchy and I don't blame him – if the ground gives way under him, we'll never get the digger out.'

'Can we get a tracked 360 digger and some of that temporary roadway matting?' Bringing in one of the enormous machines was the only thing I could think of which could cope with the conditions.

'The contractor is sending one over and I've ordered some of the matting. I'm hoping it will all be here after lunch.' I raised a sceptical eyebrow and George pulled a face. 'Well, miracles do happen, and the contractor owes me a favour.'

'Well, let's hope we get lucky.' I nodded towards the yellow machine. 'Tell him to stop – it looks far too dangerous. We'll wait until everything arrives and is in place.' Frustration gnawed at me. 'This is our last chance. If we don't find anything today, I think we're going to have to pull the plug on it.'

I hated admitting defeat, but putting all my faith in the memory of an eighty-three-year-old man was always going to be a gamble.

George frowned and shrugged. 'This is one of the most likely locations for finding a crash site I've been involved with in all my time as an archaeologist,' he said. 'Don't give up just yet, Jen, please. The plane could be lying several metres down in this ground.'

'And if it's there and buried way down, how do you think we can raise it?'

'Perhaps we won't be able to. But we'll at least discover which plane it is and who the pilot was.' He shrugged. 'Let's just go through the process and see if we can find it first.'

I reluctantly agreed and left him to it. I walked over to where the remaining volunteers were dredging through a heap of spoil.

Scott looked up as I approached.

'Is this something of interest, do you think?' he said, holding up a mangled piece of metal. 'It came out of the last bucketful.'

I took the bent and twisted piece from him and my pulse jumped. It was light – far too light to be from an old bit of farm machinery. There was no rust on it, and it looked like a crushed tin can, the metal concertinaed in on itself.

As if it had hit the ground at speed . . .

I looked at Scott and grinned. 'I think it might be very interesting, yes. Good work, Scott.'

He smiled back. 'What is it, do you think?'

'I can't say until we clean it up and take a closer look,' I said, shaking my head. 'Probably a piece of the fuselage covering or wing which was ripped off on impact.' I turned the metal over, rubbing away the damp sand and mud still clinging to it. My fingers found the blunted edges of a rough, circular hole and a small frisson ran through me. I gently cleaned the muck away from it. 'Bingo.'

Scott watched me keenly. 'What have you found?'

I showed him and his eyes met mine, widening in shock.

'A bullet hole?'

I should have known he would know what it was – he had probably seen plenty like it in his time.

I nodded. 'I think so. Probably from a German machine-gun if it's part of the plane we are looking for.'

'So, there is a plane here somewhere? We've just got to find it.'

I looked at him, his face bright with excitement. I couldn't keep a grin from my own face. He reminded me of the thrill of finding something on my first dig. I nodded and smiled, then put my hand up as a caution.

'We mustn't get ahead of ourselves, though. The number of planes that flew over this place during the war was huge. Plenty of them would have been struggling to get back to their base, damaged and bullet-ridden. Bits would fall off at any time, I have no doubt.'

His excitement seemed undimmed.

'Yeah, but it's the first thing we've found that might mean something, right?'

I couldn't help but laugh. 'Yes. Yes, it is.'

Chapter 8

Bella

John Gardner was waiting at the side of the airstrip when Bella landed the Curtiss Robin the next day. The flight had been smooth, and Uncle Gavin a more relaxed passenger than her father.

Bella ran over to her dad, and put her arms around him in a hug.

'I missed you.' Her voice was muffled against his chest.

He unclasped her arms and stepped out of her embrace, shook hands with Uncle Gavin, then turned and hobbled over to where he had parked the truck.

So, that was the way of it.

She wasn't forgiven, and her dad could hold a sulk for weeks. Bella blinked hard, lifted her bag and followed the two men. Self-pity rapidly turned to frustration at her father's refusal to forgive her for proving herself.

Dammit, I'm not the one acting like a child. If he wants to play his stupid games then let him. He's going to end up a lonely old man the way he's pushing us all away.

Later the same evening, she and Aiden walked across to the far paddock to check the horses. Their feet kicked up small spirals of dust which caught in the final rays of the lowering sun and turned their boots golden.

'What the hell did you do that has had Dad in such a blue since he came home?' Aiden's gaze stayed on the horizon. Bella was used to the fact that he rarely looked at whoever he was talking to; as if he was afraid to meet someone's eye and see what they thought of him.

She shrugged. 'I didn't obey him.'

'You've spent your whole life disobeying him; it must have been something major for him to be giving you the silent treatment after so long.'

Bella stopped and put her hand on his arm, pulling him round to face her.

'It doesn't matter what I did. What matters is that he will never see me as anything other than a kid – and even worse, as just a girl.' She searched his face – almost a mirror of her own. Aiden managed to hold her gaze for a moment then lowered his eyes. 'I can't bear it. So, I've decided to go to Scotland as soon as possible rather than wait until next year. I've written a letter to Granny Mack, asking her if I can stay with her.'

'But, you can't.'

The words burst out of him, surprising Bella.

'Don't tell me what I can or can't do. Who the hell do you think you are?'

Aiden's face twisted, his cheeks reddening.

'I didn't mean it like that. I'm not telling you what to do,' he mumbled. 'All I meant was, please don't go. God knows what'll happen if you do.' His voice rose, its tone bitter. 'If you aren't here, then I won't come back next year after I finish school.'

Bella couldn't think what to say, her head full of confusing images of all the times she had fought with Aiden, belittling his abilities and lack of competitive spirit.

'Why?' she said. 'When I'm gone things'll be easier for you, surely?

You won't have your horrible big sister bullying you all the time, telling you to sharpen up your polo strokes.'

She gave him a playful punch on the arm.

Aiden shook his head, avoiding her eye. He had missed his final year at school in Scotland after their mother died, remaining at Bindalong at their father's insistence. As siblings they had become almost strangers during the time Aiden had spent in Scotland, staying with their grandmother during school holidays. Bella hadn't seen him for over five years until this past year. Living in the same house hadn't brought them any closer though – they were chalk and cheese in every way except appearance.

She felt a pang that soon he would be out of her life again, and who knew when they might see each other next. A worm of guilt and despair made her squirm – she had made his life even more of a misery since Mum died, instead of being someone he felt he could turn to.

And now, he was about to disappear back to the life he knew better than this one. As the reality hit her, Bella realised how much she would miss him, how much she had got used to him being in her life. She wanted to make up for the times when she had been beastly to him; to show him she could be a better sister. But even if they both ended up living in Scotland, Aiden would be at school and who knew where she would be – she couldn't stay with Granny Mack for ever and wouldn't want to. It was a depressing thought.

'Strange as it might seem, not everything's about you,' he said. 'I know you need to compete, be the best, test yourself. It doesn't mean I feel the same.' He rubbed his face, passing the back of his hand across his eyes. 'I want to study art and the classics, play my violin in an orchestra, go to concerts – I can't do any of that here.' He shook his head. 'You and Dad have never understood me – always thought of me as a wet blanket, not *man* enough.' Bella couldn't stop the flush running up her back, though Aiden didn't seem to notice or care. He continued, 'I might as well speak a foreign language. I think Mum knew I wasn't cut out for this life even when I was very young, but she didn't understand either. Susan does, but she's so frightened of Dad she's no help.'

Bella felt weighed down by his words. She couldn't deny any of what he said, but jumped on his final comment.

'Susan? You're kidding. All she does is try to belittle Dad and turn him into an old man before his time. She's part of the problem.'

Aiden turned on her. 'If you gave her half a chance and got to know her, you wouldn't say that.'

He marched on towards the paddock and Bella watched him go, not knowing what to say. Finally, she ran after him and caught up as he reached the gate. Putting a hand over his to stop him opening it, she pulled him around to face her again, trying to make him look at her, to see the truth in his eyes.

'Tell me then. Tell me what I don't know about Susan and how I've misjudged her.'

For once, he held her gaze, his expression fierce.

'Open your eyes, Bella. It's Dad who does the controlling – you know that better than any of us – why else do you want to fuck off and leave?' He dragged his hand out from under hers and opened the chain on the gate. 'You know he hits her, don't you? That's why she spends her time trying to appease him. It's her way of keeping him happy.'

'That's a lie.'

'No, it's the truth. And if you ever thought of anyone other than yourself, you would see that.'

Aiden pushed the gate open and strode across the paddock towards the mob of horses dozing under a stand of gum trees.

Bella stared after him. Her brother might be many things, but he didn't lie. Flashes spun through her brain; snippets of memories. The woman her father had brought into their home indecently soon after Mum died; who seemed glamorous and light-hearted compared to the rest of the family who were drowning in grief.

How dare Susan be so happy to have reeled in Dad? Fury snagged at the edges of Bella's mind at the way her stepmother tried to cheer Aiden and her up. To be a new mother to them – as if that could ever happen?

The change in her had occurred gradually, making Bella ever more suspicious about her relationship with Dad. Thinking back, she realised that what she had seen as grasping and needy could just as easily be recognised as someone doing their best to protect themselves. The trying overhard to please, the anxiety about Dad's ailments, the timid suggestions. Gone was the cheerful, gregarious woman her father married, replaced with a silent shadow.

A shiver ran up Bella's spine. How could she have read Susan so wrongly? Aiden was right; she was so caught up in her own selfish needs she'd been blind to everything going on around her.

She ran after him. It was almost sunset and darkness would follow quickly, so she matched his pace and they reached the horses a moment later. Mini whickered and came over first. She fed her a piece of apple, then stood resting her forehead on the horse's neck, drinking in the warm smell of her, trying to block out the shock of her brother's words. Mini held still for a moment and then shook herself and wandered away. Aiden walked through the rest of the mob, running his hand over a couple of them, talking nonsense in a low voice to them.

Bella watched him, seeing how the horses responded to his quiet manner by lowering their heads and following him as he moved. He had changed since Mum died – grown from a short, stocky teenager into a slimmed-down version of himself who stood the same height as her – a young man, on the verge of adulthood. She was too hard on him; they only had each other, and needed to stick together.

After checking the water trough they turned back the way they had come, their shadows and those of the gum trees stretching long and thin ahead of them as daylight bled out of the sky.

They walked in silence until they were back at the gate, then Bella couldn't stop a torrent of thoughts and emotions from spilling over.

'Why didn't you say something before? I believe you, and I don't know how I could miss the fact that Dad has been making Susan's life a misery these past months. How could he do that to her?' She swallowed the lump in her throat. 'And apart from anything else, I have been a bitch to you. I'm sorry, Aiden. I've been so caught up in my own self-pity about Mum, I've not even asked how you're doing.'

Her brother's face flushed, lit by the last rays of the dying sun.

'I should have spoken up sooner, but you had such a blue against Susan, I thought you would back Dad.' Bella wanted the earth to swallow her. Did he really think so badly of her? 'I ought to have known you wouldn't ever think it was okay for him to do those things,' he said, hurriedly.

'I can't believe he's capable of hitting a woman – any woman,' Bella managed to say, before she covered her face with her hands and leant against the gate, an image of the poor horse her father almost whipped to death flashing through her head. She *knew* how violent he could be. Guilt swamped her, leaving her overcome by her own culpability. After a moment she wiped her eyes on her sleeve. 'I should have seen how unhappy Susan is. It's my fault, I've made her life a misery as much as Dad has.'

'Don't be an idiot. There's only one person to blame here.'

Aiden's voice had a steel in it Bella had never heard before. She noticed the set of his jaw and how cold his eyes were.

'What can we do, though? Who would we tell? Nobody will believe that the great John Gardner is a wife beater.' A thought hit her. 'You don't think he did the same to Mum?' She whispered the words, lead in her gut at the thought.

Aiden's laugh was a harsh bark.

'Do you honestly think Mum would have put up with being bullied? Would you?'

'I hope she didn't have to, and no, I don't think she would have. But you know what he can be like – his temper and sulks. He's never grown past throwing tantrums when he's crossed or doesn't get his own way.' Bella kicked a stone. 'Damn it. I can't believe we haven't known what he's like all these years.'

'Mum did a good job of shielding us from the worst of his rages, I guess.'

Tears ran down Bella's cheeks again. She had just lost the father she thought she knew and loved. It was too much; her mother gone and now this.

'One thing's certain,' she said after a moment, in between sniffs. 'I'm definitely leaving. When do you go back to school? We could go together.'

Aiden's head snapped up as he fastened the gate.

'Together? You're not serious? I leave next week. Do you honestly want to be seen travelling with your wee brother?' He glared at her. 'You loathe me hanging around you, you've made that very plain since I've been back.'

Bella hung her head.

'I know I've been the worst sister, but the longer I stay, I know I'll say or do something I'll regret, and will no doubt make things worse for Susan.' Her throat closed on the words. 'Please, Aiden.'

He ran a hand through his mop of red curls, and huffed out a long breath. After a few moments during which Bella couldn't breathe, he put his arm around her shoulders and squeezed.

'Well, you're the only sister I have, so we'll just have to put up with each other,' he said, pushing hair off her forehead. 'Will you have time to get all your papers and tickets in order?'

Bella nodded, words falling out of her mouth. 'I've got almost everything organised, already. I will be ready by the time you need to leave.'

Aiden gave her shoulder another squeeze.

'Okay. One more thing . . . perhaps you could show Susan a bit more kindness, until you leave? I think she'd appreciate it, and it might help her stand up to him. I don't know what else we can do.'

It was as if the tables had been turned and he was her big brother, instead of her being the older sister. Bella buried her face into his shoulder. She didn't deserve his gentle treatment and it brought on yet more tears.

He let her cry, until finally she raised her head.

'We could tell the police . . .' she said.

'And say what? That we think our father is hitting our step-mother? Do we have any proof?' He raised his shoulders and she shook her head. 'And if they looked into every case of men hitting their wives, half the state would be up on battery charges.'

'I suppose you're right. I know one thing – no man will ever raise a hand to me. I'd kill him if he did.'

Aiden smiled and rubbed tears off her cheek.

'He'd either be stupid or crazy to try such a thing,' he said. 'Look, if you're set on coming to Scotland immediately, of course it makes sense for us to travel together.' Linking arms with her, they walked back towards the lights of the homestead. Aiden talked as if he was thinking out loud. 'This is my final year at school and I don't know what I want to do once I'm finished. Only thing I do know is that I won't come back here and do what Dad's family has always done. It's not the life for me.'

Bella thought back to the conversation she'd had with Aunt Pegs a few days earlier. If Aiden didn't want the station, then who would take it on? She would have bitten her father's hand off if he offered to let her take charge. But now? Now, she couldn't wait to be as far away as possible from Bindalong.

Chapter 9

Jennifer

The piece of metal Scott found lifted my spirits, and the optimism I had about finding the plane returned. I was impatient to see what else we could dredge up from the boggy ground near the river. Waiting for the new equipment to arrive and be put in place had my hands itching, but experience had taught me that I must let those who knew about such things get on with their work and not try to rush them.

By mid-afternoon, the driver was ready to go again.

George and I stood back and watched the huge machine extend its telescopic arm and take a bite out of the hole which had already been excavated. Lifting a bucketful of mud, sand and water, the driver swung the giant arm, opened the bucket and deposited its contents onto a fresh bit of grass. Water leaked away, leaving a mess of detritus which spread like a stain over the ground.

The temptation to run over and start examining what was there was almost overwhelming, but I stuck my hands in my pockets and remained still. Health and Safety was a strict regime on-site, and I would be the first to condemn anyone jumping in before the digging was finished.

George grinned at me. 'That bit of wreckage has got you buzzing, hasn't it?'

I nodded and smiled back. 'Thank God Scott found it. I really thought we'd drawn a blank here, even though the old guy, Terry Bristow, was convinced about what he saw all those years ago. Looks as if he was right.'

'Yeah, but one small bit of metal does not a whole plane make, right?'

'I know, I know.'

My words came out more sharply than they should have, but I couldn't help it. I didn't need George reminding me that it might be the only thing we would find. It was such a difficult site, and the plane could be so far down we might never find the rest of it.

I walked over to where Scott and Ginge worked on the spoil heaps from the morning dig.

'How are you getting on?' I said, as Scott stood, straightening his back and easing his leg. 'Take a break, if you want. There's no rush and this kind of work takes a while to get used to.'

Ginge immediately stopped what he was doing, took a packet of cigarettes out of his pocket and wandered away to the gate. At least he had taken my words to heart. I watched him go, thinking how young he looked; his pale, spotty face with no sign of a wrinkle or stubble could have belonged to any schoolboy.

'You wouldn't think he's old enough to join up, never mind do the stuff he did before he got medivac-ed out of Afghanistan, would you?'

I glanced at Scott, unaware he had been watching me.

'He does seem very young.'

'Yeah, don't be fooled. He's as sharp as a tack and as hard.'

'Did you serve together?' Felt like biting my tongue. 'Sorry, that's none of my business.'

He shrugged. 'That's okay. I never met Ginge before coming here to help, but he's one of those who likes to talk about his time out there.' He rubbed mud off the trowel in his hand. 'We've all been through the wringer, one way or another, and everyone handles it differently I guess.' Shifting his weight from one leg to the other, he gazed at me. 'I've been around enough pain and grief in the past few years to recognise when someone is hiding it. The signs are there, if you know what they are.'

I tried to keep my face still, heat racing up my back. Was he talking about me? Did he guess? I thought I could be professional and leave Ben out of my working day, but having this bunch of volunteers working alongside for the past few days made me realise how hard it was.

'It must be tough for such young, active people like you to have to leave a job you love and find a new way of life,' I said. 'I can't imagine how difficult that would be. The armed forces must be a very different way of life to civvy street.'

'Yeah. It is.' For a second, Scott's face changed, and I glimpsed devastation in his expression. He drew in a breath and smiled at me. 'This – working here this week has been by far the best thing I've done since I came out of the Marines. It's like a treasure hunt or something; I can't wait to find more stuff.'

'If you're interested, I could tell you more about what we're doing?'

'Would you? Yeah, I'd like that, thanks. It would be good to know exactly what we're looking for and why.'

'Come on, let's get out of this wind and find a coffee. I'll fill you in on what we do in this team.'

We walked over to the site hut in the corner of the field which sat alongside a catering van that was owned and run by a small group of women who kept us supplied with coffee, cakes and sandwiches. It was a relief to get out of the ever-present wind, which seemed to find its way inside whatever clothing I chose.

Sipping hot drinks and munching on fruit cake, I pulled out a laptop from my backpack and showed Scott the company website.

'As an archaeological company, we specialise in retrieving airplanes from the First and Second World Wars. You'd be surprised how many were never recovered, or even known about. Plenty of pilots managed to get out and survived the crash, but if the planes were too badly damaged, they were just left to rot into the ground.'

'Sometimes it still happens today,' Scott said, through a mouthful of cake. 'It's just too difficult to go in and retrieve it.'

'I would have thought with all the hi-tech gubbins in today's planes and helicopters, the powers that be would want to do their best to get them back.'

He nodded. 'Some of the new stuff, yeah. And they do their best to recover everything, so it doesn't fall into the wrong hands, but it's not always possible.'

'That might be the reason so much was left back then, as well,' I said. 'New planes were being produced all the time, with better technology and materials. Having said that, it must have been devastating for families when the crew disappeared with their plane and nothing was done to find out what happened and where they died.'

I dug my nails into the palm of my hand, keeping my mind on work, not thinking about Ben and where he might be.

Scott sat without saying anything, his expression blank, eyes hooded. Again, too late, I realised I must have stepped onto territory I had no idea about. I wondered what trauma he had endured to end up here.

The rest of the volunteers wandered into the hut. They all looked cold and bored, their clothes damp and grubby from digging in the mud. Sitting at the tables, cupping their hot drinks, I felt bad for them. Did they really want to be here? Or was it part of their rehab they had to get through?

I rose and went across to them.

'I know the start of this dig has been slow, and it must seem as if nothing is happening,' I said. 'The good news is that Scott found the first solid evidence of a plane wreckage this morning. It hopefully confirms that we are in the right place. And with the

51

bigger equipment that's arrived this afternoon, we should find more wreckage in the next day or two.'

'What happens if you don't?'

Ginge, sharp and combative. Scott was right.

'Well, if we can't find anything else to prove a plane crash site, then we will put the field back to how we found it, and move on.'

The disappointment of finding nothing was part of the job. I couldn't deny it, but my gut refused to acknowledge we wouldn't find anything.

'Seems like a whole lot of hard work for nowt,' he said.

'It might feel like that, but what we do is important to many people.'

'It's not them freezing their bollocks off guddling around in the shit, though, is it?'

A couple of the men laughed, nodding.

'You're right, there is little reward so far, for the work we've done,' I said, trying not to tell him he could fuck off if that was his attitude. 'You're all volunteers, and as such, you're very valuable to us. But, you don't have to stay. You're free to go whenever you want.'

He dropped his gaze and shrugged.

'Nowt better to do, I suppose. Cake's fucking ace, too.'

He winked at me and grinned, and I had to smile. Cheeky little git, I bet he could be a pain in the backside. Well, he could try his best to wind me up; I wouldn't rise to it. I returned to my coffee to find Scott reading the company website on my laptop.

'It's good to have someone showing an interest,' I said. 'I'm not sure Ginge and the others share your enthusiasm.'

'Yeah, well, I guess it's not everyone's idea of a good way to pass the time.'

'I'd have thought anyone who has been in the forces must like working outside and be used to being cold and wet.'

Scott shrugged, not looking up from the screen.

'It's part of the job. Doesn't mean you have to enjoy it.' He shut down the website and closed the laptop. 'But you're right, it's one of the main reasons guys join up. They love the outdoors and can't stand the idea of sitting behind a desk in an office every day. It was for me.'

'The Royal Marines, though. They're pretty hardcore, right?'

'The best, that's what they are.'

'You must miss it.'

He sighed, examining his hands for a moment. Then he looked up at me.

'Every day. Every fucking minute of every fucking day.' His eyes shone and he rubbed a grubby hand across his face. 'Sorry. You don't need to hear about my shite life. Excuse me.'

He rose, picked up his mug and left me sitting on my own, pondering my own shite life.

Heading back outside, I found the wind had dropped and the sun was shining, though banks of cloud sat on the horizon over the sea. Still, it was nice to feel warm for a change. I walked over to where they were still digging, casting a long glance at the growing pile of spoil. The hole had expanded to more than double the size it had been at lunchtime and the telescopic arm seemed to disappear into the depths each time it went in. By the time I reached it, the driver had stopped, obeying a frantic wave from George, who stood at the far side, leaning over the edge and inspecting the innards.

'How's it going?' I said, coming alongside him.

He grinned and pointed. The bottom of the hole was filled with brown liquid mud. Sticking above it was the sharp edge of a piece of metal which disappeared into the side of the hole.

My pulse skipped and I mirrored his grin.

'Well, isn't that a fine sight?' For the first time in months, the fog of despair lifted. I wanted to dance; to jump down into the hole and put my hands on it. 'Is it safe to go down and take a closer look?'

'Not a chance,' was George's quick reply. 'That mud would

suck you in so you'd never get out. We'll need to step out the sides first, then cut out steps down into the bottom. If the ground is too unstable, we'll fix ladders. Then we'll try and pump most of the water out. I'll get it sorted, but you'll have to wait until tomorrow.' He fixed me with a look I knew too well. 'Come on, Jen, you know all this. We can't afford to cut corners at this stage.'

Frustration and impatience fought with common sense. He was right, of course, but it didn't stop me arguing with him.

'Find a rope and tie me on. All I want is one quick squizz, just to see what we've got. No one else need know.'

I put on my most persuasive voice, but George was unmoved by my entreaty.

'Fuck's sake, Jen, don't even suggest it. Who is Health and Safety officer, on this site?' I rolled my eyes. 'Me. That's who, and you know who would get shafted if you did anything so stupid and someone found out.'

'Sorry. You're right. It's just so close; all I want to do is put my hands on it.'

'Yeah, well, one of us has to act like a grown-up around here.' We turned as someone hailed us. 'Shit, that's all I need. What does he want?'

Dominic minced his way across the soggy ground in his Italian loafers, looking even more out of place than when I had seen him on the first day. There hadn't been a sign of him since then, though he had sent me a text asking for updates.

I put a hand on George's arm, knowing his antipathy towards our boss was on a par with my own.

'I'll talk to him. You go and sort out with the driver, and organise the stuff we'll need tomorrow, so we can get down and take a proper look at what we've got.'

He nodded, throwing a last dismissive glance at the approaching figure, before striding across to the waiting driver. I turned and walked over to meet Dominic.

'Bloody hell,' he said, when I led him to the hole. 'That's a crater, not a hole. I hope it's worth it; must be costing me a fortune.'

I didn't rise to the bait. The company wasn't his, it was owned by a charity. Dominic was one of four directors.

'We finally got some evidence, earlier today,' I said. 'The ground being so unstable, we had to bring in all this extra equipment, just to make it safe.' I pointed to the shard sticking out of the side of the wall. 'It was worth it to find this.'

He looked unimpressed.

'What is it? Doesn't look too special, could be a bit of old farm machinery, for all we know.'

I bit my lip and drew in a breath.

Keep your temper, Jen.

'The piece we found earlier is made of aluminium, and this is almost certainly part of the same wreckage.' I paused, crossing my fingers that I was right. 'In other words, I'm pretty sure this is the plane we were tipped off about.'

'I hope you're right,' he said. 'Where is everyone? I didn't take on those knackered ex-Army scroungers so they can spend their time swilling our coffee and filling their faces on cake.'

Every muscle in my face tightened. Why did he have to be such a bigot? Relaxing my hands, I smiled.

'They're a great help, but we've done as much today as we can do, so yes, they're swilling coffee and having a break.' I glared at him. 'They've earned it.' I turned away and began to walk back across the field, Dominic following in my wake. 'And if I hear you being so derogatory about them again, I shall put in a complaint against you.'

'Oh, get off your high horse, Jen. You know I'm right – they're a bunch of losers, free-loading off the government the lot of 'em.'

I stopped dead and whipped around, colliding with him so he slipped on the wet grass and landed on his backside.

'You are a fucking disgrace, Dominic.' He scrambled to his feet, mud and grass sticking to his chino-covered arse. I stabbed a finger into his chest as he backed away from me. 'And don't call me Jen. My family call me Jen. My friends call me Jen. You are neither.'

I marched away before I burnt any more bridges.

Damn. Now I'd done it.

Chapter 10

Bella

When Bella told her father she had changed her mind and planned to leave for Scotland with Aiden, he barely acknowledged her words.

'Do what you want, Bella. Nothing I say will affect your decision, will it?' he said, loading his plate with mutton pie. 'Pass the spuds, Aiden, mate, will you?'

Bella bit back the words she had planned to say. If he wanted to continue behaving like a sulky schoolboy, then let him. She turned to Susan who sat beside her, the tension coming off her stepmother in waves.

Would her words have consequences? Would Dad take his temper out on his new wife?

She pushed her plate away, nausea rising at the smell of the meat.

'Susan, would you mind helping me pack, please? I've never been on a long trip before and could do with some advice as to what to take with me.'

Her stepmother twitched so violently she almost knocked her water glass over. Bella grabbed it before it fell and righted it. She placed a hand over Susan's, giving it a small squeeze.

'Of course,' Susan stuttered. 'Of course, I'll help you. I'm not sure I'll have much advice that's any use, but I'd be happy to give you a hand.'

Bella caught Aiden's eye. He tipped his head and a half smile came and went in a moment. She didn't look at her father, but was well aware of him watching her from his place at the head of the table.

The next few days were spent packing up her things, organising tickets for the same ship as Aiden, and breaking the news to Greg and the rest of the station hands.

'We'll miss you,' Greg said, when she told him she was leaving. 'But I suppose we'll just have to manage without you for a while. What'll you do over there? Can't see your gran'ma letting you sit around making her place look untidy, like you do here.'

Bella grinned and made a face at him.

'I'm going to finish getting my full pilot's licence as soon as I can. Mum and I discussed it when we were making plans for me going to Scotland,' she said. An image of her mother flitted through her mind's eye. 'That's only for you to know, okay? I've told no one else, so don't go blabbing your mouth off.'

Greg raised an eyebrow and fixed her with a stare.

'Yer ma was quite a lady, wasn't she? And you're a proper chip off the block, ye know,' he said, his head on one side, as if examining a horse's conformation. His face became sombre. 'So, you and the boss have fallen out big time, then? If you haven't told him, there must be a reason.'

'Nothing you need to know about,' she said, wishing she hadn't said anything.

Greg looked at her sideways and put an arm around her, squeezing her gently.

'Well, go safely, Bella. Things won't be the same around this place with you gone.' He lowered his gaze and scuffed the ground with the dusty toe of his boot. 'Don't make much sense workin' all them young ponies without you here to take 'em on.'

A lump closed Bella's throat and she turned away so he wouldn't see the glint in her eyes. She couldn't deny how much she would miss Bindalong and the only life she had known.

The only thing pulling her onwards was her grand plan. When she had decided to continue flight training while lying in bed unable to sleep, it had seemed logical. She wanted to keep flying. Amy Johnson had told her to follow her dream and not let anything or anyone stop her, so that's what she would do.

In the cold light of day it seemed far more daunting. Telling Greg made it real. She couldn't go back on it now.

Bella and Aiden took the train the day before the ship was due to sail from Sydney, and stayed with Uncle Gavin and Aunt Pegs for a night. Greg had been the one to drive them to the railway station, John Gardner barely even acknowledging they were leaving. He had shut himself in his office, saying he had accounts to do. It was Susan who had waved them off from the shady verandah, tears in her eyes. Bella had held it together until they drove out of the gate at the end of the mile-long track to the main road, then broken down, stuffing a fist in her mouth to stem the sobs. Greg had cleared his throat, said nothing but patted her shoulder while continuing to negotiate the corrugated ridges of the dirt road.

Once they boarded the train, Aiden became a bag of pent-up energy and nerves. He was going back to the life he had known since he was a boy of eleven and couldn't contain his impatience to return. During the long rail journey, he regaled Bella with everything he missed about Scotland and staying with Granny Mack.

For Bella it would be the first time she left Australia, the first time she would be meeting her grandmother, the first time she must stand on her own two feet. The enormity of what she was doing brought waves of self-doubt.

What am I doing? Granny Mack won't want me cluttering up her place in Edinburgh, I'll just be in her way. How do I find somewhere to finish flight training?

It's never going to happen . . .

. . . and so on, the mass of butterflies in her belly making her want to throw up.

Aunt Pegs took one look at her when they arrived, and gave her small tasks to do, keeping her hands busy and her mind occupied with gossip about people she had never met.

After dinner, they listened to the radio, the Empire Service news programme being a nightly routine for Uncle Gavin.

'That dingo, Hitler, is a power-hungry dictator,' he said, turning up the sound to hear the latest news about the troubles in Europe. 'I don't care what anyone says, he's not after a peaceful settlement. And now Mr Chamberlain, the French and the Italians are kowtowing to him about this border wrangle with Czechoslovakia.' He flicked his newspaper open and began to read, continuing from behind the *Sydney Morning Herald*. 'I don't know what the German people were thinking, letting him take over.'

'Darling, the Germans had been in dire straits for years, and he promised to lead them out of the depression, didn't he? No wonder he's popular,' Aunt Pegs said.

'I don't know much about it,' Bella admitted. 'But surely, after the Great War, nothing will come of it? I mean, it was the war to end all wars, wasn't it?'

'That's what they said,' Uncle Gavin agreed. 'But politicians – you can't trust them an inch. There are storms brewing in Europe. Mark my words, this is only the beginning.'

Aunt Pegs frowned at her husband, hidden behind his paper.

'I'm sure there is nothing for you two young things to worry about. The politicians know what they're doing, they won't let things escalate like last time,' she said.

'Pah, I wouldn't count on it,' he said.

The next day, as Bella and Aiden made ready to go to the docks and board their ship, the newspapers announced that the Munich Agreement had been signed, and part of Czechoslovakia now belonged to Germany.

As she waved to her aunt and uncle from the ship, Bella wondered what might await her and Aiden when they reached their destination. A worm of excitement sent a shiver through her and she grabbed Aiden's arm, a similar elation to that of flying taking over from the anxiety of the past few days. It was real; she was on her way to starting her new life and nothing could stop her.

After all, nobody in their right mind would let Herr Hitler start another war, would they?

Chapter 11

Jennifer

At home that evening, I couldn't settle to anything. Why had I let Dominic get to me? I had worked under him for almost two years, knew what he was like and had always been able to bite my tongue and let his uncaring and selfish views wash over me.

Rosie had gone out to meet a friend, her mood a little elevated after our talk the previous night. I was glad she had come to me, and hoped it was a tiny step forward for her. It was bad enough her parents couldn't talk to each other; I couldn't bear the thought that she might shut down and keep her own grief bottled up too. Peter had eaten a quick supper with me and then disappeared back into his study, his routine unwavering.

It was one of those early spring evenings which give a hint of summer, the lowering sun casting a pink and golden light across the High Weald. I needed to get out of the house; remove myself from its deafening silence, do something physical to try to banish my thoughts. I grabbed the dog leads and walked down to the footpath which meandered through the local National Trust estate, Sally and Deefa running ahead along the familiar route, their heads down, examining every scent.

My mind still churned over the argument with Dominic, nausea in my stomach that I might not have a job by the morning. I knew I would have to send a grovelling apology, though the thought of doing it stuck in my throat.

I followed the dogs without conscious thought, coming out onto the lane at the next village to ours and turning towards the cottage that had always been a sanctuary for me. The curtains were closed to the deepening dusk, but a chink of light showed around the edge of the kitchen window and I hurried up the short gravel drive to the backdoor.

Knocking lightly and lifting the wrought-iron latch, I let the dogs in ahead of me and entered the warm, low-ceilinged room.

'Grandpa? It's me, Jen,' I called into the empty space.

An answering shout led me to the small, cosy sitting room, a wood stove giving off enough heat to run a steam engine. My grandfather sat in front of it, his long, thin feet so close it was a wonder his toes weren't singed. Sally trotted over to him and hopped onto his knee and Deefa flopped down in front of the stove with a sigh.

I dropped a kiss on top of Grandpa's white hair.

'Hello,' he said. 'What brings you here at this time of night? Is everything all right?'

His eyes behind the spectacles looked worried momentarily, then seeing me smile, cleared and returned to their habitual sad stoicism.

'It's a beautiful evening and the dogs and I needed some exercise.' I took off my jacket and sat in the armchair on the opposite side of the fire. 'And I haven't seen you for a few days. How are you?'

'Me?' he said, as if I might be addressing someone else in the room. 'Fine. Fit as a fiddle. What about you? How's work?'

'Work is busy, as always. We've just begun a new dig near the Romney Marsh coast. It's been a slow start – the site is so sandy and wet we've struggled to find anything, but today we discovered the first evidence of a plane.'

Grandpa leant forward. 'Well, that sounds exciting. What are you looking for? Spit? Hurricane? Bomber?'

I smiled. At ninety-six, his body might be failing him, but his mind was as sharp as ever. His interest in my work came, I suspected, from his time in the war; something he never talked about, and which I respected, though I would have loved to know about it.

'I'm not sure, to be honest,' I said. 'The old boy who gave us the tip-off is adamant that it's a Spitfire, but after all these years I'm not sure his memory is as solid as he thinks it is.'

'There's nothing like the sound of a Merlin engine. You don't forget that noise.'

'Yeah, that's what he said. We might know more in the next day or so, if we manage to lift the wreckage that was uncovered today.'

If I still had a job by then.

Grandpa pushed Sally off his knee and levered himself forward.

'I'm forgetting my manners. Would you like a coffee? Glass of wine?'

'Don't get up, Grandpa. I would love a coffee. I'll get it, though. Do you want one?'

He shook his head and leant back in his chair, rubbing his thigh with a misshapen hand. The firelight glinted off the metal strap of his watch as it slid down his wrist and caught my eye, making me realise how much weight he had lost recently.

'No thanks, but you could get me a Scotch while you're there.'

I gave him a thumbs-up, went and made myself a coffee and poured him a dram of Glenmorangie single malt in his favourite glass, put it on a tray alongside his usual small jug of water and returned to the sweltering room. I offered him the glass and held the jug over it, dribbling in the required amount of water until he put his hand up.

'Is your leg bothering you again?' I said, when I was seated once more with coffee in hand.

He shrugged, sipping the whisky and savouring the taste with his eyes closed.

'No more than usual. I've lived with it for so long I would miss it if it suddenly went away,' he said. 'It's not much fun being so old, you know. I'm just lucky I've got you close by.'

'We're the lucky ones, Grandpa. You're my rock, you know that.'

I let the elephant in the room remain, crowding our conversation but going unnamed.

We sat in silence while we finished our drinks, the fire making me drowsy. Eventually, I pulled myself out of my thoughts and gazed across at the old man whose head had dropped forward onto his chest, the empty whisky glass in danger of slipping from his grasp as he dozed.

My chest tightened. He looked so vulnerable, the sags and bags of skin covering the fragile bones of his face belying the strength of the man. He was a constant support in my life and that of my sister since our parents had been killed in a sailing accident two decades ago. My mother's widowed father had taken over grandparenting duties, childminding my two after school, taking them to swimming lessons and all the other activities they did when they were small.

I gently took the whisky glass from him, and checked the stove had enough logs banked inside it to do him for the evening. I knew he would sit there, dozing and reading, until the early hours, before he took himself to bed. Old habits die hard, he had told me once.

I put a hand on his shoulder and gently roused him.

'I'm off now, Grandpa,' I said, as he opened his eyes and sat up, apologising. 'You carry on with your snooze. I'll drop in tomorrow and let you know how we get on with the dig, if you like?'

'I'd like that. You know I love to hear how you're doing,' he said, putting a hand up to me. 'Give my love to Rosie – tell her she's always welcome here if she wants to visit.'

'She knows. But I'll remind her.' I kissed his cheek. 'Night, night. I'll see you tomorrow. Come on, Sally, Deefa. Time to go, dogs.'

'Goodnight, Jenny Wren.'

It was pitch dark outside, and it took a while before my eyes adjusted and I got my night vision. A half-moon rose slowly ahead of me as I retraced my steps along the footpath. It was enough to light my way through the ancient woodland with its venerable oaks and beeches on either side of the wide rides. During the daytime they were full of walkers and horse riders, but at this time of the evening everything was calm. I was tired and my mind had quietened. I walked slowly, breathing in the scents of the countryside I knew so well, enjoying the solitude. Even the dogs had given up on their evening hunts and trotted in single file ahead of me. A feeling of peace came over me while I walked. I should do this more often; I had almost forgotten how good it felt to be on my own, the familiar path under my feet.

Too soon, I came to the gate which would lead me back to the village, and home. Except it hadn't felt like home these past months; more like a hollow shell where Peter, Rosie and I skirted around one another, together, yet separated by the walls we had built.

Peter was in the kitchen. On the table was a bottle of red wine, almost empty. I tried to maintain the calm state of mind I had found on my walk, but the glass in his hand told the tale of another evening when he would rather spend his time drinking alone than spend it with me. His look of guilty defiance was all I needed.

Sally wasn't so judgmental and skipped over to him, pawing his knee for a pat. He ruffled her ears, which seemed to satisfy her and she flopped into the middle of the dog bed, baring her teeth at Deefa, who gave in and lay on the floor in front of the range, thumping his tail in good-natured acquiescence.

Oh, to be a labrador.

'Nice walk?'

At least he wasn't past words, yet.

'Lovely, thanks. I went to see Grandpa, stayed for a chat and a coffee.' I washed my hands and put the kettle on the hot plate, more for something to do than because I wanted another drink. 'The walk home in the moonlight was beautiful, really calm.' I paused. 'Peaceful.'

'I'm glad.'

He stood, staring into the depths of the wine-filled glass, twirling the stem so some of it sloshed over the side onto his hand.

The silence extended, growing until it became a living beast, lying in wait for one of us to dare to break it. The whistle of the boiling kettle made me jump and brought Peter to life. Still not meeting my eyes, he mumbled something and walked towards the door into the hall.

'Peter.'

He stopped, his hand on the doorknob.

'Can we talk about Grandpa?' Nothing. 'Please?'

He turned slowly, a sigh escaping him. He knew what I wanted – had wanted for the past couple of years – we had argued enough about the subject in the past, but it had been shelved by unspoken, common consent.

'Why?' he said. 'You know my thoughts on having him live with us.'

I felt my face tighten, and consciously relaxed the muscles in my jaw. I couldn't deal with an argument.

'I don't like the thought of him living alone. He's become so frail, since . . .' The knot in my throat wouldn't let the words out. I swallowed. 'He could have the downstairs spare room and bathroom. And I thought I could clear out my study and turn it into a little sitting room for him.' I was gabbling, desperate to make him see it could work. 'I'm sure he would like to keep his own space, and we could bring some of his things here, to make it familiar for him.'

'It's so like you, Jennifer; you're such a control freak. Always trying to organise other people's lives for them, whether they want you to or not. Have you even asked your grandfather if he wants to leave his home?'

Peter glared at me, his eyes bloodshot and mean with drink.

'Don't throw this back at me as if it's my fault. There's no point asking him if you refuse to have him here, is there?' My voice rose. So much for keeping calm and rational. 'He's almost ninety-seven. How can you be so callous as to refuse to let me look after him in his last few years?'

He threw his hand up, the wine spilling again.

'You know what? You do what you want to do, just like always. Who am I to stop you?' He turned as if to leave, and then spun round, spitting out words as if they were knives. 'After all, the last time you organised someone's life it ended well, didn't it?'

'What on earth are you talking about? Whose life?'

He stared at me as if I was stupid.

'Ben. Our son. Who else? You gave him the money to go on that mountaineering trip, even though I said he should stay here and get a job for the summer.' He swigged the wine. 'If he hadn't gone . . .'

His voice cracked, and he threw the wine glass across the kitchen, where it smashed against a cabinet, scattering fragments over the floor. The dogs leapt up and shot under the table. Peter stalked out of the kitchen, slamming the hall door behind him.

The shock hit me as if I had been assaulted. I sank onto a stool, shut my eyes and waited for the waves of horror to stop.

So.

The truth of his silence for the past months was out.

Me.

It was my fault.

Peter laid the blame squarely at my feet. How could he think such a thing?

And how could we come back from it now he had said it?

Chapter 12

Britain – 1940
Bella

Bella gazed out of the window of the tram at the busy streets of Edinburgh, thinking back over everything that had happened since she had been there. Eighteen months since she and Aiden had landed in Scotland. Eighteen months which had been full of new experiences, new achievements, new adventures – and the outbreak of war with Germany.

Granny Mack had taken her in and been a willing conspirator when Bella had laid out her plans. Using her wide network of friends and contacts she found her a place at a flying school down in Oxford where she could continue training for her full pilot's licence.

'You young lassies should have the opportunities which we never had in my day,' she said. 'Unless your daddy was gae rich a young lady had no hope. It wasn't seemly. Huntin', shootin' and fishin' by all means, but the main objective was to "come out" as a deb and bag a rich husband.'

'But I don't have enough money, Granny. Dad has all but cut

me off, so I can't ask him and I'll never afford it on the allowance from my trust fund.'

'Och, darling girl, never bother yourself. I'll lend it to you. You can pay me back when you've got it.' The old lady patted her cheek. 'What use is having money if you cannae have fun with it, and seeing you and your brother happy is all that matters to me, now your dear mother is no longer with us.'

She dabbed at her eyes with a tiny handkerchief and Bella blinked back her own tears, knowing how much her grandmother grieved for her daughter.

She had been awarded her licence just as war broke out and itched to join the Royal Air Force as a pilot. The recruiting officer laughed in her face.

'We dinnae take pretty wee things like yersel', he smirked. 'The WAAFs are recruiting just along the street, I'm sure they'd be happy to take you. Can you type?'

Bella had stared at him, thrusting her licence in his face, but he wouldn't even look at it and eventually she had stalked out, too embarrassed and angry to say anything, aware of the grins on the faces of the young men lining up behind her.

'Hey hen, I'll tak ye for a ride, if you want,' one of them called as she reached the door, and the whole queue laughed.

She had marched back to the joker, stared him in the eye and retorted that she wouldn't go anywhere with him if her life depended on it, then turned away and left to a chorus of whistles and catcalls.

It was the lowest moment since she had left home, but she was determined to be involved in some way, so gave in and joined the Women's Auxiliary Air Force, signing up for anything which would take her outdoors and not be confined to an office.

When she heard that female pilots were being recruited for the Air Transport Auxiliary, flying airplanes around the country to wherever they were needed, she applied immediately. If she couldn't fly in battle, she could at least be in the air doing something useful.

Watching the male pilots taking off in bombers, Hurricanes and Spitfires, while she and the other girls were allowed to fly only Tiger Moths and other noncombat airplanes left her frustrated. She was glad to be flying but knew she was as good as they were, so why couldn't she be treated equally?

And now, here she was, on her way to meet Aiden, who had finally finished school and would no doubt be itching to join up. She could imagine him as an RAF pilot, he was just as skilful as she was in the air. Since she had moved to Scotland they had met up once or twice and written to each other regularly, their relationship becoming closer even as the world fell into turmoil.

Anticipation at seeing her brother for the first time in months made her jump up as the tram approached the station. She rang the bell for the stop, then hopped down onto the busy street.

Waverley railway station, in the centre of Edinburgh, swarmed with people. Bella pushed her way through the crowd, aware she was late, too hot in her Air Transport Auxiliary uniform with the press of other bodies around her. Reaching the platform, she craned her neck to see over the heads of those already waiting for passengers to descend from the train. It sat, hissing and spitting like a sleeping dragon, steam and smoke making her eyes water and scratching at her throat. She pulled her scarf over her mouth and continued to scan the crowd.

Aiden's bright mop gave him away the minute he stepped down onto the platform, and Bella raised her hand, waving and shoving her way through until she reached him. She stopped in front of him and he grinned, wrapping his arms around her and swinging her round before planting her back on her feet.

'Look at you,' he said, standing at arm's length and surveying her. 'That uniform suits you, you look like you could fight the world and win.'

Bella laughed. 'Hah, as if the powers that be would allow that to happen.' She hugged him. 'Is your trunk in the baggage car? We should get it – Granny Mack is expecting us and will be furious if we're late.'

Aiden nodded and they navigated their way to the box car at the end of the train, where luggage was being unloaded. He handed a ticket to the porter, who arrived back with a battered trunk, plastered in labels. He gave Granny Mack's address as the place for it to be delivered, and tipped the porter. Leaving the smoke and noise of the station, they mounted the steps and walked on to Princes Street.

'I can't believe you've finished school,' Bella said once they boarded a tram and found seats. 'How does it feel to be set free?'

Her brother pulled a face.

'The way things are looking, I'll either have to go home, or join up here.' He sounded resigned, and Bella squeezed his arm. 'All I want to do is study. Did Granny Mack tell you I've been offered a place at Cambridge to read Classics?'

'No. Aiden, that's bonza news,' she said. 'You clever old thing, congratulations. This nonsense with Germany won't last long, will it? You'll be able to go to Cambridge once it's all settled down.' Bella punched his shoulder. 'My brother, the Cambridge graduate. Who would have thought that annoying little brat would turn out so well?'

He smiled and punched her back, but his eyes remained serious.

'I can't agree that peace will happen any time soon,' he said. 'Hitler won't stop until he rules Europe, or dies trying.'

'Well, let's hope it's the latter and it happens soon.'

Bella didn't want to admit that she found being part of the RAF thrilling. She got to do the thing she loved most, every day, even if it was just as a delivery pilot. She was finally doing the same thing as Amy Johnson, and who would have ever thought that was possible?

'In the meantime, you should join up over here, then we can

still see each other. The RAF are crying out for pilots, you'd hardly have to do any training.'

Aiden stared at her.

'Have you forgotten that we've discussed this? You know I don't agree with war,' he said. 'Bella, I'm against violence in all its guises. It's called pacifism.' He turned and looked out of the window at the busy street, his voice dropping. 'People call it cowardice. Do you think I'm a coward?'

'*NO*, of course not.'

Her reaction was instinctive and true, but his words hit her like a storm. Pacifism. It was a word she barely understood. How could a boy raised in the rough and tumble of the Australian outback have such views? Whatever Aiden was though, cowardly he was not.

They sat in silence until the tram arrived at their stop. Bella rang the bell and the two of them jumped off. It was only a short walk to their grandmother's house where Granny Mack welcomed Aiden and presented her powdered cheek for a kiss.

'Tea in the drawing room, please, Shona,' she said to the round-faced maid who had answered the bell she rang. 'When young Mr Gardner's trunk arrives, please ask Turner to take it up to his usual room.'

'Aye, ma'am.'

'Now, come and sit with me and tell me all your news, young man,' Granny Mack said, leading the way across a parqueted hall to a polished oak door and into a sunny room furnished with antique furniture, the walls hung with large water-colours of Highland scenery.

Sunshine flooded the place with light. It was Bella's favourite room, especially the bay window, which looked out onto a garden with mature trees and immaculate flower beds surrounding a lawn.

Granny Mack quizzed Aiden about his last term at school and his plans for the future. He was reticent about the important things Bella was itching to know, instead telling silly stories about the boys he had been at school with and what they had got up to.

Unfooled, their grandmother listened and then fixed him with a sharp eye and when he had run out of stories she spoke.

'That's all very jolly, Aiden. Now tell me what you plan to do. We are at war, the world is changing. It's time to grow up.' She tapped his arm sharply with her teaspoon. 'My cousin's son is a colonel in the Argyll and Sutherland Highlanders; I shall write to him in the morning. I'm sure he will give you a commission if I ask him.'

Shaking his head, Aiden's face paled.

'No, please don't do that, Granny.'

'Why ever no'?' she demanded. 'Yon's a fine regiment – your grandfather and great grandfather served with it.' She sniffed and dabbed her eyes with a tiny scrap of lawn, her voice catching. 'Grandpa was awarded a medal, you know, after he was killed leading his men into battle. It would be gae fitting if you followed in his footsteps and wore the Glengarry.'

Aiden glanced over at Bella, a hunted look in his eye, then dropped his gaze and fiddled with his teacup, the silence stretching. Bella desperately tried to divert their grandmother's train of thought.

What made her do it, she was never quite sure, but words erupted out of Bella before she had time to think through what she was saying. A year ago, she would have found her brother's inability to think of a reply irritating, and said something to belittle him. Now, she found herself wanting to help him confront Granny Mack's demands. Aiden had always hated being the centre of attention, all she was doing was taking the pressure off him.

'He's joining the RAF, aren't you, Aiden? Doing his bit to beat Herr Hitler and his Nazi thugs with the boys in blue.'

'What? No, Bella, you've no right . . .'

'Why that's wonderful, dear boy.' Granny Mack put her teacup down, rose stiffly and approached Aiden, who stared at Bella with horror, the colour leaching out of his cheeks. Granny Mack bent and took his face in both hands and kissed him. 'Your mother would be so proud of you.'

Bella couldn't bear the look Aiden gave her, and turned away. A sense of something sliding around in the pit of her stomach made the shortbread she had picked up seem inedible and she replaced it on her plate.

What had she done?

'How dare you?'

Granny Mack had gone to have a lie-down before dressing for dinner. Aiden sat with his head in his hands, elbows on his knees, speaking through gritted teeth.

'You had no right to say that and you know it,' he said. 'Why? Why did you after what I told you?'

Bella stood in the bay of the drawing-room window, looking out at the garden, seeing nothing. She shook her head.

'I don't know. I thought it would get her off your back.' She turned and dropped onto the sofa beside him. 'I'm sorry, Aiden. Truly. But it wouldn't be a bad thing, would it? Both of us flying – it's what we're good at, after all. And it's better than joining the Army, surely, either here or at home?'

He lifted his head and shot her a look of something she could only think of as despair.

'Did you not listen to anything I said to you in the tram? I do not believe in war. I'm a pacifist.' He enunciated each word slowly, as if she was a small child and he was explaining some difficult concept. 'Is it so hard for you to understand?'

Bella rose again and paced the room. She was ashamed. She didn't want to admit it, but it was true. Ashamed of herself for being ashamed of her brother. How could he not want to defend their mother's country of birth? She stopped in front of him.

'I shouldn't have said anything.'

'Bloody right, you shouldn't.'

'Aiden, you know what happens to people who refuse to fight, don't you?'

'There are jobs that help the war effort without fighting, you know,' he said. 'Ambulance drivers, orderlies, that kind of thing.'

'But imagine what Dad and Granny, and everyone else who knows you, will say.'

He looked up at her.

'And you, Bella. What will you say when people ask what your brother is doing? That he's staying true to his beliefs? Or that he's nothing but a bludger and a coward, not a real man who's willing to fight?' His voice rose a level, the tone cold. 'That's what you think, isn't it?'

She couldn't look him in the eye, but allowed a needle of anger to bury the shame.

'Aiden, don't make this about me,' she snapped. 'I'm not the one trying to run away from his duty to King and Country.'

'It's got nothing to do with duty.'

'Of course, it does. We are at war. Everyone has a duty.'

'And what about my duty to my own beliefs? Does that not count? How can I do something so abhorrent to me that goes against everything I believe?'

'Somebody has to stop Hitler. If everyone thought like you, we would be under the Nazi jackboot by now.' Frustration made Bella's voice sharp. 'How can you not see that?' She couldn't even look at him, much less understand him. She lowered her voice and looked out of the window again, pleading with him. 'Please, Aiden, join up; not because you must, but because it's the right thing to do.'

Bella had to go back to her unit the following morning. Dinner had been excruciating, though their grandmother hadn't appeared to notice. Granny Mack was too busy complaining about the shortage of things in the shops. How were they supposed to get by when the shelves were half empty?

She invited Bella and Aiden to spend their weekends with her. Bella knew she was lonely and enjoyed having people in her home. Judging by the way she talked non-stop she didn't expect her guests to entertain her – all she really wanted was an audience. It didn't seem to occur to her that Bella hardly got any time off, and was based in the south of England.

Aiden said very little, but mentioned he was also leaving the next day.

'But you've only just arrived. I suppose you have much more important things to do than stay with your auld Granny,' she had said. 'Are you going to the recruitment office? It's so impressive, seeing all the young men in uniform in the city.'

He shrugged. 'Perhaps. I'll see.'

Bella had bitten down on her lip to stop herself saying anything else to widen the rift between them. She hoped her words had got through to him and he realised that whatever he felt about war, it mustn't stop him from doing what he knew he should.

Saying goodbye to her grandmother with a hug and a kiss, she turned to Aiden, who came downstairs carrying a soft holdall. His face was haggard, dark shadows under his eyes.

'Shall we get the tram together?' she said.

'As long as you don't lecture me again,' he said. 'Bye, Granny. Thanks for putting up with me, and letting me leave my stuff here.'

He folded Granny Mack in a gentle hug and kissed her cheek.

'Away with ye, ye ken you're always welcome here.'

'Aye, I know. I'll be back soon. Promise.'

They walked back the way they had come the previous day and boarded a tram which would take them into the city centre.

'Where are you stationed?' Aiden said, once they had found seats.

'Hatfield. It's not too far from London.' Bella was afraid to get into another row and said nothing else until they were almost at the railway station. 'Please let me know what you decide to do and where you end up. We need to stick together.'

Aiden sighed.

'I didn't sleep last night. I couldn't stop thinking about what you said,' he said. 'You're right. How can I use my own beliefs as an excuse for not doing my bit, when everyone else is joining up? So today I'm going to volunteer for the RAF.'

He looked so downcast Bella felt a stab of guilt. She slipped her arm through his and squeezed hard.

'It's the right thing to do.'

He shrugged. 'Maybe. At least I'll be able to fly and won't have to march all over the place carrying a gun.'

'Perhaps we'll see each other, wouldn't that be beaut? I'll be delivering an airplane where you're stationed and we can meet in the mess and have a drink together.' She grinned. 'And this time I promise not to take your beer off you.'

He gave the ghost of a smile.

'Yeah, but you'll still being my bossy big sister.'

Chapter 13

Jennifer

I spent the night in the spare room, unable to face being in the same bed as Peter. Sleep deserted me, and I lay, my mind replaying his words and the look in his eyes, until my head ached. A rock sat in my chest, blocking my throat, making it hard to breathe but I refused to give in to it. I had cried enough tears already to fill a lake, and I wouldn't give my husband the satisfaction of seeing my swollen red eyes in the morning.

Eventually, I rose and sat in the kitchen with a cup of tea, trying to compose an email to Dominic, apologising for my outburst the day before. It felt as if I had succeeded in ruining my relationship with both my boss and my husband.

Well done, Jen. Played a blinder there, haven't you?

All I could think of was whether our marriage could possibly move forward from here. Peter's words had floored me, but at least now I knew what he had been thinking all this time. No wonder he could hardly bear to be in the same room as me.

He was usually so mild-mannered and easy-going, and more than happy for me to be the one who organised our family life, whether it was the kids or us as a couple. I couldn't remember him ever being set against something I had decided – not even my allowing Ben to go away the previous summer. Yes, he had suggested it would be better for Ben to stay at home and earn some money, rather than swanning around in the Alps, as he put it. But as with most things, he never mentioned it again, and I knew how much the trip meant to Ben; it would be a way to show off his skills and gain more experience as a mountaineer. More to add to his CV when he applied for jobs in the industry.

I swallowed the guilt threatening to overwhelm me. I wouldn't let myself wallow in something I could do nothing about. If I was going to get through this I had to believe that I had given our son the best opportunity possible to do the thing he was most passionate about.

Before leaving for work, I checked my emails for the tenth time – nothing back from Dominic – so either he hadn't seen my message, or wanted to sack me in person in front of the rest of the team. Nerves fluttered in my belly, but I pushed them aside; I would know the outcome soon enough.

I put my head around Rosie's bedroom door before I left. She was sitting up in bed, her head in a book. I managed a smile; it was good to see her reading again. She smiled back.

'Did you have a nice evening?' I asked.

'Yeah, it was good to see Fran. We went to the pub and talked for ages. I didn't realise how much I've missed her.'

'Talking is good. I'm glad you and Fran have met up again. She's a nice lass.'

'Yeah, she's a good friend.'

'I'm off to work. I'll see you later.'

I left her to it, took a shaky breath and quietly opened my bedroom door to get some clean clothes. Peter hadn't closed the curtains, and a ray of sun lit his face. He lay on his back, asleep with his mouth open. I stood for a moment watching him. I hadn't noticed until then how much he had changed; his face thinner, grey at his temples, lines around his mouth. Over the past few months he had gone from having a sunny, open expression, his green eyes sparkling with fun, to a closed, pinched greyness and eyes surrounded by black bags.

Perhaps I should take a hard look at myself, too. I felt as if I had aged a decade in the past six months.

While I watched, he snorted and rolled over onto his side, a rumbling snore coming from deep in his chest. I held my breath, not wanting to have to face him. Today was going to be difficult enough; the longer I could put off talking to him, the better.

Quickly tiptoeing to the wardrobe, I picked out the first things I came to and snuck back out, glad to leave him sleeping.

By the time I arrived at the site, the digger driver and George were discussing the best way to make the hole safe.

'Morning, Jen,' said George. 'God, you look rough – you feeling okay?'

'Morning. Yeah, I'm fine, just didn't sleep very well. Thanks for making a girl feel good about herself.'

He had the grace to blush.

'Sorry. I noticed you and Dominic having a bit of a set-to yesterday. Did you shove him on his arse? I hope he's not getting to you.'

'No, I did not. He slipped in his stupid, unsuitable shoes. That man would try the patience of a saint,' I said, my voice sharper than I meant it to be. I took a breath. 'Let's just say, you might be without a project leader by the end of today.'

George's eyes widened. 'Fuck. That bad, eh?'

I shrugged. 'We'll see. In the meantime, do we need to get the sides of this hole stepped out, before we can start recording?'

'Yes, that's just what we've been talking about. Frank, here, reckons it'll be the best option.'

'Okay, let's get started then, shall we? The sooner the sides are stabilised, the sooner we can get to it.' I stared down into the pit, where water had pooled overnight. 'Looks like we'll need pumps to get rid of that lot. And we should test for contamination; I'll sort out some PPE, there's bound to be fuel and oil in there.'

'I'll get the pumps organised,' he said, and went back to Frank, who had climbed into the cab of the digger.

I spent the morning putting in place everything necessary for us to comply with the strict Health and Safety protocols we worked under. The volunteers hung around, waiting for instructions, and I kept them busy sifting through the piles of spoil which had come out of the ground the day before. We had already been over them with the metal detector and I doubted they would find anything but at least it gave them something to do.

Dominic arrived just as we were breaking for lunch.

I had been keeping an eye out for him, and walked across to where he parked his car, not wanting the whole team to see me getting the sack. Being humiliated in public would be the final straw.

'Good morning, Jennifer, how are you?' he said, locking the BMW and coming to meet me. 'Today could be exciting. I hope we find what you're looking for.'

I stopped dead in my tracks. Was he joking? Playing some kind of weird game?

'Dominic, I want to apologise for my behaviour, yesterday afternoon,' I said, the words tumbling out of my mouth. 'I was completely out of line.'

He smiled at me, and I was reminded of a cat watching its prey, his eyes hooded, expression smug.

'Oh, don't worry about it. We both said things that are best forgotten, don't you think?' He put a hand on my shoulder, and squeezed.

It was all I could do not to push it off, but I made myself smile back.

'That's . . . magnanimous of you. I'm grateful.'

'This is a good team, doing important work,' he said. 'I can't see the benefit of rocking the boat, can you?'

Did I detect a hint of a threat in his words? Perhaps, but relief flooded through me, and I bit down on my lip. The words he had used about the volunteers rang in my head, and I hoped he realised that having me around worked both ways. I was prepared to call him out if he continued to show such disrespect, and he couldn't afford for that to happen.

'I suppose not,' I said. 'The team has just stopped for lunch, but we should be able to start recording what we find, this afternoon. It'll take time – it's messy in there and we'll have to go slowly – but with luck we should know what we've got by the end of today.'

'Excellent.' We arrived at the marquee, where the rest of the team were sitting eating. He put his hand up and nodded to them. 'Hello, everyone. I hear things are moving on, so I just want to say good luck this afternoon. I'm sorry I won't be here to give you all a hand, but I look forward to seeing the results very soon.'

I stood behind him, not quite believing what he said. Did the man ever do any practical archaeology, or just leave it to the rest of us and live on the publicity? I knew he was highly qualified and had been involved in some big projects in the past, but now he seemed happy to leave the dirty work to the rest of us and spend his time applying for sponsorship to fund our work. It was vital someone did, but it was the last thing I would want to do.

Each to their own, I guessed.

Tension still sang in my veins; I didn't know whether he was playing with me and I would find myself out on my backside in a day or two, or if he really meant what he had said. There was nothing I could do about it. Even if I made a complaint about him, it was my word against his. No one else had heard his words; he wasn't stupid enough to say anything derogatory in public.

I would just have to watch my step, and stay out of his way as much as possible. Dropping in for ten minutes every few days was fine by me, the less time he was here the better.

'Find a pew and I'll get you a coffee,' I said, leading him to an empty table. 'Black, three sugars, right?'

'I'm meeting a couple of chaps for lunch in twenty minutes, so I don't have time, I'm afraid,' he said. I noticed the suit under his sheepskin coat for the first time. More schmoozing, I presumed. 'I just wanted to drop in and see everything was under control.' He gave me his full-wattage smile, whitened teeth gleaming in the gloom of the hut. 'Which, of course, they are. You and George make a great team, Jennifer. I would hate to lose you.'

I eyed him for a moment before replying.

'Don't worry, Dominic, I don't plan on going anywhere. Enjoy your lunch.'

He nodded and said goodbye, leaving less than ten minutes after he had arrived. I watched him go, trying to work him out and failing. As the BMW purred its way out of the gate, I shook my head, still baffled, and went to find something to eat, excitement for the afternoon's work and what we might find bubbling under my skin.

That afternoon we worked to make the huge hole safe for us to go down into it and start examining the enticing shard of metal. By the end of the day, we were able to climb down and stand on the bottom of the pit, our eyes level with it.

I loved this part of a dig. The first time I put my hand on something which had lain buried for decades or centuries felt such a privilege, I always thanked my lucky stars for having the best job in the world. George and I began to scrape away the silty sand around the metal, which we could see was the edge of a wing of an airplane. If the plane was in one piece, or the majority of it was intact, we would need to dig a lot more earth out before we could bring it up.

By the time we had dug as far into the ground as we could along the top of the wing, I was as confident as I could be that it wasn't a broken piece. We left it for the night and climbed out of the hole. Tomorrow we would dig again, this time at exactly the right place.

I caught George's eye and we both grinned. Old Terry Bristow was spot on. A plane had crashed here, and I would lay bets on it being a Spitfire.

I couldn't wait to uncover it.

Scott must have noticed our excitement. He hobbled over to where we stood, discussing exactly what we planned to do the next day.

'Is it the same as the bit I found?' he asked.

I nodded.

'Yes. We're almost sure we have a Spitfire down there.' I saw the spark in his eye. 'This is when things get interesting. Exciting, isn't it?'

He gazed down into the hole. 'Yeah, it is. How will you get it out?'

I talked him through the basics.

'But before we do all that, we'll go down and record it in situ, so that we know exactly how it was lying and then if anything breaks during the lift, we can rebuild it just as it was in the hole. That way, we'll be able to discover what happened and why.'

'So, it's a bit like being a detective, then? You're like the SOCO team on the TV, putting together what happened at a crime scene.'

George laughed. 'That's not a bad analogy. It's more or less what we do with something like this.'

'Can't wait to find out more,' Scott said. 'It's fascinating.'

'I think we have a new convert to archaeology,' said George. He stuck his hand out and Scott took it, looking a little confused. 'Welcome to the team. Be prepared to get cold, filthy and wet in the next few days. If you still love it by then, I'll know you're the real deal.'

It was Scott's turn to laugh.

'I'm a bootneck, mate. Our default setting is being wet, cold and dirty. I reckon I'll be able to hack it. See you tomorrow.'

He walked back towards the gate, and George frowned.

'I thought he was a Royal Marine? What's a bootneck?'

I shrugged. 'Not a clue, but I like him. He's got a good attitude and is smart. It's great he's so invested in what we're doing. Come on, I'm dying for a cuppa. We can finish planning what we're going to do tomorrow, before we leave.'

Chapter 14

Bella

As the battle for air supremacy raged throughout the summer, Bella and the rest of her unit at the Air Transport Auxiliary base at Hatfield were kept busy ferrying airplanes of every description all over the country. She got used to flying different types of aircraft and having only the vaguest idea of where she was supposed to be taking whichever machine was allotted to her on any given day.

At the beginning of another long day of hopping from one airfield to another, she gazed up at a flight of Hurricanes passing overhead. Frustration nipped at her senses.

Why can't I do that? I'm just as good a pilot as any man.

Later that evening, back at base and off duty, she sat with some of the other pilots in the mess. The talk was all about the latest successes against the Luftwaffe and what heroes the RAF boys were.

'Why is it always you men who get to have all the fun?' Bella said, when one of the retired WWI pilots began praising the boys in blue again. 'Any of the women here could do the same job just as well as the RAF lads.'

There were some heads nodding in agreement from her fellow ATA women, but the men held little truck with the idea.

'You girls are far too sensitive to cope with being fighter pilots,' said one. 'You're not strong enough either. You'd never cope with the hours it takes to fly sorties, day after day, sometimes multiple times a day.'

Heat ran up Bella's back.

'Funny how we can cope with two or more trips a day every day, ferrying planes around the country, then.' She leant back and put the back of her hand up to her forehead in a mock swoon. 'But no, we would never have what it takes to fly with the fighter squadrons.'

Veronica, a South African who had a temper almost as short as Bella's, laughed.

'Damn right, Bella. We're all far too fragile to do a man's job,' she said. 'Oh, wait though . . . women *are* doing men's jobs all over the country.'

'And doing them just as well as men do them,' said Jackie, another pilot, joining them and swallowing half a pint of beer in one long draught.

The argument continued with no backing down on either side, and Bella came away from it still as frustrated; angry once again that her sex excluded her from doing what she wanted – to train as a Spitfire pilot and join her brother and his comrades in defending the country.

One thing the men had argued about was true and wasn't restricted to the women. Everyone was permanently exhausted; there was little or no time off and Bella had no energy to wonder how Aiden was getting on. They had learnt to fly the tiny Curtiss Robin at the same time, before he left for boarding school in Scotland. He was so short that Mum had made a cushion for the seat so he could see out. Mum had been an excellent instructor – patient and good at instilling confidence in her two children. Being so young, they were not allowed to fly alone but Bella didn't care as long as she was given the controls.

She had no fears that Aiden wouldn't pass out and be awarded his wings, but where he would be stationed or how long it would take him to finish training, she had no idea.

Eventually, a letter came.

Written in haste, Aiden's scrawl was barely decipherable. He had passed basic training and was being sent on to another base for advanced fighter-pilot training, where he would get to fly Spitfires and Hurricanes. There was no hint of excitement; Aiden was doing his duty as she said he should.

If that was me, I would be over the moon.

Bella's discontentment continued to grow. Every time she climbed into one of the Tiger Moths or Dominies, she resented it. What had begun as an adventure became humdrum and boring. The women were only licenced to fly the small single-engine airplanes and had to watch the men taking off in the larger bombers as well as Spitfires and Hurricanes. Nevertheless, she applied to train for her licence to fly Class 2 airplanes, more in hope than anything else. She would no doubt be turned down simply for being a woman, but she had to try.

Otherwise, she might as well be a bus driver.

'Second Officer Gardner, the commander wants to see you.'

Bella looked up from reading through her ATA pilots' notes in preparation for flying a Proctor up to one of the training camps in the north of England.

What had she done – or not done? The CO didn't normally order subordinates to her office. Brushing down her uniform jacket and rubbing her boots on the back of each calf to rid them of any dust, she checked her hair was tidy and followed the orderly, butterflies revolving in her belly.

Perhaps it was news on her application. Keeping her fingers crossed as she marched across the parade ground to the administration building, she allowed herself a small nugget of hope. It would be something, at least.

Commander Ross looked up from a sheaf of papers as Bella entered her office. She had barely spoken to her since she had been at Hatfield. The commander was a small woman in her thirties and a great ambassador for all the women in the ATA.

Her expression was sombre and Bella's mood dipped. Her application had been turned down, or she had done something so wrong (the barrel roll she'd pulled last week, maybe?) that she was about to get a proper dressing-down.

'Second Officer Gardner, please sit down.'

Bella frowned. What was this about?

She sat opposite her commanding officer, her mouth dry, heart pumping a little faster.

Commander Ross steepled her hands on the desk, the finger-tips white where they met. She cleared her throat and looked at Bella.

'I'm afraid I have some bad news for you,' she said. 'You might have heard on the radio that there was a serious train crash yesterday.'

Bella nodded. What did it have to do with her?

'You have a brother – Aiden?'

Another nod, and a knot the size of a rock in the pit of her stomach. She couldn't open her mouth, though a hundred questions fought in her head.

'Aiden was on the train that crashed, on his way to start Advanced Flight Training.'

She tried to speak but nothing came out. Cleared her throat and tried again. 'Is he dead?'

Commander Ross shook her head. 'No, but he has been injured. I don't know to what extent; he's been taken to hospital in Leeds. I am giving you compassionate leave as of now, so you can go and see him.'

Not dead. Hurt but not dead.

Shock and guilt crashed through her, making her stomach heave. Thoughts spun through Bella's mind making her dizzy. It was her fault he was on that train. She would never forgive herself if anything happened to him. She had bullied Aiden into doing something he hated and went against everything he believed in. Chances were that he would be killed in action even if he survived whatever injuries he had just sustained. Why had that never occurred to her until now?

The room seemed to be disappearing down a dark tunnel. She gripped the edge of the desk and leant forward, trying to clear her head.

'Miss Gardner, are you all right?' The CO hurried around the desk to her, crouched and took her hand. 'Put your head between your knees and breathe slowly. That's it. You've had a shock, it's natural you feel faint.'

After a few moments Bella's head cleared and she sat up.

'Has my father been told?'

Commander Ross nodded. 'I believe so. The CO of the training unit notified all the families – your brother wasn't the only pilot who was injured. There were five of them from the same training squadron on the train.'

'I'm so sorry.' It didn't sound like her voice. 'Please may I leave now? I must go to him, there's no one else here, only our grandmother.'

'Your family are Australian, aren't they?'

She nodded. 'My mother was from Scotland, originally, but moved to Australia when she married my father. She died a few years ago. We've always had strong ties here, it's why Aiden and I volunteered when the war started.'

Bella stopped. Why was she gabbling?

'I'm sorry your mother passed away. It must be very hard for you, being so far from home.'

She nodded, Commander Ross's sympathy undoing what little composure she had. Blinking furiously, she tried to keep the tears from falling. The Commander scribbled a note and passed it to her.

'Take this, in case anyone queries why you are leaving. Go now, and I hope your brother recovers very soon.'

'Thank you, ma'am,' Bella said, as she rose and saluted.

Chapter 15

Jennifer

On my way home, I stopped in at Grandpa's, finding him in his garden kneeling in the soil, planting out broad beans. I gave him my arm and he levered himself to standing.

'Hello. Two days in a row. I'm a lucky man,' he said, kissing my cheek.

I hugged him.

'I couldn't wait to tell you about my day,' I said. 'We definitely have a Spitfire, buried way down – it must have gone in at full speed, I think.'

'I'm glad the man who gave you the tip-off was correct. I thought he would be – it's not the kind of thing anyone would forget, even if he was very young when he saw it happen.'

I nodded.

'You're right. And I should learn to trust my instincts. Mr Bristow was sure, but it's been so hard to find, I was beginning to wonder if he had mis-remembered it. It could have gone down in the sea, for all we know, or crashed somewhere else.' I grinned. 'Anyway, I wanted to tell you. It's been quite a day.'

He put a hand on my shoulder and eyed me shrewdly. 'I'm sure it has been. Is there anything else? You look exhausted.'

I shook my head, a tightness in my throat. 'Anyway. I'll keep you up to date with how it all goes and what we find.'

'Why don't you come in and have a cuppa with me? I've finished here.'

'That's a lovely idea, and thank you, but I'd better get home. I am tired and I've still got to write up my notes from today.' I smiled at him. 'If I sit down it will be very difficult to move again – you know how much I love your cosy kitchen.'

'You know the door is always open. Next time come for supper – and bring Peter and Rosie with you.'

'That sounds lovely, I'll do that.' I kissed him and gave him another hug. 'Bye, Grandpa.'

'Bye, my love. Look after yourself.'

Peter was in the kitchen when I got home, feeding the animals. I hid my surprise and wondered if I should say anything. Rows between us were so scarce that I had no idea how to get over the vitriol he had spewed the previous evening. Should I act as if nothing had happened? Go in with all guns blazing and defend myself against his unfair words? Or sit in sullen silence?

I suspected it had been a way of shedding some of the bottled-up grief and anger he bore. But what if I was wrong? What if he absolutely believed I was to blame for Ben's death? How could we get over such a massive wall between us? It was hard enough trying to learn to live without our son; could I live without my husband to lean on as well?

I couldn't even imagine it.

The dogs ignored me until they had finished gobbling their food and then Deefa did his usual party trick of carrying his empty bowl to me, dropping it with a clang on the stone flags. I stroked his head and picked it up, taking it to the utility to wash.

'I'll do that,' Peter said, taking it from me. 'You look exhausted. Sit down and I'll make you a cuppa.'

He looked almost as wretched as I felt.

'Thanks.'

I dropped onto the sofa, Sally following me and hopping onto my knee. I had no idea how to navigate this. I had been prepared for another fight, or for Peter shutting himself away again and not speaking to me, but his gentle words almost undid me. I calmed myself by stroking Sally, over and over, fighting the tears I had promised myself I wouldn't shed.

I watched Peter moving around, filling the kettle, putting coffee into mugs, lifting milk out of the fridge; all the things we did every day for each other, which I never took note of. The tiny habits he had – sniffing the milk for freshness, putting a hand on top of the handle of the kettle, as if he could speed up its boiling. Things which normally made me itch with irritation, but now I realised I would miss if he wasn't here.

He brought the coffee over and sat beside me, blowing over the top of his mug, always impatient to drink it before it had time to cool down a little.

We sat in silence for a while. I didn't know what to say; how to begin the conversation I knew we needed to have.

'I'm sorry,' he said, eventually. He put a hand over mine and squeezed, gently. 'What I said last night was unforgivable. And yet, I hope – no, I beg – you to forgive me.'

I turned my hand over and gripped his.

'I had no idea you felt that way. Why didn't you say something sooner?'

'Thing is, I don't. Blame you, that is.' He gazed into his mug. 'I've been blaming myself for not being more insistent that Ben stay here and work last summer.' His voice was quiet, but the bitterness and guilt in it twisted my heart.

'Peter, nobody is to blame.' I put my hands on either side

of his head and turned him to face me. Even then, he couldn't look at me. 'You know what Ben was like; so passionate about climbing and mountaineering. It was what he was meant to do, what made him happy. How could we prevent him from following his dream?'

'We're his parents. It was our duty to keep him safe.'

'He was an adult, who made his own decisions.' His words, flung at me the night before, came back to me. 'But you're right in one thing. If I hadn't let him persuade me to lend him the money for the trip, he might still be here today. I can't forgive myself for that.'

Peter put his arms around me.

'I shouldn't have said what I did. I'd drunk too much and wanted to lash out.' He wiped a tear from my cheek. 'This is the hardest thing I've ever had to go through, and I can't do it without you beside me. Please, forgive me.'

'I do. You know I do.' I gazed into his grief-filled eyes. 'But please don't keep shutting yourself away. If we are ever going to find a way to live together without Ben – all of us, including Rosie and Grandpa – we must lean on each other. I can't see how we can do it otherwise.'

He nodded. 'I'll try.'

I leant into him and he put his arm around me.

'And, Jen . . . I'm sorry for being so stubborn about your grandfather. It's just one more thing I can't deal with right now.'

'I know, and I understand, really I do. I'll make more effort to go over there, make sure he's okay.' I pictured him as I'd found him earlier, kneeling in his garden, planting beans. 'I don't think he's ready to give up his independence, anyway, knowing him. I just worry about him.'

'I know you do, and he's done so much for us and the kids over the years. But there's enough grief in this house, already, don't you think?'

I couldn't deny it. Grandpa seemed perfectly capable of taking care of himself, still. I made a vow to go and see him every day, even if it was only for ten minutes. It was something, at least.

'He invited us all for supper,' I said. 'But I would like to get him to come here. Would you mind? It's a bank holiday next weekend, so what about Sunday lunch?'

'Yeah, why not? It would be nice to see the old boy.'

'I'll drop in again after work tomorrow and ask him.' I took his mug from him and rose. 'I'm starving. Why don't we order takeaway? I can't be bothered to cook tonight.'

'Good idea. I'll go and see what Rosie wants.' He stood and put his arms around me. 'I love you, Dr Dawson.'

I kissed him.

'I know.'

Chapter 16

Bella

Bella didn't reach the hospital in Leeds until the next day.

Twenty-four hours of terror that Aiden's injuries were so serious he would be dead before she could get to him. By the time she found him, she was sure it was too late. The harassed nurse who showed her to the ward he was in said he was alive, but unconscious.

Bella dragged a chair across to his bed and sat, relief overwhelming her so she could hardly breathe. Her brother lay on his back, eyes closed, an ugly purple bruise covering one side of his face and disappearing into his hair. There was no other sign of injury she could see, but he lay so still she leant in close to him and put a hand on his skinny chest to feel it rise and fall.

He lived.

'Aiden, I'm so sorry,' she said in a low voice, trying not to break down, gently brushing a curl of red hair off his forehead. 'I should never have pressured you into joining up. It was wrong. Please forgive me.'

A sob wrenched its way out of her mouth and she stuffed a fist into it to stop anymore escaping. What good would crying do?

Was she crying for him or herself? Guilt, grief, self-pity? All or any of them wouldn't help Aiden, and would make her feel more wretched than she already did.

She sat for an hour, talking to him as if he was awake, holding his hand, fussing with the worn white sheets that covered him. The ward was full of young men and the sounds infiltrated their way into her brain. Someone sobbed and cried for his mother, and a patient screamed in pain and was shushed by the nurses tending to him.

The room was cold, although rays of sunshine came through the windows high up the wall. Dust motes hung in the stale air; Bella thought how depressing a place it was, the patients lined up in two rows on either side of the aisle which led from one set of double doors to another at the far end.

There were few other visitors; no doubt more would arrive for visiting hours.

After she had run out of things to talk about and Aiden had shown no reaction to her voice or presence, she went in search of a doctor. In a small side-room at the end of the ward she found a tired-looking man with grey hair and a moustache stained with nicotine.

'Excuse me,' she said, knocking on the open door and stepping into the room. 'Are you the doctor treating the train crash victims?'

He raised his eyes to her and nodded. Standing, he put his hand out and she shook it.

'Yes, I'm Doctor Singleton. Who are you here to see?'

'My brother, Aiden Gardner.'

'Ah, yes. Mr Gardner has several injuries, including a nasty blow to the head. When the train crashed one of the carriages came off the track down an embankment and landed on its roof. Your brother was found crushed under part of the infrastructure.' Doctor Singleton looked grave. 'It's a wonder he survived.'

Bella had never understood the phrase *she blanched* but knew that was what she did when she heard the doctor's words, her whole being shrinking away from what he said. As if part of her had shrivelled up. She managed to croak out a question.

'How serious are his injuries? He looks as if he's asleep, he's so peaceful.'

'Most of his injuries are internal. He has a head injury, and several broken ribs.' The doctor paused. 'Those we are dealing with. He's young and will mend. Much more serious is the spinal injury he sustained. We won't know how severe it is until he regains consciousness.'

'I don't understand,' she said.

'There is a strong possibility that Mr Gardner may be paralysed.'

Bella's legs buckled and she flopped onto a chair unable to take in what the doctor said. She shook her head.

'Paralysed? As in, unable to walk?'

Horror made her want to vomit, and her words came out as a strangled whisper.

'I'm afraid so. I know it's an awful shock, but if we can keep him alive for the next few weeks, then with the right treatment and therapy, your brother should be able to live a productive life.' Doctor Singleton eyed her calmly. Bella supposed he must be used to handing out such devastating diagnoses on a routine basis. How he could do such a thing was beyond her. He continued in the same gentle tone. 'Where does your family live? There are units that have been set up which specialise in these injuries. Sadly, we see this kind of thing all too often since the war started.'

His words seemed to come from far away and were hard to process. All she could think about was that it was her fault Aiden was in this state and she should be able to do something – anything – to help him, and yet she couldn't.

Never had she felt so helpless, so culpable.

'Miss Gardner?' The doctor repeated his question. 'Your family?'

'What?' She found it hard to articulate words, her mouth dry, the lump in her throat threatening to strangle her. She tried to swallow and croaked out an answer, giving Granny Mack's address. 'When will he wake up, do you think?' she asked. 'I need to be with him. He'll be terrified if it's as bad as you think it might be.'

'He's showing signs of regaining consciousness,' the doctor said. 'He may wake in the next twenty-four hours or so.'

Bella thanked him for his candour and said she would return as soon as she could. For the moment she needed to get away, try to collect her scrambled thoughts.

She focused on the practicalities of what she had to do. If nothing else, she could be with Aiden when he discovered that he may well have lost the use of his legs. It helped steady her shattered emotions. It might be too little too late, and she could never take back all the things she had said and done to upset him when they were children, but she would do the best she could. She must be strong, now more than ever before. Her brother needed someone to lean on, and she would be that support.

First, she had to telegraph her father and ring Granny Mack.

Her pass was for a week. She took a room at a small guest house, close to the hospital, determined to be there when her brother finally regained consciousness.

Guilt haunted her like a ghost. Exhausted and battered by everything she had heard, defeat snagged at the edges of her mind, something she had never acknowledged before. She couldn't imagine anything worse than not being able to move.

Never riding again, never walking or running or dancing.

Never flying an airplane.

How would Aiden be able to come to terms with something so devastating?

Perhaps it would be better if he didn't wake up, after all. Maybe it would have been better if he had died in the crash.

Treacherous thoughts she banished as soon as they popped into her head.

One thing she knew. She must make amends to her brother. How she would do that, she had no clue, but make amends she must.

Aiden regained consciousness the following afternoon while Bella was sitting with him. The morning had been awful; she had spoken to Granny Mack who broke down in tears while they were on the line. Bella had no idea how to soothe the old lady's shock and sorrow, it was difficult enough for her to withhold her own sobs while her grandmother wept.

Eventually, she had to ring off, promising to call again when Aiden woke up. Next, she had to compose a telegram to send to her father. Although she knew he had been notified already, it seemed a particularly brutal way of breaking the news. So few words which would have such a devastating impact.

Returning to the hospital she did at least find some kind of stoical calm sitting at Aiden's bedside holding his lifeless hand. Doctor Singleton assured her that her brother was close to waking and Bella noticed movement behind the closed lids of his eyes, as if he was in the middle of a dream or something.

She woke from a light doze at the sound of her name.

'Bella?' Aiden's voice was a croak but it made her jump. He coughed and groaned. 'What happened to me? Where are we?'

She put a hand to his face and stroked his forehead, pushing the same errant lock of curls gently back.

'Shh, it's all right, you've been injured and are in a hospital.'

He groaned again. 'Everything hurts . . .'

He moved his head from side to side and Bella's heart lifted a fraction. Perhaps the doctor was wrong; if Aiden felt pain and could move his head, maybe his injuries weren't as bad as was feared.

'I'll go and find the doctor,' she said, patting his hand. 'He said to call him when you came round. I'm sure he will be pleased to see you looking so bright.'

'Please don't leave me,' he said. 'I don't feel bright, I feel as if I've been crushed under a steam roller. Please tell me what happened, I don't remember anything. Did you come all the way from home to see me? Is Dad with you? I must have been unconscious for weeks.'

Aiden's eyes met Bella's, fear and pain in them. She caught her breath. How could he not remember all the time he had spent in training?

'I'm not going anywhere,' she said. 'But Doctor Singleton will want to see you as soon as possible. I'll come straight back, I promise.'

She hurried out of the ward to the small office just outside, where Dr Singleton was writing a report. He looked up when she ran into the room.

'He's awake?'

She nodded. 'Please come. He's very confused. Can't remember anything.'

The doctor rose and came around his desk, talking as he led her back into the ward.

'That's quite normal for someone who has had a head injury. It takes a while for the brain to reset itself. His memory will return gradually, I'm sure.'

Bella's pulse slowed a little at his words. It made sense that Aiden would take time to recover. At least he knew who she was.

She watched while the doctor examined Aiden, shining a light in his eyes, listening to his chest and taking his temperature. He wrote the results on a chart which hung on the bottom of the bed.

'Now, young man, you've been in a nasty accident and got yourself pretty bashed up,' Dr Singleton said to Aiden after he had finished. 'I am going to give you something for the pain and to help you sleep, and then tomorrow we will do a few more tests and see how you're recovering. How does that sound?'

Aiden stared at him, his eyes huge in his face. He gave a tiny nod, then spoke in a frightened whisper.

'Can you tell me why I can't feel my legs, doctor?'

* * *

The next days passed in a haze of grief and fear for both Aiden and Bella. After a battery of tests Dr Singleton diagnosed Aiden with paraplegia. His spinal cord had been severed halfway down his back and he had completely lost the use of the lower half of his body.

He would be wheelchair bound for the rest of his life.

The rest of his injuries gradually healed and his memory began to return, until the only thing he didn't remember was the train crash.

Bella contacted the ATA base and asked to be posted somewhere closer to where her brother was going to be sent – a spinal unit which had been opened in central Scotland, not far from Edinburgh and Granny Mack. Commander Gower sent her papers and new orders to join an airfield in Fife in a month, giving her time to help Aiden get settled and see Granny Mack. She packed up her brother's few things, including his dusty and torn RAF uniform, with dark stains of dried blood on it. Inside a pocket she found orders for him to present himself at an airbase in Yorkshire, where he had been going when the train crash happened and changed both their lives forever.

She had the uniform cleaned and packed it into a bag. She read the blood-stained orders and returned them to the envelope they had been in. She kept them away from Aiden and put them with the identity tags she had removed from around his neck at his insistence.

'At least I don't need to keep up this charade any longer,' he said to her when she took them from him. 'Perhaps this whole mess is God's way of telling me I should have stuck to my guns and refused to sign up.'

'Don't say that, Aiden, please. It was an accident, that's all,' Bella said. 'Just an awful accident.'

She had turned away and put the tags in a pocket, unable to face her brother and witness the suffering on his face, guilt and grief sitting side by side like a pair of lead weights in her belly.

All she wanted to do was make amends to him. But what could she do? He needed ongoing specialist care, the nursing staff at the spinal hospital turning him every two hours to prevent him getting pressure sores. He couldn't even take himself to the lavatory.

What she wanted to do was run away and hide, but that would be cowardly and she knew the guilt would stick to her no matter how far she ran. She needed to do something practical – sitting around wallowing in misery watching her brother lose his sense of self was torture.

Granny Mack came to the rescue. She brought Aiden's violin and his paints with her when she came to visit him. It was the first time Bella saw him smile. He caressed the instrument as if it were a living thing and the first time he played it they all cried, the haunting music tearing a hole in Bella's soul.

That night, while she lay unable to sleep, her body craving the release of hard physical exercise, aching to be up in the air, free from all the grief and regrets, a worm of an idea came to her.

Could she pull it off? Was she brave enough to even try?

Would it be enough to make the guilt go away?

What did she have to lose? She couldn't continue in the same way, had to do something positive or else she would go mad.

The next day she went to see Aiden and said she was going back to work. She would visit again as soon as she could. Kissing him on his cold, white cheek, she walked away hoping he didn't notice the tears on her face. It was the hardest thing she had ever done, but she didn't look back, determined to carry out her plan.

Chapter 17

Jennifer

The sense of anticipation and muted excitement infected everyone the next morning. The trench remained water-free, thanks to a dry night, and the shard of metal stuck out temptingly, about four metres down. The huge tracked digger rolled in and began extending the pit to the side, above where I hoped the rest of the plane lay, taking off thin tranches of wet sandy soil and carefully depositing them on a clear bit of land. George and I stood in front of the enormous machine and to one side so the driver could see us, and inspected each bucketful as it dropped to the ground.

Within a short time we began to find more evidence. I knew it was unlikely we would find the plane in one piece; the impact would have ripped it apart, even in such soft ground. It had disappeared immediately from sight into the marsh though, and I held out hope that even if it wasn't whole, the main body of the Spitfire might still be there.

Sometime around mid-morning, George put his hand up and halted the machine. I peered into the trench with him, and saw what looked like a long, thin slice of wood lying about two metres down. He brought a ladder and a pair of metal stakes which

106

we hammered deep into the ground. He tied the ladder to the stakes and we climbed down onto the firm sand and examined it. I carefully dug around one edge of it with my trowel and it became apparent what we had. We were standing beside one of the laminated propellor blades which had been torn off, and had lain for more than seventy years waiting to be found.

George and I had a short confab and decided to carry on digging by hand. The risk of damaging what was there by using the machine was too great, even though it would be much quicker. The pit was wide enough for four or five of us to work in, and I got Scott and Ginge to help us carefully dig further down, with the other volunteers working in pairs to get rid of the spoil with shovel boards at each step.

It was slow work, but worth it when we eventually came to a much bigger piece of the fuselage, followed by one of the Browning machine guns and the second of the three blades.

George, with his H&S hat on, stopped work while we got hold of the munitions disposal expert we normally called on. He examined the gun carefully; there were more than likely still rounds of ammunition in it, and it would need to be made safe before we moved it.

The rest of us sat and drank coffee, the ex-service personnel unfazed by having lethal weaponry on-site, unsurprisingly.

Once we could start work again, recording everything meticulously in situ took up most of the morning, but the buzz and energy were palpable, even among the volunteers who hadn't seemed enthusiastic beforehand.

I was thrilled by the level of preservation; there was some corrosion, which was to be expected, but it was minor compared to many sites I had worked on. Being undisturbed in an environment of almost neutral ph made it easy to identify what we found. I hoped we could find the main body of the plane in as good a condition and be able to work out what happened on that day so long ago.

Late in the afternoon, when everyone was flagging, muscles aching from long hours bent over scraping away at the dirt, we found it. The Spitfire had gone into the watery hole nose first, perhaps after landing on its belly and sliding along for a distance until it hit the bog, and the tail and one wing had snapped off. I hoped the poor pilot had managed to bail out before it went down.

Scraping away at more mud and sand, my trowel hit something and sent a shiver up my spine like the feeling of dragging chalk on a blackboard. I put the trowel down and used my gloved hands, rubbing away the last few centimetres until the top of a Perspex frame appeared. My breath caught in my throat.

I scraped some more of the sand and mud away from around it, until I was sure of what it was, then sat back on my heels, heart thudding. It looked undamaged and still in place. That could only mean one thing and might scupper our whole operation. The licence we had been given by the Ministry of Defence allowed us to lift a crashed plane.

A crashed plane without its pilot.

The Perspex frame I had uncovered was the cockpit hood – if it was still closed it meant one thing.

The pilot had gone down with his Spitfire.

And that opened a whole new massive can of worms.

At the end of the day, after George and I had confirmed that the cockpit was intact, we called a halt to the dig and sent the volunteers home until we knew whether we could get permission to recover the body of the pilot.

I phoned Dominic.

'Fuck,' he said. I could picture the expression on his face. 'You're the licence-holder, Jennifer, so you'll have to apply to the ministry for an exhumation and talk to the MOD. We'll have to wait and see if they'll give you a permit to carry on.'

I agreed. Why there was no record of the plane crash, I had no idea. But it was such a chaotic time of the war, when the

Battle of Britain raged across the skies of England and France, I could only surmise that it had been accepted that the Spitfire had gone into the sea. I would need to do far more research and see if I could pin down who it might be. There was only one sure way of doing that.

I went to find George, who was busy going through the pieces we had already found.

'We need to find the ID of the Spitfire,' I said. 'If we're going to get anywhere with the Ministry of Justice we need to know which plane it is and who the pilot was.'

He narrowed his eyes and stared at me. 'I hope you're not suggesting what I think you are.'

'Look, everyone else has gone, it's only us still here. It wouldn't take long to dig a bit further back and find the squadron letters. At least then, I would have some idea who I was looking for.'

'Jen, are you out of your tree? You know what would happen if anyone gets wind of what we did.'

'Well, I haven't notified the ministry yet, and I told the others that we suspected there was more live ammo and needed to close the site until we were sure it was safe. Come on, it won't be dark for hours, so what are we waiting for?'

'I can't believe you. This goes against everything we should be doing. The only thing we should be doing is covering it up against the elements.'

'It doesn't go against anything. We aren't disturbing anything, or trying to move the remains of the pilot – if they are still there. And who's to know how much we had uncovered before we found the cockpit? All I want to do is identify what we've got. Surely that's okay, isn't it?'

George grumbled some more, but I knew him too well to think he wasn't as desperate as I was to know what we had found.

We took trowels and buckets and went back to the trench. An hour later, after loosening more of the compacted sand behind and below the cockpit, we could make out one side of the plane.

Most of the paintwork had disappeared, but it was still possible to make out the pale grey letters either side of the blue, white and red roundel with the faded yellow circle encompassing it.

I took a couple of photos and jotted down the letters in the small notebook I always carried. An L and a Z were plain to see in front of the roundel. On the far side, the damage was greater, but I thought I could make out either a B or perhaps a P.

A shiver ran down my back.

'Right, that's enough, Jen. We need to stop and get everything covered up,' George said.

'Yep, just one moment.' Drawn to the battered cockpit, I wiped the side of the Perspex hood with a piece of cloth and peered through the scratched and bent glass. There, still with his belts attached, was the body of the pilot. 'Whoever you are, we've got you now. We'll take care of you, it's time you went home.'

I laid a hand flat on the top of the hood, whispering the words, then followed George out of the trench.

We covered the plane and as much of the trench as we could with tarpaulins, weighting them down and tying them to iron stanchions hammered into the ground. The dig was shut down while I contacted the Ministries of Justice and Defence and tried to persuade them to let us retrieve the body. These things are always a lengthy process and hoops have to be jumped through while they investigate everything. It was not helped by the fact that the chap I usually worked with when applying for licences was away, and I found myself trying to convince a self-important jobsworth that we weren't pulling the wool over his eyes about finding the pilot.

George and I spent frustrating days duplicating all the paperwork we had on our research into the dig site, going through it time and again to make sure we hadn't missed something which would have alerted us to the possibility of a body being inside the Spitfire.

I was surprised to receive a text from Scott Hudson asking if we required any help. I rang him back and thanked him for offering.

'This is just office work, Scott. The boring part of the job, unfortunately.'

'I'd like to see how you go about it and what's involved,' he said. 'I don't live far away, and am going spare not having anything to do.'

'Hang on a moment, and I'll ring you back.' I hung up. 'George, that was one of the volunteers – Scott – you remember, the one who was actually interested in the archaeology.'

'The bootneck – whatever that is,' he said, nodding.

'Yeah, that's him. He wants to come in and help. What do you think?'

He shrugged. 'There's nothing for him to do, though, is there?'

'He seems so keen on learning about our work, I don't want to discourage him.' I thought for a moment. 'I could set him some general research on the squadron, I suppose. When we get the go-ahead . . .'

'If.'

I scowled at him. '*When* we get the go-ahead to lift the plane, we need to know where it was from and who is inside. He can do all that.'

George put his hands up. 'Yeah, whatever . . . he's an easy guy to be around. I've no problem with him being here.'

I smiled my thanks and called Scott back.

'It won't be as interesting as finding the Spit, but if you want to come and see what we do, you're welcome. You might get put to work, making the tea or something.'

He laughed.

'That's okay, I make a great hot wet.'

'Sorry?'

He laughed again. 'Bootneck slang for a brew. Tea. Any hot drink. Another thing we are expert at.'

I wasn't sure if I was having my leg pulled but laughed anyway, and said I would send him the office address and we would see him the next day. Something about him lifted my spirits; in a way he reminded me of Ben, which should have made it tough to be around him, but actually felt comforting.

Scott was waiting at the office door when I arrived the next morning, reminding me of an over-keen sheepdog. He had an energy which was infectious, and I soon discovered he was also methodical and quick in doing what I asked of him.

I showed him the letters we had uncovered on the side of the Spitfire.

'These are the code letters of the squadron the plane came from,' I said. 'I'd like you to do some research online and find out which one they belong to. Once we know that, we can see if they reported any pilots MIA on the date in question.'

'How do you know the date?'

'Terry Bristow swears it was his birthday, which is as good a confirmation as we can hope for, but to be on the safe side I want to look at the days either side – say, at least a week before and after.'

He nodded. 'Makes sense. Right, I'll track down the squadron and take it from there, shall I?'

'Thanks, that'll be a huge help.'

It didn't take him long to get back to me.

'The letters belong to 66 Squadron,' he said. 'It was based all over the south of England in 1940, ending up at Biggin Hill, until it was moved early in 1941 to the South-West. The squadron was involved in the Battle of Britain.'

'Great. Thanks for that. I'll get in touch with them and see if they'll let us have a look at their records.'

'I can do that for you, if you're busy.'

'I would be happy for you to, but there are certain proto-cols involved in these things, and I think it'll be better coming from me.'

'No worries. Back to making the tea, then,' he said, grinning. 'I'll put the kettle on.'

Late in the afternoon and many cups of excellent tea later, George and I were moaning about the long weekend coming up, and how busy the roads would be, how crowded the nearest beaches and coastal walks would get. Even though the weather forecast was inclined to cloud and showers, everyone from London would head for the countryside or the coast, clogging up the local lanes and parking in stupid places.

'I hate bank holidays,' said Scott. 'They aren't recognised in the forces, thank God. Now I'm out of uniform, there's no one I want to spend it with and it just seems like a massive commercial break anyway – I mean, why bother? Why not let everyone take an extra days' holiday when they want to, instead of making everyone take it at the same time?'

'Hear, bloody, hear,' George said. 'I won't be doing anything, that's for sure.'

'My grandfather is coming for lunch on Sunday, that's as much as we're doing,' I said. 'None of us has felt like doing any fun stuff this past while, anyway . . .'

I stopped and the silence grew.

George put a hand out and squeezed my arm. Scott looked at him and then me, then dropped his gaze. A flush ran up my neck, and I rose, collecting up the mugs.

'Look, why don't you both join us for lunch on Sunday?' The words rushed out of my mouth before I had even processed the idea. What was I thinking? Although Peter and I had brokered a truce, life at home was still far from easy. And yet, maybe it would be good to do something different. 'It'll be very traditional, but I do a mean roast leg of lamb. And Grandpa is fascinated with this dig.'

George looked at me with a frown. 'Are you sure? I wouldn't want to impose on your family.'

I nodded. 'George, nothing will bring Ben back, and I, for one, am worn out with it all. Doing something normal for a change will be good for us.'

Scott looked uncomfortable.

'What am I missing?' he said. 'Who is Ben?'

'Ben is my son— *was* my son. He disappeared in an avalanche on a glacier last year while mountaineering in the Alps.'

The bare facts. I closed my eyes for a moment and opened them to see Scott watching me. His face was unreadable, except for the compassion in his eyes.

'I'm sorry. That must be devastating for you and your family,' he said. I inclined my head, slightly. 'Lunch sounds a nice thing to do. I appreciate you inviting me, I would like to come, thank you.'

I cleared my throat.

'Great, it'll be good to have company. It's been too long . . .'

Chapter 18

Bella

'Pilot Officer Gardner reporting for duty, sir.'

Bella handed over the log book and torn, dirty orders she had found in Aiden's uniform with a shaking hand. She found it hard to breathe.

Squadron Leader Henry Faulkner took them, frowned then glanced up.

'Ah, yes, Gardner, at last. I've been expecting you. You got mixed up in that train smash I believe. I trust you're fully recovered?'

'I am, sir, thank you.'

Her reply came out in a croak. She cleared her throat and tried to slow the hammering in her chest.

'Very good, very good. We need all the pilots we can get at the moment and that crash cost lives. Terrible thing. You've missed the batch you were meant to be with, but a new group started last week so we'll slot you in with them.' He scanned Aiden's training record, then looked over the top of a pair of half-moon spectacles. 'Your training record so far looks excellent, so I'm sure you will do well here.' The squadron leader called through the open door and a corporal appeared. 'Show

Pilot Officer Gardner to his billet, Corporal. He's a bit behind the rest of the intake. Bring him up to speed so he can hit the ground running, so to speak.'

'Yes, sir.'

The corporal led Bella to one of the long wooden buildings at the edge of the RAF base where she would be billeted while training.

Her heart thudded even faster. How could she pull this off? Surely someone would realise she wasn't Aiden? His uniform fitted her well enough, after she had had it cleaned of the dust and debris from the crash. Surprisingly, the blood had come out of it and although the material was scuffed and marked, it had withstood the battering it had taken when half a train fell on her brother.

The corporal barely looked at her, however; she supposed all he saw was another officer recruit in the same uniform as the rest.

Still . . . she must not relax for a moment.

Cutting off her hair had left her with a cold neck. Vulnerable. Exposed.

It was a small price for getting into flight training, and one she was prepared to pay on Aiden's behalf – and, she admitted to herself – to get to do what she wanted more than anything; to fly in battle and play a full part in the war against Germany. She had spent nights lying awake justifying her plan to herself. Telling herself she was atoning for her treatment of her brother. That it was her fault he now had to spend his life in a wheelchair.

The rest of the recruits were out but by the time she had unpacked – and hidden the few pieces of her own clothing, toiletries and supply of sanitary towels well out of sight – she heard voices. Gathering herself, she went out to meet her new co-trainees.

The group of young men had finished morning training and come in for lunch. They introduced themselves and took her off to the mess, chattering like a mob of airforce-blue magpies.

Not normally shy, Bella found herself tongue-tied, terrified of giving something away by how she acted or what she said. Her ATA experience seemed of little use to her, it was like starting school all over again.

Over the next few days, she discovered the group was like any other bunch of young men; a mix of all sorts. Some were quieter than others, some were pushy, some lazy, some cleverer or could run faster or shoot better. She did her best to blend in to the background, not attracting attention to herself in any of the classes and training they did.

Which worked well until the first time they were allowed to fly.

There had been moans from some about the amount of time they spent in the classroom, or taking apart bits of equipment, or doing calisthenics. What good was that to an airman? All they needed to do was practise flying the damn planes, not learn how to take them apart; the ranks could do that.

Eventually, they were deemed fit to climb into the cockpit of an airplane.

As soon as Bella left the ground, her mood soared. Having the months of experience flying different airplanes, she quickly adjusted to the unfamiliar controls of the Hurricane she had been allotted. Half the group were in the air with her and she checked her position, throttling back a little to stay level with the planes on either side of her. Their orders were to make some simple manoeuvres which she did with no trouble, and then land smoothly back on the airfield. It was only later that several of her fellow recruits asked how she had made it look so easy.

One, a tall dark-haired chap with a chipped front tooth, who had introduced himself as Johnnie Winters when she first arrived, sat down next to her in the mess at dinner.

'Is that the first time you've flown a Hurricane?' he said, guzzling shepherd's pie as if his life depended on it. 'You must have done more flying than just the basic course.'

'Well, when you grow up on an Australian cattle station in

the bush, miles from anywhere, flying a plane is something you get taught pretty early.' She smiled, remembering learning how to take off and land on the rough airstrip at Bindalong. 'I guess I must have been around fourteen when I was first allowed to take the controls.'

'Golly, you're a long way from home,' Johnnie said. 'Your accent doesn't sound English, but I couldn't place it. Australia, eh? Yorkshire weather must be a shock.'

She shrugged and smiled. 'I've been in Britain for a while at school, that's why I volunteered here. And I wanted to fly.'

'It beats being in the Army, certainly. Where do you go on leave, though? It's too far to go all the way back home, surely?'

Bella liked the way this young man seemed to care about where she was from and whether she had somewhere to go to. Maybe they would be friends.

But she couldn't allow herself to get drawn in or give too much away.

'I have relatives in Scotland,' she said. She rose. 'Nice talking to you, Winters. I'm quite tired, think I'll turn in early.'

'Call me Johnnie. I don't hold with all that public school surname stuff.' He smiled at her and stuck out his hand. 'Good to talk to you too. Sleep well, old chap.'

Bella shook his hand, thinking how strange it still felt. How she had changed the way she took someone's hand – keeping her wrist firm and taking Johnnie's hand with a strong grip.

That night she slept better than she had since she arrived, dreaming of flying Spitfires instead of Aiden, whose life was ruined thanks to her interfering. One day she would tell him what she had done – if she managed to pull off her masquerade and survived to tell the tale. Would he thank her? Or would he think she was totally mad for putting herself through something he thought was intrinsically wrong on every level?

* * *

118

The next few weeks passed in a haze of stress, training and sleepless nights. For Bella, the easy part was training. Flying came as naturally to her as breathing and she enjoyed learning the theory as much as the practical side of being a pilot.

Navigating her way through the minefield of social interaction with her fellow trainees, on the other hand, left her stomach churning with dread. The station hands she had been around her whole life at Bindalong were nothing like the well-to-do young men she trained alongside. They talked of things she had no idea about; politics, sport, theatre.

And girls. The urge to laugh out loud at some of the conversations she heard was hard to contain, and she would have loved to set them straight on a few things.

As the days shortened, cricket practice ended and rugby became the sport of preference during recreation time. Bella was drawn to any sport and still daydreamed about playing polo but stayed on the sidelines with one or two others and watched Johnnie Winters and the rest practising kicking penalties, passing and tackling. They came off the field covered in mud, arms slung across the shoulders of their teammates and shared a communal bath afterwards. A good enough reason not to join in, no matter how much she was ribbed for not taking part.

Everyone smoked. Cigarettes, pipes, even cigars. She had only tried smoking once, and almost choked, but if she were to fit in she must do what the rest did, so she practised until she could blow smoke rings along with the best of them.

Her monthly cycle was her main worry. She managed to wash and change in private, but what she would do when her period appeared she hadn't worked out. In the end it was easy enough, she invented a stomach upset which meant a rush to the bathroom at odd moments. Whether she could get away with such a story every few weeks would remain to be seen.

She was a part of the training squad but apart from them, and couldn't ever be anything else.

Was this what being at an English public school had been like for Aiden? Had he been an outsider or had he fitted in? Knowing her brother, she thought he might have been the former. He found it difficult to make friends, was a loner by nature. It was hard to imagine him being part of a rugby team with the machismo and bravado that went along with it.

Yet, as far as she knew from his letters home, he had never complained about going back to school each September after spending his summer holidays with Granny Mack, so perhaps there were others he had been friends with, who were more like him. She hoped so. She knew so little about his life once he was sent away to school at eleven years old. They had never been the closest of siblings and grew more distant the older they got, their paths diverging until it felt as if they had almost nothing in common. He hadn't even been very enthusiastic about flying.

She regretted bitterly that she had made his life a misery when Aiden spent the year after their mother's death at home. It was not his fault he was the blue-eyed boy in their father's eyes and she was 'just' a girl, but she had chosen to blame him and became a jealous bitch towards him. If she could turn the clock back and replay those months differently, she would do so in a heartbeat.

She telephoned the hospital or Granny Mack whenever she had the chance to ask after Aiden. He had progressed to being in a wheelchair during the day and was stoical about his circumstances on the face of it. Thank God for his violin, her grandmother said to her, it was the saving of him. But still the thought of him sitting on his own, day in and day out, shut away from the outside world, was enough to break Bella's heart all over again.

She ran into Johnnie one day as she was hurrying back to the mess after another update from the doctors. Dispirited and fighting back tears at the news that Aiden was becoming morose and depressed, she stumbled and he grabbed her arm to stop her falling.

'Woah, steady on, old chap, what's the rush?' Johnnie said. Seeing the distress on her face, he put a hand on her shoulder. 'Is everything all right? You look in a bit of a state.'

Bella kept her gaze on her feet, blinking furiously.

'Sorry, Johnnie,' she said, after a moment. 'Fine. Everything is fine.' She managed a smile. 'Must go. Sorry.'

She slipped past him and broke into a run, needing to escape his sympathetic eyes and cry in private.

Later, she sought him out in the mess.

'Apologies for my behaviour earlier, mate,' she said.

'Nothing to apologise for. You seemed in a bit of a funk, I hope there's nothing wrong.'

She shrugged. 'I'd just had some bad news. My sister is in hospital and very unwell.'

She had decided to tell him a version of the truth. Having someone to talk to might make it a little easier to cope with.

'Oh, Lord, I'm sorry,' Johnnie said. 'This blasted war.'

'It was an accident. Nothing to do with the war, but thank you.'

He waved away her words. 'Is she at home in Australia, then?'

'No, she's been over here for a couple of years. I hope I may be allowed to go and see her.'

'The powers that be will give you special leave, won't they? Have you asked?'

She shook her head. Johnnie was very kind, but she didn't want to be drawn into having to answer his questions, she would be certain to say something to arouse his suspicions.

'I will do. I need to go and find out how she is, it's bloody hopeless on the telephone. Thanks for your concern, Johnnie, I'll let you know how I get on.'

'Think nothing of it, old chap. I hope your sister recovers soon.' He grinned, the chipped tooth giving his face an appealing lopsided appearance. 'I'd like to meet her, one day. If she's anything like her brother, she must be quite a gal.'

Heat shot up Bella's neck and into her face. She smiled, trying to hide her embarrassment.

'Maybe you will. I think you'd get on well with her.'

Bella was given leave to visit the spinal unit and noticed the difference in Aiden immediately. He was fading away, his face almost cadaverous, the skin waxy and tight across his sunken cheeks. His freckles stood out in dark contrast and appeared to have grown; splodges of brown pigment marring the paleness. He put on a brave face for her, complimenting her on her new, short hairdo, but she could see it was an act. Before she left, she went to see his specialist.

'He's not eating enough, is he, doctor?'

The doctor grimaced and spread his hands. 'For people with the kind of injuries Mr Gardner sustained, the digestive system becomes sluggish and is prone to infection,' he said. 'Getting enough nourishment into him is a problem.'

'Is he in pain? I mean he's starving to death, by the looks of it, so he must be, mustn't he?' Anger rose in a shockwave. 'How can you leave him to suffer in such a way? It's cruel. If he were a horse or a dog, I would shoot him and put him out of his misery. You must be able to do something.'

'I can assure you, Miss Gardner, we are giving your brother all the care we can.' The doctor spoke in a clipped tone. 'We are at the forefront of new treatments here. Your brother is having a new type of physiotherapy which hopefully will help him.'

'But will it be enough, or will his system shut down completely and it will be too little too late? I hate seeing him so low and in pain.'

'I understand. But we are not God, Miss Gardner. There is only so much we can do.'

Bella's anger folded in on itself and grief took over, her throat choked with sobs she refused to let out. She went back to his room and kissed Aiden's cheek, said goodbye and left. She had no idea when she might be able to return – what if she were posted to the other end of the country after training? The training that, by rights, should be what Aiden was undertaking. Thank goodness for Granny Mack, who had taken it upon herself to visit her grandson as often as possible. How hard must it be for her, having already lost her daughter?

At the railway station she changed back into uniform, wiped off her lipstick and slicked back her short hair. She slunk out, hoping she wasn't seen coming out of the ladies' lavatory dressed as an RAF officer. Nobody shouted at her or gave chase, though the hairs stood up on the back of her neck and it felt as if everyone was watching her. She made her way to the platform for her train. The skirt, blouse and pair of shoes she had kept to wear to the hospital were well wrapped up in a bag. She would hide them again in the bottom of the small chest of drawers next to her bed.

It all felt surreal.

What on earth made her think she could live in a man's world and get away with it for more than a minute? Aiden wouldn't care, in fact he would think she was mad. So why carry on with such a dangerous charade? Finally, she came to her senses. As she straightened her uniform jacket and smoothed her hair back again, it only took a second to know the reason. She might kid herself that she was doing it for her brother, as some kind of atonement. In truth, it was far more straightforward than that.

She was doing it because she *had* to fly and needed to prove she was as good as any man.

As the recruits got closer to the end of their training, they spent longer flying, practising manoeuvres, learning how to dive and spin – to survive – in a dogfight. They practised coming out of a stall, what to do if their landing gear was damaged, how to bail out – though they didn't practise that particular action while in the air, the RAF was short enough of planes as it was.

Soon enough, they passed out and were awarded their pilot's wings. The group were given orders to present themselves at their operational training units and prepare for front-line duty. It was the end of their time together; they would be posted all over the country to wherever they were needed.

On their final evening, they gathered in the mess. For the first time in weeks, Bella felt high with success, and nervous at what lay ahead. This was it, in a few days they would be flying into battle against the Luftwaffe and the deadly Messerschmitts that were doing a good job of ripping the heart out of the RAF.

Tension sang in Bella's veins so she could barely sit still. The rest of the group were quiet and twitchy, swilling from tankards, their eyes averted from others. Only when enough beer had been consumed did the men became voluble, the noise level rising as they vied with one another over the best story of their short time together.

'Do you remember when Jonesy almost jumped without a 'chute . . .?'

'Yes, but Thomo having L and R on the back of his hands beats everything . . . who would imagine being a pilot and not knowing your left from right . . .?'

'. . . and Gardner flying so low he almost knocked the sar'nt-major's hat off when we were doing manoeuvres, I thought he was going to have an apoplexy. Old chap, it was the funniest thing I've seen. I nearly choked . . .'

And so on, into the night, until they wandered back to their beds, arms across shoulders, weaving unsteadily in the dark. Johnnie linked arms with Bella on one side and on the other with Jonesy, a short, dark-haired Welshman who was the best rugger player among them.

Bella had sipped her beer slowly, watching the others get drunk, their tongues loosening as the alcohol lowered their natural reserve. She couldn't afford to let anything slip, was terrified of saying something that might give herself away. These young men reminded her so much of Aiden, bringing back the memory of him being drunk after their last polo match together, when she had been so hard on him for letting a much older, stronger and more experienced player get past him.

Would the guilt ever leave her?

It would be easy to fall into the trap of matching their banter, tempting to best them in an argument. After so many weeks together, her awe of them had gone; most of them were still boys, on the cusp of manhood, and the thought of them fighting against the Germans filled her with fear.

Johnnie was a little older, more mature and considered. She hoped they would be posted to the same squadron. It would be comforting to have him alongside her. They had become good friends; he was easy to get along with and good company. But Bella refused to admit she would miss his friendship if they had to go their separate ways. She didn't need anyone else to lean on; she had made her own way this far, and would continue to do so.

Before they parted for the night, Johnnie stopped and said goodnight.

'From tomorrow, it becomes real, doesn't it?' he said, his face serious in the near darkness. 'I've got to admit, old chap, I'm nervous as a kitten. I hope we make it through, but if we don't I want you to know that it's been a pleasure getting to know you.' He paused, swaying slightly. 'You're by far the best of us, I know you'll do fine. Me; well, I'll do my damnedest to stay alive and if I can take down a few of the bastards, I'll be happy.'

Bella had no idea what to say. Men like Johnnie and the rest of them didn't say things like this. But then, they were living through extraordinary times and who knew if they would all be alive by the time the war ended. She blurted out what had been on her mind.

'Johnnie, all I hope is that we get posted to the same unit. You're a good mate and we can look out for each other in the air and on the ground if we stick together, can't we?'

It was all she could say.

Chapter 19

Jennifer

Peter and Rosie were less than happy when I told them at supper that we had two extra guests coming for Sunday lunch.

'Mum, how can you do that? I don't want to have my bank holiday ruined by a couple of strange old crusties wittering on about crashed planes,' Rosie said. 'Can I eat up in my room, instead?'

'No, you can't, young lady. You're old enough to be able to sit through a meal, and be polite. And George isn't a stranger, you've met him before.'

'Yeah, when I was, like, twelve or something. Basically, a kid.'

'Well, you can show him how much you've grown up, then, can't you?' I smiled at her. I would probably have felt the same at her age. 'Grandpa is looking forward to seeing you. He's missed you.'

She dropped her gaze and sighed.

'I've missed him, too.' She paused for a second. 'I don't know what to say to him . . .'

I rubbed her hand, gently. 'I think you'll find you don't have to say anything. He understands, perfectly.'

She blinked away the glitter of tears. 'Okay.'

'Okay.'

I cleared the plates. Peter had said nothing, which was all I needed to know.

Later, as I got into bed, he put his book down and removed his glasses. 'Why didn't you tell me you were going to invite people for lunch?'

Why did he have to have this conversation when I was dropping with tiredness?

'I told you I wanted to invite Grandpa.'

'That's not who I meant and you know it.'

I shrugged.

'We were talking about the bank holiday at work and neither of them had anyone to spend it with. I just blurted it out. I know I should have waited and discussed it with you first. I'm sorry.' I didn't want a row. We had walked around on eggshells since Peter had apologised for his behaviour, everything still felt raw, even though we were trying. 'You know George, and Scott is really easy-going. It's only lunch; a couple of hours or so. We can surely manage that, can't we?'

'We'll have to, won't we?'

He put his glasses back on and picked up the book again. Discussion over.

I sighed, put my bedside light out and closed my eyes. Would it ever get easier?

'Rosie, can you go and collect Grandpa later this morning, please?' I said, while I continued peeling potatoes and vegetables, the aroma of slowly roasting lamb teasing my nostrils. 'You can take my car. He said he'd be ready by eleven thirty.'

She lay on the sofa, still in her pyjamas with Sally curled up beside her, watching an old black-and-white film on the small TV which sat in the corner.

'Okay. What's the time now?'

'Almost eleven.'

'Yikes. Come on, Sally, time to shift yourself, I haven't even had a shower yet.' Rosie pushed the terrier onto the floor, stood and stretched, then came over and put her arms around my middle, laying her head between my shoulder blades. 'That smells wonderful,' she said. 'Sorry I was a spoilt brat the other day, when you told us we had guests for lunch.' Her words were spoken into my back, muffled by my T-shirt.

'I know it was a surprise. I shouldn't have sprung it on you and your dad like that,' I said. 'He wasn't happy either, but it's only lunch. A few hours of eating, drinking and chatting – not too much to ask, is it?'

I could feel her smile on my back, and the gentle shake of her head. She kissed my spine and then was gone.

'Grandpa had better be ready when I get there,' she called from the stairs.

'He will be.'

I smiled to myself. He had never been late for anything in his life.

George and Scott arrived within a few minutes of each other, at noon. Grandpa was, by that time, ensconced in the large leather armchair beside the fire, which usually had at least one dog or a cat sleeping in it, and was nursing a dry sherry.

The introductions over, I left Peter to make small talk while Rosie and I put the finishing touches to lunch.

'Bloody hell, Mum, you might have told me how buff Scott is,' she hissed. 'I expected him to be like George.'

'What do you mean – *buff*? And *like George*?'

'You know – buff – as in hunky, good-looking. And George is kind of nerdy, and old. He's even older than Dad, isn't he?'

I laughed and promised myself to never, ever divulge this conversation to poor George. He was a perfectly average-looking middle-aged man and one of the nicest people I knew.

Trying to see Scott through the eyes of my nineteen-year-old daughter though, made me realise how unalike the two men were.

'I suppose Scott is quite good-looking,' I admitted in a low voice, hoping no one else was listening. 'But don't be so mean about George. He's one of the best people I know.'

'Yeah, I know he is. But I'm sitting next to Scott. End of.'

'No, you aren't. I want you to sit next to Grandpa. You've hardly seen him recently.'

She huffed. 'In between them?'

'A rose between two thorns? Okay, then, you can sit at the end of the table. But don't you dare flirt with Scott.'

She batted her eyelashes at me. 'Me? Flirt? Never.'

I narrowed my eyes and gave her a look.

It hadn't occurred to me that she and Scott were much closer in age than the rest of us, even though he reminded me of Ben. He seemed so much older than Rosie, years of experience sitting heavily on his shoulders. I hoped I wouldn't regret my rash decision to invite him here.

'Go and tell them lunch is ready, will you?'

I took the food through to the dining room, then put another log on the wood stove, knowing Grandpa would think it was chilly after the warmth of the kitchen, and waited until everyone sat down.

'Peter, do you want to carve the meat, please?' I said, placing the joint on a side table. 'I hope everyone likes lamb.'

There was a general rumble of accord. Peter picked up the knife and steel, and sharpened the blade before carving thick slices of the pink meat. Putting the serving dish in the centre of the table, he and I sat down.

'Please, help yourselves.'

Everyone was too polite, at first, the conversation stilted. Only Scott and Rosie chatted together, quietly, at the opposite end of the table from me, until he said something and she almost choked on her food, trying not to laugh, her eyes wide with horrified amusement.

'That's awful,' she said.

He raised his eyebrows. 'I know, right?'

'Tell everyone else. I can't believe it really happened,' she said.

We all looked at Scott, and he seemed momentarily nonplussed to have the eyes of everyone on him.

'Okay. Well, we had this sergeant when I was training, who was a right sadistic sod. If things weren't up to scratch he made the whole troop do extra reps of press-ups, or something equally disgusting, usually in the rain in the middle of the night.' He paused. 'One day he came in and inspected our dorm, and all he could find was one dead fly on the windowsill. We got done for keeping illegal livestock, and neglecting it so badly it died.' He shook his head and grinned. 'Like I said, he was a right sadist.'

Peter snorted, a laugh rumbling up from his belly. 'That sounds extraordinarily unfair,' he said. 'What were you training for?'

'Royal Marines, sir.'

'Ah. It sounds very tough.'

Peter went back to his lunch, nodding to himself. I guessed he didn't see much in common with our guest.

Grandpa had a wide grin on his face as he gazed across the table.

'Hmm, sounds a bit different to my day,' he said. 'The most we did were a few calisthenics, as far as I can remember. I suppose the ethos being drummed into you is that you're all responsible for everything and everyone within the troop.'

Scott nodded. 'Exactly.' His face grew serious. 'A kind of all for one and one for all. Like the Three Musketeers.'

'You must have been very close to the men you worked alongside,' Grandpa said, quietly. 'I know I was.'

'You too?' Scott regarded him for a moment. Grandpa nodded, once. 'Makes it hard to leave behind, doesn't it?'

'Indeed. Though in my case it was a very, very long time ago.

But it's impossible to forget an experience like that, when one is so young.'

I watched both their faces and then caught Rosie's look. This was supposed to be a way for us to move forward and enjoy company again, but it was turning into something intensely personal. I shied away from it going anywhere near the mention of Ben.

I stood up. 'Would anyone like second helpings? Scott, have some more lamb, there's plenty. And roast spuds too.'

He looked at me and smiled. 'I would love some more, thanks. It's delicious.'

The atmosphere lightened and I continued the business of seeing to the filling of plates. From there, it got easier, though I could see Grandpa was waning. He managed a small dish of trifle and then fell silent.

I went and helped him up from his chair. His gammy leg always pained him more when he was tired.

'Why don't you come into the kitchen and have a snooze beside the fire? Then I'll get Rosie to run you back after tea.'

'That's a splendid idea, old thing,' he said, leaning on my arm.

I settled him in the armchair again, and put a rug over his knees, then put the kettle on to make coffee for the rest of us. Before it had boiled I heard a gentle snore and smiled to myself. I was glad he and Scott had hit it off; Grandpa's life before I remembered him had always been a closed book. It was nice to hear even a tiny snippet about it.

Returning to the dining room with a tray full of coffee cups, I found George and Peter in deep conversation about a documentary they had both watched recently. Scott and Rosie, meanwhile, sat at the opposite end of the table, discussing skiing. At least my family seemed to be enjoying having company to talk to. I doled out coffee and then stacked the tray with dirty crockery. Scott immediately stood up and began to help me.

'Please, there's no need. You sit down and drink your coffee. I'll just get these out of the way.' I smiled my thanks at him.

'Seems harsh that you cooked it and now you have to clear away too,' he said.

'Hah, don't you worry, I have two slaves here who will do the washing up.' I winked and laughed.

Rosie pulled a face.

'Won't be me. I have to take Grandpa home and make sure he's tucked in for the night,' she said. 'Bad luck, Dad, looks like you drew the short straw.'

Peter looked up. 'What have I drawn the short straw on, now?'

I dropped a kiss on top of his head.

'Nothing, nothing at all.' I sat down again. 'George and Scott, thanks for coming. It's nice to have you here. It's been a while.'

For a moment no one said anything, and a tremor ran down my back. I could picture Ben sitting in his usual place at the table, bickering with Rosie about whose turn it was to wash up. I closed my eyes for a second, needing to centre myself and stay in the here and now. There was no point in looking back. No point at all.

Chapter 20

Bella

There was no leave granted between being awarded their wings and starting their next posting. Guilt dogged Bella that she was unable to get away and visit Aiden, but she managed a short conversation with him by telephone before she left the training base. It didn't feel enough, not nearly enough, but she couldn't say everything she wanted to. The words just wouldn't come out the way she meant them to, so perhaps it was just as well. He told her that he was on a trial regime, which was helping – he had a better appetite and his system seemed to be holding up. She promised to write and to phone again when she had a chance.

Grief hung around Bella's neck like a noose at the thought of not knowing when – or if – she would see her brother again. At least her father had re-opened communications and wrote to her at least twice a week, asking how Aiden was and instructing her to tell Granny Mack to let him know if there was any change in his condition. As if that miracle was ever going to happen.

The Royal Mail being what it was, she received nothing for weeks and then a sheaf of letters all arrived together at the post office box she kept in the local town under her own name, just before she was posted. She buried them at the bottom of her kit bag, unable to look at them and the desperate hope they contained. She scribbled a quick note to Granny Mack, telling her she was being transferred and would let her know the address once she was settled.

She thanked her lucky stars that she and Johnnie were posted to the same squadron. They spent the next day on a train southbound to the capital and then on to their base at Duxford. Johnnie had a copy of *The Times* which he buried himself in for the first part of the journey. Bella pulled out her battered copy of Banjo Patterson's *Old Bush Songs*, although she knew them all by heart. The book was a comfort in its familiarity and brought back memories of Bindalong, before her mother's accident.

A bookmark slipped out of the worn pages and landed on the floor between her and Johnnie, who sat opposite. He lifted it and glanced at the picture before Bella could grab it.

It was an old photograph of her family in front of Bindalong homestead, taken when she and Aiden were about eight and ten. The pair of them were in scruffy dungarees, shoeless, and each sat on a pony bareback, cut-down polo mallets in hand. Her parents had their arms around each other and they were all grinning at the camera. She recalled it had been Greg who took it, before the accident which lamed him for life.

'Gosh, is this you and your family?' he said, peering at the grainy image. 'I can't tell which is you and which is your sister. You're very alike.' Bella held her hand out, heart thumping, but Johnnie stared at it for a moment more. 'Is this you?' he said, pointing at Aiden. 'I guess it must be, as the other has pigtails. You could be twins, though.'

He handed the photograph back to Bella, who quickly hid it in the book. How stupid of her to forget it was there. Heat prickled in her hairline and her hand shook.

She could remember that day so clearly; the heat on her back, dust in her eyes and throat as she and Aiden galloped across the training field trying to hit the polo ball their dad had thrown ahead of them. A memory of the thrill of speed as she urged her pony to go faster in her determination to beat her brother.

The day had ended badly, their parents having a blazing row over some tiny matter, her mother's quick tongue more than a match for Dad's blustering bullishness. She remembered sitting at the top of the stairs, willing them to stop shouting at each other. A door slamming and Mum running up the stairs holding her cheek, her eyes wild, red hair in disarray. She had almost tripped over Bella, who shrank against the wall trying to stay out of her way.

'Go to bed, Bella,' she had said. 'You shouldn't be up.'

Bella had run to her room, jumped into bed and pulled the covers over her head, not wanting to think the things that ran around her brain, trying to blot out the expression on her mother's face and the angry words she had heard.

With hindsight she wondered exactly what kind of marriage her parents had had. Did her dad ever lift a hand to Mum? The thought made her feel sick. She closed her eyes and tried to block the images that flitted through her mind.

Johnnie seemed unaware of her reaction and had gone back to his crossword. The tedious journey continued, their carriage emptying and filling with different passengers at each stop. Finally, after changing at King's Cross in London, they embarked on the last leg to Duxford, arriving tired and hungry.

The adjutant of 92 Squadron cast a baleful eye over Bella and Johnnie as they stood before him. He sat at his desk, looking more like a bank clerk than anything else. However, his WWI ribbons said otherwise, and they threw him a smart salute.

'Who are you?' the adjutant said.

'Gardner, sir, posted to 92 Squadron.'

'Winters, sir, and likewise.'

'We've had no notification of your arrival, but that's nothing new and not your problem. I suppose you're fresh out of training?'

'Yes, sir,' in unison.

'Oh good, just what we need. Another two who'll need baby-sitting. Don't suppose you've flown Spits, either?' Bella and Johnnie shook their heads. The adjutant sighed. 'My name is Gowling, and I can tell you the CO is going to be less than impressed we've been sent a couple of wet-behind-the-ears recruits to look after, when he requested fully trained, experienced pilots.' He stared at them for a moment. 'Log books please, gentlemen. Let's see how bloody awful you are.'

The two handed over their training logs and continued to stand at attention while Gowling scanned the pages detailing their results over the past weeks and months. Bella wiped sweaty palms down her thighs, hoping he wouldn't notice.

'Mr Gardner, how old are you?'

She rapidly did the maths in her head. Aiden's birthdate was exactly two years and two months after hers.

'Almost twenty, sir.'

'I didn't ask how old you almost are, Pilot Officer. How old are you – exactly.'

Heat travelled up Bella's neck. This was not the start she imagined.

'Nineteen years and seven months, sir.'

Gowling shook his head, muttering about sending children to do a man's work. He said nothing to Johnnie.

'Right, gentlemen, the CO is away until tomorrow morning, so I suggest you go and find your quarters and get settled in. I'll send for you when the boss is back.'

Later that evening, they found themselves in the officers' mess, along with those of the squadron not on duty. Bella had taken particular care with her uniform and appearance. Still, her hands shook so she rammed them in her trouser pockets, trying to assume a relaxed demeanour. Johnnie was in a high good humour, and after they had been introduced to one or two other pilots by Gowling, he seemed to fit in immediately, drinking beer and chatting to a small group at the bar.

Bella stood a little apart, her stomach churning. She had calmed down enough to be able to hold a tankard of beer but hadn't drunk any of it. Why did she think she could do this? Her deception would be discovered before the evening was out; all she wanted to do was hide in her room and hope the world would disappear.

'Digger, another beer, old chap?'

Johnnie's voice broke into her thoughts. She started, almost spilling her drink.

'What? No. Sorry, Johnnie, I'm still going, thanks.'

'Are you all right? You look a tad seedy, if you don't mind me saying.'

She managed a smile and nodded. 'Perfectly fine, mate. Bit tired, that's all. It's been a long day. Think I might turn in early.'

'Absolutely, old chap. Won't be far behind you, after I've bought these fellows a beer.' Johnnie wafted his tankard in the general direction of the group he had been chatting with. 'They seem a good bunch, don't you think?'

Bella nodded again. 'I'm sure they are. Just not sure they're going to be thrilled at having us two novices in their midst.'

Johnnie smiled at her. 'Well, I s'pose it's not long since they were as *wet behind the ears* as we are.' He lightly punched her shoulder. 'Come on, Digger, buck up, old man. You're as good a flyer as anyone else here. Aren't you excited to finally be doing what we've trained for all this time?'

Bella looked up into his eyes, which sparked as if catching the flames in the open fire behind her.

'Let me have a good night's sleep and I'll be as excited as the best of 'em tomorrow,' she said. 'Here, finish this for me. I can't face it.'

'Blimey, you sure you're not sick?' Johnnie laughed and took the tankard. 'Well, night, night, old chap. I hope you sleep well and feel more the thing in the morning.'

'Night, Johnnie.'

She raised a hand to the others and left, hurrying back to her room as if she was escaping something unseen but terrifying.

Chapter 21

Jennifer

Back at the office after the long weekend, I got in touch with the squadron we now knew the Spitfire belonged to, asking if it was possible to do some research and identify who the pilot might be. They surely must have records of men who were officially still missing in action, their bodies never recovered.

I gave them the site co-ordinates and the date we thought the Spit had crashed. Until we had the licence to recover the body there wasn't much more we could do. Recovering the pilot's dog tags and log book would tell us exactly who he was, but I was impatient. It might be weeks before we were given permission to continue the dig, and the thought of kicking our heels until then was enough to sour my mood.

In the meantime, George, Scott and I went through the finds we already had, cleaning them up with a soft dry brush and trying to work out what parts of the plane we had found. Basic skills that Scott picked up quickly, handling each item with care and respect.

Just as we were coming to the end of cleaning, I received an email from the squadron. The period that included the date Terry

Bristow assured us was when he saw the Spitfire come down was one of the deadliest for their pilots. The squadron had been involved in dogfights over the Channel every day during that time, and some of their pilots were lost and not recovered, shot down over the water. The planes were never found and it was understood that they lay on the seabed. One pilot bailed out and was found, eventually, when his body was washed up on the coast a week later. The others were still missing.

Reading the email for the second time, frustration gnawed at me. Not only did we not have a definite identification for the man we had found, it also made it very apparent how many other potential sons, husbands and brothers never came home and lay at the bottom of the sea or buried in the ground, forgotten by almost everyone.

I knew from some of the previous planes we had recovered that our pilot could easily be younger than Ben or Rosie. I imagined the effect it must have had on his family, never having a body to bury, or knowing exactly where he was. I only hoped that we could identify our man and finally let his family know what happened to him. As hard as I tried to look on each small piece of information as a positive thing which could help the dig move forward, it sent me into a spinning vortex of grief for my own son, all over again.

Scott came into the office to find me in a mess. I turned away, trying to control the tears, shaky breaths giving away my reaction to the message. He no doubt wanted to run away, but stayed and sat in the chair opposite me.

'I can see you're not okay, so I won't ask if you are,' he said. 'Is there anything I can do? Do you want to tell me about it?'

I shook my head.

'There is nothing anyone can do,' I managed to say.

'Is this about your son . . . um, Ben?'

I nodded and turned the laptop around so that he could read the email.

'Our pilot was probably younger than Ben. It just got to me.' I wiped my eyes. 'Stupid, really. Young men have been getting killed in wars for millenia.'

Scott scanned the email, then turned the laptop back towards me.

'I lost a couple of close mates in Afghanistan,' he said. 'One was nineteen and the other twenty-three. I understand.'

I looked up, and saw the grief in his face. He had more than likely gone through more trauma already than most people would do their whole lives.

'Was that when you were injured, too?' I bit my lip. 'Sorry. You don't have to answer that. It's none of my business.'

'It's okay. Sometimes it helps to talk about it. Other times, it feels all wrong. Is that weird?'

'I don't think so. How we deal with grief is a very personal thing. There isn't a right or wrong, is there?'

He shook his head. 'No, I don't think there is.' He drew a breath, as if girding himself, his eyes becoming distant. 'We were on a recce of a village, way out in the desert . . .'

I remember dragging an arm across my face, wiping the dust and sweat away before putting the scope back up to my eye and focusing on the collection of rough buildings 400m below. A heat haze warped my vision, the afternoon as hot as Hades.

Nothing stirred. Anything living, with an atom of sense, would be indoors hiding from the sun.

Mad dogs and all that . . .

A movement beside me sharpened my concentration. Chris 'Noddy' Holder, my corporal, nudged my arm and tipped his head towards the village. A man dressed in a long white dishdasha, with a traditional kaffiyeh on his head, appeared from behind the biggest building. Over his shoulder was slung an AK-47 and I noticed a large dog on a chain tied to a wall slink out behind him. A second man followed him and seemed to be unarmed. I re-focused the spotting scope and homed in on the two faces.

I put the scope down.

'Neither are him,' I whispered. 'No scar.'

'Fuck it,' Chris muttered.

I continued my surveillance of the Afghan village; hiding place, according to our source, of Ahmed Rafiq – warlord, opium poppy producer and heroin supplier – it would be good if we could finally be rid of him, but he was adept at evading capture. The only photo circulating of him was years out of date and only one thing made him stand out – a three-inch scar down his right cheek which ended at his top lip, giving him a permanent sneer.

A breeze sprang up, as dry and desiccating as the desert sand. It put us on the wrong side, coming from behind our small group of four and wafting towards the village. I kept my sights on the guard, and saw the dog raise its head and sniff the wind, looking straight at the spot where we lay hidden. Its hackles went up and even from this distance I could hear its volley of barks.

'Fuck.' I shuggled down the slope. 'We've been compromised. Come on, time to withdraw before that bastard lets his dog off. I'll cover first. Let's move.'

Setting off at a low run, the other two commandos, Robbo Ivinson and Hamish 'Mish' Chambers, followed Noddy back down the hill while I kept eyes on the village, rifle at the ready. I'd already been in comms with our base, letting them know the OP had been compromised. Once I was as sure as I could be that we weren't being followed, I set off after the others.

After covering ten kilometres we reached the Snatch Land Rover we had left hidden in a deep gulley, three days earlier.

Jumping into the front passenger seat, I let my corporal drive, while the other two climbed into the back, keeping their guns close. Noddy set the vehicle into reverse, and the Land

Rover skidded and bounced its way out of the wadi back to the dirt road which eventually led to the village we had been watching. Noddy did a hand-brake turn onto the track back towards base, and gunned the accelerator pedal, making the tyres spin on the loose, sandy gravel.

'Cum'n, you fucker, shift yer arse,' Noddy spat, as the tyres bit and the Landy jumped forward.

I kept my eyes on the wing mirror, dreading the sight of sunlight reflecting off a vehicle behind us. Noddy kept his foot flat to the floor and the vehicle bucked and shuddered on the rough road, the rest of us hanging on to stop ourselves being thrown around like rag dolls. After ten minutes, he slowed down a little as we came to the small town we had passed through three days before. I kept my attention on the empty road behind us, while Robbo and Mish scanned the buildings. The single street had shops on either side, closed until the heat abated and people came out of their houses to buy food and drink mint tea. I checked my watch. It was past time for opening. Where were the people? I shifted my focus onto the shops. A face in a window, withdrawn as we passed. A man, fumbling with a key, hurrying to get inside. What was going on?

Noddy didn't seem to have noticed anything suspicious, too busy thinking about the cold one he would down when we got back to base, I reckoned, but the other two wore frowns and muttered at the deserted street.

We breathed a collective sigh as we reached the end of the row of buildings and nothing had kicked off.

The Land Rover hit the improvised explosive device as we sped and left the town.

Scott paused, looking wrung out, his eyes distant.

'It's the impressions of the aftermath that have stayed with me. I wake at night and am back there, in that hell . . .'

The screams of the other men. My leg, mangled and shattered, after I was thrown through the windscreen and across the road by the force of the IED. The fact that I couldn't feel any pain as I dragged myself back to the upside-down vehicle and made frantic attempts to help the others. The scorching metal of the Land Rover on my hands, as the fire burnt Noddy alive. How, no matter how I pulled and ripped at it, I couldn't get the twisted metal of the driver's door to open. The devastating injuries to Mish and Robbo in the back.

The choppers coming to our rescue; one on the ground and one in the air, circling and keeping watch for enemy approaching.

They sent Noddy home in a body bag. Me, Mish and Robbo spent months in hospital and then rehab, our careers and lives in shreds. Six months after returning to Britain, Robbo wheeled his chair out of the rehab unit, down the drive and into the patch of woodland across the road, where he liked to sit from time to time. There, he took his commando knife, opened his wrists and bled out.

Sweat stood out on Scott's forehead and his hands shook.

'I still can't hear the sound of a chopper without turning into a wreck . . .'

We sat in silence for a few moments, Scott breathing deeply as if he had been running hard, or something. I tried to assimilate what he had told me but everything he said was so outside my experience that he might have been telling me the plot of a film he had just watched.

It felt unreal . . . as unreal as picturing my son lying under tons of ice and snow on a mountain, somewhere.

Chapter 22

Bella

The next morning, Bella and Johnnie stood in front of the CO, Squadron Leader James Henderson, a tall, rangy man whose craggy face looked as if it had seen too many late nights.

'Well, gentlemen,' he said, after they had saluted him and given their names. 'I can't have you in my squadron, I'm afraid. We're on twenty-four-hour stand-by, and neither of you has any experience flying Spits. I should have you posted tout de suite.' He sighed, picked up a pipe and began filling it from a leather pouch of tobacco. When it was filled to his satisfaction, he tamped it down, placed it between his lips and sucked on it without lighting it. He continued speaking with the pipe clamped to his teeth and his eyes on what was on the desk in front of him. 'However, good pilots are hard to find, and your log books tell me you have potential.' He tapped a booklet and looked up at them. 'I am not going to throw you straight into the fray – that would be akin to child murder in my view – I'm going to give you a few weeks to show me you're worth having. You will live, breathe, eat – and eventually fly – Spitfires.' Removing the pipe, he speared them with his eyes.

'Don't let me down, gentlemen. We need all the good men we can get. Dismissed.'

Bella and Johnnie saluted again, left the office in stunned silence, and were met by the adjutant, Gowling, who must have known their outcome. He grinned at their expressions.

'Right, let's get you started. You've got one chance to impress the boss. Don't fuck it up, gentlemen.'

'No, sir, thank you, sir,' Bella said.

'Don't call me sir.'

'No, si . . . adj, sorry.'

Her head spun with a mixture of terror and excitement. They were on probation with no second chances, and must make the best of it. Bella glanced sideways at Johnnie, whose face gave nothing away, apart from a twitch of his lips.

The next week reminded her of being back in training and that feeling of being out of her depth while at the same time being elated to be around airplanes all day every day. The first time she walked over to her plane, her parachute slung over her shoulder, the oxygen mask swinging annoyingly beside her cheek, she could barely breathe. The two ground crewmen looked at her with resignation on their faces. She could almost see their thoughts – *here's another one we've got to baby-sit.*

Well, she would show them.

They helped strap her into the cockpit, shut the small door, and she was alone in a Spitfire for the first time. Anticipation, and a deep-seated contentment, settled over her, as if she had found her home, the place she was meant to be.

It didn't mean there were no challenges. The Spit was so different to anything she had flown before, either in the ATA or in training. The power of the Merlin engine astonished her. Smoke enveloped the cockpit for a moment when it started up and there was a flash of flame from the twin exhausts. She found all she could see was the huge nose in front of her while she taxied to the end of the runway, and swung the Spitfire from side to side as she'd been told to.

Letting off the brakes at the end of the runway, she slowly opened the throttle. A surge of power pushed her back into her seat and she laughed out loud as adrenaline sang in her veins. The strength of the torque pulled one wing down and she quickly adjusted and straightened up. The plane seemed to fling itself into the air and she hung on to the stick for dear life until everything settled down and her heart rate slowed a little.

Feeling a little more in control, she changed hands on the stick and pumped the undercarriage up, feeling as if she were rubbing her stomach while patting her head, the concentration making her head spin.

It was physically far more demanding than anything she had experienced before, her arms and shoulders aching with effort. There was so much to remember but as she practised some basic manoeuvres she relaxed and began to sing.

Making a long, slow turn back towards Duxford, she thought of Aiden, and wondered how he might have handled such a machine. He was as good a pilot as she was, and she hoped the Spitfire would have engendered the same response in him. Sadness tugged at her, that he had never got the chance to feel its power and grace in the air. She tried not to let in a sneaking moment of gratitude that his tragedy had given her this opportunity.

She would honour him by being one of the best pilots in 92 Squadron.

Bella was brought back to earth, literally, as she approached the aerodrome. She and Johnnie had been warned about the number of pilots who never walked away from their first landing of a Spit.

She selected 'wheels down' and pumped until a green light came on and the word 'down' appeared. Good, wheels were down and locked. She breathed a sigh and concentrated on bringing the plane in straight and level. Everything seemed to be happening very quickly and as she got flaps down and sailed lower, she couldn't see anything beyond the nose obscuring her view.

Praying she was on course she glanced down to the side and saw the hedge at the end of the field flash past. Trying not to panic at the speed, she slowed some more, then felt a solid bump as the wheels hit the ground. Cutting the throttle, she prayed she wouldn't brake too hard and end up with the nose ploughing into the ground. Allowing the plane to roll across the uneven grass, she steered off the runway and came to a stop.

Shaking, the sweat trickling down inside her Sidcot suit, she sat for a moment, trying to make sense of what she had just done.

She was a Spitfire pilot. Nobody could take that away from her, whatever happened.

Walking back to the barracks, Bella relived the past hour, her mind still in the clouds going over all the things she could have done better. A slap on the back made her jump and she spun round to see Johnnie with a wide grin on his face.

'Wasn't it the best thing you've ever done?' he said, ripping off his flying helmet and holding his arms out like a small boy playing at airplanes. He made a tight circle and stopped in front of her, his eyes alight with excitement and happiness.

Bella laughed, joining him in his game for a moment.

'Yes. Yes, it was. The very best thing I have ever experienced,' she said, linking arms with him. 'Now we can call ourselves Spitfire pilots – how many people can claim that? We are such lucky buggers.'

'Luck has nothing to do with it – we're just fucking excellent at flying. Don't do yourself down, Digger, my friend. I caught sight of you landing and it looked as if you've been doing it your whole life. You're a natural, old chap.'

Admiration shone out of Johnnie's face, and heat rushed through Bella's body. She laughed and brushed off his compliment.

'Well, I've trained with the best, haven't I? Now, last one back to the mess buys the beer.'

She set off at a run, her parachute bouncing on her shoulder, her flying boots and Sidcot suit hampering her strides. Johnnie made an attempt to keep up with her but soon dropped to a jog.

'You win,' he yelled. 'I'm buying.'

Bella glanced over her shoulder at him and slowed, thankful she could stop. The pair of them flopped down on a bench outside the mess, sweating and blowing hard.

After a long draught of cool beer, Bella felt better and could look Johnnie in the eye again.

Johnnie slouched back against the wall, his eyes closed, face up to the rays of the sun. He'd loosened his flying suit and scarf and she could see the pale skin of his throat where a pulse beat steadily. She was very glad that he was the one she had been paired up with; they made a good team, were on the same wavelength.

She shook her head.

Don't get too friendly, don't get too close—

She couldn't afford to let her guard down.

Keep everyone else at arm's length.

'Penny for 'em.' Johnnie opened one eye and smiled. 'As if I can't guess.'

Bella jumped and knocked her tankard over.

'Oh damn. God, I'm so clumsy, how the fuck I can be a pilot I've no idea.' She laughed, covering her embarrassment.

'Exhaustion, old thing. No surprise, really. Come on, I need a bath and a shave before dinner. They won't let us into the dining hall if we're stinking like this.'

He rose, pulled her up, and, linking arms with her, dragged her back to their barracks. Bella's legs had turned to jelly and though she tried not to lean on him, she had no choice, trying to ignore the warmth and intimacy of his arm through hers.

The two pilots were given every opportunity to fly as often as they wanted to or could persuade their ground crews to let them. Their planes were old and had been flown for hundreds of hours but they were kept prepared and in good shape.

Bella and Johnnie went out together, flying in formation, practising stalls, dives, screws and rolls, getting used to throwing the machines all over the skies above the countryside and coast. They had already done training in dogfighting and now they spent hours honing their skills, until flying a Spitfire became as easy and routine as riding a bicycle.

After another afternoon of waiting until those of the squadron who were on duty had taken off before they could get into the air and spend an hour chasing each other around the sky, the pair walked back from the aerodrome as Spitfires began arriving back. Watching the first couple land and taxi across to their bays, they could tell the others had been caught up in yet another fight with the Luftwaffe. Bullet holes peppered their wings and one had lost its tail.

'Wonder how many poor bastards won't make it back this time,' Johnnie said.

Bella heard the drone of a plane arriving which sounded like a wounded animal, metal screeching on metal. The Spitfire seemed to crawl over the far hedge, missing it by a few feet, and then appeared to drop straight down onto the runway, landing on its belly and skidding across the rough turf until it came to a stop with one wingtip dug into the earth. Smoke and the red flicker of flame came from the fuselage.

'Get out of there,' Bella muttered to herself.

She set off to run and help, but Johnnie put a hand on her arm and stopped her.

'It's okay, they've got it covered.'

He pointed, and she could see fire trucks and an ambulance racing towards the stricken plane. Slowly, the cockpit opened and the pilot's arm appeared in a wave. Bella's heart pounded in her throat somewhere, yet she couldn't look away. The flames licked higher, consuming the rear part of the plane, just as the rescue teams reached it.

Hoses sprayed water over the fire and a team of men helped

the pilot out of the cockpit. His legs looked to be injured and they helped him to a stretcher and into the ambulance.

Just as it seemed all would be well, another plane appeared with one wing shot to pieces and one of its wheels hanging down. Bella imagined the pilot realising what was going to happen and frantically pulling up on the stick, trying desperately to gain enough height to clear the obstacle. And he almost succeeded, but for the hanging wheel, which hooked onto the open cockpit, flipping the Spitfire over onto its back so that it slid a hundred yards down the runway, one wingtip gouging a trench as it went.

It eventually stopped with one wing up in the air and the cockpit buried into the ground.

Bella and Johnnie dropped their parachutes and raced across the runway towards the plane. More emergency vehicles arrived just as they got there, the teams efficiently working together to get the pilot out. The two young pilots stood to one side and let them do their job, only jumping to when someone yelled at them to help get the cockpit door open.

Bella could see the pilot was dead, his head at an angle which told the tale of his demise. She was shocked to see it was Paul Smallwood. He was one of the group who had made them feel welcome when they first arrived.

What a tragic waste.

The sortie cost the squadron two lives, and two pilots hospitalised. The ground crews worked around the clock patching up the damaged Spits and the CO ordered two replacement planes.

The mess was a quiet and sombre place. Exhausted pilots spent their time off-duty drinking tea, reading or sleeping in the sagging armchairs.

Bella felt even more of a fraud. What on earth was she thinking, imagining she could do this job? Never mind keep up her charade in front of the whole squadron. She might as well come clean and take whatever punishment she deserved or run away and lose herself as Bella Gardner.

The lure of the airplanes kept her there though. It was as if she had an itch which just had to be scratched – never mind that scratching it might make her bleed or worse.

Two days after they helped extricate the pilot from the crashed plane, the CO called her and Johnnie into his office.

'Right, gentlemen, your training time has ended. Tomorrow, I'm placing you in Blue Wing. Toby Cranston is your flight commander. Questions?'

Bella glanced at Johnnie. His face was impassive.

'No, sir.' Their words together.

'Good luck, both of you. Dismissed.' The CO's voice sounded hollow and tired.

Bella and Johnnie saluted and left. There was no going back. Tomorrow they would fly their first sortie.

Chapter 23

Bella

Two weeks later, they were still alive. The days merged one into another in Bella's mind. Sleep badly, eat, wait, fly a sortie, land, wait, fly another, land, wait again. Fall into a doze at the slightest opportunity.

Tension and fear sat side by side within her and she wondered how long she could control them. She had seen other pilots blanche at the prospect of going out again after surviving a sortie where some of their fellows didn't make it. It was something they all had to face: fear, and how to overcome it so they could do their job.

Johnnie stopped his easy-going chattering and spent his time wandering around the aerodrome by himself when he wasn't on stand-by. Dealing with his fear in his own way. Bella understood, but missed him; his enthusiasm, his humour, the solidity of having him alongside her. They had gone through so much together already, yet now she needed him more than ever, he couldn't help her.

The missions they had flown so far had been protecting bombers flying to cities in France to attack German-held factories.

Apparently, she and Johnnie had been lucky in that they had met little opposition apart from flak and anti-aircraft guns. The Luftwaffe must have been taking a holiday, so the joke went.

It did little to instil confidence into Bella. If this was easy, what the hell would it be like to be set upon by a squadron of Messerschmitt 109s?

The next day the two new pilots were assigned to fly sorties again, beginning at dawn. Woken by her batman at 4.30am with a steaming mug of tea, she dragged herself out of bed after a night of fitful sleep, every muscle aching with fatigue. Washing her face with cold water, she dressed in the pre-dawn gloom, wrapping her breasts tightly with a crepe bandage over which she pulled a vest, relieved as always for her flat chest and lack of cleavage. Being skinny had its compensations.

Funny how people saw what they expected to. None of those she worked with every day had questioned her gender, or even looked at her sideways. Why would they, unless she did something stupid and gave herself away?

Others had already gathered in the mess for breakfast, though few ate more than a piece of toast. Bella couldn't face eating anything but filled a large mug with coffee, drinking it black and very sweet. Turning away from the large urn, she almost bumped into Johnnie and just avoided spilling it down his chest.

'Woah, careful,' he said.

'Sorry, Johnnie,' she said. 'This stuff had better wake me up a bit, I'll be useless otherwise.'

'Sleeping badly?'

She nodded. 'I'm so tired, but still can't sleep at night.'

'Me too.' He poured himself some coffee, took a piece of buttered toast, and followed her to a table. 'Well, here we go again. Funny how *this* is what I've been dreaming of for months. The reality isn't quite the same, is it?'

'It's the hanging about, waiting, that's the worst, don't you think?' Bella spoke in low tones. 'My stomach's in knots the whole time.'

153

Johnnie grimaced. 'It's hellish, isn't it? And we've only just begun. We survived the first week, so apparently we have a good chance of not copping it.' He rubbed a hand over his face. 'We're not out of the woods yet, though. Not by a long shot.'

'Do you think we'll get used to it? The ones who've been here a while seem relaxed enough . . . does it just become routine?'

He shrugged. 'I have no idea. Ask me again in a month – if we're still alive.'

'Don't speak like that, mate. We'll get through this, I have to believe it.'

'You do know the odds are against us, don't you? All we can do is pray to God and hope he's watching over us.'

'It's a cruel god who allows this despicable war to happen.'

'Amen to that.'

They took off in formation, flying south towards the Channel above the Stirling bombers carrying their lethal loads. Johnnie and Bella were in the middle of the flight, and Bella looked across at him as the early morning sunlight glanced off the Perspex of the cockpit. Johnnie gave her a thumbs-up and she smiled.

Her nerves disappeared as soon as she got airborne. The cockpit felt as familiar and comfortable as her bed, and she settled herself in the seat, enjoying the feeling of being part of the sortie with everyone around her. Making tiny adjustments to speed and height happened without thought after the hours they had put in, practising for these moments.

It was a serene, beautiful morning, the autumn colours of the English countryside lending a patchwork of russets, greens and reds beneath her. As they crossed the White Cliffs, Bella looked down at a sea which sparkled as if it were covered in diamonds. How could something so wondrous have such terrible deeds happening above it?

A squawk on her r/t and Toby Cranston's sharp voice brought

her back to the job in hand. Looking up, she realised she'd dropped slightly out of formation.

'Sorry, Blue One.'

'Stop fucking daydreaming, Blue Four.'

'Right, TC.'

Heat prickled under her flying helmet and she wanted to kick herself. It was like being told off at school for being caught looking out of the window. Only, at school she wouldn't get shot at.

Minutes later, the French coast appeared as a dim shadow on the horizon, which quickly sharpened into the low country around Boulogne. Empty white beaches lapped by a gentle tide belied the defensive cordons of barbed wire and concrete outposts. Puffs of white smoke began appearing all around them as they flew through flak coming from the German posts around the town. The bombers droned on, seemingly impervious to it.

The r/t squawked again.

'Right, chaps, this is where things begin to get tasty. Keep your eyes peeled for 109s and any other Hun bastards.'

Heart rate increasing, hands sweating on the stick, her eyes dry and sore from staring into the sky all around her, she was aware of all these things but put them aside as her senses sharpened.

'Blue Leader, got a sighting at two o'clock. Looks like a pair of 109s, but they're miles away.' It sounded like Eric the Red, sitting on Cranston's shoulder at Blue Two. 'Christ, not just a pair, there must be a dozen at least. Don't think they've seen us yet.'

'Thanks, Blue Two, I can see 'em. Let's just keep schtum and get these big boys to their target and then see where we are. Keep eyes open, everybody, there may be others.'

Bella could just make out the gleam of sunlight on a cockpit, a pulse thumping in her head making it ache. How could the Germans not see them? Three bombers and a dozen Spits were hard to miss. But they had the sun on the right side of them, so perhaps it hadn't given them away, yet.

Five minutes later they were over the target – a bomb-making factory on the outskirts of a large town north of Paris. The Stirlings dropped their loads and Bella watched them hit both the target and part of the town itself. Small puffs were all that she could see from the height they flew at, but horror filled her at the thought of the innocent French civilians who had no doubt been killed while still in their beds.

The planes began a long turn to starboard, still shadowing the bombers, and before long were on the return path to home. So far, so good, and as they crossed the French coast again, she gave Johnnie a thumbs-up when he looked across at her and grinned.

'Blue leader, this is Magpie, you have a large formation coming up fast on your port side.' The voice over the r/t was the radar controller back at base. 'Looks like multiple bandits.'

'Thanks, Magpie. Can't see 'em yet, though we saw something on the way in.'

'They're closing on you, Blue Leader, you should be able to see them, now.'

'Blue Leader, this is Blue Three. I have 'em, they're above us, we must be in their sights. Fuck, we're toast unless we can break.'

'Okay, chaps, go get the bastards.'

Bella swivelled her neck in every direction and caught a glimpse of sunlight on a canopy. Damn, it was so hard to see anything, the rising sun almost blinding her.

Beware the Hun in the sun had been dinned into them all during training, and that was exactly where they were.

Planes began peeling off in pursuit of the enemy, rolling and turning away to try and get the advantage back over the 109s. The Stirlings droned on, on their own now.

Within a moment all hell seemed to break loose and Bella flew without consciously thinking about what she was doing. A 109 latched onto her tail, its cannon spitting shells. She flung her plane into a steep climb straight into the sun, leaning forward to beat the G force, then sat it on its tail and rolled away. The pilot stuck to her and all she could do was fly for her life, trying to evade him and not being able to fire a shot.

Left, right, up, down and sideways, she didn't even think about what she was doing. Had he hit her? Probably; but at least her plane seemed to respond to everything she asked it to do, so it must be minor damage.

Desperate to escape or at least turn the tables on her pursuer, she took the Spitfire straight up again, past twenty thousand feet, clasping her oxygen mask across her face, fighting the G, black dots flashing in front of her eyes. The Luftwaffe pilot followed her and kept following. How long could he keep going? Without conscious thought, she stood the plane on its tail, flung the stick hard over and tipped it into the tightest of turns. The plane juddered, at the edge of it structural integrity, signalling a potential stall, but she held it there, confident she could pull out of the turn before the German got near her.

The 109 would never manage a turn like that, and coming around she found herself below and behind the Messerschmitt and chased after it, the hunted becoming the hunter. Setting her sights, she opened fire and continued firing as the plane spun and twisted trying to shake her off.

'No you don't, you bastard. Let's see how you like having the tables turned on you.'

She copied every move he made, seeing the damage her guns were doing. One of the engines had smoke pouring out of it and a lick of flame brightened and grew. The 109 dropped lower, gaining speed as it lost control, and she followed, concentrating on sticking with it, oblivious to everything else going on. A moment later, the pilot appeared, his parachute opening above him.

It felt like hours since they had begun their dance of death, but was probably less than five minutes.

Bella turned away, hoping the German would get picked up before the cold waters of the Channel killed him. Her hands shook so hard she could barely keep them on the stick, and sweat stung her eyes, blurring her vision. She climbed again, wondering where everyone else was. The skies were empty above her; surely the rest of the squadron hadn't bolted for home already? Clouds were building from the west, so perhaps she just couldn't see where they were.

Another 109 appeared below on her port side, flying back towards France. He didn't seem to have seen her, so she dropped a little lower and made a tight turn, coming up right behind him and waited until she had a clear shot. She must be almost out of ammunition but it seemed too good a chance to miss, and even if she only did some damage, it would be one less German in the air for a while.

She fired, sticking like glue while the pilot twisted, climbed, screwed and rolled, trying to evade her guns. She thought she got a few direct hits in before her magazines were emptied, but had to let the German flee after a few minutes of frantic flying.

She turned and set a course for home, exhaustion making her dizzy. Where were the others? How had Johnnie got on? It was strange the way everyone disappeared so quickly – was that normal?

'Magpie, this is Blue Four. Returning home.'

The r/t crackled, then a voice.

'Good show, Blue Four. What's your position?'

'No idea. I'm still over the Channel, but can see the coast. Will let you know as soon as I can.'

'Roger, Blue Four.'

Now she found herself shivering, old sweat cold against her skin. It was hard to concentrate and the Spit seemed to have developed a list, one wing dipping slightly and pulling her away from the coast. It was all she could do to keep it straight. Her shoulders and arms ached as if she had carried a heavy load for miles, the muscles screaming with each movement.

'Soon. We'll be home soon, mate.'

She spoke aloud, coaxing the plane to keep going.

It was only ten minutes from the coast to the aerodrome.

Only ten minutes to stay awake, stay focused.

When the base appeared below her, it was the most beautiful sight she could remember. Circling the runway, seeing it was clear, she dropped over the hedge and flopped down onto the turf, fighting to keep the damaged wing clear of the ground and letting the Spit rumble along the rough grass, until it slowed enough for her to make a turn and stop not too far from dispatch.

Her ground crew ran across and directed her in, holding the wingtips to guide the plane under cover. Bella unfastened the safety belts and pulled off her flying cap. Closing her eyes, she let her head fall back; she had never felt so tired.

The squadron was stood down for the remainder of the day, and the rest were already in the mess by the time Bella bathed and changed and dragged herself there. It was still not even ten o'clock and the sun had just climbed above the stand of burnished beech trees at the eastern end of the runway. How could it be so early? It felt like the sun should be at the far end and dipping below the horizon.

She piled a plate with bacon, sausages and eggs, and filled a large mug with tea. Looking for a spare seat, she scanned the room. Johnnie wasn't there, and now she noticed one or two others missing. Carefully placing her tray on a table, her appetite gone, she approached Toby Cranston.

'Hello, Digger,' he said, using the nickname the squadron had christened her with. 'I hear you got a kill – impressive on your first dogfight, well done.'

'Thanks.' She brushed off his comment. 'Did everyone make it back?'

Her voice sounded wrong. Rusty, as if she hadn't used it for a while. Her heart up in her throat somewhere, making it hard to get the words out.

Toby Cranston looked up from his bacon and eggs.

'Colin ditched, but was seen floating and there were fishing boats about, so we're hoping to hear something soon. Dodger bought it, I'm afraid. Went down in flames, poor sod.'

'What about Johnnie? Is he here, I've not seen him?'

'Johnnie's around somewhere. He took a hit but definitely made it back.' He looked at her with a shrewd eye. 'You two have done well, so far. You're good pals, aye?' She nodded, unable to say anything. 'Look after each other. It's a tough game and you need someone to offload to.'

Bella nodded again and left her flight commander to his breakfast, making a dash for the door before anyone saw her break down. Learning that one of the squadron had been killed and another was missing somewhere in the English Channel saddened her, but couldn't prevent her overwhelming feeling of relief that Johnnie was alive and kicking.

Gazing at the field with its boundaries of trees and hedging still throwing shadows across the runway, she saw a lone figure wandering along the far side. Pulling her jacket closer around her, she leant against a gate post and waited. Ten minutes later, Johnnie stood in front of her.

'God, I'm so glad you're home in one piece,' he said, interrupting her same words. 'When the rest were back and no one had seen you since you went haring off trying to escape that 109 . . .' He cleared his throat and looked at his boots. When he glanced up again his eyes were bright. 'Let's just say I didn't rate your chances.' His face lit up in a smile and he punched her lightly on the arm. 'Should have known better and had more faith. You're a fucking ace pilot, old chap.'

Bella wanted to put her arms around him and bury her head into his shoulder, but had to content herself with giving him a playful shove and laughing off his comments.

'I have no idea how I did it, but I ended up right behind him and got the bastard. He bailed out, so'll live to fight another day.' She was glad the pilot hadn't gone down with his plane. That was no way for a young man to die, even if he was a Hun. They made their way back to barracks. 'How did you get on? TC said you'd taken a hit.'

Johnnie nodded, his face sombre.

'I was lucky not to end up in the drink. So impressed with myself for giving one of them a pasting I forgot there were still a few of the buggers around.' He grimaced. 'Won't make that mistake again. He snuck up behind and almost had me. I got out by the skin of my teeth. Plane's a bit shot up, but it's all superficial, thank God.'

'We did all right, then, for a pair of newcomers, didn't we?'

'Digger, you're right, old man. We did just fine – we're still here, and that's what matters. Now, I could eat a horse. Breakfast, old chap?'

'Absolutely, old chap.'

He laughed at her and they wandered back across the lawn, their steps leaving prints in the still dewy grass.

Chapter 24

Jennifer

Scott's story left me wondering how anyone could come back from such physical and mental trauma. Selfishly, I was secretly relieved that at least Ben hadn't had to endure something so hideous.

I found myself in awe of the young Marine's resilience and strength. He managed to present himself as someone who didn't let his past prevent him from doing what he wanted. But of course, that wasn't the truth of it; he had had no choice but to give up doing the thing he loved most. The strength of mind to leave it behind, carry on and rebuild his life showed the metal of the man.

I didn't realise until a couple of weeks later, that he and Rosie were still in touch and had met up at the local pub a couple of times for a drink. I raised an eyebrow when she mentioned it, on her way out one evening.

'What?' she said. 'He's a friend, that's all, and far more interesting to talk to than most of my old school-mates.' She looked a little wistful. 'He reminds me of the students from uni. Like he hasn't spent his whole life in this backwater.'

I smiled. It was a good sign that she was missing her university friends, but I knew better than to push her.

'Scott's a good lad, I'm glad you two get on well,' I said. 'Just . . .'

She put a hand up, palm out. 'Don't, Mum, okay? *Just* nothing.'

I nodded and let her go, hoping it wouldn't end in tears . . . two damaged people, what could possibly go wrong?

Over the next weeks, Rosie looked better, less pale, more like her old chatty self, though grief hit her, just as it hit me and Peter, at the most unlikely of times. The smallest of things triggered extreme reactions in all of us. Since the bank holiday weekend, we had all managed to keep the channels of communication open, at least on the surface. Peter and I had stopped tiptoeing around each other, he drank less, and I came home earlier and spent the evenings with him.

We began taking the dogs out together after work. It was easier to talk while walking, without the pressure of being sat together. While our relationship was nowhere near back to where it should be, it was a vast improvement on the frozen silences of the past six months.

After being persuaded to make a pitstop at a local pub on the way home one evening, I realised how much I missed physical contact with Peter. Our sex life had become non-existent, and we barely shared a peck on the cheek anymore. Sitting in the beer garden on our own, with the low spring sun on my back, I leant into him and kissed his mouth. He pulled away a little and then kissed me back with a passion that surprised me.

'I miss you,' I said, when we parted.

He put a hand up to my cheek for a moment, looking into my face, as if seeing me for the first time, then stood up, took my hand and pulled me up.

'Come on, we're going home.'

I raised an eyebrow and he gave me a small grin. 'Oh . . . okay. Come on, dogs, we're off.'

We hurried home, closed the kitchen door on the dogs, then ran upstairs and fell into bed, making love as if it was the first time all over again, exploring each other's body, rediscovering the passion that had been lost for so many months.

The next morning when we came down to breakfast Rosie took one look at us and put a hand up.

'Eeeww, take it someplace else, you two, that is too much this early in the day.'

'I have no idea what you mean,' I said, knowing my face must be beaming.

She shook her head in disgust, picked up a bit of toast and marched out of the room, muttering something about parents knowing how to behave at their age.

Peter and I looked at each other and burst out laughing.

'Coffee?' I said, when I could get a word out.

'Thank you, if that's all I'm going to get this morning.'

He waggled his eyebrows in a decidedly *Carry On* way and I collapsed in a heap again. From the sitting room a loud voice shouted something about *still being able to hear us* and *growing up*, which added to the hysteria.

It was a big step forward for both of us. We promised to keep talking, keep loving each other, knowing it would take forever to go back to how we had been before, but at least we wanted to find our way there together and that was what mattered.

I didn't broach the subject of Grandpa moving in with us again. It was too soon, and Peter and I were still too fragile. I was concerned about him living on his own, though. He had grown more frail, his leg giving him more pain, his appetite tiny. I sent Rosie over with all his favourite treats each week, and instructed her to stay and keep him company for a while, instead of dropping them off and disappearing. I went to see him as often as I could on my way home from work, and at weekends took the dogs along the path through the woods to his cottage and made lunch for him or helped in the garden.

Sitting with him one evening, he asked how Scott was.

'He's doing well at work,' I said. '*And*, he and Rosie have met up a couple of times for a drink together at the local.'

He grinned. 'He's a fine young man. Been through a lot though, I reckon.' He gazed into the fire. 'You can see it in his eyes.'

'You're right. He told me what happened to him in Afghanistan.' I shook my head, remembering the devastation on his face. 'It was horrific.'

'So many lost. Such a waste of young lives . . .'

I wasn't sure if he was talking about the war in Afghanistan or World War II. Since he had joined us for Sunday lunch, he had mentioned it once or twice, though never said anything about his own experience. But he was right, whichever he meant. We chatted on for a while longer, until I could see he was drooping. I rose, put on my jacket and kissed his cheek.

'I'll see you tomorrow.'

He smiled up at me. 'Goodnight, Jenny Wren. Oh, I meant to ask, did you get your licence yet?'

I shook my head and held out crossed fingers. 'I'm hoping to hear in the next few days. I'll let you know how we go.'

The licence was granted a couple of days later. We had convinced them that we had no knowledge of a pilot still being aboard the Spitfire. Now we could continue the task of raising the plane and hopefully discover who he was.

So far it had been a lovely spring, the weather mild and dry. It was Sod's law that the weather forecast showed a massive low coming across the whole of the south of England for the next few days, just when we wanted to get cracking again. By the end of the day, it was predicted to grow into a full-on storm.

'Shit.' George frowned at the app on his phone. He was never normally one for expletives, and I looked up at him in surprise. He showed me the map, with its tightly coiled isobars right over Kent. 'Looks like we'll have to wait a bit longer before we get back to digging.'

My words were considerably worse than his, at least in my head. I bit my lip in frustration. Would nothing go right with this damn dig?

'I hope the trench doesn't get too flooded. God knows what damage it might do.'

'Well, I guess the plane has been buried in water and sand for seventy odd years, so as long as the wind doesn't get too wild and rip off the tarp, and the wreck doesn't move, we should be okay.' I rose, dragging my coat on. 'Let's go down there now and check everything is secure.'

George shook his head. 'Sorry, don't have time. I have a meeting in half an hour.'

'I'll go. It won't take long to check.'

'I don't like the idea of you going on your own,' he said. 'I know you – you'll jump down in the trench if something needs doing. There should be two of us there.' He checked the app again. 'The storm looks like it won't hit until the morning. Let's do it on the way in here tomorrow.'

'This storm is moving so fast it might hit the coast overnight. You know what these things are like.' I put my hand up. 'I promise I won't go into the trench, okay?'

'Hah, as if I believe you.'

'For God's sake, George. Trust me on this. I will not do anything rash.'

Scott came in from clearing up the tiny kitchenette and looked from me to George. 'Shall I leave again? What's up?'

George shook his head and said nothing.

'I want to go and check the site is secure before the storm hits,' I said. 'George doesn't trust me.'

George glared at me. I glared back.

'Why? What's the problem in you going?'

'Health and Safety,' George muttered.

'There should be two of us, in case we need to enter the trench to make sure it's safe.'

Scott nodded. 'Makes sense. What's the problem?' he repeated.

'George can't come. I'm happy to go and check it on my own, and won't do anything stupid, obviously.' I rolled my eyes at my colleague who steadfastly ignored me.

'I'll come if you need another pair of hands. I can follow in my own car and head home afterwards.'

'You aren't H&S qualified and you're a volunteer. It's not appropriate,' said George.

'For fuck's sake, George, will you lighten up, just for once?' I snapped, then stopped and took a breath. 'Look, how about this. Scott and I will go and take a look, and if it all seems okay, then fine. If anything needs to be battened down, I'll phone you and we can come back later and do it after your meeting.' He looked unhappy, and I didn't blame him. Health and Safety was a shit job, and a huge responsibility. 'I swear we won't do anything stupid. And Scott will not be allowed anywhere near the trench.'

'I suppose it will have to do.' He sighed. 'Someone has to check everything is safe and secure. Just, please, be sensible, Jen.'

'I will, don't worry.' I picked up my bag. 'Come on, Scott, let's go and take a look before the rain comes.'

At the site, everything looked as it had the last time I had been there to inspect it. Mr Bristow's grandson, who ran the farm for him, kept an eye out for any trespassers on our behalf, but it was so isolated that I doubted many people knew it was even there. Still, WWII memorabilia was always good to make money from, and I wouldn't put it past the odd local to go and have a walk around with a metal detector and scavenge anything they could find.

We had erected a temporary wire panel Heras fence around the site and hung 'No Entry' signs on it, and as far as I could tell it was undisturbed. Scott and I walked around the perimeter, checking it was still firmly in place.

'This all looks fine,' I said, raising my voice against the strengthening wind. 'As long as we don't get a hurricane or something,

I can't see any problem with it. I'm just going to take a closer look at the tarps covering the trench and make sure the fixings haven't come loose.'

'I'll come and help,' said Scott.

'Okay, but stay back from the edge of the trench, please. George will bust a gut if anything happens while he isn't here.' Scott laughed. 'What? I don't want to have to tell him you fell in the pit and got buried in wet sand.'

'Sorry,' he said, still grinning. 'I think, sometimes you forget what I did in a former life.'

I couldn't help seeing the funny side, too. 'Fair play, this is kid's stuff to you, but we work in the risk-averse world of Health and Safety here, so do as I bloody say, okay?'

He gave me a mock salute. 'Yes, ma'am!'

'Don't be an arse. Idiot. Come on, we can get inside the fence, here.'

We inspected the tarp tie-downs, and the stanchions, making sure nothing was loose. One rope had pulled away and frayed, the whole thing beginning to flap, pulling on the iron stanchion and raising it out of the sandy ground with each gust. I pulled a handful of plastic ties and a hammer from my backpack and used them to bash the thick iron pole deeper into the ground and double-tie the rope back onto it making the tarp taut again.

The temptation to lift the tarpaulin covering the Spit was overwhelming, my hands itched to undo one corner and check it was okay.

'You promised George you wouldn't go in,' said Scott, quietly into my ear.

I jumped, almost forgetting he stood beside me.

'Yeah, I know.' I sighed and turned away. 'It's hard to leave it there without seeing if it's safe, though.'

'I wouldn't say anything, if you thought it was necessary,' he said, not looking at me. 'And it would save George and you having to come back later.'

'Don't tempt me.'

'No skin off my nose. I can stay here, see you're okay.'

'Scott, shut up, you're not helping.' I glanced at him. He was still staring at the trench. I wondered how much he wanted to see what was in there. Didn't matter. We weren't doing it. 'Anyway, the ladders and ropes are all locked in the Portakabin, and I don't have the key, George does. Come on, let's go, and keep everything crossed the storm isn't as bad as they're predicting.'

We turned, went back through the fence and secured it again. Walking against the wind back across the field to the gate, where our cars were parked, I couldn't help but do a little prying.

'Rosie tells me you two have gone to the pub together, a couple of times.'

'She's a nice girl,' he said, looking a little uncomfortable. 'Bit like her mum.'

'Hah! Don't try and butter me up, young man. Just . . . she's still very fragile, you know . . .'

We were at the gate and he stopped, giving me a look.

'I know. And she's very young. We have a lot in common. I promise not to hurt her.'

I smiled at him. 'I have no worries on that score, I'm glad she's getting out and seeing people again.'

'And what about you?'

'What about me?'

'You're still fragile, too. If you ever want to talk, I'm a good listener.'

He looked so serious . . . and so young. Something squeezed in my chest, making it hard to breathe. For a moment, our positions might have been reversed, and for all his youth I was the one who felt out of my depth, and had no idea what to say or do.

I tried to smile.

'That's very kind of you. I'll keep it in mind, but really, I'm fine.' I pulled my car keys out of my pocket. 'Let's get out of here, shall we? I'll see you tomorrow.' I opened the car door. 'And Scott . . .'

He looked back at me. 'Yes?'

'Thanks. For coming with me, and for the offer. I appreciate it.'

'No worries. See you in the morning.'

Chapter 25

Bella

A few days after Bella and Johnnie had been involved in their first dogfight, the CO sent a memo round saying 92 Squadron was being moved to an airbase in south Wales. Their time of baby-sitting bombers was over for now, they would be helping to protect the South-West, and in particular Bristol, from the bombs of the Germans.

With everything packed up, they flew to their new home on a cool, crisp October morning in formation, all twelve Spitfires in the air at once. Bella flew side by side with Johnnie, enjoying the view of the English autumn countryside, so unlike the dry red land of home. It brought on a feeling of contentment she hadn't felt since training. The cockpit was warm, she was relaxed and comfortable; the stress of the past weeks receded and she allowed herself to enjoy the ride.

Their new base was set in beautiful country, close to the border with England, with the Welsh mountains overlooking them. The coast was nearby and from the air she could see a long empty beach of white sand stretching away in a gentle curve. Johnnie looked over to her and she grinned and pointed downwards. She saw him glance down and then nod and give her a thumbs-up. Perhaps they would have time to go and discover it for themselves. The prospect of a swim with Johnnie in the cold Bristol Channel wasn't as unenticing as she thought it might be. She shook herself – what a stupid idea. It was impossible, of course – and yet she dreamt that one day Johnnie might know the real Bella, and that he would like her as much as he liked Aiden.

Their new posting changed the way the squadron worked. They were sent out in small numbers whenever Control warned them of possible enemy planes approaching, so were on continual stand-by, sometimes at thirty minutes and sometimes at ten.

Those on ten-minute stand-by spent their time at the marquee down at dispersal, trying to relax in the moth-eaten armchairs, reading, drinking tea, chain-smoking and sleeping. As the weather became colder and the days shorter, the stewards kept the place as warm as possible by banking up the open fire, which smoked horribly when the wind was in the north.

They lost another couple of men, and received more newly qualified pilots. On the evening two new faces appeared in the mess, Bella had just come off stand-by and looked forward to being able to relax for the first time in almost a week. She stood at the bar talking to Toby Cranston about the latest sortie they had been on, and how there seemed to be more ME110s in this part of the country.

'Hello, Aiden, fancy meeting you here, old chum.'

Someone stood at her right shoulder. Bella froze. Was this one of the recruits she had met in training? She didn't recognise the voice. Her belly turned to liquid, praying this wouldn't turn into the thing she had dreaded most. She didn't know what to do – should she turn and shake his hand? Ignore him?

TC gave her a look as if to say someone is speaking to you, and she was left with no choice. She turned slowly to find a short, stocky young man with blond hair, grinning at her. His grin faded and confusion replaced it on his face.

'Oh, sorry, I thought . . .'

'Mate! Hello. How are you? Long time since I saw you. I had no idea you were in the RAF.'

She rabbited on, speaking rapidly, not letting him get a word in edgeways, all the while trying desperately to place the face from the many photographs of cricket and rugby teams and theatrical extravaganzas Aiden's school insisted their pupils send home.

The young man continued to look totally dumbfounded, and Bella drew him away from the scrum at the bar to a quiet table in the corner by the fire. She sat down opposite him, put a hand up as he opened his mouth to speak and fixed him with a glare.

'Don't. Just don't say anything.'

'You're not Aiden. You look like him, but you aren't him,' he hissed. 'Who are you? I didn't know he had a brother. He only has a sister, as far as I remember.'

'Well, you don't know everything, do you?' Bella's heart was up in her throat somewhere and hammering so hard she was surprised the whole room couldn't hear it. 'What's your name? I remember you from photographs Aiden sent home from school.' Her memory clicked over and she recalled who he was. 'You're Stephen. Stephen Collingwood-Smith or something like that. I'm right, aren't I?'

The young man nodded.

'Yes – it's Collingwood-Smythe, actually. But you still haven't told me who you are.'

'I'm Aiden Gardner. That's all you need to remember, mate.' Bella leant in close, recalling what Aiden had told her about Collingwood-Smythe and his cronies. 'And you *weren't* friends with Aiden. In fact as far as I recall, you were one of the little shits who made his life miserable for most of his fourth year. Just because he was small and quiet, and preferred to play violin than sport.'

It was the only time Aiden sent a letter just to her, instead of to the whole family. He admitted that a group of boys took great

173

pains to make his life unpleasant, named names but wouldn't say what they did. She had given him a few suggestions of ways to stand up to them. The next time he wrote he said it wasn't an issue anymore, the ringleader had been caught stealing and was expelled.

Collingwood-Smythe blushed and couldn't look at her, picking at a thumbnail until it bled.

'It was years ago, and we were boys. I'm not proud of my behaviour back then, I was in with a group of chaps who thought they were better than anyone else.' Now he raised his eyes and stared at her. 'But that doesn't alter the fact that you are *not* Aiden.' He paused, as if weighing up what to say next. 'Look, I don't want to cause any trouble. It's my first posting, and to be honest I'm shitting myself, I'm so scared. Can't we just keep all that stuff between us and get on?'

Bella searched his face. Was he just saying that to shut her up about the bullying? Could she trust him to keep his mouth shut? At least he hadn't guessed who she really was, which was something. And in reality, there was little she could do if he decided to tell the CO. Thinking it through though, she wondered if anyone would believe him – or care? She had become an integral part of the squadron and built solid friendships with the other pilots as well as Johnnie. It would take a lot to convince them he was telling the truth.

'Why would I want to tell anyone you were a monstrous little bully when you were a boy? It's water under the bridge as far as I'm concerned. I just hope you've learnt that it's not the way to get on in life. No one here will have a bar of you if you start that kind of nonsense in the squadron.'

He nodded, his face glum. 'I know. I need all the help I can get while I'm here.'

She took pity on him. 'Well, this is the best bunch of blokes you could ask for. You couldn't be in a better place than 92 Squadron.'

Johnnie wandered over carrying a couple of tankards, sat down and placed one in front of her. Bella smiled her thanks.

'This is Stephen Collingwood-Smythe, one of the new boys, who just so happened to be at school with me. Stephen, meet Johnnie Winters.'

Johnnie put his hand out and the pair shook.

'Pleased to meet you, Stephen – or do we call you Steve?'

'Stephen is fine, thanks.'

'So, you and Aiden were at school together. Small world, eh?' Johnnie grinned and winked at Bella. 'Any little snippets you can share that might embarrass the hell out of this poor sod? He's always pretty reticent when it comes to schooldays, which makes me suspect there's history there to be discovered.'

Stephen flushed and glanced at Bella who glared at him.

'Well, Johnnie, all I can say is that Aiden was one of the quiet ones, and I rather think he's changed a lot since those days.'

'Ha! A diplomatic answer if ever I heard one.' Johnnie laughed. 'What are you drinking, old chap? I'll stand you a beer if you want.'

'Thanks, that's very decent of you. A beer would go down well.'

Johnnie rose and threaded his way through the crowd to the bar. Bella waited until he was out of earshot.

'Thank you.'

Bella had a day off the following day – the first one since they moved to Wales. She borrowed an old bicycle from one of the other pilots, filled a Thermos with coffee, grabbed some bread and cold bacon and cycled to the beach she had seen from the air.

It was a cold, windy day and sand whipped up around her in vicious swirls as she walked along the clean white sand. It felt good to stretch her legs after being on duty for so many days. She imagined galloping Mini into the sea and smiled to think how strange it must be to ride in water. It had been an age since she had thought of home and she allowed herself to wallow in a little homesickness for a while. The polo season would be finished by now, and hot summer weather would have dried everything up. The thought of some heat in her bones instead of the damp and cold of the British autumn brought a longing she hadn't felt in months.

Guilt nagged at her. It was an age since she had written to her father. Since Aiden's accident she had kept in regular contact with her brother, but hadn't allowed herself to think about home. The appearance of Stephen Collingwood-Smythe had rocked her world, bringing up half-buried memories of the childhood she had shared with Aiden. She had a lot to be sorry for in her treatment of her brother back then. How could she be so self-righteous and angry at Stephen when she had also bullied Aiden mercilessly? She was his big sister – she should have been on his side and looked after him, not treated him so shabbily.

Not given to such introspection by nature, Bella picked up her pace until she broke into a run, pounding along the sand, the wind in her face making her eyes stream. At least that was what she told herself when she stopped at last where the beach ended in a rubble of rocks, sobbing for air, hands on her sides. Collapsing to her knees, she put her head forward and hugged herself until she became as small as possible, tears falling while a howl ripped its way out of her.

Eventually, she cried herself to a halt. Exhaustion dragged at her, but she rose, brushed wet sand from her trousers and turned to retrace her steps. Somehow, the wind and sand made it feel as if she had scoured her inner self as well as the abrasion she could feel on her face. She was more at peace, lighter than she had been since she had taken Aiden's uniform and transformed herself. The guilt remained, she would carry that forever, but the weight seemed less crushing.

More than anything though, she began to wish she could let Johnnie see who she really was, let him know Bella Gardner. She had tried so hard to keep him at arm's length, but since they had been posted to 92 Squadron, they had grown closer than ever. Her feelings for him had changed over the past months, from liking him as a comrade into something much deeper and scarier, so that now she was completely confused. All she knew was that she wanted him to see the real person behind the mask she had so carefully constructed. Perhaps when this shitty war was over – if they both survived – the time would be right.

Chapter 26

Jennifer

The forecasted storm veered away into the Channel and Kent only caught the tail end of it, so after a twenty-four-hour delay, the whole team re-assembled on-site.

By the end of the first day, we had fully uncovered the main body of the Spitfire and removed the Perspex cowl of the cockpit. Extricating the pilot needed time and care, though, and George and I considered the best way to go about it.

We had both been involved with extracting human remains in previous digs, but personally I had never been on a dig where the body was so well preserved. I found myself enormously moved by the pilot's presence. I couldn't help wondering if Ben would be found eventually in a similar state but pushed the thought away. I must not allow myself to fall down that hole, not now when I needed to be focused and at my most professional.

The rest of the team were subdued by the sight of the body. It was held in place by the shoulder straps. The pilot's head hung forward; he might almost have been asleep. The water had done a good job of preserving everything, his uniform, flying helmet, goggles, parachute all still easily identifiable, even though the front of the plane had been pushed backwards on impact.

It was evident that the Spit had landed on its belly, probably sliding along the marshy ground until it hit the water-filled hole, its nose went down and it sank out of sight. The fuel tank was bent but intact, thankfully, so the ground-water was uncontaminated, though I suspected there would have been very little fuel left if the pilot was on his way back to base after a sortie. The tail was missing, perhaps snapped off when it crashed.

Did he bring the plane down and try to land? Or was he so badly injured that he lost control? Or, as Terry Bristow had asserted, did the local coastal defence team shoot the plane down? If the last, wouldn't it have been seen by them? Or had they been the ones who claimed it had crashed into the sea? It was possible; the site was so close to the coast and if the weather had been bad, or the light poor, with no crash site evident, it would seem the most logical answer.

I had found no record of an RAF plane being shot down by friendly fire in this location, so either they had lied, or neglected to report it. Or Terry was wrong. It didn't make any real difference, but I wanted to get to the truth of the matter. It felt like a missing piece of the jigsaw.

The following day, we brought in heavy machinery to lift the Spitfire out of its grave, positioning slings under it and carefully bringing it up to the firm ground alongside the pit. George and I had discussed whether to try and get the body out first, but it was such a difficult job we decided against it. I had spent the final hour the day before recording everything in situ – photographing and doing all the paperwork.

Once the plane was out of the ground, it was evident the engine block had prevented too much damage. The plane must have sunk when it hit the water. Over time, the ground above had dried up and left no sign of the Spitfire lying below.

Forgotten by everyone except one old man.

* * *

Once we extracted the body of the pilot from the tiny cockpit, I had him taken to the lab where I did my forensic work. The rest of the team remained and carried on cleaning and recording what we had found. There was still much that was missing – the tail, the other wing, the rest of the guns and part of the undercarriage.

'Do you mind if I come with you and see what you do in the lab?' Scott asked, as I was packing up my kit, ready to leave.

I was surprised at his question. 'Don't you want to stay and help here?'

'Yeah, of course, but I want to learn everything there is to know about this business,' he said. 'If it's not possible, that's okay, there's loads going on here to help with.'

'You can come if you want, I don't mind. I'm not sure you'll find it very interesting though. It's slow work. Lots of recording and paperwork.'

'Thanks, I'd like to. I guess it's kind of a post-mortem, right?'

'Exactly like a post-mortem examination. We want to know what happened here, and the pilot's body might help to give us the answers.'

I liked his enthusiasm for all aspects of the job. Inspecting long-dead bodies wasn't for everyone.

At the lab, I changed and gave Scott a lab coat. The body was already on the table and my lab assistant had carefully cleaned off the mud and detritus that had seeped into the cockpit over the years.

I looked it over carefully, before touching it. The pilot's flying suit and leather helmet were still in good condition, thanks to where it had been buried for more than seventy years. His boots were flattened and misshapen, goodness knew what the feet and leg bones would be like. They had taken the brunt of the force of the crash. The rest was in remarkable condition and a thrill of anticipation ran up my back at the prospect of discovering more about our man.

Carefully removing the clothing, I discovered a hole in one leg of the flying suit.

'Scott, look at this. What do you think?' I raised an eyebrow at him as he looked at the stain still evident around the hole.

'He was shot?'

'Yes, it looks like a bullet hole, don't you think?'

'Is that blood?'

I carefully scraped a bit of the fragile, stained material away and with forceps placed it into a container.

'I'll get this tested. We'll know soon enough, but I think you're right.' I measured how far down the leg the hole was and then went and checked the body. 'See here? There's a chip in the femur right where the hole would have covered it. If it nicked the femoral artery the pilot was as good as dead before he crashed.'

'Any chance of finding the bullet?'

'Very unlikely, given where it's sat all this time. There are always tons of bullets lying around on solid ground, but in a bog like the one this poor chap ended up in, goodness know how far down we would have to go.'

Scott's mouth compressed into a tight line as he stared at the thigh bone with a notch out of it.

'No evidence of a tourniquet?'

I shook my head. 'If he was in the middle of a dogfight he wouldn't have had time to think about anything other than beating the enemy and surviving.'

Once again, my mood dipped at the thought of this young man battling for his life against his opponent. Had he been terrified? How could he not have been? I prayed he didn't suffer and his end was quick.

Dragging my thoughts back to the present I tried to detach myself from who the pilot might have been in life and concentrate on the job. At the very least I wanted to get him home to his family, whoever and wherever they might be.

I hoped there would be some evidence of skin and possibly

hair, and I was right. The preservation was as good as it could be after so long, especially the hair, teeth and nails. There were fragments of skin remaining, too, and I carefully photographed and then collected everything, and collated what we had.

I gently took the dog tags from around the pilot's neck and a badly corroded watch that still hung on the bones of his wrist. The dog tags were clogged with mud but I hoped I could clean them up and they would reveal his identity. Perhaps then it would be possible to track down his family and reunite them after so many decades of their not knowing what happened to him. Perhaps one of his family might like the watch as a keepsake. I put it with the dog tags to clean up later.

It struck me, as I continued my examination of the skeleton, that our man must have been very young but the further I went, the more confused I became. Measuring the pelvis, the skull and the long bones of the arms and legs, something didn't add up. Bodies varied so much, I thought perhaps he must have been on the small side – perhaps he had been built like a jockey or similar. I took a DNA sample from his femur and hoped I would get some answers.

'What's up?' Scott said, making me jump.

I'd forgotten he was there.

'Nothing, really. I'm just a bit confused.' I looked over the body again, taking in the size of the bones, the shape of the skull and jaw. Shook my head. 'I've got an overactive imagination, that's all.'

'What happens now?'

'We'll do our best to find his family.'

'That must be very satisfying, being able to reunite them after so many years.'

'It is.'

There it was again, sitting on my shoulder, ready to pounce on me at any moment. I dropped my head and closed my eyes for a second.

'Are you okay?' Scott's voice was gentle.

I nodded. Breathe . . . in, out, in, out . . . in. Opened my eyes, met his.

'One day, I hope someone will reunite us with Ben.'

He said nothing, just kept his eyes on mine, waiting . . .

I blew my breath out, managed a small smile, and carried on with my work.

I dropped in to see Grandpa on the way home. The storm had left his garden looking bedraggled, leaves and twigs scattered across the small lawn and the vegetable beds sodden, with puddles of water lying in the dips. The bare soil looked black and rich as liquorice, the tiny bean plants standing up bravely, undaunted by the weather. The evening sun made the tiny space gleam in its soft light.

Grandpa sat in his sunroom, dozing in an ancient, rickety rocking chair. A cat lay curled up on his knee. He opened his eyes as I came in, confusion clouding them for a moment, then clearing and he smiled.

'Hello, Jenny Wren.'

I leant down and kissed his cheek. 'Hello. I'm sorry I woke you. Who is this? You didn't tell me you were getting a cat.'

He smiled and stroked the tabby fur. The cat stretched and clawed his leg, purring under his hand.

'She's not mine, she lives next door. I think she likes this room when the sun's on it – like me – don't you, puss?' I sat on a stool next to him, rubbing the cat's soft ears. She hopped across onto my lap and Grandpa laughed. 'Typical cat. No loyalty. How was your day?'

'Productive – at last,' I said. 'Good job the storm wasn't as bad as predicted. The site was water-tight and nothing came to harm, thankfully.'

'Did you get the Spit out?'

'We did. And the pilot. Both in amazing condition thanks to where it crashed. I've spent the afternoon examining the body.'

He pulled a face and gave a theatrical shudder. I grinned; it was a familiar response.

'I can never quite understand how my granddaughter ended up specialising in cutting up bodies.'

'Because it's one of the most fascinating aspects of the job. I love uncovering the secrets a body can tell us. How they lived, what they ate, how they died, were they sick, or injured, had they led a healthy life?' I laughed again. 'But you know this, already. I realise I'm a broken record.'

He patted my hand and smiled. 'I'm glad you do a job you love and which gives you so much satisfaction.'

'Yeah, I'm very lucky. Scott came and watched me. He's really got the archaeological bug, I think. I'm glad we've helped him find a new passion. He's gone through a lot for such a young guy, it must be so hard to change your whole life like he's had to.'

He shifted his gaze away from me, his eyes suddenly hooded. 'Indeed.'

'I suppose it must have been the same for thousands of people when World War II ended. All those soldiers coming back home, not to mention the women who had done a man's work for years and then had to go back to being a wife and mother. Six years of upheaval and fear and then it's over and back to normal life. I can't imagine how difficult it must be to adjust to something like that.'

I spoke lightly, expecting him to shut down as usual, when the subject was raised.

He nodded.

'It was much harder than any of us who survived imagined it would be,' he said. 'The war was terrible, and yet we got to do things we would never have dreamt of doing. And the camaraderie was everything; going through such extraordinary times together. Leaving all that and going back to civvy street while we were still so young, expected to drop back into "normal" life as if we had left it yesterday . . .' He huffed out a breath. 'Let's just say it was the most difficult time of my life.'

I squeezed his hand.

'But then you met Grandma and got married. Or was that during the war?'

'Oh, no, I didn't meet your grandmother until after the war. She probably saved me from myself, to be honest. God knows what I would have done if she hadn't made me her mission in life.'

He lapsed into silence, his head nodding. It was, by far, the most he had ever talked about his wartime experiences to me. I wanted to know more. Who knew how much longer he had; it felt important to know about him as a young man.

'I've always wondered which service you were with during the war. You never talk about it.'

'Why the RAF, of course.' He sounded surprised. 'One of the reasons I'm so proud of you being involved with the work to recover lost planes.' He gripped my hand. 'So many who never made it back home . . .'

Of course. If I hadn't been so self-absorbed I would have realised.

'Were you a pilot?'

He nodded. 'Until I was injured. Got consigned to a desk job after that.' He rubbed a gnarled hand over his face, as if the memory of whatever befell him was still fresh in his mind. 'Probably why I'm here today – and you, for that matter. I could have been one of the ones who never made it back, and someone else would be digging the plane out of a bog.'

'I've never thought about it like that,' I said. 'Imagine all the generations who never were, because their forefathers were killed in wars.'

'It's a sobering thought.'

'Well, I'm very, very happy you are here.' I quickly rose, not wanting my mind to take the route I knew it would, following this conversation. 'Shall I make you a cup of tea and something to eat before I leave?'

'A piece of toast might be nice with marmalade and a chunk of cheddar.'

'Coming up. You stay where you are and enjoy the sunshine. I'll bring it on a tray.'

Busying myself, I put bread in the toaster and the kettle on to boil. Set a tray with a mug and plate, took a jar of marmalade and the butter dish out of the larder, searched for the cheese in the fridge; doing my best to not think of anything and failing. I placed my hands on the worktop in the kitchen and hung my head. Picturing Ben as a father had never been part of my grief . . .

. . . he appeared in my bedroom that night, as he had every night, walking through, holding the hand of a small boy who closely resembled him. He didn't look at me or say anything, too busy talking to his son who wanted to know who the old people in the bed were . . . breaking my heart all over again.

Chapter 27

Bella

Bella arrived back at base from her day at the beach as a chill mist came in off the sea, turning the twilight into damp half-light, where droplets hung from every dead stalk of grass and cobweb as if they were covered in a layer of lacy diamonds.

The lights on the aerodrome gleamed dully and she could just make out the dim shapes of planes that had been on stand-by being rolled under cover at dispatch. Thank God she didn't have to fly tonight, she couldn't think of anything worse in this type of weather than flying by instrument alone – blind to all intents and purposes.

Returning the bicycle to its owner and offering to buy him a beer as a thank you, she wandered over to the mess. It was half full, the atmosphere heavy. A rough day, then – it always took a while and a few tankards of beer to loosen tongues when things hadn't gone well.

A cold lump of foreboding crept into the pit of Bella's stomach. She stood at the door for a moment, scanning the room. The CO was there, and most of the pilots she'd come to know well. Stephen Collingwood-Smythe stood on his own at the bar, a whisky in front of him.

187

She approached him and he recoiled at seeing her. His face was white and behind his eyes she could see terror – and something else – guilt? Shame? God, what had happened?

'You look like you need that,' she said, nodding towards the untouched Scotch.

He glanced at it, seeming not to know what it was, then picked it up and threw it down his throat, choking on the rough alcohol.

'Steady on, mate, you'll be as sick as a dog if you carry on that way.' She banged his back until he stopped coughing and rubbed tears out of his eyes. 'Tough day?'

He nodded, his face grim.

'It was hellish,' he whispered. 'I did something terrible.'

His chin trembled. He dragged in a breath and clamped his lips together, holding it until he had control of himself.

The foreboding returned. Bella excused herself and went to find Toby Cranston. He was talking quietly with Gowling the adjutant, who nodded once or twice and then left.

'Evening, TC. The new boy, Collingwood-Smythe? He seems in a bit of a stew after his first day. Was it a rough one?' She had to know what happened. Who hadn't returned.

Toby Cranston sighed and shook his head.

'It wasn't out of the ordinary, Digger; at least not for those who've been doing this for a while,' he said. 'And compared with Duxford, this is a walk in the park, don't you think?'

Bella nodded.

'The sorties are much less . . . exciting . . . if that's the right word.'

Flying after German bombers and chasing them away from Bristol docks and the south-western coast lacked the nervous tension of dogfighting with 109s.

'Today we got mixed up with a flight of ME110s just over the coast around Plymouth, flying defence for six Heinkel bombers, heading for Bristol.' Toby took a long swig of his beer. 'We were above them and they didn't see us until we got on their tails and gave 'em what for. Pretty good stuff, actually, we took down a few.'

'That's good. Less of the buggers to return.' She nodded her head towards Stephen, who still stood at the bar, nursing another Scotch. 'Why is he in such a blue?'

'The stupid bastard came up and started shooting while some of our lads were in front of him. Took out poor old Johnnie.' Toby put a hand on her shoulder. 'Sorry, old chap, I know you two are good friends.'

Bella's head spun.

TC was still speaking but she couldn't hear anything except a roaring in her ears and a blackness closing in on her. Shaking her head, she pinched her wrist as hard as she could and the swoon stopped.

'Pardon?'

'Johnnie's been taken to hospital in Plymouth. The adj was just off the telephone and they reckon he might lose a leg.'

'You mean he's not dead?'

'What? No. He managed to land in a farmer's field after that stupid arse took out his undercarriage and half his tail.' Toby shook his head again and puffed hard on his pipe. 'If he'd done that to a fucking Hun he'd be a hero, but look at him – the CO's taking him off active duty for a while. We can do without fellows who damage our planes and almost kill their own side.'

Bella's gaze drilled into Stephen's back. She wanted to march back over to where he stood on his own swilling another Scotch and scream at him, whale into him with her fists, kick him to the ground and stamp him into a bloody pulp. Anything to release the pressure building in her head at the thought of Johnnie lying injured in a hospital bed. She found she was shaking – her rage white-hot in her blood.

She closed her eyes and took a breath; tried to calm her mind. There was no good in blaming Stephen, much as she wanted to. He obviously felt bad enough as it was. Johnnie was still alive and all she could hope was that he would recover and she would see him again. In that moment all she knew was how much she wanted – no, *needed* – to tell Johnnie how she felt about him.

'Thanks for telling me.' Bella hadn't heard most of what TC had said. 'Do you think I could get a pass so I can go and see Johnnie? Poor sod must be feeling pretty low, don't you think?'

Toby narrowed his eyes.

'You'll need to okay it with the CO, and you know how short we are, Digger. With Johnnie gone and Stephen no use to us, I can't see him being happy to have pilots swanning off for a day.' He seemed to consider his words, taking his pipe out of his mouth and tamping more tobacco into the bowl. Replacing it between his teeth and putting a match to the fresh tobacco, he spoke around the stem as he puffed. 'If he thinks we can spare you for a twenty-four-hour pass, then so be it. But if you're not back here by tomorrow night I'll have your hide.'

'Thanks, TC, I'll go and ask.'

'And give Johnnie my sincere condolences. It'll be the end of his flying career, I don't doubt.'

She nodded, turned and marched back towards the door, hoping he didn't notice the shine of unshed tears. As she passed Stephen, he caught her eye and smiled. To her overemotional state of mind it looked like a smirk and she couldn't resist leaning into him.

'If Johnnie dies because of you, I will personally come and tear your fucking head off your shoulders.'

Stephen's face paled under the flush caused by the drink he had taken.

'I'm sorry, really I am,' he said. His voice rose as Bella fixed him with a wild stare. 'It was an accident. It wasn't my fault he flew in front of me.' His words became slurred and self-pitying. She thought he might actually cry. Looking down into his empty glass for a moment, he seemed to come to a decision and when he glanced back up into Bella's face, she saw his eyes take on a mean look. 'Anyway, you can't touch me – I know you're not Aiden Gardner, so keep away from me, or you'll be sorry.'

She grabbed the front of his jacket and pulled him towards her, not caring who saw her, too angry to think straight.

'You weaselly little bastard,' she hissed at him. 'Do you think anyone gives a fuck about anything you say after the stunt you pulled today?' She pushed him away again. 'Tell the world. See if I care.' As she walked away, she realised the mess had gone completely silent and every man in the room was staring at her. 'WHAT? Johnnie might be dead and it's this little shit's fault. Maybe you lot don't care, but I do.'

With that, she stalked out of the room, her mind in complete turmoil, knowing she had overstepped the mark by a very long way.

Chapter 28

Jennifer

Once the team had recovered as much as we could from the site, we brought everything back to base, to begin the huge job of cleaning, recording and collating all the pieces of the Spitfire we had found. This wouldn't be one of those sites we could go back to at a future time, if we felt it might give us more evidence of the crash. The road development would see to that.

Terry Bristow came to see me on our final day as we dismantled the safety fence, and the Portakabin was towed away.

'I were right, then, eh, Doctor Dawson,' he said, a hint of *I told you so* in his voice. 'Said it were a Spitfire, all along.'

'You did, Mr Bristow, and I can't thank you enough for bringing it to our attention,' I said. 'It's been one of the most rewarding digs I've been involved in. We've recovered the plane and the pilot. That's a lot more than we sometimes find.'

He harrumphed. 'Wish my old man were still alive, then I'd tell him I were no liar, miserable old bugger that he were.'

'I'm sorry you're losing your land to the new road. That must be a blow. This is a special place, it's so wild and empty.'

'Don't be sorry. I ain't. Got it taken off us as compulsory

purchase and paid a pretty penny in compensation. It'll set my lad and his son up very nicely. This place never made money as a farm, ground's too wet, see.'

I gazed around at the rough, marshy land, a curlew keening overhead. This ancient landscape would soon be erased in the name of progress. It made me momentarily sad, but I understood the old man's words.

'Well, I'm glad it's worked out well for you, then.' I shook his hand. 'Thanks for all your help. Goodbye, Mr Bristow.'

'Bye, Doctor Dawson.'

The volunteers had mostly left, except Scott, Ginge and Linda, one of the women, who seemed to have taken a shine to the young redhead.

'Gonna miss coming here,' Ginge said. 'Bin a good way to fill the days.'

'What's next for you?' I said.

'Hopin' to get back to me unit, if the doc reckons I'm ready.' I must have shown my surprise. He tapped the side of his head. 'Got me noggin straight now, ain't I? Dunno what else I'd do if they won't let me back in.'

He suddenly looked very young and vulnerable.

'Can I help?' I said. 'I could write you a reference or some-thing, perhaps?'

Ginge blushed, his freckles hidden in the crimson of his cheeks.

'Would you do that for, me, Doc? Fuck, I thought you might chuck me out, cos I can be a right gobby cu . . . bugger, when I want.'

I grinned at him.

'Yes, you can, but you've stuck with it and turned up every day, when some of the others didn't. I'd be happy to do that. One thing though . . .'

He looked sideways at me, narrowing his eyes. 'Wha'?'

'Well, I can't call you Ginge in a professional reference, can I? What's your name?'

He blushed again, and Linda laughed.

'Shut it, you,' he snapped at her. He eyed me with a defiant glare. 'It's Walter. Walter Wiggins.'

I smiled, and jotted it in my notebook. I guessed he'd undergone a fair bit of stick for it, even Scott had a smirk on his face.

'Thanks, Walter. I'll pop an email to the charity and they can send it on to you. Will that do?'

He grinned. 'Cheers, Doc.'

'Right, let's get out of here. I have a pile of broken Spitfire parts to sort out.' I paused at the gate. 'Thanks all of you, for the help you've been. It's not been the easiest dig, but without people like you volunteering, it would have been a damn sight harder.'

There were nods and goodbyes and you're welcomes, they climbed into the waiting minibus and left.

When I got home, I found a text from Scott.

Is there any chance I can stay on and help in any way?

I wasn't surprised. He was so keen, but I felt guilty that we may be taking advantage of him, and he would end up being an unpaid dogsbody.

I phoned George.

'Scott wants to carry on helping. What do you think?'

'I don't know,' he said. 'You've spent far more time with him than I have. Is he any use, or will he just get in your way?'

'I'd be happy to have him around, but we can't pay him.'

'I think as long as he knows he's still helping on a voluntary basis then it's fine. It's up to him.'

'Okay, I'll make it plain he's not getting paid.' I sighed. 'I suppose I'll have to run it by Dominic as well. If he drops in and sees some random guy helping us, he'll not be happy.'

'Yeah, probably a good idea. I'll see you tomorrow.'

'Thanks, George, see you.'

I rang Scott.

'You're welcome to carry on volunteering with us, if that's what you want,' I said. 'I'm sorry, but we can't pay you anything though.'

'Great, thanks,' he said. 'No worries about paying me, I wasn't expecting anything. I just want to learn as much as I can, and pick your and George's brains.'

'So, you want to take archaeology seriously?'

'I do, yeah. I don't know what I would need to do to get accepted to study it at university, but I'm going to give it my best shot.'

'Well, you're in the best place to do that. And if you need help with it, I'm happy to sit down with you and go through the admissions process. Do you have any A Levels?'

'Yeah. Geography, maths and psychology of all things, a right hotch-potch of subjects. Not that they have ever done me any good. All I ever wanted to do was join the armed forces.'

'Well, they could very well be of use to you if you want to study archaeology. Let's look at what you need to do, tomorrow, after work.'

'Thanks. That'll be great. I'll see you tomorrow.'

'Okay. Bye, Scott.'

'Cheers, Jennifer.'

Over the next few days, try as I might, I couldn't get the pilot out of my mind. Until the DNA results came back, there was no more I could do, and it went against all the rules to try and track down his family – that was the task of the MOD or his old squadron.

But it didn't mean I couldn't do a bit of digging. Frustratingly, after I had cleaned up the dog tags I still couldn't make out the pilot's name . . . a couple of letters I thought I could make out, maybe a G or was it an O at the beginning of the surname? And I was sure the final letter was an R, stamped into the circular vulcanised tag. The rest were indecipherable.

I turned to the watch. I could tell by the size of it that it wasn't a regulation RAF-issue timepiece. This one had a smaller face and a metal link strap. Did it mean something special to our man? I knew pilots didn't always wear the watch they were issued with and supposed if they were attached to one given as a present it was understandable.

This one was badly corroded but I cleaned it up as much as I could, gently removing the mud encasing it until the face and strap were free of any detritus. It always moved me, working on something personal which had belonged to a long-dead serviceman. How many times had this young man wound up his watch? Looked at the time? Taken it off and placed it on a bedside table, ready to strap it back on his wrist when he rose the next morning? Holding it in my hand made him feel closer to me, and I felt honoured to be doing this job I loved.

Turning the watch over to make sure I had cleaned away every speck of dirt, I rubbed my thumb across the back of the battered case. It wasn't smooth. I did it again and turned the lamp at my side to focus the light on the scratched metal. There, I could see several lines of tiny writing.

It was inscribed. I grinned.

'Yes. Now maybe, we can get somewhere,' I muttered.

The corrosion meant that much of the writing was gone, but I took a magnifying glass, a piece of thin tissue paper and a nub of charcoal and placed the paper over the back of the watch. Gently rubbing the charcoal over the paper, I prayed the indentations were enough for me to make out the words inscribed beneath.

When I took the paper away, laid it flat on a board and shone the lamp right on it, I blew a raspberry of exasperation. There was too much damage to the metal. Despite the random scratches and pits of corrosion I tried to make sense of what I could understand.

D.g . . . . t. . . v.
. W
D 0

There was no way I could decipher the inscription, so I was no further forward in discovering who the pilot was. We would have to go back to the squadron and try to work out who he was from their archive records.

Frustration nagged at me, but there was nothing else I could do for now.

You're a scientist, Jennifer. Get a grip.

I decided to do a search through the archives for anything relating to a plane crash in the area around the date Terry Bristow was sure it came down on. It felt as if I was doing something useful. After scrolling through umpteen newspaper reports I found one, which made my pulse jump.

The *Kentish Express* had a report on the shooting down of a German plane into the sea by the local coastal defence team on Terry Bristow's birthday.

Was this our man? Had the Spitfire been mistaken for an enemy plane and been brought down by friendly fire as Terry had asserted all along?

I changed my search parameters to include friendly fire but came up with nothing. Not surprising. I guessed those kinds of accidents were kept out of the press. It wouldn't do much for morale if the general populace knew how many 'blue on blue' fatalities there were.

It looked as if I had come to another dead-end. I rubbed my eyes and stretched, frustration making me cranky. Closing the laptop, I rose and went to make tea for everyone.

Admitting I was getting nowhere with the search for our man, George suggested searching for any surviving pilots from the same squadron.

'There's bound to be an old-boy's network,' he said. 'There might well be one or two still alive who would remember him, though they'll be well into their nineties by now, I guess.'

'Worth a shot, isn't it?' Scott said. 'Would you like me to see what I can find out?'

I nodded. I could do with a break from the frustration and intensity of constant failure.

'That would be a help, thanks.'

I kept thinking about the newspaper article and whether the

ack-ack crew had mistaken our plane for a German one. If the visibility had been bad – rain or fog perhaps – or it had been dark, wouldn't the gun-crew have asked for solid identification from their command post? So many questions I couldn't answer. I wished there were some physical evidence we could use to prove one way or another what had happened. It was unlikely I would get what I hoped for. So far, we hadn't found any stray bullets, either German or British.

I went back to working on the Spitfire, cleaning and identifying small bits of mangled metal that had come out of the wet ground after the metal detectors had done their work on the spoil heaps. It was like constructing a giant jigsaw. Trying to work out which part of the plane they might have come from was something I always took satisfaction from, especially with a site that yielded so many well-preserved pieces.

Still, I felt deflated that I hadn't got further in the search for our pilot's family or with piecing together exactly what had happened to him on that fatal day. George worked on the opposite side of the pile of finds, humming quietly under his breath. He must have picked up on my mood because after another hour of slow, painstaking work he looked across the table at me, a frown furrowing his forehead.

'Jen, it's Friday afternoon, why don't you go home? You look knackered. I can get on with this on my own, and Scott's here if I need another pair of hands.'

'I am a bit tired. Not sleeping too well, at the moment,' I admitted. 'Perhaps, I will.'

'Go and spend the rest of the afternoon with Peter and Rosie. You've been burning the candle too much. It's no wonder you're tired.'

'Fat chance, they'll be doing their own thing. I might go and see Grandpa, though. Help him with his vegetable garden.'

'Do that. I'll see you on Monday.'

'Thanks, George. If Dominic should happen to come looking

for me, can you make up an excuse? Tell him I'll call him next week.'

'No worries. Have a relaxing weekend.'

The garden was bathed in late afternoon sunshine when I pulled up outside Grandpa's cottage. He was dozing in a garden chair, a trowel and gloves on his knee, one hand hanging down almost touching the ground that he loved so much. The cat stalked up to me when I opened the gate and wound itself around my legs.

'You've made yourself at home, here, haven't you?' I said, quietly, running my hand along its back and tail. It arched its back and then trotted ahead of me along the path.

The vegetable plot was pristine, regimented rows of beans, peas and lettuces growing well, now the weather had warmed up and the days were longer. One side had Toblerone-shaped rows, where potatoes peeked their green shoots out of the top. Feathery carrot tops lined up alongside onion setts. So much work, and I knew he would give most of the produce away, there was far too much for one elderly man with the appetite of a sparrow. I couldn't imagine him not doing it though, gardening was as much a part of who he was as his limp.

I stood for a moment, looking at my grandfather, taking in how gaunt he was becoming. I wondered what it would take to persuade Peter to agree that he should live with us. Sighing, I sat in the twin chair to his, and leant back, closing my eyes for a moment, enjoying the garden's serene atmosphere. It was a restful place, only birdsong breaking the silence. Bone-deep weariness dragged at me, the temptation to let myself slide into oblivion almost overwhelming. I could sleep here.

Ben's nightly foray into my dreams was both a balm to my soul and a knife in the carefully constructed carapace I thought I had succeeded in building. Part of me dreaded him assailing my sleep each night; I was exhausted, nerves strung as taut as high tensile wire. The flipside was the terror of not having the dreams – my assumption that if they stopped it meant I was forgetting him. In rational moments I knew that would never happen but my fragile psyche refused to accept it. To have such a clear vision of him each night left me devastated every time, and yet there was a comfort there I yearned for and needed.

I woke suddenly to find Grandpa standing over me.

'Hello, Jenny Wren, I didn't mean to disturb you. You looked very peaceful.'

I sat up, my face hot from the sun on it, and pushed hair back off my forehead.

'Ugh, I didn't mean to fall asleep, sorry.'

'Teatime?'

'Yes. You sit here. I'll make it and bring it out.'

He creaked his way into his chair again, and I went and made a pot of tea and found some Jaffa cakes in the biscuit tin, my head fuzzy with sleep. Bringing everything outside on a tray, we sat and sipped our drinks while munching in silence.

My mind turned to the pilot, trying to think of other avenues to explore which might reveal more information on him.

'Are you still in touch with any of the other pilots you flew with during the war?'

'That's an odd question.'

'Yeah, I know. Sorry. We're trying to learn more about the pilot we've found and who he was. George suggested there may still be ex-RAF pilots who knew him back then. I wondered if there was some kind of club or ex-servicemen's association you all belonged to.'

'There aren't many of us left, now, I'm afraid, but I sometimes meet up with odd fellows. On special occasions, like Remembrance Sunday and so on.' He grew still, eyes distant. 'Which squadron was he with, have you discovered that?'

'Sixty-six, I think.'

The colour leached out of Grandpa's face and tea slopped over the side of his mug. He dropped it, and shook his hand, putting his other hand over the burn.

'Damnation.'

'Are you okay? Here, let me see.'

'I'm fine, just my stupid old hands that can't hold a cup steady anymore.'

'You've gone as white as a sheet, Grandpa. Are you sure you're okay?'

'Don't fuss, Jennifer. I said I'm fine.'

He didn't look fine, he looked like he was in shock, his face pale and hands shaking. I poured him more tea and he leant back in the chair, his eyes closed. I watched him closely. God forbid he was about to have a stroke or something. Was his face dipping at one side? Had he dropped the mug because he had lost the use of an arm? Was his pallor because the blood wasn't circulating around his body as it should? Was he in pain?

'I think we should go indoors, and I'll get you settled before you get cold.'

'Since when did you become such a fusspot? There's nothing wrong with me.' He answered without opening his eyes.

'That's as maybe, but I'm not leaving until you're inside, by the fire.'

He heaved a sigh of annoyance, and opened his eyes. 'If I tell you something, will you leave me in peace?'

'Depends what it is. I'm not promising anything.'

'I hate bossy women.'

I grinned at him. 'Tough, you're stuck with me.'

'Just like your mother – and Grandma, for that matter.'

'Come on then. What are you going to tell me?'

He looked down and inspected his hands, picking soil out of a thumbnail. Blowing out a rasping breath, he told me.

'I was with 66 Squadron for a while. After my flying days were done, they gave me a desk job and 66 was where I was sent.' His voice grew shaky. 'It was a terrible time; the Battle of Britain took so many lives – both Allied and German – and being on the ground was almost as bad as being in the air – at least for me. Waiting for them to return, never knowing whose would be the next photo to have a cross through it. I still can't bear to think about that time.'

My pulse jumped at his words. He had been with 66 Squadron? How bizarre and unlikely a coincidence. Perhaps he had known and worked alongside our man, although I knew how often pilots changed squadrons, so it was more than likely they never crossed paths. Still . . . excitement sang in my veins and I itched to ask him more about those days. I could see the toll my snippet of information had had on him, though, so I pushed away all the questions I wanted to ask. They could wait.

I crouched down in front of him and took his cold hands, holding them gently between my own warm ones. No wonder he never talked about his experiences. They were all so young, it must have been terrible.

'I'm sorry I've reminded you of that awful time, Grandpa. Come on, let's go inside, you're frozen.'

He allowed me to help him rise and leant on me as we walked slowly across the garden to the backdoor. Inside, he sat in his usual chair, still pale and shaky while I checked the burn. I gently bathed it with cold water, relieved to see the skin wasn't blistered, thinking again that he had lost more weight, his wrists like sticks so that his old watch hung as loosely as a bracelet. Perhaps I could get a jeweller to take a couple of the links out of it for him before it dropped off his arm and he lost it in the garden. I busied myself stoking the fire and then banking it so that he wouldn't have to put any more logs on it before he took himself to bed.

'Shall I put the TV on for you?'

He shook his head.

'Sit for a moment,' he said, nodding at the chair across the fire from where he sat.

I did as he said.

'Have you identified the pilot? From what you've told me, the Spit must have crashed around the time I was with 66 Squadron. I might have known him.'

He looked bereft, as if the subject had dredged up such awful memories he was grief-stricken all over again.

I shook my head.

'No, not so far. His dog tags are too corroded to make out the name. All I can guess is that his surname might have begun with a G or an O. He was wearing a watch with an inscription on the back that was unreadable. It wasn't regulation issue, but that's not unusual, as far as I know. It wasn't compulsory to wear standard issue, was it?'

He shook his head then covered his face with his hands and stayed like that for so long I started worrying all over again. He rocked backwards and forwards, whispering to himself. When he eventually stopped and dragged his hands down his cheeks, he looked every one of his ninety-six years. I knelt in front of him.

'Are you all right? I'm worried about you, Grandpa, please tell me if you're not feeling well.'

He shook his head. 'I'm fine, Jenny Wren, don't worry about me. It's just a shock to learn that someone from my old squadron is the pilot you've discovered, and that the poor sod has been lying in a bog all these years.'

'Of course – it's bound to be. Shall I leave you in peace? Promise me you'll call if you feel unwell. I can see the news has knocked you for six. I don't want you keeling over from all this excitement.'

'I promise,' he whispered. He took my hand and kissed the back of it. 'And I will tell you all about it, just not right now.'

I dropped a kiss on top of his head and left, quietly closing the door behind me. My mind spun.

He'd tell me all about it.

It struck me as an odd thing to say. Well, I would just have to be patient and wait until he was ready to talk.

It was the most extraordinary coincidence, though. Who would have thought it – that my grandfather might have known our mystery Spitfire pilot. There was so much I didn't know about his life . . . and I was beginning to suspect my grandfather was a bit of a dark horse.

Chapter 29

Bella

Bella was given a serious dressing-down that evening, but was allowed to take the next day off to go and see Johnnie. The CO recognised how strung up and distressed she was and as one of the squadron's best pilots she was let off, albeit with a caution to stay away from Stephen.

She caught the earliest train possible to Plymouth the next morning. It was full of troops – both Army and Navy personnel – and she had difficulty finding a seat, but didn't care. She would stand all the way if that was what it took. All she could think of was Johnnie, hoping he wasn't in too bad a state to see her.

She hitched the small bag higher onto her shoulder, gripping it tightly, feeling faintly sick. Was she mad? Perhaps, but she was determined to go through with her plan, dreamt up overnight when she had lain awake dreading seeing him badly hurt.

If, for whatever reason, it was the last time they would spend together, she didn't want him to go on thinking she was Aiden. She needed him to know *her* – Bella – and how she felt about him. If she had learnt anything over the past few months, it was that there were no guarantees in this shitty war. Life was short and she must make the most of every moment. She couldn't continue to lie – to herself or to Johnnie.

On the train, she locked herself into the lavatory, removed her uniform and changed into the blue silk tea-dress Aunt Pegs had bought her, put on some lipstick and brushed her hair into a more feminine style. Then she placed a small cloche hat on her head, stepped into a pair of low-heeled court shoes and looked in the mirror.

'Hello, Bella.'

She had spent so many months wearing a man's uniform that she stared at her reflection for a long moment, barely recognising the woman looking back at her. Lines had appeared at the corners of her mouth and her freckles had paled in the cool British climate. But it was the eyes which had changed the most. Dark and guarded, she was no longer the Bella Gardner who had left Australia. She shook her head and stuck her tongue out, turning away from the image.

She folded her uniform and carefully stowed it in the bag, then slipped out of the bathroom and squeezed her way to the other end of the train, wishing she had thought to bring something thicker to cover herself. The fine dress material was no defence to the chill weather or the eyes of the sailors that followed her as she stepped onto the platform at Plymouth railway station.

At the hospital she was met by a fearsome-looking woman in a matron's uniform who questioned her as to her relationship with Flight Officer Winters in a voice which could have been heard on a drill field from fifty yards away.

'He's family,' Bella said.

'What family? Only immediate relatives are allowed in to see him,' the matron barked.

She really was a sergeant-major in disguise.

'Brother.'

'Identification, please.'

'Sorry, I don't seem to have it with me, I was in such a hurry to see Johnnie – he might be dying for all I know and you're standing there telling me I can't see him? Excuse me, but I don't think so.'

She had had enough and swerved past the woman and set off at a run along the corridor with a sign saying *Wards* above the entrance. She had no idea where she should be going but anything was better than arguing.

Passing double doors at intervals, she poked her head into each one and none of them had patients in them with obvious injuries. They all looked like sick people. No use at all.

Where was he? The hammering in her chest increased with each failure to find him and panic threatened to overwhelm her. She couldn't come all this way and not see him, it was impossible. She would find him, if she had to rip this damn place apart to do it.

At the far end of the corridor, she came upon the final set of doors and stopped. Pushing the door open, she saw a long double line of beds, similar to the ward Aiden had been in, with half or more of them occupied with men. Some had a leg or arm raised in the air, some were bandaged.

Halfway down one side lay Johnnie, covered up to his neck in blankets, a cage affair over his legs, his face so white Bella thought he must be at death's door. She made a sound – something between a cry and a yelp – and he looked straight at her without the slightest sign of recognition.

She tried to compose herself, slowing her breathing and wiping her hands surreptitiously down the sides of the blue dress. She lifted her chin and walked down the ward until she stood at the side of his bed. There was no going back, it was now or never.

He stirred and groaned, a confused frown on his face.

'Hello, Johnnie.'

His eyes widened and he struggled to sit up. She put a hand on his shoulder to stay him and sat on the edge of the narrow bed.

'Sshh, don't move.'

She stood again and brought a chair across and sat on it.

'Aiden?' he whispered.

Bella nodded then shook her head. 'Yes. And no.'

'I don't understand.' He tried to sit up again, and she took a pillow from the next empty bed and placed it behind him then helped him sit.

'Johnnie, tell me how you are, first, then I'll tell you the truth. I had to come and see you – couldn't bear the thought of you lying in hospital all beaten up. Nobody seemed to know anything back at base.' She took a breath, aware she was gabbling but needing to know he was not about to die, as she'd imagined.

'Base? Wait. You *are* Aiden. Why are you dressed as a woman?' His voice rose in disbelief.

'Sshhh.' She looked around, hoping nobody was listening to them. 'I'm not telling you anything more until you promise you'll live.'

'Of course I'll live, you idiot. I only smashed my leg and shoulder when the Spit landed on its nose,' he said, grunting as he moved so that he could see her better. 'No thanks to that brainless new boy, Stephen. He shot me up, went totally doolally, spraying bullets everywhere. It's a wonder more of us weren't hit by him.'

'I heard. TC told me. Stephen is terribly blue about it and I said some awful things to him. I'm not sure he's cut out for this business.'

She closed her eyes for a moment at the memory of her row in the mess. Regret snagged at her and she shook her head to clear her mind.

Johnnie winced. 'Sooner he leaves the better, if you ask me.'

'How bad are the leg and your shoulder?'

'Well, I won't be flying again any time soon, the doc told me. Need an operation on my leg to set the bone properly. Think I'm lucky not to have lost it, in all honesty.' He looked bereft. 'Not ready to give up on this job. What will I do, old chap?' He paused. 'Sorry. If I don't look at you, I still think you're Aiden.'

She put a hand on his arm, where he'd laid it on top of the white sheet.

'Johnnie, listen to me. I am Aiden, at least for the past six months I've been him.' She wasn't sure how to tell him the truth, how it would sound to tell him she had stolen her brother's identity. She wasn't even entirely sure in her own mind anymore why she had done it. 'Aiden is my brother. He was badly injured in a train crash on his way to Advanced Flight Training and will have to spend the rest of his days in a wheelchair.' She stopped, her throat closing at the memory of her brother the last time she had seen him, his body shrunken and still. Swallowing away the image, she continued. 'My real name is Bella. I'm Aiden's sister.'

His mouth fell open as she spoke and he stared at her until she flushed under his scrutiny.

'What? You really *are* a woman? You've been disguised as a man all this time and nobody knew? How? How in heaven's name did you do such a thing?'

His voice rose once more, outrage and disbelief on his face.

She looked around again and shushed him, then shrugged, smiling in spite of herself.

'Nobody expects an RAF pilot to be a woman. You all saw what you expected to see. Aiden and I are . . .' her voice cracked and she swallowed, willing herself to carry on '. . . very alike. Similar height, same build, same hair colour. People who don't know us well always mistake us for twins. It wasn't all that difficult.' She sighed. 'We learnt to fly when we were still kids – the story I've told you about my family is true, I just switched us around. I came to England to get my full pilot's licence a year before war broke out, and joined ATA as soon as I heard they were recruiting women as well as men. The flying was fun to begin with, but women are only allowed to fly the small trainer planes – Tiger Moths and so on. I wanted to fly Hurricanes, Spitfires. Be a proper airman.' She paused; even the word *airman* infuriated her. That life seemed aeons ago, so much had changed since then. 'Aiden wanted to go to university when he finished school and had won a place at Cambridge. He hated the idea of fighting, full stop. Not because he was afraid, but because he abhors violence of any kind. My brother is a pacifist, and yet I bullied him into joining the RAF – told him it was his duty. And he almost died and has had his life ruined because of it. What kind of sister does that make me?' Her eyes prickled and she shook her head. 'It's my fault my brother is wheelchair bound so I decided I should take his place and keep his name alive and do what he would have done.' She took a long breath and looked at Johnnie. His eyes were glued to her face. 'And it's everything I wanted to do and so much more. The flying, the camaraderie, even the dreaded dogfights. I was made for this life, Johnnie, and I'm damned good at it.'

He grunted. 'Better than most, I'd say.'

She smiled. 'I don't know about that. All I know is that up there, flying my Spit, I know who I am. Does that make any kind of sense?'

He nodded. 'It does. It makes perfect sense to me and most of the squadron, I should think.'

Bella looked down at her broken and grubby nails. She should have brought gloves to wear – they were not the hands of a young lady.

'There's only one thing that's gone wrong with my grand plan.'

'Let me guess. Stephen Collingwood-Smythe?'

She smiled in spite of her turmoil.

'Yes, there is Stephen. I almost had a heart attack when he said Aiden's name the other night. But even he didn't guess I'm Aiden's sister, he thinks I'm a brother Aiden never mentioned.' She smiled again. 'I don't think he's too much of a bright spark.' Bella gazed at Johnnie's face, the face she had come to know as well as her own. 'He's not the problem. You are.'

'Me? Why? I can't deny your story is crazy, but I believe you.'

'Why are you the problem? Because I never planned to fall

in love, and yet here I am. Head over heels in love with you, Johnnie Winters.' She blurted it out in one long breath before she lost her nerve.

He stared at her for so long she almost got up and ran. What an idiot. Why did she have to tell him how she felt and ruin everything? And yet, the devastation that had hit her on hearing Johnnie had crashed made her realise he was far more to her than just a friend. She wanted him to know – needed him to know – how she felt.

'Say that again.' Johnnie's voice wobbled.

'I'm in love with you. As a girl loves a boy. You know, romantically.'

He turned his head away from her and defeat was a leaden lump in her throat. She had ruined things and for what? Some kind of grand romantic gesture? Hah, that went well, didn't it? She shivered in the chilly room and stood up. She had failed and would just have to accept it. At least she wouldn't have Johnnie around anymore, she could forget about him – if that was possible.

He grabbed her arm and she flopped down onto the chair again, a spark of hope in her soul.

'Bloody hell. This is a lot to take in. A. Lot.'

He lay back against the pillows and closed his eyes. Bella kept her eyes on his face and saw a small smile lift the corners of his dry, cracked lips followed by a frown, which knitted his eyebrows into a line.

'Bloody hell,' he repeated. 'We've been such good chums since we met, gone through so much together, haven't we?' His eyes opened. 'I don't know what to say. It's too much to take in right now.' He scanned her face and must have seen the pain she couldn't hide. 'Can I have some time to think? I'm damned flattered, it's not every day a gal turns up at a chap's bedside and tells him she's head over heels about him. It's just . . .' He tailed off and turned his head away.

Bella swallowed the lump in her throat. If he didn't feel the same way, there was no way back to the easy friendship and camaraderie they had built over the past months. Had she ruined all that for the sake of her own selfish needs? It was too much to hope that he felt the same way – and to blindside him when he was at his most vulnerable was probably the stupidest stunt she had ever pulled.

'I'm sorry, Johnnie,' she said, clearing her throat and blinking hard. 'I shouldn't have come. You've had a terrible experience and are lucky to be alive, and all I can think of is myself.'

He shook his head and winced. Closed his eyes for a moment and then opened them and met hers.

'Don't be sorry. I'm very happy you came, but as I said, it's a hell of a lot to take in. I have no idea whether I'll be able to walk again, much less if I can ever fly again.' His expression darkened, grief stark in his eyes as they searched her face again. He dropped his gaze and rubbed his cheek with his uninjured hand. 'I must have been blind all these months. How could I not see you're a girl?'

Bella managed a weak smile. 'Like I said. You saw what you believed. Who would suspect a girl of spinning lies and deceit to join the RAF?'

'You've got more balls than most of us chaps.'

'Thank you, I'll take that as a compliment.'

He managed a small grin. 'I need time to consider everything. I can't be a burden on you or anyone else and until I know how – if – I'll recover, I can't think of anything else, never mind make decisions. I'll write to you. Is that okay?'

Bella nodded, fighting tears – thinking how typical of him to consider others before his own needs.

The fearsome matron chose that moment to throw open the doors of the ward, glare around and fix her eyes on Bella.

'You shouldn't be in here, young lady. I told you it's relatives only, and I do not believe you are a relative of Flight Officer Winters.

212

Yet here you are pestering him, when he should be resting in preparation for a major operation.'

'Matron, this is Miss Gardner, a very close friend of mine, who I am more than happy to see.'

'That's as may be, young man, but you need to rest. Come on, miss, out with you.'

The matron made sweeping gestures with her arms, as if Bella were some kind of flotsam that needed clearing out of the way. She rose, placed her hand over Johnnie's and left, looking back as she reached the door to see his eyes fixed on her.

'I'll be back – and I'll write,' she said.

'Please do. I'm counting on it.'

The return journey to base seemed interminable, the train was packed and stopped every few minutes without, it appeared, any reason. Bella wanted nothing more than to crawl into a corner and hide so that she could give vent to her pent-up emotions. Her mind rocketed from one extreme to another: haranguing herself for admitting her feelings to Johnnie and ruining their friendship forever, then swinging wildly the other way and finding a tiny kernel of hope when she remembered the look he gave her as she was marched out of the ward by the matron.

She couldn't stay still, and pushed and shoved her way up and down the corridor of the train as it made its slow way north. She hid herself in the lavatory again, removed the lipstick and redressed in her blue RAF uniform before she left the train. Once she arrived back at base, she hid the bag of women's clothing in the bottom of her wardrobe before she bumped into anyone she knew.

Most of the squadron were still out on sorties and she was glad of the quiet so she could compose herself and get back into Aiden's skin.

Toby Cranston approached her in the mess as soon as he came through the door.

'Well?'

'Evening, Toby.' Embarrassment chased its way up her back as she recalled the scene she had caused the day before. 'Sorry about what happened yesterday. I was in a bit of a state.'

It was hard to look him in the eye, more of a fraud than ever, after today.

'I can't blame you, knowing how you and Johnnie are such pals, but you need to keep your temper in check,' he said. 'Anyway, enough of that; don't keep me in suspense, Digger. How is he?'

TC chewed on his pipe as if his life depended on it. He looked exhausted. They all looked exhausted. Too many sorties on too many days with too few pilots.

'He's pretty bashed up, and has to have an operation on his leg to set the bone properly, but is putting on a brave face and seemed happy to see a friend.'

Bella kicked herself. That made him sound as if he just needed a few days in bed. He couldn't come back to flying which was devastating for him.

'Well, if I'd just survived a nosedive like he did, I would be pretty relieved about it, I suppose.' He shook his head. 'We'll miss him though. He's such a bloody good pilot, and there are few enough of you around.'

'He feels awful that he can't fly again in the foreseeable future, but knowing Johnnie, he'll do his damnedest to get back in a plane again as soon as he can.'

'He'll get sent to a rehabilitation centre, once he leaves hospital, poor sod.'

'I'm afraid I didn't have time to learn anything about his care after the operation. There was a dragon of a matron who didn't take kindly to me ignoring her instructions that only family could visit him.' Bella grimaced. 'She kicked me out smartish once she found me talking to him.'

'Well, at least you got to go and cheer the old bugger up. I'm sure he appreciated you making the effort.'

She hoped he didn't notice the flush creeping up her face.

'He seemed to, TC, yes. I just wish he was near enough that we could all go and visit him when we have the time. Do you think they would move him up to Bristol or Chepstow or somewhere nearby?'

She could only hope.

'No idea; none of the other banged-up boys have been. Most go home to recuperate.'

'Johnnie's family are from Somerset, I think,' Bella said. 'Maybe he'll be moved closer once he's well enough.'

'Let's hope so. It's tough on all the family. But at least it's one letter I don't have to write to his parents.'

'Thank God for that,' Bella whispered.

'Indeed. Now, you look like you need a drink, Digger. Beer?'

She nodded and thanked him, though all she really wanted to do was be alone with her thoughts. She felt as disconnected as if she had been cut adrift and was floundering in choppy seas. Each time she thought of seeing Johnnie again her heart banged in her chest and her stomach filled with butterflies. She refused to contemplate his upcoming operation and the long recovery he would undergo. It was frustrating not to be there to give him some moral support.

She pushed away the possibility that he might not want to see her again after the shock she had given him today. It was something she couldn't even begin to contemplate.

Chapter 30

Jennifer

I returned to work after the weekend to find there was a letter from the squadron thanking us for raising the plane and finding their missing pilot. As we had guessed, the Spitfire had been reported as lost at sea, after no sign of any wreckage was found on the coast or inland.

The results of the pilot's DNA test were also waiting for me.

I read them three times to make sure I wasn't imagining what was there. Had the lab mixed up our sample with one from another source? It seemed unlikely, all the correct references were there. Did I inadvertently get some foreign DNA on the sample? Absolutely not. Our protocols were rock solid, and even though there were times when I was tempted to bend rules in things like Health and Safety, I would never compromise something so vital with sloppy procedures.

By eliminating any mistakes, it must mean the results were correct. I stared at the report one more time, for the results turned everything we thought we knew about the pilot on its head and threw up even more questions. No wonder I was confused when I examined the skeleton – the bones belonged to a woman.

I knew women flew planes during the war. The Air Transport Auxiliary delivered all kinds of planes around the country to wherever they were needed, and had a cohort of women from across the Allied world who were trained pilots and flew everything from Tiger Moths to Lancaster bombers by the end of the war.

But they never flew in battle.

So why was a woman flying our Spit? Had we got it completely wrong, and it was a case of wrong place, wrong time? Perhaps the woman was flying it to another airfield and had been caught up in a dogfight purely by chance.

But our woman *was* an RAF pilot, the dog tags confirmed it.

So why was a woman wearing them?

I was more confused than ever.

Perhaps my grandfather might hold the key to the mystery, but would he tell me? After all, as far as I knew he had never told anyone else about that time of his life, so why should he want to break his silence now?

Or maybe there was a simple explanation and I was overthinking it. It didn't stop a ripple of excitement running up my back. A mystery that had lain dormant for more than seventy years might now be revealed.

Finding any remaining family might provide the answers. It was frustrating to have to leave that search to others, but I knew it was a line I shouldn't cross. The squadron would notify them. I would just have to rely on my powers of persuasion and get Grandpa to tell me what he remembered and hope that he could help.

I stopped off at his cottage on the way home from work, guilt worming its way up my spine at how upset he had been at hearing which squadron the Spitfire belonged to. I hadn't mentioned it again over the weekend, just checking in with him each evening and making sure he was well. He hadn't offered any more information and I hadn't pushed him. He seemed quieter than usual, but otherwise okay.

Throughout the weekend our conversation had played on my

mind, making me re-evaluate how I approached the work we were doing. All the planes we had recovered so far had crashed without their pilot, and I hadn't thought too deeply about the young men who flew the skies and kept Britain safe from invasion during the war, too caught up in the excitement and satisfaction that archaeology gave me as a scientist. I hadn't looked further than the physical condition of the plane, how it had got there, how we were going to retrieve it; all the practical elements of the dig. The human cost had been shoved into a corner of my mind, out of harm's way. To consider it – especially since Ben's accident – was a dark place I didn't want to explore.

To discover my own grandfather had been one of those pilots and almost lost his life when he was so young pulled me up short and made me face the fact that for each of those plane wrecks there was a human cost. And seeing the distress my words had caused Grandpa brought home to me the depth of comradeship and love for their fellow aviators there must have been among those young men.

As well as the families who never had a body to bury. Who had lived out their lives always wondering where their sons, husbands, lovers, brothers were lying.

No wonder Grandpa was so upset.

I hoped by discovering exactly where the plane had crashed and the identity of the pilot, that the family could at last have some closure, and it might help bring them some kind of peace.

Not knowing was by far the worst thing, I knew that much.

One overriding question still hung in my mind.

Who exactly *was* our pilot?

And how the hell did I explain to my frail grandfather that one of his fellow pilots, and possibly a close friend, was a woman?

Chapter 31

Bella

Bella persuaded Gowling, the adjutant, to contact Johnnie's parents and enquire how he was recovering, a week after she had seen him. The adjutant reported back that the operation on his leg went as well as could be expected, considering the damage the crash had caused.

A few weeks later Johnnie was moved to a rehabilitation centre in an old manor house close to Bridgwater Bay. His family lived on the Somerset Levels, so were nearby, and it was near enough for his friends from 92 Squadron to visit occasionally – those who still survived.

Bella bought herself a second-hand Ford car, a tiny rust bucket which backfired at every opportunity, but which she managed to scrounge petrol for from the quartermaster when she said it was for visiting Johnnie. Although she had written to him while he was in hospital and he had replied to her, he had made no mention about her visit and admission of her love for him. His letters seemed impersonal, giving nothing away of his own feelings, and made Bella seethe with frustration and anger at her own stupidity for jeopardising their friendship.

The first time she had a chance to go and visit him at the rehab centre, she badly wanted to go alone, but when TC heard where she was going, she couldn't deny giving him and a couple of the others a lift too.

She noticed how much going along in a group raised Johnnie's spirits. He tried his best to join in with the banter and joshing which was part and parcel of the normal camaraderie between them all, but underneath it all Bella could see how low he was. Even though the rehab centre was in beautiful parkland overlooking the sea, and it was a period of cold, clear weather with sharp frosts each night, he seemed far more depressed than when she had seen him in hospital. The operation had saved his leg but left it shorter than the other. He was in considerable pain, even after the wound site healed. Having to learn to walk in a whole new way brought untold stress on the rest of his body, which left him exhausted.

When she had an evening pass, she went to see him on her own, taking the risk of going as Bella, even though some of the staff now knew her as Aiden.

'What are you doing?' he hissed at her, when she walked into his room. 'Someone will recognise you, surely?'

'Will they? So far, I've walked past two nurses who've seen Aiden before and they didn't bat an eyelid.' She pulled a chair up next to him. 'And hello to you too. Aren't you glad to see a friendly face?'

He gazed up at her from his chair where he sat huddled in a thick dressing gown in front of a bay window which caught the evening sun. There were new lines around his eyes and his face had a cold, pinched look about it. The room was large, and though the sun gave the impression of warmth it was freezing.

'Hello.' He looked tired. 'Of course, I am. I'm so down in the dumps at the moment, I need cheering up.'

'Well, I'm just the woman to do that,' she said, winking in an exaggerated way, so that he couldn't help laughing.

'Silly arse,' he said, his expression returning to its default

220

gloomy expression. 'I miss our friendship, you know. No matter how I try, I don't think I can go back to thinking of you as Digger. Everything has changed – and not just because of this.'

He slapped his thigh as if it was a recalcitrant horse.

Bella sighed. It was just as she had feared. He didn't love her and couldn't go back to being her friend and comrade. Her throat tightened and she looked away, trying to control the urge to beg him to reconsider. She had to leave with a tiny bit of self-respect and pride in place. She knew it must be the last time she came to see him; she couldn't bear being close to him knowing he rejected her. The prospect was too overwhelming to consider. She blinked back a threatening tear and cleared her throat.

'I won't come again if it's too difficult for you. I'm sorry, Johnnie, so very sorry. I only wanted you to know who I really am, and what you mean to me.'

The words she wanted to say remained unsaid. She couldn't tell him she loved him again. It would be the end of any hope for their friendship. She stood, wanting only to run away and find somewhere to let her tears fall.

He grabbed her hand. 'Don't go. Please . . . Bella. Don't go.'

His voice sounded choked, the words tumbling out, her name sounding strange on his tongue.

She dropped back into the chair and gazed at him, noticing how much he had aged, his face thin, lines of pain drawn on his cheeks, his eyes dull and bloodshot.

He leant across and traced the line of her jaw with his fingers, ending at her chin. Drawing her face towards him he kissed her gently on the lips. Bella pulled back instinctively, shock rippling through her. Johnnie's face was so close to her own that she saw the smile creeping up to his eyes.

'Can I try that again? Do you mind?' he said, stroking a stray tear away from her cheek.

She nodded, unable to speak for a moment, then her words coming out in a squeaky pitch quite unlike her normal voice.

'Yes. Yes please, I would like that very much, and no, I don't mind in the slightest.'

He kissed her again, his lips cool against her own, then pulled her down to his level, so she knelt in front of him. He leant forward and held her face between his hands, tenderly pushing a wave of red hair from her forehead.

'I must be a blind fool not to have seen who you really are before now,' he said. 'We've been in each other's pockets for months and nothing you've said or done made me doubt you were anyone other than my pal, Digger.' Johnnie shook his head, his finger following each contour of her face. 'I'm very glad you've come clean though, now that I've had time to think about everything. I have no idea how we can make this work without giving ourselves away, without giving *you* away, but knowing how long you've done it for so far, I'm sure we will find a way.'

Joy swept through Bella like a warm wind on a cold day. She wanted to dance, to sing, to throw her arms around Johnnie and never stop kissing him. She felt as if she must be grinning like the cat that stole the cream. Blowing out a shaky breath and hoping he couldn't tell how much of an effect his words had on her, she took his cold hand and kissed the palm, relief sitting side by side with her newfound happiness.

'Well, the first thing is to get you better,' she said. 'You know how hectic things are at the base, I don't know when I'll be able to come and see you again. I want you to promise me you'll do everything the doctors and the whatchamacallits – phys . . . something?'

'Physiotherapists.'

'That's the one . . . you must listen to them, Johnnie, and do all the exercises they give you, so you get fit again.' She put her arms around his waist and lay her head on his lap, marvelling at being able to touch him in such a way at last, and how right it felt. 'I know you're strong enough to get over this, and I'll help whenever I can. I hate seeing you so down and confined to this place.'

'You do realise I shall be posted somewhere else once I am fit again, don't you?'

Her head shot up. 'Why? Won't they let you stay with 92 Squadron?'

'I have no doubt I'll be given a desk job. They won't want a lame pilot in charge of a Spit. I couldn't even climb into the cockpit.'

'But you'll get stronger and fitter. And you're such a good flyer, there are few enough of those around. They need every experienced man they can get. I'm sure I've heard about a chap who lost both his legs in a flying accident and is still a commissioned pilot.'

She jumped up, her head in her hands trying to remember the man's name.

'You mean Douglas Bader, don't you?' Johnnie said. 'He is an exceptional case, though. I doubt many injured pilots with a gammy leg get a second chance like he has.'

She dropped down beside his chair again and grabbed his hand.

'But it gives one hope, doesn't it? If he can get back in a Spit, there's no reason for you not to be allowed to, surely?'

His shoulders sagged and his head drooped. Bella wondered fleetingly why she was being so pushy. Was it just to raise his spirits? Or for her own selfish needs; that she couldn't bear the thought of him not being by her side every day? God knew, the chances of them both making it to the end of the war were minimal. She should be grateful that he had a valid reason to be stood down as a pilot. At least he would be safer on the ground.

Johnnie straightened in his chair and squeezed her hand.

'Well, it's up to the docs and the brass. I will do my best to get back to full fitness; that's all I can do.'

Bella hugged him again, wishing she could do more to help him.

A quiet tap on the door and it opening was enough to make her jump up and retake her seat next to Johnnie, her pulse jumping. She straightened her skirt over her knees as a nurse entered the room.

'I'm sorry, miss, it's time for Mr Winters's medication and visiting hours are over,' the rather stern-looking woman said. 'Our patient needs to rest. He tires quickly.'

Bella glanced at Johnnie and saw how his cheeks had reddened. She wanted to slap the nurse for speaking about him as if he wasn't sitting right in front of her. She stood up, took his hand and gave it a squeeze, then leant down and kissed him on the lips. Raising an eyebrow at the nurse, she gathered up her handbag.

'I will see you again soon, darling,' she said, dropping a slow wink as his mouth dropped open and he blushed even more. Walking across the room, she stopped for a moment in front of the nurse, tweaking her jacket and speaking in a low voice so that Johnnie couldn't hear. 'If you speak like that in front of Mr Winters again, I will see to it that your highers hear about it. He's one of the finest men you'll ever meet, not an imbecile. Have some respect, woman.'

The nurse stared at her and paled. Bella raised her eyebrows again, then carried on through the open door, her heart banging against her ribs and her mouth still tingling from the kiss.

Chapter 32

Jennifer

Rosie and Scott were sitting snuggled up on the sofa in the kitchen when I walked in. Rosie jumped up, her face turning beetroot. I tried not to smile at her embarrassment and bent to say hello to the dogs, who were weaving themselves around my legs. Ginger lay curled up on Scott's lap and hissed at her. Had he found a new best friend to replace Ben? I squashed a prickle of resentment – he was a cat – they had no loyalty when it came to their favourites.

'Evening. Have you fed these three?'

'Evening, Jen,' said Scott, not in the least fazed by my entrance.

'Dad fed the animals an hour ago,' Rosie said. 'Where have you been? You're not usually this late.'

'I dropped in to see Grandpa and stayed longer than I meant to.'

'Why?' Rosie pounced on my words, her voice strained with anxiety. 'Is Grandpa sick?'

'No, he's fine.' I put my arms around her and pulled her into a hug, which she wriggled out of impatiently. Or perhaps, she didn't want Scott to see. I stepped back obediently, not wanting to embarrass her more than I had already. 'Grandpa and I got talking about his time in the war. Our work raising the Spitfire has really interested him and I've been keeping him up to date with the progress we've made.'

Scott eyed me and smiled.

'Once a military man, always a military man, eh?' he said.

I shrugged. 'It would appear so. My grandfather has never, ever talked about what happened to him back then, but today he opened up a tiny bit.'

'So, what *did* he do in the war?' Rosie asked.

'He told me he was in the RAF,' Scott said.

My head snapped up. 'Did he? It's more than he's ever told the family, as far as I know.'

I tried to banish the slight jealousy at learning my grandfather felt comfortable enough with a stranger young enough to be his great-grandson to tell him something he had always withheld from his own family.

'It was no big deal. We got chatting when we were at lunch here, and discussed the forces and all that. Sounds like he had quite a time of it.'

'His leg has always pained him. I knew it happened in an accident but not that it was during the war.'

'How old was he when the war started?' Rosie asked.

'Twenty-one. He was almost twenty-two when he joined the RAF,' I said.

She frowned. 'Not that much older than me, then?'

'Makes you think, doesn't it?'

'I can't even imagine having to go and fight an enemy.'

She flopped down beside Scott again and he took her hand.

'I joined the Marines when I was eighteen, and was sent to Afghanistan not long after I'd finished training,' he said. 'I'd just had my twentieth birthday.' His expression was bleak and he looked down at Rosie's hand he still held. 'All the training in the world doesn't prepare you for the real thing. Nobody knows how they'll react when they go to war.'

Rosie leant in against him, saying nothing.

I left them to it and went to find Peter, who, as always, was in his study.

'Hello, you,' I said. 'Have you seen those two in the kitchen?'

'Hello, yourself. Which two? What have those dogs been up to now?'

I laughed and put my arms around him. 'Not the dogs. Rosie and Scott, snuggled up on the sofa, looking very at home together.'

Peter eyed me with a frown that pulled his brow out of shape.

'I'm not happy about them getting so close,' he said. 'She's too young for him, and he's got his own problems. Rosie doesn't need any more baggage to deal with.'

I leant away from him. 'I thought you liked Scott?'

'I do. He's a grand lad. But not right for Rosie.' His tone was flat, his expression stubborn.

'I understand why you think that, but I disagree. She's more like her old self since meeting him, and I suspect if anyone can help her learn how to live without Ben, it's Scott.' Dropping a kiss on top of his head, I sat down with him. 'And, when it comes down to it, she's an adult. We have no right to interfere and I wouldn't want to.'

Peter looked away from me, but not before I caught the shine in his eye.

'I can't bear the thought of her being hurt. She's been through enough.'

'I know, and I get it. You're her dad, and it's hard-wired in you to protect her.' I leant in to him and kissed his mouth. 'But it's time to let her make her own decisions. And if he makes her even a little bit happy, then surely that's a good thing?'

He dragged out a sigh. 'I suppose so.'

He still couldn't look me in the eye, and I knew we had a long way to go to regain the relationship we had always enjoyed and to some extent taken for granted. A lump forced its way into my throat at how broken we still were as a couple. I was exhausted with trying to shore up our shattered marriage, but would fight to the end for it.

We were both making more effort to spend time together, although we still hadn't talked about Ben. That was a wall which seemed insurmountable to me, but which we were going to have to break down sooner or later if we were ever to lay our son to rest. I changed the subject to familiar territory, hoping it might persuade him to lighten up a little.

'Grandpa talked about his war days, today. It's the first time I've ever heard him mention what he did,' I said. 'He was an RAF Spitfire pilot. Can you imagine?'

'Goodness, if I had to guess, I don't think I would have said that,' Peter said, a wry smile crossing his face. 'It makes sense of his enthusiasm for your latest work project, doesn't it? Is that why he told you what he did? And is that where he hurt his leg?'

I nodded.

The same emotion hit me as when I'd considered that I would never have existed if Grandpa had been killed. I swallowed the lump in my throat. I refused to go back down the rabbit hole of Ben's death and him never having children.

Peter seemed oblivious. I was becoming good at masking my thoughts and emotions.

'Have you discovered anything more about the body in the plane?'

'The DNA report came back.' I paused, still not quite able to believe it. 'It's the strangest thing; the pilot was female.'

'Really? I thought fighter pilots were always men. That can't be right, surely?' He frowned. 'Have you asked them to run the tests again?'

I shook my head.

'It actually confirms what I suspected from examining the pilot's remains. I thought he – she – must have been very young or perhaps small and slight.' I said. 'But you're correct. Only men

228

could fly in battle, yet here we are, with a dead woman wearing the dog tags of an RAF pilot.'

'There were women pilots, though, weren't there? I'm sure I've read about them.'

'Yes, there were a good number who worked in the Air Transport Auxiliary, ferrying planes all over the place, but they were never trained as fighter pilots. It was deemed too much for a woman to contend with.'

It was all I felt I could tell him, for the time being. I still didn't know how our mystery woman managed to get away with her deception.

Tomorrow, I would try and winkle more information out of Grandpa and see if he had any clue as to who his mysterious comrade-in-arms might be.

Chapter 33

Bella

Christmas came and went, with barely a pause in operations. The mess orderlies did their best to make things look festive, and there was a carol service for those who wished to go. Bella received a letter from Susan, which surprised her and made her cry. Her father was a changed man, barely said a word to anyone, wasn't interested in Bindalong business, just sat in Aiden's room staring into space.

All he wanted was to bring his son home, but judging from what Aiden had told her, Bella knew it was the last thing her brother would do, even if it was possible. He showed such strong resilience and stoicism, it made her immensely proud of him. His letters were full of plans to continue his education as soon as he was strong enough to live independently. His last letter had amazed her.

I see this as an opportunity to do all the things which seemed impossible when war began. I will go to university, I will play the violin, I will paint.

God has given me a second chance and I mean to grasp it with both hands.

He never seemed to doubt her story of continuing to fly airplanes for ATA. One day, when peace reigned once more, she would tell him what she did. Until then, all she could do was carry on with her charade and pray they both lived to see each other again.

Bella spent New Year's Day with Johnnie. His rehabilitation was almost finished, though the limp would remain with him for life. He had been stood down as a pilot and assigned a job at a base just south of London. He tried to look cheerful when she arrived, but she could see the bleakness in his eyes as she walked into his arms and kissed him.

'That makes me feel a little better,' he said. 'I'm afraid I'm not very good company at the moment, old thing. I can't wait to leave this place, but we're going to be miles apart. God knows when I shall see you again.'

'Well, we will just have to make the most of today, then, won't we?' she said, stepping out of his embrace and taking a square package wrapped in brown paper out of her bag. She held it out to him. 'Happy Christmas. I'm sorry it's late.'

Johnnie took it from her and kissed her cheek. 'Thank you. Don't move, I have a little something for you, too.'

He put his hand in the pocket of his dressing gown and gave her a velvet-covered box tied with a blue ribbon. Bella wondered how he could have got hold of something so fancy-looking. In her heart she hoped it wasn't jewellery – surely Johnnie knew her well enough to realise that she never wore any.

They opened their presents and burst out laughing at the same moment.

'Great minds think alike, eh?' Johnnie said, taking the watch out of its box and strapping it to his wrist. 'I love it, thank you.'

Bella giggled as she gazed at her own present – a silver wristwatch with a sturdy strap.

'It's perfect, Johnnie. I shall wear it every day,' she said, admiring the timepiece before putting it on.

'Check the back,' he said.

Glancing at him, she turned the watch over. On the back was an inscription in tiny writing:

Digger, with love, JW
Dec.1940.

Her eyes filled with tears and she brushed them away, laughing through them.

'Look at the back of yours.'

Johnnie eyed her with a grin and took the watch off again. Bella had also had it inscribed.

Johnnie, my heart is yours, Bella

'Bloody hell, talk about reading each other's minds,' he said.

He grabbed her in a hug and they kissed, passion growing until Bella thought her legs would give way. She pulled out of the clinch and pushed the hair off her forehead, trying to slow her racing pulse and control her breathing. If they carried on like this they would never get out of the place and it wasn't at all what she had planned for their last day together.

'Come on, we're going out; your doctor agrees you need a change of scene.' She arched an eyebrow. 'He didn't ask what kind of scene. I hope you'll like what I have planned for you, so you'd better get out of that dressing gown and smarten up a bit.'

Johnnie's cheeks had turned a deep pink and he grinned at her, the first proper smile she had seen in weeks.

'Where are we going?'

'It's a surprise. Move it, Winters, we haven't got all day.'

He hobbled over to a wardrobe and took out a tweed jacket and a tie and allowed Bella to knot it for him. Once he was ready, he saluted her.

'Flight Officer Winters ready for duty, sir!'

She giggled. 'Idiot. Where's your coat?'

He pointed to a hook on the back of the door where his RAF coat hung. Holding it out to him while he struggled to get his recovering shoulder into the sleeve and then passing him his walking stick, she opened the door and waved her hand low in front of her.

'After you, sir.'

She drove them to the nearby Quantock Hills, where a pub with a thatched roof stood in the heart of a small village. The low winter sun brightened the ancient stone building and made the mullioned windows glint, as if each tiny pane was hewn from diamonds.

Inside, she led him to a small bar and ordered two tankards of beer and a plate of sandwiches. They sat at a round table in a nook under one of the tiny windows, and after taking a long drink of beer, Bella excused herself.

'Won't be long,' she said, bending and kissing him. 'And don't eat all the sandwiches; I'm starving.'

'Not promising anything, so you'd better be quick.'

She laughed and trotted out of the room.

At the reception desk, she signed them in as Mr and Mrs Winters. The middle-aged receptionist put her head on one side.

'You seem awful young to be wed, the pair of you,' she said. Heat raced up Bella's face and she dropped her gaze, shoving her left hand in her pocket, out of sight. 'But then, this war is making widows of so many young maids, you should make the most of the time you have together, I say.'

Raising her eyes, Bella caught a hint of a wink and couldn't help but grin.

'Thank you, we intend to,' she said.

'I hope you enjoy your stay, Mrs . . . Winters.'

The woman handed over a large, old-fashioned key and asked if they needed help with their luggage.

'No, thank you, we can manage.'

Bother. Why hadn't she thought about bringing any other clothes? Hurrying back through to the bar, she sat down just as their lunch was served, and the two of them ate, drank and chatted as if nothing had changed from the pals they had always been.

After they had refused coffee but accepted a small dram of whisky, Bella rose again.

'You look tired, Johnnie. I think you should go and rest.'

'What? No, I feel better than I've felt in weeks. I don't want to waste a moment of this day.'

'Well, I hope you won't think you'll be wasting your time.' She arched her eyebrows and his cheeks coloured. She took his hand and helped him out of chair. 'Come with me.'

She gave him an arm and they slowly mounted the narrow staircase until they arrived on the first-floor landing. In front of them were three doors, and Bella checked the fob of the key she had been given. Unlocking the middle door, she pushed it wide and drew Johnnie inside. His face had paled as he climbed the steep stairs, pain written in his eyes. Now he looked at her, a hint of a smile pulling at the corner of his mouth.

'What have you cooked up?'

She didn't answer, but gently removed the coat from his shoulders and pushed him slowly onto the counterpane of the double bed. He put his arms around her waist and rested his cheek against her shoulder.

'Are you sure about this?' he said, his voice muffled.

In answer she pulled away, and removed his shoes, placing them side by side with her own. Then she sat beside him and wrapped her arms around him.

'I've never been so sure in my life.'

She kissed him, his mouth warm under her lips, and he returned her kiss with passion, pulling her down until they lay across the bed. His hands ran down her back and her body responded in a way she'd never experienced before, until her bones turned to liquid and her breath came in quick gasps.

This was going way too quickly, and they had the whole afternoon. Using every bit of self-restraint, she sat up.

'Wait,' she said. 'I want to do something for you.'

Johnnie frowned, backing away slightly. 'What do you mean?'

She unbuttoned his shirt and removed it, then pulled his vest over his head. His body was thin, the muscle tone in his arms and shoulders she remembered from the summer, gone. Too shy to go any further for the moment, she pushed him back onto the bed and told him to turn over.

'Your physiotherapist said your back and shoulders are always aching with having to accommodate your leg.'

Taking a small bottle from her handbag, she put a few drops of lotion onto her palms, and began to massage him. Gently at first, then, as she found all the hard knots and tender spots, working harder, remembering how the horses enjoyed being rubbed down after a hard polo match and how relaxed it made them.

Five minutes later, Johnnie groaned.

'You're going to have to stop,' he said in a husky voice. 'I can't bear it.'

Bella's heart dropped. How could she have got this so wrong? She was so naive, how could she ever think Johnnie would agree to this clandestine afternoon? Perhaps he couldn't bear for her to see him in pain and so low? What else could it be? Embarrassment?

'I'm sorry,' she said, trying to keep the catch out of her voice. She stood up straight, easing the crick in her shoulders. 'Am I hurting you? I thought it might help with the pain.'

'Come here.' He pulled her down beside him. 'You have no idea the effect your hands are having on me . . .'

Pressing her close so their bodies fitted together, Bella giggled.

'Oh. I see . . .' She ran her hands up his back and then down his chest until she came to the waistband of his trousers. 'Well, perhaps you'll feel better if I undo this button? And this one? And this one . . .'

'Yes, yes, that's better, much better. It's a bit chilly in here though, don't you think? It'll be warmer in bed.'

Dragging the rest of their clothes off each other, they pulled the counterpane back to find a thick eiderdown, heavy woollen blankets and fleecy cotton sheets. Sliding into the comfort of the feather mattress, Bella squeaked as Johnnie ran his cold hand down her belly and then sighed as he kissed her again and his hand kept travelling.

She had never had a lover; never felt the kind of passion he awoke in her that afternoon. They made love, snoozed, then made love again. Once it was dark, they dressed and went downstairs for a quick supper, then wandered back up to the haven of their room.

Bella finished massaging Johnnie's back and legs, which led to more love-making. Afterwards, they lay in each other's arms talking about their dreams, as something which they could never expect to happen. It was impossible to think about the future, for no one could do anything other than live in the present.

When the war is over was not something they said. Nobody knew better how fragile life was, and while Johnnie had been allocated a desk job until he was fit again, Bella would be back in the air tomorrow, and who knew what that would bring?

The next morning Bella tried not to show how miserable she felt as they ate a quick breakfast before returning to the rehabilitation centre. Thousands of couples had been torn apart over the past few years. She and Johnnie were no different and would have to get on with it as best they could. Johnnie barely said two words, his face closed and pinched.

As they parted, she tried to be optimistic.

'Perhaps the squadron will be moved again, back to the south-east, and we will be close enough to see each other.'

He shrugged.

'Depends on how hard they want to hit Europe, I suppose. And who knows how the top brass decide where to send all the squadrons.' He took her hand, squeezing it hard. 'Just promise me you'll go on being the best of the best. That way, I know you'll come home safe.'

'Hah. That's always supposing there isn't a hotshot Luftwaffe pilot on my tail, who's better than I am.'

He kissed her.

'There's no fear of that. You're twice the pilot of any of those boys.' He tried to smile. 'Just stay out of the way of Collingwood-Smythe. He's more lethal than the Huns are.'

'Poor Stephen, you underestimate him. He got his first kill this week, did I tell you? He was quite stunned I think – and so were the rest of us.' She hugged him. 'I must go. I'm on stand-by from three o'clock. Seems a bloody silly time of day to start, if you ask me. We'll only have an hour or two of daylight.'

Johnnie shivered inside his greatcoat.

'Ugh, night flying is awful. Let's hope the Germans stay at home.'

'Second that. Write to me, please.' She put her arms around him under the coat, snuggling in against the thin wind. 'And you will remember to address it to Aiden, won't you?'

He laughed. 'I would love to be a fly on the wall if anyone discovers your real identity.'

Bella shivered, not from the cold. 'Please don't make a joke about it. It gives me nightmares.'

He kissed her again.

'I still can't understand how I never suspected a thing. All those weeks of training and flying together.' He shook his head, scanning her face. 'I must have been blind. One thing's for sure – your career as an actress will be a certainty.'

She stopped his words with a finger to his lips.

'Don't say that . . . please . . .' She kissed him for the final time. 'I must go. Goodbye, Johnnie.'

She climbed into her car, not wanting him to see her tears as she drew away.

Chapter 34

Bella

The winter dragged on with long, dreary days of low cloud, rain and sleet. It was the thing about England Bella hated the most. At least Australian winters were short, and the sun had warmth in it. Here, the sun hardly peeped over the horizon, and when it did it was a poor watery version of itself.

The squadron continued to be on stand-by, which meant long hours in the marquee at dispersal, hunched around the wood-burning stove, a mug of tea cradled in hands which never felt properly warm.

Bella had a perpetual cold which added to her woes. Not someone who suffered ailments, she despised herself for not being able to shake it off. Lying in bed, her chest heavy with a cough which felt as if it would crack her ribs, she resolved to ask the squadron doctor for a remedy.

Yet how could she? He would undoubtedly want to examine her and listen to her chest. She turned over and hit the lumpy pillow a few times. She would just have to get on with it. A cold was a cold, and would clear up eventually. The local chemist's shop would have something she could take, surely?

Finally nodding off, she dreamt of her mother, who would drip eucalyptus oil on her pillow when she had a sniffle and give her a hot lemon drink to soothe her throat. She woke with her head banging, homesick for Bindalong, the scent of gum trees and the chuckling call of a kookaburra or the liquid song of a currawong.

Feeling as if her head were stuffed with cotton-wool, she had no choice but to join the others who were on stand-by that morning. The CO looked at her with a frown.

'Digger, you look like shit, old man. That cold not clearing?'

She dug up a smile. 'You know how to make a bloke feel good about himself, sir, if you don't mind me saying.'

He grunted. 'I don't want you flying if you're as under par as you look.'

'In that case, half the squadron would be permanently on sick leave looking at the ugly mugs in here.' She turned the smile up a notch to a grin. 'I'll be right, sir.'

'I hope so, Digger. If it doesn't improve in the next couple of days, I want you to see the doc. That's an order.'

'Right, sir.' She dropped her gaze. It wouldn't happen. 'If this bloody weather would improve, it might help.'

'Depressing, isn't it?'

'Bloody right, sir, and makes our job even more difficult.'

'Well, let's hope the Huns think it's just as difficult and stay at home.'

The phone rang and the marquee fell silent. Toby Cranston looked up from his newspaper and nodded to Stephen Collingwood-Smythe who happened to be nearest.

'Get that, would you.'

Stephen picked up the receiver, listened and jotted something on a pad. He put the phone back in its cradle.

'Three needed to check out a sighting of possible bandits just south of Bristol.'

'Right, Red Section, you're on. Good luck, chaps.'

The pilots in Red Section swallowed the dregs of their tea and disappeared out into the foggy morning. Bella would rather have gone with them than be left to let the day drag on, but poured another mug of tea and sat as close to the fire as she could get, with a two-day-old newspaper on her lap. Perhaps she could catch a few winks of sleep at least.

She fell into a doze, and woke to someone shaking her shoulder. 'Come on, Digger, we're off.'

Struggling to make sense of what was being said, she put her head in her hands for a moment, then dragged her fingers through her hair and stood up, stretching and trying to clear her head.

'What's going on?'

'A dozen or more spotted down along the coast,' TC said. 'Let's see if we can chase the buggers back across the Channel, shall we?'

He quickly gave orders for where he wanted everyone to fly and the group pulled on their thickest jackets over the Sidcot suits they already wore. Grabbing parachutes, flying helmets and gloves, they were ready to go in a couple of moments.

Running up to where her ground crew had already pulled out her Spitfire, Bella was helped with her parachute and then into the neat space of the cockpit. She worked automatically as she performed the pre-flight checks, gave the okay to the two men on the ground and started the engine.

Rolling out into her place alongside the others she glanced to her left and gave her number two the thumbs-up, then taxied onto the runway. Nine Spitfires all taking off at the same time was always a thrill, and her spirits rose as they left the ground, made a long loop and headed south in formation.

Her head cleared, she forgot about her cough, and settled down to the business in hand, hearing ground control give the last co-ordinates of the enemy planes and which direction they were headed. Setting a course to hopefully intercept them, she cursed the cloud. They flew low, keeping just below the blanket of white, but even so visibility was poor. Rain ran off the Perspex hood and Bella's eyes ached from concentrating on seeing where they were going.

Trying to see anything in this is going to be impossible. It's like trying to find that bloody needle in a haystack.

Looking down, she made out a white line of surf as they crossed the coast.

Her radio crackled.

'Fuck, it's going to be even harder now.'

'What's that, Blue Two?'

'Nothing, Blue Two, just letting off steam. This cloud is making our job impossible. Keep as high as you can, chaps. I don't want anyone taking a bath today.'

She could barely make out the two planes alongside her, and for a moment felt lonely. It was easy to imagine she was the only plane in the sky on a day like this. A pain built behind her eyes and made her head feel like someone was hitting it with a hammer. She would love to close her eyes and rest them for a moment. Shaking her head, she stared all around as a dim gleam escaped the clouds and briefly lit up the water three hundred feet below.

A flash of something made her sit up and stare harder. Was that a cockpit hood catching a ray? The cloud covered the gleam and it was gone, but she could see a little further, the weather was clearing slightly.

Come on. Come on, show me where you are.

Another tiny break and another ray hit the water, and there they were. A group flying almost down to ground level, nothing much more than shadows, relying on the dreadful conditions to protect them.

TC's voice broke in just as Bella was about to report her sighting.

'Magpie, this is Blue Leader, I have eyes on bandits at six o'clock, heading south. They must be on the home run. They're almost swimming, the sneaky buggers.'

'Blue Leader, how many?'

'At least five. Bloody visibility is still not helping.'

'Good spot, Blue Leader. Try and creep up on the buggers. Give 'em what for.'

TC raised his voice over the r/t. 'Tally ho, chaps. Let's go.'

They were above and behind the German planes. Bella could see now they were ME109s, and smiled. None of them had made any evasive manoeuvres and seemingly had no idea they were about to get pounced on.

'Blue Leader, I'm taking that bugger on the right, who has broken formation a bit. Teach him to sit tight on his leader's arse. Blue Three, keep a lookout for any other bandits lurking above and behind us, will you?'

'Roger, Blue Two.'

She pushed the stick forward, dropping lower and speeding up, keeping the Messerschmitt she had spotted out on the wing in her sights. Jonty Hart, one of the latest replacement pilots, flew Blue Three on her left, slightly behind her, and stayed with her until they were directly behind the German planes, then latched onto one at the back of the group.

The enemy planes suddenly split and began twisting and spiralling, desperately climbing to try and escape the Spits. Jonty stuck to the tail of his enemy and Bella hoped he would get through the day unscathed. Then she gave all her attention to her own job, she couldn't help him, they were all on their own. The German planes were so low already there was no hope of diving to get out of trouble and Bella followed her target doggedly, as he twisted and spun, staying with him and firing as soon as she could, before he disappeared into the cloud and would be lost.

She hated being so low, there was no room to play with; all she could do was try to stay a little above him, so he had to remain under the clouds. Sticking to his tail, she let off bursts of fire, every few seconds, and saw the puffs as she hit his fuselage. Grey-white smoke erupted and became a trail as glycol leaked out. She'd caused damage, but not enough to put him out of action.

She was sweating, throwing the Spit around as she doggedly stuck with the German. One last round and she had him. The nose of the 109 dipped and the plane went into a dive. Something had gone catastrophically wrong, either with the controls, or maybe she had hit the pilot.

'Bail out,' she muttered.

The plane had less than three hundred feet before it hit the water. The pilot had no chance to get out in time. It went in nose first and sank immediately. No hope for the poor bugger.

There was no time to ponder, she was dangerously close to getting wet herself. Pulling hard on the stick, sweating with the effort, she grunted as the G force hit her stomach with the sudden change of direction. The Spitfire climbed and in a moment she was back up at cloud level. The sky was empty.

She could only assume the 109s had either had the chance to hide in the clouds, or else turned on the juice and high-tailed it for home. She got on the r/t and reported she was heading home with a confirmed kill under her belt.

Another young man on the bottom of the sea, joining so many others in a watery grave.

Chapter 35

Jennifer

Arriving at the cottage the next evening, I was surprised to find it in darkness, the undrawn curtains at the windows casting accusatory stares at me. A shiver of anxiety ran through me and I hurried up the path to the back door, finding it half open.

'Grandpa?' I ran into the kitchen and across the small hall to the living room. It was empty, though the fire was laid in the stove – Mary, the carer who came in each morning to help, would have set it ready to light. 'Grandpa,' I called again, trying to stem the rising sense of worry.

A movement caught the edge of my vision and I whipped round. The cat rose from the window seat, yawned and stretched, giving me a dirty look before hopping down and leaving me to my worrying.

I ran upstairs and found both bedroom doors and the bathroom door closed. Drawing a breath, I tapped on Grandpa's bedroom door, and opened it quietly, hoping he was just having a snooze. Not wanting to disturb him, but needing to know. It was empty, the bed tidily made, his dressing gown and slippers at their usual stations. With a rising sense of panic, I barged open the two other doors to find both rooms empty as well.

Racing downstairs again, I checked the sunroom and as I was about to leave noticed the cat again, sitting beside a lumpen shape in the deepening shadows of the back garden.

'No, no, no.' I reached him in seconds, and knelt beside his unmoving body, taking his hand in mine, trying to rub the cold out of it. I dragged my phone out and hit 999, waiting for what seemed like an age before the operator asked which service I wanted. We had a quick conversation while I gave her the details and she said an ambulance would be on its way immediately. 'Grandpa. Grandpa, can you hear me? Please, wake up, come on, come on.' I leant into him and put a finger on his neck, where I felt a tiny beat. 'Thank God, oh thank God, come on, Grandpa, please wake up, please.'

I ran back inside, took the duvet off his bed and found a thick woollen plaid blanket in the sunroom, raced back and wrapped them around Grandpa's still body, tucking the blanket as far under him as I could. Using the torch on my phone I tried to see if he had hurt himself, but found no sign of injury. His face was white, shadows turning it cadaverous in the light of the torch. I put my jacket under his head and brushed the thin white hair back from his cold forehead. Lying beside him, I wrapped my arms around him, hoping the heat from my body might help to warm him.

Was it a heart attack, or a stroke? Had he slipped and banged his head? Whatever had happened, I didn't know how long he had lain there, unconscious and growing colder with every moment.

It seemed an age until I heard a siren and through the sunroom windows saw flashing blue lights coming along the lane. I crawled out from under the covers and went to meet the paramedics.

By the time the ambulance reached hospital, Grandpa had been hooked up to fluids and his vital signs had improved a little. His body temperature was better but his pulse and blood pressure were weak and low. I followed in my car after sending Peter a message telling him what had happened.

I remained in the waiting area while Grandpa was whisked away on a trolley. I spent the time pacing up and down, trying to stay positive, fighting black thoughts crowding in and sucking me down.

Eventually, a doctor, who looked no older than my children, appeared and ushered me into a small office.

'Will my grandfather live?' were the first words out of my mouth.

The doctor gave me a kind look.

'He is comfortable and stable, for the moment,' she said. 'He's remarkably robust for a man of his years, but it will take a while for him to recover.'

'Was it a stroke? His heart?'

'We can't find any sign of either a stroke or cardiac problems. His blood pressure is very low, though, and I suspect he may have become dizzy and fallen. There's a bump on his head, and evidence of slight concussion.'

'Is he conscious?'

'He is, though confused and exhausted.'

'Can I see him?'

'Yes, but only for a few minutes. He needs to rest.' The doctor rose and held the door for me. 'Five minutes, no more.'

Hurrying along a corridor to a small room, I entered as quietly as possible in case I disturbed him. Grandpa lay on his back, eyes closed, his face pale, cheeks hollow. He seemed to have shrunk, and looked so vulnerable I blinked back tears and swallowed a sob.

I don't care what Peter says, he's coming back to live with us.

I pulled a chair across to his bedside, sat and watched him. After a moment he opened his eyes and looked at me.

'Hello, Jenny Wren.' He knew me, which was something. I took his hand, warm now, thank goodness. 'How did I end up here with a sore head?'

'I hoped you could tell me, Grandpa. I found you on the garden path, unconscious.'

He closed his eyes again and frowned. 'Goodness, that must have been a shock. Are you all right?'

Thinking of me, rather than himself. Typical.

'Never mind me. How do you feel?'

'Bit woozy, to be honest, old girl.'

'The doc said I can't stay more than a few minutes; you need to rest. I'll pop back to your cottage and bring you some pyjamas and so on.'

His eyes opened.

'But I'll be home by tomorrow, won't I? No need to put you to any bother.'

'Grandpa, I think they'll want to keep you in for a wee while, until you're a bit more yourself,' I said, gently. 'And it isn't a bother, at all.'

He opened his mouth as if to argue, but then heaved a sigh and nodded slightly.

'As you wish. I do feel a little tired.'

'I should go and let you sleep.' Noticing his watch and glasses lying on a small shelf beside his bed, I picked them up and put them in my bag, thinking I would take them with me and keep them safe. I rose and kissed his cheek. 'I'll be back in the morning.'

I left, fighting tears again. It seemed impossible to think I might lose him, so soon after Ben.

At home, exhaustion hit. Peter took one look at me, sat me down and gave me a large mug of tea.

'You need to eat,' he said. It was the furthest thing from my mind. 'You're no help to anyone if you fall apart. Let me make you an omelette or something.' I almost laughed and he caught my expression. 'What? I can make an omelette – at least, I used to be able to. Soup then? I can at least open a tin.'

I rose and went and put my arms around him, laying my head against his chest.

'Thank you. Soup will be lovely,' I said, inhaling the familiar smell of him. 'Where's Rosie? Have you told her?'

Peter shook his head.

'She's been out all afternoon, so I haven't spoken to her. I thought it was best to wait until you got back and could tell us how your grandfather is.' He took my shoulders and held me away from him, scanning my face, his eyes anxious behind his glasses. 'I'm sorry I've been so stubborn about having him live with us. I feel awful that he was hurt and nobody found him for goodness knows how long.' He let go of me and dragged his hands through his hair. 'If you hadn't gone to see him, he could have lain there all night.'

'But I did go, and have been going every day these past months.' I managed a small smile. 'Does this mean we're not going to have another fight over him coming here? Because it's all I've been thinking about since I found him.'

'No, we're not going to fight about it anymore.'

'Thank you.' I blinked back tears and kissed his cheek. 'Now, where's that soup? It's not often my husband makes my supper, I can't wait.'

Grandpa shook his head when I said I wanted him to come and live with us.

'That's very kind of you to offer, Jenny Wren, but I'm happy in my cottage, thank you. Who'll look after my garden if I'm not there?'

'Grandpa, I'm worried about you. I know you want to remain independent, and I respect that, but what if I hadn't come to see you the other day? You might have lain in the garden all night until Mary arrived the next morning, and probably would have died of hypothermia.' My voice rose and I had to pause and pull in a breath. I sounded more like a nagging wife than a concerned granddaughter, so I continued in a gentler vein. 'Please, come and stay. At least while you're recuperating. You can have your own sitting room, so we won't bother you unless you want us to, and I promise to take you over to your garden every day, if needs be.'

A forlorn expression crossed his face and I felt mean for pushing him. I could understand his wish to keep living the life he had built for himself since Grandma died, it must feel as if he was no longer in control.

Was Peter right? Was I a control freak who had to interfere in everything? His words had been thrown at me in drunken anger, but it didn't mean they weren't true.

Grandpa was silent for so long, I wondered if he had lost the thread of our conversation. Eventually, he sighed and raised his eyes to meet mine.

'I suppose it makes sense,' he said. 'I'm just a stubborn old man who likes to think he's still capable. These past few days have proved that isn't the case.' His voice grew husky and he cleared his throat. 'I promised myself I would never leave my home unless it was in a box. The reality is somewhat different, eh, old girl?'

'Does that mean you'll come?'

He nodded and tried to smile. 'Shall we call it an extended visit?'

I hugged him and kissed his cheek.

'We can call it whatever you want, I'm just happy you've agreed to stay.'

Chapter 36

Bella

Gowling put his head around the door of the mess, where Bella was eating a late breakfast after an early sortie which had been a false alarm. An overly skittish coastal watch thinking they had spotted a flight of enemy bombers, which turned out to be RAF.

'Digger, the boss wants you in his office.'

She lifted her head, pulse beating a little quicker as always, when she was singled out.

'Thanks, adj. Can I finish my breakfast first, or is it urgent?'

'You know the boss. Doesn't like to be kept waiting.'

She slurped the last of her coffee, rose with a piece of toast in her hand and made her way across the parade ground to the offices, munching as she walked in the early spring sunshine.

What could he want? She had done nothing out of line, so far as she could remember. The lead weight in her belly at the thought of being found out made her regret the extra coffee and toast she'd thrown down her throat.

Squadron Leader Henderson's door was open, and she knocked then waited until he raised his eyes from the papers he was perusing and nodded for her to enter.

'You wanted to see me, sir?'

'Yes, Digger, come in and take a seat, old man.'

Would she ever get used to that most English of terms? The boss was not an officer to stand on formalities, but 'old man' and 'old chap' always brought a smile to her face.

She sat opposite him. This was out of the ordinary, so must be something official. Her stomach clenched.

The CO looked across at her, his face serious.

'You've been a great asset to the squadron, Digger.' He stopped and cleared his throat.

Fuck, what was he going to say? Surely, they weren't grounding her?

'Thank you, sir.' Her voice sounded tinny and far away.

'Sixty-six Squadron over at Ibsley need a flight commander, tout de suite. One of theirs bought it a day ago. Your orders are to go and take over.'

Bella stared at him.

'Excuse me, sir?'

'You're moving on, young man. You've been promoted and not before time, I might add. 66's gain is our loss.'

The CO rose and stuck his hand out. Bella slowly stood, not sure her legs would support her, and shook his hand, then saluted. He continued to talk, going over the arrangements of her departure. She barely took any of it in.

Part of her wanted to laugh at the absurdity of it all. Mostly, she wanted to scream, run away and hide.

Fuck.

The next twenty-four hours passed in a whirl of packing, goodbyes and travel arrangements.

She found time to dash off a letter to Johnnie, needing to vent her anxiety to someone who would understand. The one bright moment was when she remembered Ibsley was where he had been posted to. It made the move seem somewhat serendipitous.

She was given a final night send-off of too much drink and maudlin speeches by the CO and her friends. Stephen Collingwood-Smythe got very drunk, came over and threw an arm around her neck.

'I hope we can let bygones be bygones, old chap. I don' care if yer not *you know who*,' he said, with an exaggerated wink. 'You're the bes' pilot here. I'll miss you.'

Heat prickled in Bella's scalp and she held her breath. Please God, don't let him let the cat out of the bag at this late stage.

'Stephen, for a man who nearly killed half our own men, you've turned into a bloody good pilot yourself. Look after yourself, mate.' She raised her tankard of beer and saluted him with it, then leant in and whispered in his ear. 'If you ever let on, I will find you and shoot you myself.'

His face paled for a moment, until she winked and grinned.

'Ha, yes. Very good.'

They clinked tankards again, and Bella hoped he would keep his word.

The next day she drove the little Ford across the country to Ibsley, just south of London. If she had to be transferred anywhere, it was the one place she would have chosen above all others. Johnnie was there – doing what, she had no idea – but to know he was close by made the move bearable. She just hoped they could remain 'mates' in the eyes of everyone else. How she would manage it, she couldn't imagine, but it had to be done.

She reported to the CO, Squadron Leader Vince Morrison, who seemed a decent sort.

'I've heard good things about you, Mr Gardner, from the CO at your old squadron. He says we're lucky to have you.'

Bella kept her eyes on a calendar on the wall behind the CO's desk.

'Thank you, sir, the squadron leader is a kind man to say such things.'

'Well, your record speaks for itself, so no false modesty, young man.' He waved Bella to a chair, and sat down himself. 'In all honesty, the winter has been dire. We've lost too many good men, and those who are left are exhausted and on the verge of burn-out. After losing another flight commander a couple of days ago, the squadron are as down as I've seen them.' He gave her a tired smile. 'I'm hoping you may be the one who can bring us some luck. God knows, we need it.'

Bloody hell.

The last thing she wanted was to be seen as some kind of talisman or good luck charm. The squadrons based in the southeast of England had taken the brunt of the Battle of Britain. The worst of it might be over but there was still plenty to do to keep the skies over Britain free of enemy bombers. It wasn't surprising their pilots were at the end of their tether. What was needed was fresh personnel with good flying experience. Like her – only a hundredfold. Not raw recruits who didn't have the wits to stay alive longer than a few days, or worn-out men with battle fatigue.

She sighed and tried to banish the dread lying in her belly. She had a job to do, and she would do it for as long as she could, as well as she could, until she was told to stop or until she was stopped by a pilot who was better than her.

The CO was still speaking, and she realised she had missed half of what he had said.

'I'll take you over to the mess, and introduce you to anyone who is around. Your batman can take your gear and unpack for you.'

Panic fluttered in her breast.

'Thank you, sir. I would prefer to find my billet first, if that's all right.' She tried a smile. 'I'm a particular sod, who likes things done in a certain way. Why don't I join you in the mess in half an hour and I can meet the rest of the chaps, then?'

He looked at her with a tight-lipped smile; obviously she was upsetting his plans before she had even started.

'Very well,' he said, after a moment. 'Shall we say 1600 hours in the mess?'

She glanced at the wristwatch Johnnie had given her. 'Perfect, sir. Thank you.'

He shouted a command, and an orderly poked his head into the office.

'Show Flight Commander Gardner to his billet, Jenkins.'

'Yes, sir. If you'll follow me, sir.'

Bella saluted the CO, picked up her duffel bag and followed the orderly outside and across to the barracks. Once he showed her where she was billeted, she dismissed him. The room was almost a replica of the one she had had with 92 Squadron, and it didn't take long to unpack her things and hide her own clothes out of sight at the bottom of the wardrobe.

Where did Johnnie spend his days here? He wouldn't have received her letter yet, she realised. She hoped to God he wasn't in the mess when she walked in; he would have almost as big a shock as when she had appeared dressed as Bella in the hospital.

She had that scratchy, nervy feeling she got when she hadn't flown for a while. All she wanted to do was get back in the air and do the job she loved. Being flight commander meant more responsibility. It occurred to her that she knew nothing about being in charge and what it entailed.

She would just have to come clean to the CO and ask for some guidance. The lives of other men were now in her hands. Lives she knew nothing about. The thought hit her as if she had been punched in the stomach, knocking the wind out of her. She flopped down on the bed and wished Johnnie was with her. He would steady her nerves.

For a moment, loneliness engulfed her; a grey cloud of nothingness, through which she couldn't see a way forward. She put her head in her hands.

What was she doing?

She didn't belong here – she was a fraud in every sense of the word. It was impossible, but she had put herself in this situation and would have to get through it as best she could.

As always, she thought of flying and how to get out of the cloud. She could always go low and sneak along at ground level, keeping out of sight and out of trouble. Or, she could climb until she shot out of the murk into the sun where she could see and be seen.

Not the safe option, but then, how many times had she taken the safe route? Where was the fun in that? She belonged above the clouds, and that's where she would stay.

She wandered over to the mess at four o'clock, mentally preparing herself for meeting men who might easily have many more hours of flying experience than she had. Squadron Leader Morrison introduced her to the rest of the pilots and soon she was sitting in a group with a mug of tea in her hand, trying to remember names.

Feeling more relaxed, realising these men were no different to her fellow airmen at 92 Squadron, she could not miss the signs of fatigue and stress on most of the faces. One young man told her it was his first week of operations. His hands shook slightly, making the tea in his mug slop over the top.

'Oh, Lord, I'm such a clumsy oaf,' he said, reddening.

'My first week I almost tipped my coffee down the CO,' Bella said, making up the story, hoping it would help him a little.

His eyes shone a little too brightly.

'Did you feel all at sea? I do. Like everyone else knows the score except me.'

The poor boy looked utterly miserable.

'All you need to remember, is that every single man in this room has been where you are now.' She smiled. 'And you're part of the best air force in the world. Isn't that a wonderful thing? I still kick myself that I'm doing the thing I love more than anything every single day.'

'I was so excited when I got my posting. Somehow, the reality is a lot more daunting.' His face brightened with determination. 'But I will do my very best to be an asset, while I can.'

'Good man. That's all any of us can do.' A sixth sense made her look across the room to where a tall figure stood in the doorway, staring at her. 'Oh. Excuse me . . . James, isn't it? There's someone I should say hello to.'

She rose and tried to appear calm as she walked over to where he remained, his eyes fixed on her.

'Johnnie, how good to see you again, mate. I had no idea you'd been posted here.'

'Hello, Digger, I thought I heard your Aussie twang across the room. What the hell are you doing here? 92 get sick of you?'

She laughed. 'Something like that.'

The CO wandered over to them. 'You two know each other?'

They both nodded. Bella tried to keep her eyes from locking with Johnnie's, sure it would be a give-away that they were far more than friends or acquaintances.

'Went through training, sir, then posted to 92 Squadron together.' Johnnie leant on his stick, shifting his weight. 'Until I had an unfortunate incident and ended up here.' He appeared far more relaxed than Bella felt under the scrutiny of Squadron Leader Morrison. 'Digger here is one of the best pilots you could hope to have in the squadron, sir. We're more than lucky to have him.'

He caught her eye and dropped a quick wink. Bella's face felt as if it was on fire.

'Digger, eh? One doesn't need to be a genius to see where you got that from with your surname.' Johnnie and Bella burst out laughing together. The CO looked from one to the other. 'What did I miss?'

'Sir, Digger comes more from my nationality than my name,' she said. 'Johnnie says I still have my Aussie twang, but perhaps the edge has been rubbed off a bit after spending so much time with you Pommies.'

'It never occurred to me that it fitted your name as well,' Johnnie admitted.

The CO seemed a little put out, harrumphed and wandered away to speak to someone else. They were left to themselves and found a small table to sit at in a quiet corner of the room.

'You might have warned me,' Johnnie said, in a low tone. 'I almost had a fit when I heard your voice.'

'Sorry. I only had twenty-four hours' notice. I wrote to you but things happened so fast the letter will still be on its way.'

'Why are you here, anyway?'

'They lost one of their flight commanders and needed a new one. Guess who's been promoted?'

'Goodness, congratulations. It's well deserved, that's all I can say.'

'Thank you.' She paused. 'You realise I'm completely out of my depth, don't you?'

'You're one of the best in the business. I can't think of anyone more suited to the job.' He gave her a look which sent all the wrong signals to her body. 'Wait until you're up in the air, and you'll forget all the doubts.'

'Stop looking at me like that,' she hissed. 'But thank you. You're probably right. It's down here on the ground that's the problem.' She slid her foot up his leg, making him jump, and raised an eyebrow. 'Anyway, how are you? Is being part of the ground staff horribly boring?'

'I'm very well, considering,' he said. 'The leg is a bind, but I get by and I'm a lot better off than many of the poor sods who fell out of the sky.' He rubbed his neck inside his shirt collar, as if he were too warm. 'The job is okay, and at least I'm still useful. They move me around a fair bit. At present I'm in Control, so you might hear my dulcet tones on the r/t from time to time.'

'You realise this is going to be torture?' She butted in, voicing her thoughts. 'How can I pretend to be your mate when all I want to do is fall into bed with you?'

'Shhh. Bloody hell, old man, keep it down.' He sat back in his chair and perused her face and body. 'Seeing you like this – in uniform, as part of the squadron – makes it easy to think of you as Digger. I called you old man just like I always did.'

'Well, I'm glad you think it's so easy. I'll have to avoid you like the plague, it's the only way I'll stay sane.' She rose. 'I suppose I should go and talk to some of my new colleagues.' Bending slightly, she whispered, 'What I would prefer is to feel your hands on my body, and your mouth kissing me in parts only you know.'

Johnnie's mouth dropped open and his face flushed scarlet. She smiled and raised her eyebrows. That would teach him to think of her as a man.

Chapter 37

Jennifer

While Grandpa remained in hospital, Peter and I cleared out my office and set up the desk in a corner of the dining room. It wasn't perfect, but the only other space was Ben's bedroom and I definitely wasn't ready to take that step.

We brought Grandpa's favourite armchair from the cottage, plus one or two of his other bits and pieces, his television and a load of books. I hoped it would help him feel at home and settled. The spare bedroom and its en-suite bathroom were right next door and the kitchen just along the hall. With Rosie still knocking about and Peter working in his office all day, there would be people around should Grandpa need help or want company.

Peter's doubts about having him live with us seemed to have disappeared – or at least he accepted that Grandpa needed a bit of extra support. The two men had always had a good rapport, so I hoped the extra pressure of living under the same roof didn't alter that.

When he was allowed out of hospital and I brought him home – after a diversion to check on his vegetable garden – I found my pulse racing as if I'd run a marathon when I pulled up in the drive. Grandpa sat next to me staring at our house as if he had never seen it before and he was about to be committed to prison or something. My heart ached for him – perhaps it was exactly how he was feeling – that he had lost his independence and freedom, and was expected to live according to our rules from now on.

'I know this isn't what you want, and I understand how hard it is for you to accept,' I said. 'I promise we'll only come and "visit" you when you want us to. You can have as much or as little privacy as you want, it's totally up to you. If you don't want to eat when we do that's fine, whatever works for you is okay with me.'

He put a hand over mine on the steering wheel.

'You don't need to worry, Jenny Wren. I've had plenty of time to think while I've been laid up. Sometimes we have to accept the inevitable, and I know living on my own is a thing of the past.' He gave me a rueful smile. 'I'm fortunate to have you all willing to put up with an old codger like me in your home. There's one thing, though. I seem to have mislaid my watch and glasses. Have you seen them?'

'Oh, sorry, Grandpa, I completely forgot. I picked them up the night you were admitted to hospital. If you look in my bag, there, you'll find them.' I felt a twinge of guilt at taking his things and not telling him. 'I noticed your watch strap is getting very loose. Would you like me to take it to a jeweller and have them take a couple of links out of the strap? I would hate you to lose it – I've never known you wear another one. It's like it's part of you.'

He lifted the watch out of the bag, rubbed the back gently as if he were stroking it and, gazing fondly at the ancient timepiece, shook his head.

'This was given to me a very long time ago. It would be wrong to change it.' He heaved a sigh that seemed full of sad resignation and yet again, I was filled with guilt at making him give up his independence. Then he lifted his eyes to meet mine and there was a shadow of his usual grin. 'Now, why are we still sitting in the car? I could murder a cup of tea and a piece of Rosie's gingerbread.'

I grinned, hoping he didn't notice my unshed tears.

'Coming right up, sir. Let's get you in and comfortable and you can have as much cake as you want.'

When it came down to it, we all adjusted to Grandpa living with us remarkably quickly. From a purely selfish point of view, it made my work days far easier, as I could go straight home and spend as much time as both of us wanted with him. Rosie became chief tea and coffee maker and moved on to being Grandpa's partner in crime when it came to his nightly dram of Scotch.

Peter went about his daily routine as if there wasn't an extra body in the house, which didn't surprise me. His ability to bury himself in work had long since ceased to be a source of friction. I had conceded that battle years ago when I realised that, for all intents and purposes, I was a single parent during the working week. Peter's single-minded passion for his research came before everything else.

I wondered if it was part of the reason Ben's death hit him so hard. He had missed out on so much family life and now it was too late.

It took Grandpa a few weeks to recuperate from his fall. He became exhausted quickly and seemed content to sit and read or watch TV, even though the weather was beautiful. I offered to take him down to his garden as often as I or Rosie could, but he waved my suggestion away, saying he would go another day. In the meantime, I took matters into my own hands and spoke to the neighbour who owned the cat. She promised to keep an eye on his cottage and take care of the vegetable garden until he was ready. I wondered if he dreaded going back? Was he afraid that if he returned to his cottage he would find it too hard to leave again? He didn't seem to be missing it, but it was hard to read him, at times.

Meanwhile, I didn't raise the subject of our unknown pilot again. The less stress Grandpa was put under, the sooner he would recover fully. All that could wait – even though I was itching to get to the bottom of the mystery.

Chapter 38

Bella

Bella had no time to worry about anything, as her wing was on stand-by from seven o'clock the next morning. She had been allocated Red Flight, which had lost its flight commander in their last sortie over the Channel. Following the two pilots she would be leading down to dispatch as dawn was breaking, it all seemed so familiar she wondered why she had been in such a state of panic the day before.

She introduced herself to her ground crew and carefully checked over the Spitfire she had been given. Putting her hand on the nosecone felt the same as handling a strange horse for the first time. Each one was different and she wished she had the time to take her new beast for a trial spin before taking off into battle. Would it list to one side? Was the throttle stiff, or would it be as skittish as a nervous horse? She would find out soon enough.

The two members of Red Flight, Tom Furniss and Alan Broadbent, seemed fine men. She had bought them each a beer the evening before, and had a chat with them. Tom was a sergeant pilot from the Black Country, with an accent she found hard to understand. He seemed as steady as any of the chaps she had flown alongside in 92 Squadron. Alan was a Yorkshireman with a chip on his shoulder, grumbling about the north–south divide to her within a few minutes of their being introduced. She suspected he thought he should have been made up to flight commander.

At least they had plenty of flying hours under their belts.

Their first sortie was rung through just after 7.30am. Possible sighting of enemy aircraft crossing the south coast.

'Now where do you think they'll be heading?' Bella asked, as the three of them ran from the dispatch hut to their planes, already being prepared for take-off by the ground crews.

'Who knows?' Tom said between breaths as he ran.

They took off together, flying alongside one another, wing-tips almost touching. Bella immediately relaxed and hummed to herself as she became accustomed to the new Spitfire. She had spent so long in the one she had flown with 92 that it felt strange at first, but this new machine was well tuned and didn't seem to have any peculiarities. Perhaps a touch heavy on one side, the wing having a tendency to dip if she relaxed too much. She adjusted the trim and made a mental note to let the boys on the ground know.

Reaching the south coast, they stayed high, each of them looking out for German planes. The sky was clear and as the sun climbed higher, sweat ran down inside Bella's suit. She put on sunglasses, craning her neck in all directions, trying to spot anything that shouldn't be there.

The three of them began long sweeping turns, crossing the coast and flying inland and then back out to sea, but saw nothing. After they had been up and down the same area twice, she opened the r/t.

'Okay, chaps, it seems like we've missed them – if they were ever here. Let's just head over to Portsmouth and see if the buggers are causing havoc there, shall we?'

They flew west along the coast, seeing nothing out of the ordinary.

Portsmouth looked quiet, the ships in dock looking as placid as rowing boats.

Bella radioed back to Control.

'Gambit, this is Red Leader. No sighting of enemy planes. No sighting of anything. Turning for home.'

'Roger, Red Leader. Come on back.'

She felt the drop in adrenaline as they flew back in perfect spring weather. The clear air gave her visibility as far as she could see, the English countryside a patchwork of browns and every shade of green as it woke from its winter slumbers. Contours flattened out and villages might have been plasticine models. Nothing seemed real.

How easy it would be to keep going, forget about the war for a while and just soar through the air for the hell of it. Everything was simple while she sat in the cockpit and only had to think about flying. Why couldn't the rest of life be so straightforward?

She was glad it wasn't Johnnie's voice on the r/t for her first morning, she needed time to get used to the idea of working on the same base as he did. Knowing he was so close and they couldn't be together filled her mind as she guided the Spit back to Ibsley.

Somehow, they must find a place to go where there was no possibility of anyone recognising them, otherwise she might go mad.

Red Flight had been back at base for two hours when another shout went up. Bombers seen out in the Channel with a phalanx of 109s around them. They would take off with three Hurricanes from a different squadron.

The boys on the ground had re-fuelled the Spits and made sure their armouries were full by the time Bella, Alan and Tom took off again. Tension pulled her stomach into a knot as she was strapped into the cockpit, but as soon as they left the ground and joined the other fighters, she forgot about it and concentrated on finding the enemy planes as quickly as she could.

Setting a course that would, hopefully, intercept the Germans, it only took the Spitfires a few minutes to reach the coast. From the information given it seemed most likely the bombers were heading for the Essex coast, staying out over the water and out of range of coastal defences.

'Right, chaps, keep your eyes peeled – we'll do a sweep along the coast up towards the mouth of the Thames and see if we can spot the buggers.'

'Roger, Red Leader,' came back at her.

The fine, clear conditions had deteriorated and cloud was beginning to build out to sea. Still, there was good enough visibility to see a group of bombers and their guard dogs.

Now, where are you?

Bella scanned the sky around her, above and below. They were flying at fifteen thousand feet; above the wispy clouds but still able to see the ground. She checked behind her, giving Alan a thumbs-up where he flew on her right flank.

Ten minutes of searching and Bella began to think they had guessed wrong. Perhaps the bombers were away to the west, dropping their deadly loads on part of London. This was where she felt out of her depth, hadn't had the experience of making decisions that might be the difference between life and death for people on the ground as well as in the air.

'Red Leader, this is Red Two. Bandits, nine o'clock at angels ten.'

Bella fixed her gaze below and to her left-hand side. There they were, just as Alan had said, flying at ten thousand feet. Four Junkers with their cohort of three 109s just above.

Unaware of the hunters above them.

She quickly craned her neck and looked straight up, checking there wasn't additional cover of more Messerschmitts higher up. But the cloud had steadily grown and she could see nothing past a couple of hundred feet above her.

Well, if I can't see anything, neither can they.

'Okay, those bandits haven't seen us yet. Let's go and surprise them.'

Within a moment, the three Spits and the Hurricanes dropped out of the sky and latched on to the enemy planes, Bella picking out one on the outer edge of the group.

The Luftwaffe pilot immediately climbed and spun, trying to get above and behind to regain the advantage, but Bella stayed with him, sitting the Spitfire on its tail and following the 109's every move, rolling over and above and coming down directly behind him. Her guns already primed, she aimed and fired, hanging on to every evasive move he made, keeping her bursts short to conserve ammunition.

Out of the corner of her eye, she saw one of the Junkers on fire and spiralling out of the sky into the water. Two tiny figures appeared with open parachutes. The rest of the crew went into the water with their plane. She had no time to feel anything, the 109 pilot still keeping up his twisting and turning, spinning and diving, trying everything to get away from her.

'No, you bloody don't,' she muttered, spraying another burst into the fuselage. A flicker came from the engine, which grew into a red flame, quickly engulfing the plane.

Bella watched as the 109 fell into a death dive straight into the sea. It could have been something on a cinema screen; nothing to do with her, her mind detached from the reality of what had just happened. She pulled her gaze away as the plane disappeared below the steel grey water and climbed back up to ten thousand feet, searching for another target. The Germans were in disarray, one bomber lost, another with half a wing missing and pitching to one side. Alan, though, had a 109 above him on his tail, and seemed unaware of the danger he was in as he clung doggedly to the Messerschmitt he had in his sights.

She climbed another thousand feet and made a tight turn to come in above and behind the 109 close enough to see its number. She chuckled that she was fourth in a line of deadly firepower and hoped there wasn't another German on *her* tail. The pilot in front of her suddenly realised he was in her sights and set his plane on its end and went into a steep climb. She was ready for him and stuck as close as she could, imitating every move he made, the pair of them rolling and diving, almost stalling, throwing the planes to the edge of their structural integrity.

Bella's arms and shoulders ached, sweat pouring off her as she tried to out-fly her adversary. He was good. A much better pilot than the first one she had shot down. This man had all the tricks up his sleeve, but her own reflexes and ability matched him. She clung on as if she were on a horse hell-bent on getting rid of her and stamping her into the ground; diving, climbing, spinning, rolling, they shot across the sky, neither in a position to fire a shot, intent on getting the upper hand but too evenly matched to outdo each other.

She was tiring, her reflexes slowing with fatigue. She had never come up against an opponent like this one. Bella knew she couldn't keep going much longer, but all she could do to survive was carry on in the deadly dance until one of them made a mistake.

She gritted her teeth. It would not be her. Not today, not any day. Taking a hand off the stick for a second, she wiped the sweat out of her eyes with the silk scarf draped around her neck, then groaned as her adversary fell into a steep turning dive. Well, she could stay with him for as long as he wanted to keep playing this game.

She spun the Spit and followed him, pushing the plane to its limits.

'Go home, you fucker,' she yelled into the confines of the cockpit, the screaming noise of the Merlin engine blanketing her voice. 'I'm not giving up.'

The 109 kept diving, its speed increasing until both planes were flying so fast Bella thought she might not be able to turn and climb before hitting the water.

'Pull up, you fool. Pull UP.'

She knew she could turn the Spit on a sixpence but the water was rapidly getting closer and the 109 needed more space to climb out of such a dive than her plane.

The thought of such a good pilot diving to his death was beyond her, but she didn't pull up. If he wanted to play chicken, she was more than ready to do that.

At the last possible second, just as she was sure he would never make it, the German pilot pulled out of the dive. She was almost too late, so astonished at his prowess that all she could do was watch. Coming to her senses, she threw the Spitfire out of the dive, the plane shuddering as if it would stall, while she hung on to the stick with all her remaining strength and waited for the gut-wrenching lurch as it went from a near-vertical dive into an almost vertical climb.

Almost skimming the waves, the Spitfire pulled away, and she blew a huge breath of relief. High above, the Messerschmitt waggled his wings at her and shot away back out to sea.

'Bastard,' she said. 'You nearly had me. We may meet again, mate, and next time, I'll have you. This is not over.'

Chapter 39

Jennifer

After all the relief of Grandpa recovering and the upheaval of him moving in, things went back to what had become the norm for us as a family. It felt as if Peter and I were living half a life, getting through each day the best way we knew how. Rosie spent as much time as she could with Scott, their friendship deepening into a close-knit bond, which at least made me smile.

Scott continued to volunteer for us, and eventually I persuaded Dominic to put him on the books. He applied to study archaeology and I wrote a reference for him and gave him a hand with his personal statement. He deserved a chance at a new life and I hoped he was happy and successful.

As summer progressed, the anniversary of Ben's death lay like a black hole ahead of us, dragging us all in, sucking the life out of us. There was no possibility of avoiding it, but it threatened to undo everything our family had managed to achieve over the past few months, and send us back to the broken people we had become after we lost him.

Lost.

Such an odd word to use to describe death – it made me think of misplaced instead of dead, but in our case it fitted. We *had* lost him, there was no body to bury, no grave to mourn beside. Knowing he was lying at the bottom of an avalanche entombed in ice, moving at an infinitesimal rate in the glacier that had taken his life was something I could not begin to contemplate.

Peter and Rosie had withdrawn again, just as I had, the three of us living in our heads, passing each other with eyes focused on the floor, unable to look at the pain in each other's faces. Grandpa stayed in his sitting room, watching cricket or racing or some other mindless programme on TV, with the sound down.

It was Scott who came to our rescue and made us face the reality of life now. He and Rosie had been out for a walk with the dogs, and I guess she had said something to him because when they got home he took charge.

'Rosie, put the kettle on, your family need to sit down together and talk,' he said. 'Jen, go and fetch your granddad and Peter.'

I bridled at his tone, speaking to me as if I were one of the men he had been in charge of. I was tired, my head hurt, and all I wanted was to lie down, close my eyes and make the world go away.

'Why? What is there to talk about?'

Scott looked at me with a kind gaze.

'Okay. *I* want to talk to you. To all of you,' he said. 'Please, I want to help, if I can.'

I shrugged and went to find the menfolk, both of whom had to be dragged out of their respective hiding places. When we were all sat around the table nursing mugs of tea in silence, Scott cleared his throat and began to speak.

'When I came back from Afghanistan, I was broken in both my body and my mind, and all I wanted to do was join my mates who'd been killed. Why was I the one who had got away with still being alive? Dying seemed so much easier than struggling to get through each day – and I did struggle, massively. I spent the hours when my physio wasn't torturing me inventing ways to take my own life . . .' Rosie made a small sound in her throat and I caught her surreptitiously wiping her eye. Scott put his hand over hers and squeezed gently. 'I know it's tough to hear – it's still hard to acknowledge that it's how I felt, but it's true. I was diagnosed with PTSD, which is a major problem in ex-service personnel, especially if they have seen action.'

Grandpa nodded at Scott's words, his face a grim mask.

Scott continued. 'The Marines do a lot to help those who can no longer serve, but there's plenty still to do. It's why projects like yours, Jen, are so important. They help bring us back together, give us a purpose.'

I managed a ghost of a smile. I had seen the positive effects for myself over the past few months. Scott was a different person to the withdrawn, sarcastic man he had been when he started.

'I'm glad we could help you and some of the others who volunteered.'

He inclined his head.

'What has this to do with us on a personal level, though?'

'My parents, and the parents of my mates who lost their lives, went through the same grieving process you're going through. I survived, but my folks could see the effect my injuries had on me, and grieved almost as if I had died.' He stopped again, staring into his mug of tea as if choosing his next words. 'Thing is, I got some great help from a guy who understood what I was going through – the grief and the guilt, the disconnect and frustration, the feeling of uselessness, the rage – and much more than that. The one thing he made me realise was that everything I went through had happened while I was living my dream. Being a Royal Marine was all I ever wanted to do, and I wouldn't have changed it for the world, even if I had known how it ended before I joined.' Now he looked up and fixed us all with his gaze. 'Yes, I was broken. Yes, I was devastated that I could no longer do what

I loved doing, but did I regret being a bootneck?' He shook his head. 'Not for one moment.'

There was silence around the table.

Grandpa broke it. 'I understand. I flew Spits for less than a year, and had countless friends killed or maimed during the war, as well as almost losing my own life, but have never felt more alive than I did during those few months.'

Scott smiled at him and nodded.

'I suppose what I'm trying to say is that my parents eventually came to accept that I was lucky enough to do the thing I had always dreamt of. Yes, they grieved for me and with me, but the anger they felt because my life was changed – for the worse in their eyes – they had to let go of, just as I had to.' He shrugged. 'Life goes on, and I couldn't bear the thought of my misfortune making their lives a misery. I chose to be a Royal Marine and am proud to still be one today. Ben chose to be a mountaineer, and from what I've learnt about him from you all, he died doing exactly what he wanted to do, living his best life and being fucking good at it. I reckon he would hate to see you like this.'

'He was twenty-one,' Peter said, his eyes cold and hard as he stared at Scott. 'Don't tell me I can't mourn my only son when he had his whole life ahead of him.' He slammed his mug down and stood up, shoving his chair so hard it fell backwards with a clatter. Deefa woke from his sleep, jumped up and began barking. 'Shut the fuck up, Deefa,' he yelled and the poor dog slunk back to his basket.

Rosie's face paled at his outburst, though it didn't entirely surprise me. Peter had been winding up to some kind of blow-out for days. I got up from my chair and went around the table to him, standing in the way of him leaving. I had no intention of letting him go back to the closed-in shell of a man he had been up until a few weeks ago. We had made progress as a couple and as a family. Of course, it was going to be impossibly difficult with the anniversary around the corner, but if we were to get past it we needed each other.

'Peter, please,' I said, laying a hand on his shaking arm. 'Scott's right in that we have to find a way to live without Ben. We can't go on avoiding each other, treading on eggshells, not mentioning his name in case it upsets us.'

'So, you'd rather we just carry on as if nothing has happened.' His tone was bitter. 'I can't do that, even if you can.'

I swallowed the lump in my throat and tried not to say something I might regret.

'Of course not. I'll never forget him. He's come to me every single night since he disappeared, it's impossible to get him out of my mind,' I snapped, then clamped my mouth shut.

I had never mentioned my dreams to anyone so far.

Breathe, Jen.

'But we have to survive as a family, too. What sort of legacy would it be to Ben, if we broke apart?'

Peter bowed his head, righted the chair and sat down again. 'Why didn't you tell me?'

I shook my head and shrugged. How could I possibly explain? I went back to my seat and dropped into it. Grandpa took my hand and gave it a gentle squeeze which almost undid what little self-control I still had.

'Please, you two. Could you not fight over Ben's memory?' Rosie's voice broke into my self-pity. 'Of course, we're always going to remember him. He was unforgettable. Brave, funny, outstanding at how much he achieved in the time he had.' Her lower lip quivered and she took a ragged breath. I could see how much effort it took her to stay calm. 'My brother deserves more than us drowning in a self-induced pity party. It won't bring him back, will it? And I, for one, want to thank Scott for telling us his story, it took guts.'

Her eyes shone as she looked at him, and he smiled back at her.

'I understand how tough it is for you all. And dates like Ben's birthday or the anniversary of his death will be the hardest to bear,' Scott said. 'Have you considered a way to commemorate him? I know you don't have anything physical where you can go and remember him. Is there a special place he loved to go, where you could set a bench or erect a plaque or something? It might help, and I'm sure his friends would appreciate having somewhere to go and remember him.'

We sat in silence digesting his words. The idea appealed to me, and if we could make it happen in time for the first anniversary, it might be something to focus on which would help us cope.

'His favourite place was Greystone Crags,' said Rosie, quietly, almost as if she was talking to herself. 'He loved it there. All his climbing mates still go there, bouldering and top roping and just hanging out.' She looked around the table at us, her voice growing stronger. 'And it's really accessible, so anyone can reach it from the car park, even if they aren't climbers.'

'That sounds like a good place,' Scott said. 'Can I suggest something? Why don't you all go away and come up with a few ideas and then go through them and make a decision?'

We looked at each other and nodded in agreement, though I could see Peter was still struggling. I hoped he would find his way through the turmoil I could see written on his face. We all needed to be onside with this. I glanced at Scott who was looking at Rosie, his soft expression making me want to smile. Rosie had had so much to deal with, not least her parents being unable to cope with their own grief, never mind help with hers. Scott had lifted her out of her depression and given her back to us, and for that I would always be grateful.

Later, as he said goodnight and picked up his jacket, I thanked him.

He waved away my gratitude.

'You'd have worked it out for yourselves, eventually,' he said. 'All I did was pass on what has helped me. What you're going through is awful, and I can't truly understand what it's like to lose a child, but I've seen what it was like for my own parents and how close they came with me.'

'You're a good man, Scott Hudson.'

He shook his head. 'Not really. You've done a massive amount to help me, even though you've been dealing with all of this shit too. You're going through hell and I know how that feels.'

He left, Rosie accompanying him to his car to say goodnight. When she came back in a few minutes later, she hugged me, something she had avoided doing for the past couple of weeks. I folded my arms around her and we rocked gently together for a moment.

'I like him, Mum,' she said.

'I know. I like him too. He's a good guy.'

'I don't think Dad approves though. He's so stuffy and grumpy when Scott's around.'

'You leave your dad to me.' How could I say that it was Rosie who sent Peter into a panic? 'Dad is struggling massively. He bottles it all up, but he'll come round.' I pushed a curl of hair off her forehead. 'And I'll let you in on a secret – I don't think it would matter who you brought home, if it was male, your dad would find some way of disapproving.'

She managed a smile at my words, and nodded her acknowledgement.

'Can we have another fam-con tomorrow evening, when we've all had a think about what we want to do to commemorate Ben?' she said.

'Fam Con? What the heck is that?'

'Fam-con – family confab, family conference, whatever you want it to mean. A get-together to talk about what we're gonna do.'

'Yeah, definitely. We need to make a decision. It's a good idea, I really like the thought of having somewhere that Ben loved as a place to remember him.'

'Do you think we'll ever get over what happened?' Rosie's anxious eyes scanned mine. 'I mean, how can we go back to normal?

Sometimes I wish it was before, and I could unsay all the crap I argued with him about, but then I think those are memories I'll always have, so I guess I should just treasure them, shouldn't I?'

'Oh, Rosie, I don't have any answers for you, love. Does anyone ever, truly get over the death of a loved one? Okay, perhaps if that person is at the end of a long and productive life, we can look back with fondness knowing it was well lived, but for someone as young as Ben?' I shook my head, trying to hold myself together in front of her. 'I don't think a parent can ever fully recover from the death of their child. No one expects to outlive their offspring, it's wrong on so many levels. All I would say, is that you're right to treasure every single memory of your brother, and that includes those you might regret having made.'

She nodded, a glint of tears making her eyes shine.

'It's so hard, isn't it?'

I hugged her again, burying my face in her sweet-smelling hair, my words muffled.

'It's unbearable, but we'll get through it, as a family.'

We got together the following day and found that everyone had more or less the same ideas regarding a memorial for Ben. We would ask the National Trust, who were responsible for Greystone Crags, if we could donate a bench and place it at the top looking out over the High Weald towards the sea.

Another idea had come to me during the night and I put it forward as something else we could do.

'What about donating a chunk of the insurance money to the climbing club towards the cost of a new climbing wall? Ben spent every spare moment there when he was a kid, it's where he fell in love with climbing,' I said. 'They're always fund-raising and I heard their facilities have to be upgraded to comply with the latest Health and Safety standards.'

I hated that we had benefited from Ben's death financially. The money sat untouched, it seemed all wrong to spend it.

Peter put his head on one side, a sure sign he was considering my words. After a few moments, he nodded.

'I think that's a really good idea. Why don't we go the whole hog and set up a trust or something, so it can be used to help other kids who wouldn't have the same opportunities ours have had?'

Within a few minutes the four of us were chipping in with thoughts and ideas as to how and what we could do to make the insurance money a lasting legacy Ben would have been proud of.

I got a notebook and pen and thrust them at Rosie. 'Here. Let's jot down everything so we don't forget it. You can be secretary and keep the minutes.'

She pulled a face at me but took the pad and began scribbling.

'Don't blame me if nobody can read what I've written,' she said with a grimace.

'This is only the beginning,' said Peter. 'We're talking a serious amount of money, so it's going to have to be done properly, with accountants and solicitors. It will probably be best to apply for charitable status or something, don't you think, Jen?'

'Yes, I think so. There's no hurry though, we can look into all the pros and cons, and see what works the best, both for us and the club.'

Grandpa sat, not saying much, but his eyes had a twinkle in them I'd not seen since Ben's disappearance.

'What do you think?' I asked him. 'Is there anything else you think we ought to do?'

He shook his head. 'I think it's a wonderful idea, and Ben would be immensely proud of you all.'

'You too, Grandpa. We're in this as a family, which includes you.'

'Well, I don't know that I can be of much help,' he said. 'But if there is anything I can do, you know you only have to ask.'

I took his hand across the kitchen table, feeling how fragile it was.

'Okay, I think we've made a really good start. Tomorrow, I'll get in touch with the National Trust about the bench. Peter, who's that mate of yours who builds furniture? Do you think he would do us something bespoke?'

'I'll talk to him tomorrow,' he said, tearing a page out of Rosie's notepad and making a note.

I leant over the table and put my hands out either side of me. Rosie, Peter and Grandpa took each other's hands until we were linked in a circle. For the first time the black pit in front of me receded a little and a chink of optimism let in a speck of light.

Chapter 40

Bella

A week or so later, just as the sun rose, Red Flight got into a dogfight with another group of M109s protecting a flight of German bombers heading for the Kent coast. Bella, Tom and Alan were part of a group of nine planes from two different squadrons, and flew at the outer edge of the phalanx.

The sky was misty, with a bank of high cloud threatening to obscure their view. The opposing pilots saw each other at almost the same time and there were a few moments of aerial gymnastics as each side tried to better the other.

Bella peeled off after a plane with familiar markings. She was sure this was the same pilot she had come up against before. He clocked her immediately, flipped his plane into a roll and came up behind her before she had time to react. The tables were turned on her and she had to fly at the limit of her abilities to outmanoeuvre him. It seemed as if he knew what she was going to do almost before she did, and no matter what she tried he stuck to her tail, spattering her with shots, which did little harm, but infuriated her.

Gritting her teeth, she finally managed to shake her enemy off for a second and spun the Spit on its tail so she could get above him. Climbing quickly, she almost stalled as she dropped into a spin and came down behind the German.

'Now I've got you. Let's see how you like being the mouse,' she muttered, lining up her guns and letting off a short burst which went high. 'Fuck, come on, Bella, concentrate dammit.'

Her second burst hit the tail but seemed to make no difference to the Messerschmitt's performance. If anything, it made the pilot raise his game and suddenly she was once again the hunted and not the hunter.

His next shots hit home and Bella felt something thump against her leg. She ignored it, her mind intent on preventing her enemy retaking the upper hand. She knew it wouldn't be long until she ran out of ammunition.

'I'm not letting you get away again, however good you are,' she muttered, twisting away into a dive then barrel-rolling and coming up behind him again. 'Hah, now I've got you. Take that, you German bastard.' She finally found her target and saw a stream of smoke flying out of the engine. The Messerschmitt dropped quickly and then rose again as the pilot fought to keep control of his machine. She couldn't believe it when he swung round and came straight at her, firing all the while. 'Why don't you just die?' she screamed.

Flinging the Spit into a steep climb as bullets peppered her plane, Bella glanced at her fuel gauge. It was dropping rapidly. The fuel tank must have been hit. If she wasn't careful she would end up in the Channel. She felt the change in how the Spit handled, becoming sluggish and heavy on one side. It was no use, she would have to admit he had won this round. Better to get home and live to fight another day than try and beat him with a damaged plane. She just hoped the Luftwaffe pilot would accept her surrender and let her go.

Climbing as high as she dared with the plane so unresponsive, she realised the German was not following her. Had he given up or had one of the others taken him out? Part of her hoped not, there was a connection between them – like two prize-fighters, they had unfinished business. Levelling out just below a thickening bank of cloud, she looked down at the action still going on. As she watched she held her breath when one of the RAF went on fire and nose-dived into the water. And then it seemed as if a whistle was blown for the end of the match, and within a few moments the skies cleared.

Bella sighed and for the first time took note of the pain in her thigh. A dark stain had appeared over it and moving was agony. She bit back a cry and tried to concentrate. Her plane was dropping every time she tried to level out and cruise, the strength required to hold it on a steady course sapping her stamina. Trying the radio, all she got was static.

'Well then, we're on our own. Let's go home.' She glanced at the watch Johnnie had given her for Christmas, amazed as always at how early it still was. It felt as if she had been chasing the German across the sky for hours, when it was probably less than ten minutes. She turned and headed back towards the English coast, the engine stuttering all the time. 'Come on, don't do this to me. I'm not ditching, you bloody thing. If we have to land it's going to be on British soil. It's not far, we can do this.'

Her radio squawked, making her jump and swear when a bolt of agony shot through her leg.

'Red Leader, this is Gambit, come in.'

She pressed the com button with a shaking hand.

'Gambit, this is Red Leader.'

'Digger, is that you? Good to hear you're in one piece, old man.' Johnnie's voice. She blinked back a tear.

'On my way home, Gambit. See you in the mess for a beer.'

'The first one's on me. Apparently, you've taken out one of the Luftwaffe's best pilots.'

Bella smiled at the relief in his voice. So, she had got her opponent in the end. She was too tired to care.

'Looking forward to it, Gambit. Red Leader out.'

A dark smudge grew more distinct as she neared the coast, flying lower, fighting to keep the Spitfire in a straight line. Pain overrode everything now and her head swam. She should tie her scarf around her leg above the wound, but couldn't find the energy and knew she would end up in the water if she took her hand off the stick.

Relief flooded her as she approached the misty coastline, just visible through the low-lying morning fog. She followed what she hoped was the river she had noted before it disappeared beneath the cloud.

The radio crackled again, the voice disjointed and fading in and out. All she could understand was someone wanting the code for the day. Her head swam, she couldn't seem to think straight – was it blue? Or had that been yesterday? Why couldn't they let her be, all she wanted to do was land safely and sleep . . .

She barely registered the sound of the ack-ack guns.

Chapter 41

Jennifer

The squadron finally informed us that, armed with the date Terry Bristow claimed he saw the Spitfire crash, they had discovered the name of our long-lost pilot. He was Flight Commander Aiden Gardner, one of their top pilots during the Battle of Britain, whose plane had been presumed to have gone down into the sea. During his final sortie, Flight Commander Gardner had shot down one of the Luftwaffe's ace pilots and been hailed as a lost hero. It felt like the last piece of the jigsaw had been slotted into place. The only thing I still had to do was break the news to them that Aiden Gardner was not who they thought he was. I wasn't sure how that would go.

The following Saturday afternoon, after a week in the office sorting out the final bits of paperwork to do with the dig, I put the dogs in the back of the car, thinking I would head for the coast and give them a long walk. Rosie was out with Scott, and Peter had been ensconced in his office since breakfast. A solitary walk was just what I needed; some thinking time and fresh air.

I popped my head around the door of Grandpa's sitting room to say I would be out for a couple of hours.

'Where are you going?' he said.

'Taking the dogs down to the coast for a walk.'

'Do you mind an extra passenger? I can sit in the sun and do the crossword while you walk. I could do with a change of air.'

My heart lifted. This was the first time he had wanted to get out of his room.

'I would love company. Let me get your coat and a hat though. There's always an onshore breeze down there.'

Ten minutes later we were on our way, Grandpa gazing out at the passing countryside as I negotiated the weekend traffic in the narrow lanes that led to the stretch of coast path I had chosen.

'You remember weeks ago, when you told me about the Spitfire pilot you had discovered, and that he was from 66 Squadron?' he said, after sitting in silence for ten minutes. 'I think I said at the time that one day I would tell you all about it. I think it's time you learnt the truth. Would you like to hear what happened?'

My pulse jumped. How could I say no? And how could I continue driving safely while he was divulging something he had kept secret for more than seventy years? I didn't know how I would tell him that 'he' was a 'she', but that could wait. I wanted to hear Grandpa's memories – it felt as if he knew things that might answer some of the questions which still spun round my head.

'Yes. Yes, please, I would love that. Oh, and I forgot to tell you last night that the squadron know who he was. Apparently, he was an ace pilot called Aiden Gardner.'

I heard a sharp intake of breath.

'I knew it.' His voice a whisper.

I glanced at him in surprise. I tried to concentrate on my driving, desperate to reach the beach, frustrated at the amount of traffic holding us up.

'Let's get to the car park and then I'm all ears,' I said, growing more and more impatient at the hopelessness of tourists who were unable to reverse into a passing place, or who thought driving right in the middle of the road was an acceptable way to get around. At last, though, I pulled into the car park and found a space near the dunes, which I knew would be sheltered from the wind.

Sally and Deefa immediately began their chorus of excited barking at the prospect of a walk. Yelling at them to pipe down, I wound the windows down and inhaled the fresh, salty tang of the sea. Grandpa had been silent since his declaration earlier and I hoped he wasn't regretting his offer of telling me.

'Shall we sit here and you can tell me your story?'

He nodded.

I waited. Grandpa said nothing for a while, staring at the sea through a gap in the dunes, spinning his watch round and round his wrist, an action I'd known for years he did when he was stressed. He looked as if he were miles away. I didn't try and hurry him – if he had indeed told nobody about his war experiences all this time, then I was prepared to be patient.

I wondered if he had ever shared his story with Grandma. I couldn't imagine them keeping secrets – they were the kind of couple who finished one another's sentences, and seemed to communicate with a look or a raised eyebrow. Not that they were particularly lovey-dovey or anything; Grandma was one of the most straight-talking women I'd ever known and didn't hold with gushy gestures like holding hands or giving flowers. But if someone was in need she would be right there, helping in any way that was required. She had been dead for almost twenty years and I still missed her. I knew Grandpa mourned her deeply, though he said little.

At last, he stirred, taking his eyes off the view and turning them on me and then away again.

'You know how old I am, don't you, Jenny Wren?'

I nodded. 'Of course. You're ninety-six.'

'That's right. I was born right at the end of the Great War, in 1918. When I joined the RAF at the end of 1939, just after my twenty-first birthday, I was one of the older recruits. Many of

286

the others were eighteen or younger – boys, with no experience of life, straight out of school. Full of piss and vinegar, most of 'em.' Grandpa glanced at me, a rueful expression on his face. 'We had no idea, then, what was in store for us, too caught up in the thrill of becoming pilots. Certain we were invincible.' He blew out a sigh. 'I met Aiden Gardner – Digger – after I had done basic training and got sent for Advanced Flight Training.'

'So, you did know him?'

He nodded.

'We hit it off, and became good friends right away. He was a terrific pilot who had grown up in Australia – hence his nickname – flying planes since he was a teenager. He could fly rings around the rest of us from the first day. When we passed out we were posted to the same squadron.'

'Sixty-six?'

He shook his head. 'No. Not to start with. We were sent to another at first. The squadron leader hated that he'd been sent a couple of wet-behind-the-ears boys who had never flown a Spitfire. Rather than letting us be cannon fodder for the Luftwaffe, he gave us a couple of weeks' grace to get used to the planes before letting us loose with the rest of the squadron.' Grandpa grinned, his eyes dancing for a moment. 'We had a wonderful time, playing at dogfighting in the world's best airplane. Until we had to do it for real – it was a wake-up call I can tell you. I've never been so terrified in my life.' He looked across at me, his face white and drawn. 'But we managed to survive the first few weeks and I suppose we got used to the mix of boredom, exhilaration and fear. Until I got shot up and crashed . . .'

He fell silent, his face still pale. I leant across and took his hand.

'Please. Stop if it's too hard to talk about.'

He shook his head, so much sadness in his eyes it brought a lump to my throat.

'I've tried to bury the memories for seventy years or more, but they remain as fresh as if it all happened yesterday,' he said.

'Did you bail out of your plane when it was hit?' I asked.

He shook his head again.

'No. I managed to land it. My leg got smashed up when the landing gear failed.' He grunted. 'I wouldn't have felt so bad except that it was one of our own squadron that hit my Spit. Bloody new boy, who got so overexcited at his first dogfight he sprayed most of his ammo at his fellow airmen.'

'Bloody hell, Grandpa, that must have been terrible. Bad enough to get shot at by the enemy, but for one of your own to fire on you . . . I can't even imagine how that must have felt.'

He shrugged.

'It wasn't unusual, sadly. *Blue on blue,* as it was known, was a common occurrence during the war. Friendly fire is still something that happens to this day, I believe . . . Scott would know.' He fell silent for a moment as if considering what to say next. 'Digger came to see me in hospital. And that's when he let me in on his secret.' He cleared his throat and shook his head. 'How he pulled it off for so long – and continued to do so after he told me – I have no idea.' Now he fixed his eyes on me. 'You see, old girl, my mate Digger wasn't a bloke at all. *He* was a *she.*'

I sat back and blew out a long breath. Relieved it wasn't down to me to give him a huge shock.

'So, who was she?'

He eyed me shrewdly. 'You knew?'

I nodded. 'I was confused by the skeleton; it didn't feel like that of a young man, but I thought he must have been very young and slight of build. But the results of the DNA sample came back and confirmed it. I can't believe you're the person who can reveal who the pilot actually was, though. It's beyond a coincidence – it's spooky.' I tapped a rhythm on the steering wheel setting the dogs off again. Once I had yelled at them and they had lain down again I asked the obvious question. 'Why did she do it? And why, after keeping up her charade for so long, did this mystery woman let you into her secret? I would have thought, that being such good mates, she'd have been terrified of you finding out.'

Grandpa shifted in his seat and rubbed his gammy leg. He shot me an embarrassed grin, his cheeks pink.

'Because she had fallen for me, and when I got injured she was afraid I might not make it. She wanted to come clean about who she was and how she felt.' I stared at him, trying to process his words. He laughed at my expression. 'She had such balls. I can picture her now; how this strange woman strode into the hospital ward, wearing this slinky blue silk dress and sat down beside my bed. How horribly confused I was when she opened her mouth and it was Digger speaking.'

My jaw felt like it was on the floor. 'Wow. I can understand how weird that must have been.'

He laughed again. 'There I was, not looking my best with a smashed leg and other injuries, and this elegant, strange woman sat down and admitted she was in love with me. To make matters worse she spoke with the voice of my closest friend. What was a chap to think?'

'So *how* had she got away with pretending to be a man for so long? What was it – months? And why? Why put herself in such danger for so long? I don't understand it.'

He smiled.

'Bella – that was her name – explained it very simply. Everyone expected RAF pilots to be men, so it was never questioned. And she was good. *Very* good. The best pilot I ever flew with, so who would be suspicious? She never gave us cause to doubt her. Her skill, her nerve and courage were exemplary.'

I couldn't help but be impressed.

'Still, it must have been so stressful and difficult for her. Did you not all share accommodation, bathrooms, all that kind of thing?'

'Not as officers, no. We had our own rooms, and our own batmen. I was amazed she managed to hide who she was from hers. But you know, it was the last thing anyone was looking for.'

Grandpa gazed out of the windscreen, his eyes unfocused. 'She was skinny but strong – what's the word? Wiry? Yes, that's it. A redhead with a million freckles at the first sign of sunshine. She bit her nails, they were always a mess, but then lots of us had habits born out of the stress of the job.'

'So, after she came clean to you, what happened? You said you couldn't fly again, but if you still worked at the same base, it must have been impossible not to give her away?'

He laughed, ruefully, his face lighting up for a moment.

'It was hell, actually, because by that time we were in the throes of a passionate love affair.'

'Grandpa!'

'What? We were young and in love. We both ended up being posted to 66 Squadron and found hideaways where we could meet for an hour or two. It was heaven, but while we were working we had to be *just good friends*.' He put his two fingers up to accentuate his words. 'And she was a witch, could wind me up no end and keep a straight face, so nobody would know what was going on. It was impossible but we managed and it made the times we could be together even sweeter and more precious.' He twisted his watch around his wrist, then flicked the catch, took it off and held it out to me with a twisted smile. 'She gave me this as a Christmas present.' I took it, unable to grasp that something I had seen him wearing my whole life could have such significance. 'Look at the back,' he said.

I could make out a worn inscription and peering at it closely, made out the words:

Johnnie, my heart is yours, Bella

'We bought each other the same Christmas present,' he said, a sad smile crossing his face. 'She gave me that, and I gave her a silver watch which I also had inscribed. That was how close we were . . .'

I gaped at him, then passed it back, amazed at his story. It was like something out of a romance novel. It must have been the same watch I had cleaned up. A shiver ran down my spine at the fact that all the answers to my mysterious pilot were locked in Grandpa's head all along. There was something I still didn't understand though.

'I can't get past her wanting to do it. Why would she? Did she ever tell you? It seems such an outlandish thing to try and get away with, especially as women flew with the ATA during the war. Surely, she could have joined them and flown as much as she wanted.'

Grandpa nodded.

'She joined up as an ATA pilot, but hated that being a woman meant all she could fly were Tiger Moths. Bella would have been a feminist these days, or a suffragette if she'd been born twenty years earlier. In her view, women were just as capable as men at everything, which of course, they are.' His face lost its light and he grew serious. 'But there was more to it than that. Aiden Gardner was her brother. I saw a photo of them as children once. Except for her pigtails, I couldn't tell them apart. Anyway, he was badly injured in a train crash on his way to start Advanced Flight Training at the same base I was at, ended up paralysed from the waist down. When it was clear he would be an invalid for life Bella took his dog tags, paperwork and uniform, and became him.'

'What, without telling him? Just so she could fly Spitfires? That sounds quite hard-bitten. The poor boy – he must have still been a boy, mustn't he? He was surely devastated at losing the use of his legs, and then his sister buggers off and pretends to be him. And what about her family, what did they think?'

Words tumbled out without thinking. I found it hard to get my head around Grandpa's story. Bella Gardner sounded unlike anyone I had ever known. She must have been an extraordinary woman determined to make her own way.

Grandpa shook his head.

'Her family were all in Australia and she never told them. As far as they knew she was still with ATA.' He frowned. 'She was devastated when her brother was injured. And racked with guilt. You see, he was a pacifist and wanted to be a conscientious objector, but she bullied him into joining the RAF, and blamed herself when he was hurt before he even had a chance to fight. She took his place as some kind of penance, a way to assuage her guilt. And a way of honouring him – she wanted the world to think Aiden Gardner was an ace pilot.' Grandpa fell silent for a moment, lost in his memories. 'You know, Aiden did himself proud in the end without her intervention. I never met him, but I learnt that he became a well-respected violinist. Bella told me it was all he ever wanted to do, and in the end he fulfilled his dream.' He closed his eyes. 'She would have been so proud of him . . .'

I sat, thinking what an incredible and unlikely story he had just told me. There were still questions in my mind, but it might be a step too far to ask him. If I had been a stranger he might find it easier, but to talk to his granddaughter about such painful, intimate memories might be too difficult.

'It must have been awful when she went missing.' I spoke my thoughts aloud without realising it, then tried to take them back with an apology.

He looked at me with haunted eyes.

'It was. I was on the r/t that day – the radio transmitter. When we lost contact, I wasn't too concerned at first, it happened if the plane was damaged, or the weather was bad. But when she didn't appear and none of the rest of the flight had seen her, I knew the worst had happened.' I reached across and put a hand over his. There was nothing I could say. His voice grew husky. 'We all lost friends, it was part and parcel of war, and you learnt to bury the grief and carry on. It was different with Digger. I fell apart – everything I'd been bottling up for so long burst out, except how I felt about her. I suppose nowadays they would call it post traumatic whatchamacallit or something. Anyway, I spent months in a psychiatric hospital, with the shrinks trying to get to the bottom of my breakdown. How could I tell them the truth though? That the woman I loved was lying at the bottom of the English Channel or dead in a French field . . . the irony of it all being that she was much closer to home than anyone knew . . .'

He dragged a hand across his face and pulled in a ragged breath, exhaustion making him look every one of his ninety-six years.

One more question was nagging at me. One thing I needed to ask . . .

'Were you and Grandma courting when all this was going on?'

'No.' It came out as a sharp denial and I breathed a quiet sigh. He softened his voice. 'I didn't meet Grandma until after the war, didn't I already tell you that? She saved me, to be honest. I was in a dark hole for a long time and she gave me a reason to drag myself out of it.'

'I'm sorry if all this reminiscing has upset you. Thank you for feeling you could share your story with me, it means a lot.'

He patted my shoulder.

'It all happened so long ago, it's time I told someone, before it's too late. And you're the only one I want to tell.'

'I can't even imagine how hard it must have been for you.' As I said the words, I realised I knew exactly how hard it was to mourn someone who had disappeared. I swallowed my grief. This wasn't about me. 'No wonder you couldn't cope any longer.' We sat for a moment, neither of us saying anything, then I started the car. 'Right, let's go home. The dogs can have a walk tomorrow.'

He tried to protest but I could see the toll relating his story had taken. There was no way I was leaving him alone for an hour.

Halfway home he spoke.

'Do you know, I feel better for telling you. I've carried this secret around for so long I had forgotten how heavy it was to bear. And now you've found her, I hope I can put Bella to rest for good.' He paused. 'I just pray she didn't suffer too much. That she knew nothing about it, you know?'

'I know,' I whispered. It was the prayer I said each and every night.

Chapter 42

Jennifer

The Spitfire was clean and lay in pieces in the huge shed we used for finds. George had been in touch with the squadron who expressed a desire for it to be returned to them. They had a small museum run by local enthusiasts and while the plane was too badly damaged to be reconstructed, they wanted to exhibit the main frame.

I hadn't talked to anyone except Peter about the result of the pilot's DNA, yet. It felt almost sacrilegious, and I suspected would create a furore. There would probably be denials and demands for another DNA test, which were understandable. And what might happen if the media got hold of it I couldn't guess. I wasn't sure how Grandpa would cope with the rest of the world knowing his best mate was a woman.

One thing I did know – Dominic would be all over it like a rash, and do everything to promote himself. And I suspected he would make out like he had been leading the team. I didn't want it being all about him, but I also didn't want it to be my job dealing with intrusive journalists.

Could we just keep quiet about Aiden's true identity? Would it hurt?

Personally, I couldn't see that it would, but that option didn't sit well with me. Bella Gardner had been an extraordinary woman, that much was plain. We owed it to her to give her the recognition and respect she deserved.

After Grandpa's revelation I had looked up the real Aiden Gardner. As well as being a professional musician he had written a couple of books on twentieth-century composers and was well respected in his field. The amazing thing was that he was still alive and living in Edinburgh. How on earth did I go about contacting him and telling him that we had found his sister?

Had he known what she did? I had no idea. I needed to speak to Grandpa again and see if he knew. And what would the squadron say when they learnt that the real Aiden Gardner was still alive?

The whole thing was turning into a potential minefield.

Before I told anyone else, I spoke to Grandpa.

'I've found out that Aiden Gardner is still alive,' I said. 'Do you think he knew what his sister did? That she took his identity and masqueraded as him?'

'Is he? Well, I never. From what Bella said, the prognosis for him living a long life was poor. In those days, people with paralysis often died soon after they were injured, I believe. I suppose one benefit that comes out of wars is that medical breakthroughs happen thick and fast. From that viewpoint he's been one of the lucky ones, if you can call being paralysed for most of your life, lucky.' He paused. 'I can't remember Bella telling me she confessed to her brother what she'd done. Does it matter now, after all this time?'

'You know that I should come clean and let the squadron know their ace pilot is not who they think he is, don't you?'

Grandpa nodded, a grimace crossing his face.

'Yes, I suppose so. Do you have to mention me, though?' He sighed. 'Silly question. Of course, you do – how else can you persuade them of the truth? Won't they want to know why I've never spoken up before now?'

'But why would you? Bella was lost at sea, or so everyone thought. Her secret went down with her and was safe with you. What proof did you have that she was anyone other than Aiden Gardner?'

He rubbed a hand over his face. Was the thought of going public something he was terrified of? He had always been such a private man; I knew that better than most people.

'I have a feeling once the word is out that the press will have a field day with the story, but I'll do my best to keep your name out of it, if you prefer. The squadron will want to hear your testimony about Bella's identity, though.' I smiled at him. 'But nobody else needs to know the details of your relationship with her. You needn't worry on that score.'

He gave me the shadow of a smile back.

'Do you know, I'm sure Bella would love all this intrigue. She would have loved to stick two fingers up to the old guard who didn't believe a woman was capable of doing exactly the same job as a man – and doing it far better.' His smile turned up a notch. 'Go ahead, Jenny Wren, do whatever you have to do. Let's show the world exactly how extraordinary Bella Gardner was.'

I grinned back at him.

'Right. I will contact the squadron on Monday and give them the news. I can't wait to hear their reply.' I couldn't suppress a laugh, imagining their shock. 'I think Bella deserves to be recognised in her own right, don't you? And in these days of women being part of the front line in the armed forces she'll be seen as a true heroine of her time.'

I dropped the bombshell to George first thing on the Monday morning and couldn't help laughing at his reaction. Scott walked in as he choked and spluttered coffee across his desk. I banged him on the back and he wiped tears away from his red cheeks.

'What's happened?' Scott looked from me to George. 'Should I disappear again and come back later?'

We both shook our heads.

'The DNA results have come back on the Spitfire pilot,' I said. 'He's not exactly who we thought he was.'

'Who was he, if not Aiden Gardner?'

'He was a she.'

Scott gaped at me.

'What? Are you sure? Sorry, of course you must be sure, otherwise George wouldn't be spitting coffee on his laptop. Fuck. A woman, though. How on earth did she come to be flying a Spit in battle?' He shook his head. 'So many questions to find answers to. Will it be possible, do you think, to find out who she was?'

'The most amazing thing is that I already know the answer to that question.'

'How the hell did you find that out? As far as I remember, there was nothing on the body that would give you a clue. No personal documents other than the dog tags.'

'That's right, although when I did the post-mortem I had my suspicions that the body might not be male. The DNA has confirmed it's a woman.' I paused, a picture of Grandpa's face coming to mind when he admitted he knew who the pilot was. 'The reason I know who it is though, is that my grandfather knew our pilot. In fact, he went right through with them, from Advanced Flight Training to being posted to the same squadron.' Both men stared at me, their mouths hanging open. 'For most of that time, he knew her as Aiden Gardner – Digger to his friends. But when Grandpa was shot down and laid up in hospital, his mate went to visit him and came clean. Her real name was Bella. Bella Gardner – Aiden's sister.'

'Fucking hell,' said Scott. 'Sorry, 'scuse the language, but that's unbelievable. Fancy your granddad knowing her. Who would have bet on that?'

George's eyes had narrowed and he speared me with a look that I knew well. I looked away, a flush running up my back.

'Exactly how long have you sat on this information?'

I cleared my throat, my mouth suddenly dry.

'I admit the results came in a little while ago, but I swear I only discovered exactly who she was a few days ago.' I thought carefully about how much to say. The last thing I wanted was to give away all of Grandpa's secrets. 'When we recovered the pilot and knew which squadron he – she – was with, I mentioned it to Grandpa. He's been so interested in the dig and I've chatted to him about everything we've been doing. Anyway, he said he'd been with 66 Squadron too and was clearly upset, so I left it at that. Then he had his fall and was in hospital and it all went out of my head, I was so worried about him. Now, he's come to live with us and a couple of days ago I told him the squadron had informed me that they were almost certain they knew who the pilot was – Aiden Gardner. Grandpa admitted he knew Aiden was actually his sister, Bella, in disguise. Apparently, Aiden was horribly injured after being in a train crash, so she took his identity papers, cut her hair and wore his uniform.' I shook my head at the thought of it. 'Not one person questioned who she was, can you believe that? But then, why would they? Everyone expected Aiden Gardner to be just one more young man who could fly an airplane, and that's what they saw.'

'So why did she tell him, after successfully passing herself off as a bloke for so long?'

George was still pissed at me, I could tell, but he couldn't resist being drawn into the story.

I shrugged. 'I don't know, but I imagine it must have taken its toll, being someone else in the most terrifying of times. Perhaps she wanted Grandpa to see the real person before one or other of them was killed in action.' I paused, a lump growing in my throat. That was exactly the reason, I realised. 'And then she was . . .' I whispered to myself.

George grunted. 'The bloody press are going to have a field day with this when they get wind.'

'I think it's great,' said Scott. 'A female Spitfire pilot – who'd have thought it? I wonder if there were any other women who did the same thing?'

''Course there weren't,' George said. 'How would they get away with it?'

'Well, she managed to, though I guess nicking her brother's ID helped. But women have been going to war disguised as men for centuries, haven't they?' Scott looked at me for back-up, and I nodded. 'At least it's now recognised they are as capable as men of being part of a fighting force.'

'True,' I said, thinking how different my perception of the armed forces was after a few months of getting to know Scott and his fellow volunteers. 'Right – enough of this discussion. I need to inform 66 Squadron that their pilot is not who they thought he was, and then any surviving family will have to be told too. I've learnt that the real Aiden Gardner is actually still alive – who would have expected that? It gets more complicated by the day, this charade.'

We were right when we guessed that the news of a woman being a WWII Spitfire pilot would cause a stir. It was leaked almost immediately after I told the squadron, and the media loved it. The RAF brass were less impressed and demanded a second DNA test, asserting there must have been a mix-up of samples at the lab. When the results came back the same, they had to admit Bella Gardner had indeed succeeded in being the first – and as far as they were concerned, only – woman to fly a Spitfire into battle during WWII.

To give them their due, once they had accepted the fact, their public relations office took over and lauded Bella as an extra-ordinary woman on a level with Amy Johnson and Amelia Earhart. It wasn't long before I heard of plans being made for a BBC documentary and that Netflix were interested, too.

Aiden Gardner was a resident of a private nursing home and when he was approached by the squadron, asked if I would be willing to meet him. I jumped at the chance and asked if he would mind if Grandpa came with me, to which he agreed.

He was a small, wizened old man with a shock of curly white hair and a pale complexion. He had a very expensive-looking wheelchair which he could move around by means of a joystick. He seemed as bright as Grandpa, and the two men got on well.

We spent an afternoon talking about his sister and his memories of her from when they were children. She had never told him what she had done, and why, but he didn't seem surprised.

'She was the most competitive person I've ever known,' he said. 'I knew how much she hated not being able to fly into battle. It never occurred to me she had taken my things though. I assumed the hospital had got rid of them or something, I suppose. It was so long ago I can barely remember.' His eyes lost focus for a moment and he grew silent. We sat and waited, and after a while he continued. 'I'm pleased you found her and she can come home to me and our grandmother. I do remember Granny Mack being heartbroken when we stopped receiving letters from Bella. We tried to find her but nobody seemed to know where she was, which ATA unit she was based with. Of course, now it makes sense – she wasn't with the ATA at all. But not being able to find her and know what happened took a huge toll on our grandmother, especially after our mother – her daughter – had died so young in an accident a few years earlier.'

I wondered briefly how many other families had never discovered how their loved ones died and in what circumstances. It all felt too close to home and I pushed the thoughts away. This was not about me and our family's tragedy.

'I'm glad you are all reunited now,' I said. 'We should go, we've taken up enough of your day.'

Grandpa shook hands with Aiden and they promised to stay in touch with each other. It felt as if we had closed the circle. For the first time in a long while I felt at peace.

Bella's remains were interred in Edinburgh next to her grandmother, Isobel MacKenzie, in the family plot. It made me sad to think she hadn't returned to the land of her birth, but apparently there were no family still alive there. The only other relatives were some distant cousins; a young man and his sister who lived in the Scottish Borders and lapped up the limelight around their now famous relative.

The remains of the Spitfire were put on show at the squadron museum, with a plaque next to it telling Bella's story. There was an unveiling ceremony which we were invited to, along with the volunteers and their families and one or two veteran RAF servicemen who had served in 66 Squadron alongside Bella and Grandpa. Terry Bristow had his moment of fame on the local TV news when he told his part in the story, and Grandpa was even persuaded to be interviewed as one of Bella's few remaining fellow pilots and the only person who had known her real identity. Dominic's nose was left severely out of joint when nobody wanted to interview him, which gave me a sneaking sense of satisfaction.

It was a good way to wrap up the dig and I was glad that Bella had found her way back to her family after so many years.

It gave me hope that one day Ben might return to us too.

Chapter 43

Jennifer

As the date of the first anniversary of Ben's death drew closer, Rosie took it upon herself to contact as many of his friends as she could, and let them know we were planning a celebration of his life at the indoor climbing wall. We had decided to give it a festival atmosphere, with food, music and silly games. All things Ben would have loved to have at a party in his name.

Peter and I had already approached the club and discussed our idea of a charity trust in Ben's name to help them with facilities, promotion and teaching. Everything would take months to put into place, but the management committee were more than happy to be the recipients of our donation.

The anniversary morning broke clear and sunny, the early September air cool against my skin as I took a cup of coffee out into the garden and sat in the swing seat, enjoying the late summer light. The air was alive with the hum of bees in the lavender bed as I watched the dogs snuffling along the hedge. I was determined to make this a positive day, and not allow myself to be sucked down into a pit of grief, but my overwhelming feeling was of the hole in our lives. And while I had begun to find ways of dealing with it, I knew it would always be there. As if Ben was just out of sight and we were always running to catch a peek at him.

Peter joined me, his eyes as haunted as mine probably were. He sat next to me and put an arm around my shoulders. I leant into him and closed my eyes, tears spilling over onto my cheeks. He kissed the top of my head and hugged me gently.

'Today is going to be hard,' he whispered. I nodded against his chest, my throat too tight to speak. 'But I think Ben would be proud of what we're doing.' I nodded again and swallowed hard. 'We should hold on to that, and the fact that our family will get through this. We have each other and that's what matters most.' We sat in silence for a few minutes and then he stood, offering me a hand. 'Come on, we have work to do.'

I took his hand and rose. Our arms around each other we walked back into the house.

A Letter from Corin Burnside

Thank you so much for choosing to read *The Memory Keeper*. I hope you enjoyed it! If you did and would like to be the first to know about my new releases, you can follow me on X here: https://twitter.com/write_corinmd

I hope you loved *The Memory Keeper* and if you did I would be so grateful if you would leave a review. I always love to hear what readers thought, and it helps new readers discover my books too.

Thanks,
Corin Burnside

Her Forgotten Promise

Claire has always had a special bond with her aunt Margaret, but she's astonished when Margaret suddenly begins talking about a friend called Agnes, who Margaret met working as a WAAF in World War 2 – a past Claire had no idea about. Margaret and Agnes were best friends until Agnes started acting strangely, becoming secretive and distant. Then one morning, Agnes vanished and never returned home, leaving Margaret distraught.

Claire promises to delve back into the past and help discover what happened to Agnes. But Margaret's memory is rapidly deteriorating, and apart from an old photograph of the two women, Agnes seems to have disappeared into thin air. Can Claire uncover Agnes' story before it's too late?

An utterly heart-wrenching and unputdownable novel about love, loss and sacrifice, perfect for fans of Fiona Valpy, Lorna Cook and Kathryn Hughes.

Acknowledgements

I hope that if you are reading these acknowledgements, it means you have read and enjoyed *The Memory Keeper*. Thank you for taking the time to choose to read my book.

Many people have helped me bring the story to publication and I cannot thank them enough for their support, time and encouragement along the way.

First, huge thanks to all the team at HQ Digital/HQ Stories, and especially to my editor, Audrey Linton, whose faith in me, and endless enthusiasm for the story, kept my spirits up when things took the odd sticky turn.

When I decided to include archaeology in *The Memory Keeper*, I knew nothing about the subject and very soon found myself out of my depth as to how to proceed. Step in my writing pal Anita Frank, who pointed me towards Jon Hart, archaeologist and talented writer, who became my go-to person for any and all questions regarding digging up old airplanes and bodies. I can never thank him enough for his endless patience and prompt replies to my cries for help. Always going above and beyond what I thought I needed to know, he has instilled a newfound enthusiasm in me for all things to do with archaeology. Thank you so much, Jon, you are a star.

I want to pay tribute to Operation Nightingale, which is an initiative that has been running since 2011. It was set up to assist the recovery of wounded, injured and sick military personnel and veterans by getting them involved in archaeological investigations. Wessex Archaeology is one of the main commercial providers of Operation Nightingale projects. You can read more about their work on their website.

I must also thank my patient and long-suffering family for all their help and input. To Gemma, for your enthusiasm, encouragement and belief in me. To John and Michael, who put up with my constant questions about Spitfire airplanes, the Royal Marines, the Alps and mountain climbing, among other things, I am eternally grateful.

Finally, to my wonderful writing friends in the VWG, I would not be here today without you. Thank you all.

Dear Reader,

We hope you enjoyed reading this book. If you did, we'd be so appreciative if you left a review. It really helps us and the author to bring more books like this to you.

Here at HQ Digital we are dedicated to publishing fiction that will keep you turning the pages into the early hours. Don't want to miss a thing? To find out more about our books, promotions, discover exclusive content and enter competitions you can keep in touch in the following ways:

JOIN OUR COMMUNITY:

Sign up to our new email newsletter: http://smarturl.it/SignUpHQ

Read our new blog www.hqstories.co.uk

X https://twitter.com/HQStories

f www.facebook.com/HQStories

BUDDING WRITER?

We're also looking for authors to join the HQ Digital family!

Find out more here:

https://www.hqstories.co.uk/want-to-write-for-us/

Thanks for reading, from the HQ Digital team